The Maestro

T. Davis Bunn

BETHANY HOUSE PUBLISHERS
MINNEAPOLIS, MINNESOTA 55438

It is important to note that, except as specifically mentioned within the Acknowledgments section, this particular story is entirely a creation of the author's imagination. No parallel between any persons, living or dead, is intended.

Copyright © 1991
T. Davis Bunn
All Rights Reserved

Published by Bethany House Publishers
A Ministry of Bethany Fellowship, Inc.
6820 Auto Club Road, Minneapolis, Minnesota 55438

Printed in the United States of America

Library of Congress Cataloging-in-Publication Data

Bunn, T. Davis, 1952–
    The maestro / T. Davis Bunn.
        p. cm.

    I. Title.
PS3552.U4718M3   1991
813'.54—dc20   91–6624
ISBN 1–55661–146–3   CIP

This book is dedicated to all
who seek fame and fortune
for the sake of self.

*Joy is the customary way of life of those who have received the
Spirit . . . The Spirit transforms those in whom He lives. We may
have lived without joy, or only with the kind of joy which comes
from having selfish desires fulfilled. The Spirit transforms us
into people who have joy because we have found our true destiny.
The joy we have, not the legalistic rules we follow, show we are
Christ's.*

Commentary on Romans 14:17–18
The NIV Disciples' Study Bible

Other Books by the Author

The Presence

T. DAVIS BUNN, a native of North Carolina, is the director of an investment consulting group in Dusseldorf, West Germany. After completing graduate studies in economics and international finance, Davis worked first as a university professor and then as marketing manager for a Swiss firm. His career has taken him to over forty countries in Europe, Africa, and the Middle East. Davis draws on this experience and the Holy Spirit's inspiration in crafting his stories. He shares his life and his work on the writing with his wife, Isabella.

You make the laws, let me make the music,
and I will rule your nation.

ANDREW FLETCHER, 1703

Next to theology, I give to music the highest place and honor.
Music is the art of the prophets, the only art that can calm the
agitations of the soul; it is one of the most magnificent and
delightful presents God has given us.

MARTIN LUTHER

PROLOGUE

Sunlight played over the water, golden mirrors that shimmered among the crystal-blue waves. The air blew fresh and sweet in my face, a breeze tasting both of the lake and distant snow-capped peaks. I could make out a hint of my breath in the chilly April air. The people on the ferry with me did not talk; they sang their speech with hands floating in accent to their words. Before me stretched the city of Como, a fair white maiden bathing at her lake.

It was still too early in the season for more than a handful of tourists. Two months from now summer would bring them in droves. With the heat came the hordes, the locals said, rubbing together thumb and forefinger to indicate money to be made. Today the boat-bus was filled with well-dressed Italians who knew the luxury of a little free time. The ferry was not the swiftest way to travel the lake's forty-kilometer length, but on an afternoon as beautiful as this, the panorama brought glances of approval from the most cynical of locals.

The distance from Torno, the village of two thousand inhabitants where my little stone cottage was situated, to the city of Como was eleven kilometers by car and forty-five minutes by boat. I sat on my favorite bench in the bow and wrapped my scarf up around my face to hold off the water-wind's bite. I liked this bench and daily hoped that it would be free. With my guitar case beside me there was no room for anyone else, so my solitude was guaranteed.

The boat chugged its ancient song from village to village, the cobblestone landings grooved by ten centuries of use. Fishing boats lay upturned along the water's edge, resting beneath blankets of nets. Beyond them, tiny plazas stretched like colorful mosaics, crammed to overflowing with local market stalls.

Many of the piazzas were fronted by chapels which dated back to the early Middle Ages, dedicated to the men who fished and kept the villages alive. Charming though they might be, these villages and their rocky soil were steeped in poverty before Goethe and Beethoven and Thomas Mann brought the eyes of the world and the wealth of tourism to their shores.

On the other side of the lake lay the village of Cernobbio, nestled in a narrow valley that swept back from the lake to the Swiss border. Beyond the village rose the snow-capped peaks of the Alps. In the rarified spring air, they seemed close enough to touch.

Despite the beauty of the scenery, I did not like these Thursday afternoons. My head was a little too clear, the emptiness a little too powerful. I hid behind my sunglasses on the hard wooden bench. It was time to get to work.

At the Como quay I picked up my guitar case and followed the other passengers off the boat, ignoring the scattered glances tossed my way. There were all kinds of looks and most of them were empty too. I adjusted tiny earphones and switched on the pocket tape player; my head was filled with fusion jazz as my feet beat a matching rhythm across thousand-year cobblestones.

The closer I came to the club, the more often my hand went up in greeting. I was pretty well known in Como, especially in this neighborhood—the local kid who had made it big.

The club was still locked, but I had my own key and let myself in through the massive oak portals. In the thirteenth century the hall into which I entered had been the central courtyard of a wealthy man's villa. Eleven years ago a private consortium had bought the place, reinforced the high surrounding walls, and at incredible expense laid a glass roof over the entire quad. Hanging gardens and a world-class restaurant had at first attracted a fashionable clientele from as far away as

Bologna and Torino. But in time other restaurants had opened, and business had gradually begun to fade.

Then I arrived, guitar in hand, looking for a job. I thought playing in a restaurant might be a nice change from teaching lessons to the local kids. The club's owner took me on because I was the cheapest thing going; I agreed to work for a good meal with wine and boat-bus fare. I played mostly classical compositions, the music of my upbringing. But in my private time I was becoming more and more intrigued by fusion jazz, that marriage of two worlds, rock and funk.

That lasted a little less than six months. By then we were both aware that the scene was changing. People were coming back more often, bringing their friends, staying on longer and asking for more. The club's owner requested a late set and started talking what for me was very serious money. I bought a steel string Ibanez hollow-body and a state-of-the-art drum machine, and began building a second repertoire. By my second summer they were taking reservations two months in advance and talking about keeping the place open as a late-night club.

I still used the drum machine when playing the early set, when I combined portions of favorite classical pieces with instrumentals designed around well-known hit songs. But for the Thursday, Friday, and Saturday late-night shows I had a couple of friends join me, musicians I had met doing studio work in Milan. We gained a reputation for using the sessions to perform the newest hits weeks before they were released on Italian radio. These late sets were strictly standing-room only.

My dressing room in the corner had probably once served as a guardhouse. I set my guitar case down beside the open window, its frame of stone almost three feet thick. Centuries-old iron bars kept out everything but the chilly evening air. I glanced at the lower cabinet, hesitated for a moment, then decided I could wait to satisfy that particular hunger until after dinner.

I walked through the dimly lit club, drawn toward the kitchen by the sound of laughter and the aroma of fine cooking. The kitchen door was open and members of the staff were sprawled out around the battered table where they ate their own meals. Glasses were nearly empty; coffee cups and cigarettes dangled from most hands.

"Salve, Maestro," somebody called as I entered. I waved my greetings and sat down.

Alessandro walked over and clapped a heavy hand on my shoulder in greeting. He was a very big man, well over a hundred and forty kilos and sporting a vast black beard. He was the club's owner, an honest man who had treated me well and genuinely liked my music. His greatest concern in life was that I would go off and leave him with an empty club. Or so he said.

"What you up for, Maestro? How about some shrimp?"

"They nice?" Shrimp sounded fine.

"Take a look." Alessandro walked over to the long central work station, reached inside a refrigerator and held up a tail almost as long as his hand. "Norwegian. Best there is."

"Looks good, thanks."

"Save me some of those, Alessandro," a voice called out from the kitchen's back door. "I've got some friends joining me for dinner tonight."

A cheer rose from the table as Mario's head jutted around the door. Alessandro's bearded features broke into a smile as he walked over with outstretched hand. "É il piccolo pazzo, salve," Alessandro said. The little crazy one. "How goes it?"

Mario shook his hand, smiled at the crew, gave me a wink. "Had a dream about you, Alessandro. Saw us praying together."

That brought down the house. Alessandro raised his hands in mock prayer, then made a rude gesture. "Know what you can do with that?"

Mario winked again, said, "Just planting seeds, Alessandro, just planting seeds."

Alessandro offered to do the seeds a disservice, then walked back over to the kitchen. For some reason he always liked to prepare my dinner himself. From the stove he called out, "Got something special for you, Mario. Piattino dei Profeti." Plate of the Prophets. "Bread and water, how's that?"

"Anything you serve'll be fine, amico," Mario said mildly, and to me, "How you been, Maestro?"

"You know he does it just to get your goat," I said loudly

enough for Alessandro to hear. "All you'd have to do is slap him down once."

"That's right, Gianni, that's all it'd take." He repeated his question. "How you been?"

"Not bad. All right." Mario was my oldest friend, the only friend I had kept in contact with from my childhood. It was great seeing him again, but his glowing self-assuredness, his downright happiness, was occasionally hard to take. It irritated me and appealed to me at the same time.

"You given our offer any thought?"

Mario was sound engineer for an up-and-coming band based in Germany. They were losing their lead guitarist and had been after me for two months to join them. It was only the seriousness with which he discussed the offer that kept me from thinking he was joking. Leave all this? "I've been a little busy, Mario."

"Yeah, I bet." The eyes took on a look of silent wisdom, of unspoken criticism. At moments like this I thought Mario's eyes looked a thousand years old. Mario was the most honest man I knew, and it granted him some special power all his own. That and his religion.

Mario was handsome in a tough, hard-bitten way. He was dark-eyed like me, with a full head of hair drawn back tightly from an angular face. His chin was sharp, his cheekbones pronounced, and his build as tight as a decade of dedicated bodybuilding could make it. The only thing that kept Mario from being a thoroughly frightening character was the light in his eyes. I often thought of that light in the quiet of my empty nights, after the stage lights went off and the high lost its edge and all that lay in front of me was a lonely taxi ride back to a lonely bed.

A scar running above Mario's left eyebrow gave the sharpened features a dangerous cast. Another scar under his shirt traced a jagged line from a point just below his heart all the way around to his armpit. I was one of the few people who knew the story of those scars.

The fight took place three days before he was brought to his senses and his knees, was how Mario had started the tale. It was back in the days when he still thought faith in Jesus Christ, which his brother and his brother's friends talked about constantly, was just one step short of insanity; back when he carried a knife in the pouch sewn in his right boot. He had special-ordered those boots from Texas, with metal tips hewn to stiletto points.

At the time Mario was sound engineer for one of the big German rock groups, and they were up finishing an album in a local Hamburg studio. To celebrate recording the last take on the last song, he and a couple of the musicians made for the Pauli district, a trio of streets lined with beer halls and porn shops and high-rise whorehouses, and a favorite meeting ground for losers from all over the world.

In one of the bars sporting a live sex show, Mario started trading words with an enormous Dane, a stoker on one of the ferries to Copenhagen. The shaggy-haired giant had survived a dozen fights, and met Mario's challenge with a joyous gleam in his eyes. Looking back, Mario told me, he realized he had finally found what he'd been looking for all along. Here was a man willing to fight to the death for the thrill of it, for the futility of a life without God.

The Dane treated it all as a game, and saw Mario with his swaggering braggadocio as just another notch on the fighter's blade. The fight did not last long; knife fights seldom do. The blond giant opened the skin above Mario's eye first. When Mario swiped at the blinding spill, the Dane let out a hungry laugh and told Mario, take a good look, kiddie. The next blood you see's gonna pour from a broken heart. Then his eyes became flat and wide and dark like the mouth of an empty cave, and Mario knew he was looking death in the face.

When he told me about this part Mario's eyes looked out into the distance of memories and his voice became low and very hoarse. He said, I never knew what fear was until that moment. I replied, I don't think I want to hear this. Mario ignored me, went on, I wasn't scared of dying near as much as I was of ending a life that had no meaning.

By a miracle the knife deflected off a rib instead of finding Mario's heart. Two days and eighty-nine stitches later Mario was back on the street, shaken and scared and looking for answers. He'd spent the entire time in the hospital, he told me, remembering the look in the Dane's eyes and the answering emptiness in his own heart. There had to be more, he'd repeated a hundred thousand times by then. There *had* to be.

The next day his brother had shown up with an American called Jake. Before the sun had set that day, as he told it, Mario had found a better way.

When Mario wasn't around it was easier to toss the story off as a scared man looking for a lifeline. But when he was looking at me with those shining eyes I found it harder to push it all away. His way of making God seem like a close personal friend left me both confused and angry. His inner light somehow challenged me more than anything he could ever say. It tugged at the shadows I didn't like to see inside myself. But Mario was my oldest friend. I tried as best I could to ignore his loud proclamations of faith, and looked forward to his visits more than I could say.

And in the darkness of my lonely room, especially when there was some little soft-bodied music fan sleeping beside me and making my loneliness ache even more, I remembered the light in Mario's eyes.

.   .   .

Mario sipped his water and said casually, "Jake's down for a little R and R, Gianni. He wants to drop by and hear you tonight."

That surprised me. "Jake, as in the leader of your band?" As in the man who brought Mario to religion. As in the man who wanted me to come play with them.

"That's the one," he said, leaning back and slinging an arm across the chairback. "Amy's down, too."

"She's your lead singer, right?"

"And Jake's wife," Mario said. "Amy was wondering if she could sing a couple of songs with you tonight."

"I don't know, Mario. I'll have to check with the others." We did have the occasional guest singer, but it was usually somebody well known in the Italian pop world, whose appearance on stage created a sensation. Oftentimes they were friends from the studio scene who wanted to try out a new song on a live audience, or who were just out for a night and willing to be dragged up on stage for a song. I tried to remember if we had ever had anyone nameless up there with us.

I was seeking some kind way to tell Mario that it was not

an appropriate request when the familiar face of my booking agent appeared in the doorway and moaned, "Gianni, where is a man supposed to park a car around this dump?"

Alessandro hefted a large meat cleaver and came swinging around the counter of pots and pans. "I told you the next time you showed your face around here I was gonna chop you up in little bits."

Antonio was a wispy stick figure with an oversized walrus mustache and bleak ancient eyes. He didn't move from the doorway. "Put that thing down before you hurt yourself."

Alessandro made do with one more threatening swipe; he kept up a running battle with Antonio, who he claimed was out to steal me from the club. He set the cleaver down, wiped a large hand on his apron, stuck it out, said, "How's it going, 'Tonio?"

The tired-looking man with the eternally weary eyes surrendered his hand, winced as it was swallowed. "I'm an old man, Alessandro. Bones don't heal fast as they used to."

When his hand was released Antonio Salvatore walked over to me and twisted his face into a tired smile. "You doing okay, Gianni?"

"Fine, thanks. Like you to meet a friend of mine, Mario Angeletti. Mario, Tony's the biggest booking agent in Milan."

"Wish it was true," Antonio Salvatore countered. He eased himself into a seat, asked Mario, "You really a friend of his?"

"I try to be."

"Then get him to tell me when he's coming in and making an album of his own."

Alessandro set a steaming plate in front of me, said proudly, "Scampi alla Villa d'Este. Grilled jumbo shrimp with a cream and peppercorn sauce, served on a bed of wild rice and fresh spinach. Buon appetito, Maestro."

I nodded my thanks, smelled the steamy perfume, said, "I haven't worked up any songs I like enough to want to record."

Antonio Salvatore looked at Mario, his face wearing its habitually pained expression. "Did you hear me say anything about songs? Has this old brain started spouting off without my hearing what I'm saying?"

Alessandro watched until I took the first bite and smiled my approval. "There's still some of that Gavi di Gavi left in the fridge. You want a glass, Maestro?"

"Great, Alessandro. Thanks."

Antonio Salvatore went on to Mario, "I got songwriters coming outta my ears. You know what they'd give to do songs for Giovanni di Alta's first album? I tell you what they'd give. Their mommas, their younger sisters, and rights to their first children. You ever heard this guy sing? I won't even ask you about how he plays. I'm talking about his voice."

"I've heard," Mario said mildly.

"So what's this guy doing spending his life in a Como nightclub? You mind telling me that? You think maybe he's decided it's his life's mission to keep me poor?"

"You're a lot of things, Tony," I said, talking around a bite of scrunchy-soft shrimp. "But poor isn't one of them."

Antonio passed a wrinkled hand over the thin strands of hair that barely covered his crown. "I gotta stop this. It makes me too upset. My doctor warned me about that. Said every time I made myself upset I take two years off my life. Shoulda warned me to stay outta Como."

"Don't get yourself worked up, Tony," I said, winking at Mario. It was an old story between us, this album.

Antonio Salvatore sighed his defeat, reached for an inner pocket, pulled out the inevitable papers. "Giorgio Coppa's starting his first takes next month. Wants you to work with him on three, maybe four songs."

Mario stood, slid a cassette across the table toward me, said, "You get a minute, Gianni, take a listen to this."

I picked it up, said, "I don't know, Mario, it's just not—"

"I recorded it during a session a couple of weeks ago," Mario said, riding over my words. "Lifted the vocals out, so you've got just the instruments."

Antonio Salvatore's watered-down eyes showed a flicker of interest. He said to Mario, "You play with a group?"

"Mario is sound engineer to a group in Germany," I explained.

"Germany, Holland, Belgium, Great Britain, Switzerland," Mario corrected. "You really oughtta check this out, Maestro."

"Yeah?" Antonio Salvatore focused on Mario as though seeing him for the first time. "This a German group?"

"Pretty international," I said, keeping my eyes on Mario.

"Three Germans, a Swiss, a Brazilian, an Egyptian, and two Americans—did I get that right?"

"Two Germans," Mario corrected.

"Yeah, I forgot. Your guitarist has a new job lined up in the States, doesn't he." It was not a question. Ever since he had told the group of his plans they had been pressing me to join. It surprised me; Mario above all others should know that the thought of returning to Germany left me cold. I dropped my eyes to my plate, shook my head. Whatever else Jake was, he had to be crazy.

"The Italian market's hot for foreign bands right now," Antonio Salvatore told Mario. "You guys contracted with anybody?"

Mario ignored him, said to me, "It's just three songs, Gianni. There oughtta be room sometime in the night for three songs."

I picked up the cassette, asked, "Who're they by, these songs?"

"Nobody you ever heard of, that's why I did the cassette." Mario turned for the door, said over his shoulder, "You really oughtta check them out, Maestro. It's the chance of a lifetime."

.   .   .

I carried a half bottle of wine with me back to the dressing room. Gavi di Gavi was one of my favorites, full-bodied and dry, the kind of wine I could drink slow and steady all night and not feel that dull-eyed sinking state at the end. This was very important if I expected to repeat the process the next night. And the night after that. And again Monday and Tuesday if I was doing studio sessions. It was important to know what would keep me up, and not come crashing down on my head too hard the next morning.

A hunger clenched my gut by the time I closed my dressing room door, and it wasn't for food. I practiced a sort of abstinence on Wednesdays, the day I visited my grandmother's church. Then on Thursdays I would not do anything until it was time to play. I never did. Holding off unless I was playing meant that I didn't touch anything from Sunday night until Thursday evening if I wasn't doing studio work that week. This was one of those weeks. It was tough making the distance, but it left me feeling as if I was in control. I could handle it. I wasn't in trouble so long as I could wait for either a session or the stage. And the hunger I felt after a four-day wait was a high almost as strong as what was to come.

Before I could unlock the cabinet, a knock sounded on my door. I opened it to admit Bruno, my drummer. He was originally from Torre Del Greco, a squalid little village between Naples and Pompei, best known for its export of coral carvings and able-bodied men. Bruno called his move to Milan the great escape, and maintained a sense of style patterned after the women of his village. Everything he wore was black—black boots, black trousers and shirt and string bow tie and suede vest and slouch hat and velvet ribbon to tie back his black hair. Black eyes were hidden behind black sunglasses on stage, and his drum-gloves were skin-tight black leather. In the world of modern music, Bruno was considered a conservative dresser.

He slipped a soft leather pouch from his pocket and tossed it to me. I released the drawstring and gingerly let a thumb-size ball slide into my hand. The stuff was crumbly-soft and blond, almost white. I whistled softly at the sight.

"Lebanese," Bruno said, taking a sip from my wine. "Luca brought it in from Amsterdam last night."

"He got any more?" I broke a little into my palm and put it into the glass water pipe I extracted from my cabinet.

"I'll have to ask." From long habit Bruno lit the scented candle and swung the window shut.

Carefully I uncorked the pipe, made to order by a glass-blowing friend, and poured in some of the chilled wine. My throat was very sensitive, and wine or grappa helped to lessen the smoke's sting.

I refitted the top, held a match to the bowl, and drew softly. Bruno seated himself across from me and began playing rhythmic combinations in the air. When the pipe's bulb-shaped base was filled with swirling smoke, I released my finger from the opening and drew it deep inside my lungs. I took another hit, then passed the pipe to Bruno. We seldom spoke in these first moments. There was little that could compare with the pleasure of that first rush, especially after a few days of doing without.

I first met Bruno a couple of years ago while working in a Turin studio for a singer who wanted to apply a jazz beat to a contemporary pop song. There weren't many studio musicians in Italy with the talent and flexibility to meld one range of sound—rhythm and blues, rock, funk, contemporary pop, Latin salsa—with another. Bruno was a last-ditch effort brought in by a Milanese agent, a guy who was known throughout the industry as an expert at promising the moon. The surprise was, Bruno delivered. He had all the poses that were so typical of Italian musicians, the hard-set face and the stone-cold eyes and the dead-panned speech, but he played with brilliance.

The professional music industry in Italy was as small and closed as anywhere else. Word swiftly got around, and we discovered that playing together as a unit offered us an edge. A keyboard player, Claudio, soon joined us. The weekend sessions at the Como nightclub seemed a natural addition to our work.

A couple more tokes and the pipe was set aside. I took out the cassette and reached for the portable player I used for recording sessions and song ideas.

"What you got, Gianni?"

"Something Mario gave me."

Bruno snorted. He kept his opinions about Mario to himself. He knew Mario was my friend.

"Their lead singer's out front tonight. He asked if I'd check out their music, maybe give her a chance to sing with us."

I pushed the play button and settled back. The room filled with sound. I glanced over, saw Bruno's eyebrows lift slightly. I agreed. The music was very tight, very good. Even without the vocals, the band sounded solid.

The song ended and the next began. Like the first, it had a fairly standard sort of pattern, probably chosen because it would be easy to learn. Yet the two songs were as different in beat and perspective as two songs could be and still be called contemporary. Bruno's eyebrows crawled up another notch.

The third song was as powerful as the first two, and just as different. Most groups playing contemporary music had the ability to play well only within a very limited range of musical form. This group clearly had the talent to switch from one point on the musical spectrum to something entirely different, and do so with fluid professionalism. The songs represented three points of a triangle, as distant from each other as they could possibly be. If their lead singer Amy could sing as well as her band played, it would show an amazing range of voice and control.

"That Mario's group playing?" Bruno finally asked.

I nodded. "This Amy must be pretty good."

"That's their singer's name? Amy?" Bruno shook his head. "Either she's something else or 'una pazza totale.' " A total whacko.

We played the tape several more times, with me fingering chords and Bruno drumming silent tempo and time changes. In a recording studio time was money; speed in learning new parts was essential. When a studio musician was brought in for overdubbing he was under constant pressure to learn his part swiftly and play it correctly. I went over the songs until the chords were memorized and the playing smooth, then went back and tried a few runs for the solos. I watched Bruno's face for reaction, stopping here and there to discuss timing and emphasis. My first impression solidified. This music was very strong.

Alessandro knocked on the door; Bruno got up to let him in. I re-lit the pipe, took a deep drag, passed it over. Alessandro drew the smoke in and expanded visibly. He blew out for what seemed to be forever, said, "Time to go, Maestro."

"We've got a guest singer for the late-night set," I told him.

"If she's as good as her band she's gonna bring the house down," Bruno predicted.

Alessandro split his beard with an enormous grin. "Great, just great. Nothing like the special guest to pack 'em in."

"We've never heard her sing," Bruno warned. "Right, Gianni?"

"A total unknown," I agreed.

Alessandro shrugged one massive shoulder. "If the Maestro wants her on, she's gotta be hot as they come."

I stopped in front of the full-length mirror, checked out my reflection. My jet-black hair fell in the same loose curls I'd had since I was a baby, only now they spilled over my shoulders and down my back. I wore what I did most nights—tight silver-gray gabardine pants, soft-leather black boots, and a white-on-white silk shirt. The cuffs had two rings of light elastic sewn in, so that I could push them up and out of my way if we started on some heavy runs. The shirt was cut like a flamenco dancer's, with voluminous sleeves and a long triangular flap over the chest that had to be tied shut with a little silk cable. I usually left the flap open. A girl once told me that when I was moving around the stage under the lights, I looked as if I were wearing a rainbow on my upper body. The frame of my haircut made my eyes look enormous, just like my hairdresser said it would. The slight glaze from the smoke was invisible under the stage lights. That I knew from experience.

I turned back to the room and smiled at my two friends. "Showtime."

There was a smattering of applause when I walked up on stage and sat down on the simple lonely stool. I didn't have an announcer because I didn't want one. It was a challenge I never tired of, entering into a cold room—although it wasn't so cold anymore. More and more the audiences on the nights when I played here were regulars, booking the next free night before they departed.

The guests at tables farther away continued to talk, some more loudly than others. I didn't mind. Out of the corner of my eye, I spotted Mario at one of the stageside tables, seated beside a truly beautiful lady and one of the biggest men I had ever seen. I resisted the urge to look up. It would have violated the shield, the distance the smoke's high placed between me and the rest of the world.

I picked up my Chet Atkins acoustic, adjusted the footstool, took a breath, and began.

Tonight's introduction was the first movement of a classical piece, one which almost cost me my sanity when I first learned it. At the time I was studying under a very severe guitar teacher in Germany, and he stripped this graceful piece of all its melodious fluidity and forced me to play as though the notes were intended to march off the page. This evening I held myself to his rigidity, accepting the repeated challenge from a man whom I had not seen nor heard from in over ten years. I played it precisely as he would have wanted it, but it was not enough. It never was. Being forced by this teacher to concentrate on discipline above all else had transformed classical music from the most important thing in my life into a launching pad.

Not allowing time for applause, I swung into a second song, a sort of bridge. From the careful fingering and severe timing

I used on the classical movement, I loosened into an exaggerated scale exercise, sliding up and down the neck of the guitar,
switching from minor to seventh to discord, creating a transi-
tion from disciplined classical to free-flowing interpretation. I
did not stay with it long. It threatened to bring up memories of
another time, when I would start on this little moment of wing-
stretching and hear a voice sing to me from within. I had not
heard that inner voice or followed its song since the day my
grandmother died.

With a flick of my toe I turned on the rhythm machine,
smoothly swinging up the volume with a special foot control
and allowing the bridge exercise to melt into the beat. It was
a slow-to-moderate samba. I decided on a song that almost all
the Italians there would know, "Il Nastro Rosa" by Lucio Bat-
tisti, and gradually moved away from the bridge. I was five bars
into the song when applause from the front tables signaled that
people recognized what I was playing.

Mario and company were honored with the best table in the
house. Mario knew Alessandro well, had helped us set up the
club's sound system when we opened for the weekend late-night
shows. Like many others Alessandro found Mario a great guy
who unfortunately was a little crazy over religion. That the
religion was called Christianity meant less than nothing to
Alessandro. To his mind the fervor with which Mario approached faith pushed Christianity out into the fringes where
all the other way-out sects resided. Mario read the message in
Alessandro's eyes and smiled that gentle smile, his light never
dimming.

I felt my attention drawn to his table. Well-known musicians were often guests at the club, and they were normally
very easy to keep out of my protected zone. I could hold their
jealousy and their desire to steal and use and manipulate and
belittle at a safe distance. But from Mario and his friends I felt
no threat. The enormous smile the beautiful woman wore, the
brilliant look in Mario's eyes that I caught sight of from time
to time seemed to urge me on. I took it as a challenge and played
as I rarely did.

After the set, I found the keyboard player already in my
room, busy with his little mirror. Claudio looked up from where
he was carefully chopping the white powder with his bone-

handled knife. "Mario's band sounds hot, Maestro."

Bruno lit the pipe, handed it over. I took a long hit before replying, "He's out in the front row with the singer, Amy."

"I saw her," Bruno said, taking back the pipe. "Spectacular."

"That's some giant of a man beside her," Claudio said. From the same kangaroo-skin pouch that held his mirror and knife and stash, he took out a thin silver tube. With practiced ease he drew a line into each nostril. He raised his head, eyes half-closed, and sniffed in very hard. With a finger he traced over the mirror's surface, then licked off the residue.

He held out the tube. "You want a taste, Gianni?"

"Not tonight, Claudio." I usually held myself to smoke these days. That and wine and grappa. Sometimes I'd do a little coke on Tuesdays, if the week had been a weary one and I needed an extra lift for the last few studio takes. Cocaine didn't agree with me, or rather, it agreed with me too much. The desire for marijuana or hashish or keef was nothing like what I felt after doing a couple of lines. The white powder was a spiral without an end, a drug that promised too much. I was afraid if I started on cocaine seriously, before too long the stuff would own me.

"You were hot out there tonight, Maestro," Bruno said.

"Yeah, caught the last part of your set. Sounded good, Gianni. Really good."

I toasted them with the pipe, took a final drag, said with the smoke, "Why don't we go over the girl's songs?"

We went through the music a number of times, anticipating a fifteen-minute session with the beautiful mystery woman. I fingered scattered patches on my classical guitar, the one my grandmother had given me for my fourteenth birthday. I seldom played the classical on stage because the required microhone and amplification would pick up too much background noise. But I loved this instrument and the intimacy it imparted. Claudio played complex chordings on his portable Yamaha keyboard, and Bruno kept time on the edge of the table. Claudio stopped us more often than was necessary, asking questions that really weren't important so he could snort a few more lines. Bruno accepted his invitations cheerfully, and soon both were sniffing and smiling at the shared joke of another high.

To see them so hooked on coke gave me a sense of superiority. I watched them inhale line after line, resisting my own tugging hunger, feeling strong that I could hold myself back. My smoke was not nearly as dangerous as their powder; it was not a problem so long as I could hold off on those four-day stretches. Now that the pause was over, now that I was high again, I felt I could stop smoking any time I liked. I watched the pair chop up the white crystals and stick the silver tube up their noses and felt totally in control, secure in my strength.

There seemed to be barely enough time for a full run-through of the songs before Alessandro was back, calling us for the second show. "Got a major-league crowd out there, Maestro," he said, his eyes sparkling. This was what he lived for. "Every time I try to count the crowd, my eyes get stuck on some angel. Never knew Como had so many beauties."

"Got a couple picked out for the Maestro?" Bruno asked, whacking my shoulder.

Alessandro laughed. "He's one cat who can take care of himself." The word for cat, *il gatto,* meant a tom on the prowl. "I took a look outside. We got enough people wanting to get in we could fill this place up another time over. Maybe I should put in a balcony."

I stood and moved for the door. "Give me five minutes to talk to Amy, then come on out."

Progress toward Mario's table was slowed by the people who wanted to say hello or make a show of knowing me. I avoided their eyes wherever possible, detesting the lies there, hating the empty smiles and the surging voices that sought to break through my barrier.

It was different with Mario's friends. I could sense it even before I approached the table. They were clearly glad to see me, but their attitude was one of friendly calm. I reached their island of peace and watched them rise to meet me.

"Salve, Maestro." Mario gestured with evident pride to his friends, said in English, "I want you to meet Giovanni di Alta. Maestro, this is Amy and Jake Templer."

"Mario's told us so much about you," Amy said, extending her hand. She was a sloe-eyed beauty with skin the color of café au lait. Her smile warmed me.

Jake was one of the biggest men I had ever seen, hard and dark and stern. Amy's hand was replaced by a slab of ebony. A voice from the depths of a cave said, "That was great, man. Really enjoyed your music."

"Thanks," I said, a little awed by the strength that poured from him.

"Gianni's the first Italian name I ever got right the first time."

I nodded. Correctly said, the name was pronounced like the American *Johnny*, but with a little lilt from the *i* added for Italian spice. "It's short for Giovanni," I explained.

"Right, Mario told us. After that set I understand how you earned that other name. Maestro." He pronounced it correctly, rhyming it with "my" and "throw." "Means the master, Mario told me. Did I say it right?"

"Close enough."

"Usually got somebody else in mind when I think on that word," Jake said.

"C'mon, Gianni," Mario said, still in English. "Siddown a minute."

"I don't have much time," I said, retreating from Jake by focusing hard on Amy. "I understand you'd like to sing with us."

A light gathered around the table as all three smiled their pleasure. "You had a chance to listen to the songs," Amy said, her voice a honeyed burr. "I'm so glad."

"I thought your music was great," I said.

Amy and Jake shared a glance. She appeared small only because of the giant seated beside her. I would have guessed her height at close to mine, but when she laid her hand on Jake's it shrank to the size of a child's. She turned back to me, the light in her eyes reminding me for some reason of Mario. "I'm really looking forward to singing with you," she said.

We discussed timing for a few minutes. I was pleased to hear her review the songs like a pro, and enormously surprised to find none of the overpowering ego most lead artists used to cover up their nerves. I had a different method. I never became involved in anything that I didn't think I could walk away from without the slightest qualm. That was the real reason behind my refusal to ever consider doing an album of my own. It might mean too much, and if it didn't work out, it might hurt more than I could stand. My fragile balance had been built at too great a cost to risk it on something that might never come.

Whistles and cheers filled the air as the lights began to dim.

I caught glimpses of shadowy faces as the room's depths disappeared into the darkness. Before the late-night crowd was allowed in, Alessandro cleared out the back two rows of tables and staffed the bar he had built along the entire length of the back wall. People stood six and seven deep at the bar, separated by a brass railing from those who had reservations and money for the tables.

Forms moved with practiced sureness on the dark stage. Vague sounds and little orange lights marked Bruno and Claudio settling into position. Alessandro placed my three guitars up front—the long-neck Fender Stratocaster I had searched almost three years for, the hollow-body Ibanez, and the Chet Atkins—and moved my stand-up voice mike front and center. He tapped the mike, blew one time, said, "Va bene."

That was all the crowd needed. I felt eyes turn toward me, knew that sweet sensation of adrenaline pumping up my heartbeat.

The spotlight flashed on Alessandro's bearded features. "Signore e signori. Buona sera e benvenuti al' Club della Vecchia Como!" He opened his arms and grinned to the applauding crowd, then pointed down to where I was seated. "Our very own maestro of guitar, Giovanni di Alta!"

I stood and vaulted easily onto the stage, then smiled and waved at the crowd. Conscious of Amy and Mario and Jake seated below me I strapped on the Stratocaster, glanced a nod toward Bruno, counted his timing with my head, and swung into the first bars of "Animal" by Toto.

In order to build up momentum we performed many of our songs in series, with either Claudio or me playing a bridge. "Animal" was followed with a song by Francesco de Gregori, a popular Italian singer, and from that we swung into "Urgent" by Foreigner. We paused after the third song, shared smiles over the applause. I thanked the crowd for coming, introduced the group, said we had a special guest who would open up the second set that night, and watched as the audience searched around the club for a famous face. I purposefully avoided looking toward Mario's table.

An hour for the first late-night set, half an hour off, then a longer second set with time for a couple of encores—that was the schedule on which Alessandro and I had agreed. He did not care if we took longer between sets; it meant more drinking time for the crowd. But I had to make sure I could last the night, maintain the tension and the energy and the high. The first late-night set was usually divided between favorites from the British and American rock scenes and the latest Italian hits. The second set was mostly fusion jazz. I sang lead, with Bruno and Claudio on backup. They both spoke only smatterings of English, but tone and pitch were more important for singing backup than proper grammar, and their voices were good. It was enough.

After the first set was over we returned to the dressing room, where Bruno and I passed the pipe while Claudio played with his mirror. We went through Amy's three songs one more time. They still sounded good.

Amy did not realize what a compliment it was for her to start off the second late-night set. My peaking high combined with the music's power to make me feel invincible. My life began anew in those moments. There was no future, no past, nothing but the music and the high. I could manipulate the crowd, play the most complex forms of fusion jazz and convince them to like just about anything. It was an immense thrill, one which kept me chasing after it night after night. Later on the set gradually loosened and mellowed, flowing into a quiet and sad goodbye to the pinnacle moment, a time filled with blues and love songs. All was ending, disappearing. All was a run to the next high.

We sat and smoked and waited for the intermission to end. As we prepared to leave our little room, we shared a laugh and a mock hope that Amy wouldn't leave us up there with our pants down. We carried the smiles with us back down the hall, past the waiters and their rude comments, past a back-slapping Alessandro, out to the stage and the lights and the clamor.

I thanked the crowd and looked down to where Amy was seated. She replied with a quick little wave and a grin from the heart. If she was suffering from nerves she didn't show it.

"Many of you know my good friend Mario Angeletti," I began. "He and I go back a long, long way. Mario is here with us tonight, and he brought with him the leaders of his band, Jake and Amy Templer." I switched to English and said to them, "We're very glad that you could join us tonight."

I motioned for the spotlight as they rose to their feet. The stark white lighting transformed Jake into an ebony mountain and made Amy's high cheekbones and slanted eyes look mysteriously Oriental. Clearly the crowd agreed with me. Amy was a fine-looking woman.

"Amy, why don't you join us up here for a while," I said. She rewarded me with another smile and let Jake lift her up on stage. He handled her like a feather.

She walked up to the mike, grasped my upper arm, looked at me with eyes that searched deep. Very deep. I returned the gaze, unsure of myself despite the protective high.

She said, "I've been looking forward to this for a long time, Gianni."

Amy Templer turned around, approached the mike with a smile and a wave for the crowd. "Thank you very much," she told them. "It's a real pleasure to be here with you tonight. You certainly have a beautiful city."

There was a brief cheer from the crowd, which brightened her even more. "Marvelous; some of you speak English. That will surely help me get the message across, won't it?" She took the microphone from the stand and flipped the cord to free it. "This first song is by an American artist, Mr. Bryan Duncan."

She wore a dress designed like an Arab djellabah, the long hooded garb of the desert, made from white satin that cascaded in sparkling folds to her sandaled feet. The sleeves were long and loose and embroidered with little colored baubles that twinkled like prisms under the stage lights. Her dark skin made her smile look dazzlingly white as she turned to us and waved an open-palmed invitation.

Bruno counted us down, and we began.

The first song was a soft-shoe Chicago blues that Bruno laced out with wire brushes. It started out low-key and very husky, a whisper of a song with a very nice beat. I concentrated on playing this new song correctly, and I listened. Amy was good. Very good. She carried a lot of force even when she was quiet. That was a rare ability. She did not sing at that hushed, almost monotonous level because she needed to. She did it to prepare us for what was yet to come. I hunkered down over my guitar a little and listened to the words.

Lies upon lies are said to get by.
Lies upon lies are clouds in the sky.
Pretty soon it's gonna rain,
Ya gonna get those shiny shoes muddy.
Between the fools and the wise,
A smile can be a wicked disguise.[1]

Her purpose seemed very clear, or so I thought. She was working with relatively straightforward songs, ones whose success would ride completely upon her voice. She sang the second verse with occasional surges of strength, barely veiled promises of what she held in reserve.

This was followed by a solo that on Mario's tape had been done by a sax. Claudio and I had decided that he would perform the first half, then allow me to take over and finish it up. I played the steel-string Ibanez; Claudio had his computerized keyboards switched to the sound of an upright piano. We were trying to stay true to the song's original feel by adding a hint of barroom blues.

When I began the solo's second half, Amy joined in beside me. She sang a wordless chorus to my run, rising and falling to match me in harmony. It was quite a feat.

On the final verse she cut loose and showed what she was made of. The sound powered and reached out to the crowd. And to us. I saw Claudio and Bruno exchange glances, and agreed with them. This woman could really sing.

Lies upon lies to the wheres and the whys.
Lies upon lies bring tears to the eyes.
Gonna cry yourself a flood,
Ain't gonna be no ark to save you now.
Between the fools and the wise,
A smile can be a wicked disguise.

When she was finished, she bowed low and gave the audience a smile for the applause that washed over us. I was impressed. She was carrying a new audience with songs they had never heard before, sung by a woman they did not know, and in a language many did not understand. She had the voice and the looks and something more. She shone out there. She lifted

---

[1]"Lies Upon Lies," from Bryan Duncan's album *STRONG MEDICINE* on Myrrh Records. Written by Bryan Duncan © 1989, Fanatic Music/Panda Paws Music. Used by permission.

them up. She was magnetic in her happiness.

"Thank you so very much," she said. "Bryan is a fine Christian artist whom I admire very much."

I don't think many of them really understood her. The applause sounded more like people who just liked her music. But I understood. And so did Bruno. He looked at me, then at Claudio, mouthed the word in Italian, *Cristiano?* They play this in church?

"This next song is by a musician who has been in the Christian music scene for over a decade, first with the Imperials and now on his own. 'It Was Love' by Russ Taff."[2]

Bruno made even bigger eyes at me, motioned out the count, and we hit it.

It was R & B on the hard side, gutsy and heavy on the rock. The lyrics were sharp and simple, little pushes of power that struck out with the beat. A Tina Turner sound voicing words that spoke of love from somewhere beyond man.

Amy danced a swirl of flashing lights, covering the stage with streaming white satin. The crowd was up from the tables, dancing in the aisles. It was love, she said. Love. Shining down from above. It hit me, she cried, and I swung into a solo, with Amy right there beside me crying for everyone to look up and find love. Love. A blinding light from above.

When she closed us down we were all breathing hard.

"God loves you all," she said, waving to the shouts and whistles and applause. "How could I do anything else?"

Amy Templer fitted the mike back in the stand. "This last one is older than anybody in this room. My grandmother sang it to me when I was a child. It's called 'I Surrender All,' and I don't have any idea who wrote it. Deniece Williams came up with this rendition. She won herself two Grammy awards with the album."

I signaled our technician at the back of the room to lower the lights to two spots focused on Amy's face. Both the stage and the club fell to blackness, her shadow sending out sharp light-angles above Claudio, Bruno, and me. Bruno whispered out the count, and we began.

---

[2]"It Was Love," by Russ Taff, James Hollihan Music/Tori Taff Music/Darrell Brown Music/Geffen Music/ASCAP/Tall Girl Music (administered by Bug Music) BMI.

It was a love song, a slow, sweet melody, a perch from which Amy could soar. And the words left no question of her direction.

> All to Jesus I surrender,
> All to Him I freely give.
> I will ever love and trust Him
> In His presence daily live.

The power in the words filled the room and hammered at my chest. I sought to escape by searching the only two faces I could see through the spotlight's glare. Bruno and Claudio were caught up in the music, eyes half-closed, swinging their bodies in time to Amy's soaring voice. I wondered whether anyone in the audience realized to whom the song was directed. It was difficult to understand the words of a new song, especially in a foreign language. Then again, I thought as I felt myself drawn back to listening to the song's message, perhaps I wasn't the only one so touched by the fierce emotion with which Amy praised her God.

> All to Jesus I surrender
> Humbly at His feet I bow.
> Worldly pleasures all forsaken,
> Take me, Jesus, take me now.

The crowd was breathless throughout. A few listeners reached forward, raising outstretched hands up into the spotlight's concentrated beam. A few applauded between the verses. Most held their breath along with me.

> All to Jesus I surrender
> Lord, I give myself to Thee.
> Fill me with Thy love and power,
> Let Thy blessings fall on me.

When she finished and let her hands drop to her sides, there was a long stretch of silence, then pandemonium.

I stood there behind her, watched the lights come up and illuminate the fiercely cheering audience, saw her turn and open her arms to us in thanks. Bruno and Claudio applauded and smiled in return. I was unable to respond at all. I felt trapped inside a sudden surge of memories that came and went within the space of a heartbeat, yet which seared me with their power. I could see it all clearly, feel the applause wash over me in waves, but remained imprisoned within the recollections of a time I thought buried away forever.

I looked at Amy and the crowd and the band, yet saw another place when another crowd had reacted to me with a similar sense of abandon. And in the midst of my own first great success I had felt nothing. Instead of the joy and the triumph which I saw radiating from Amy, I had been surrounded by an emptiness so great it had threatened to engulf me. I had achieved a lifetime goal, and it had been worthless.

I realized that Amy was still watching me, and felt drawn by her look of heartfelt compassion. I sensed walls coming down inside me, faces of the past forcing their way out. I made a conscious effort to push it all away, but I was driven by the love in Amy's eyes to relent, to turn within, to confront what I had been running from for so very, very long.

PART ONE

You, however, did not come to know Christ that way. Surely you heard of him and were taught in him in accordance with the truth that is in Jesus.

EPHESIANS 4:20–21

CHAPTER
1

My mother died when I was five. She was an American, born and raised in Ann Arbor, from a strong old family. My father was Italian, born and raised in Torno, a tiny village perched on the side of a mountain that faces straight into Lake Como. He was from a working-class family. His father, my grandfather, was a stonecutter and wall builder. My father met my mother when she came to Italy to study Italian and joined the class he was teaching. They fell in love, and eleven months later they married in a little mountain chapel when they found out she was pregnant with me.

My mother's family was horrified at the news, both about the marriage and about the reason, namely me. But faced with the prospect of losing touch with their favorite daughter, they made the best of a bad deal and invited them home. My mother wanted her baby born in America, so they went. They were very, very much in love, my grandmother used to tell me, and little as my father wanted to leave Italy, he agreed to take her home.

So I was born in America and lived my first five years in a little house my mother's parents gave her. I don't remember much about that time. I remember the cold. I remember the way my mother used to rock me in her lap and sing me to sleep. She wanted to be an opera singer; that was why she went to Italy to study Italian and Italian opera, and so met my father, and had me. The misfit.

I remember, too, the way they used to fight, especially the winter she died. I tried to tell my grandmother about it once, but she said I was mistaken. And if I was not mistaken I should forget it. My parents loved each other very much. That was what I should remember. So I never said anything more to my grandmother about the fights. But I remembered them. I would lie in bed and feel the wall beside my head vibrate to the power of their voices—my mother's especially. She did not sound like an opera singer then. She sounded enraged.

I think they fought the night my mother was killed, but I'm not sure; the days and nights around that time are all confused in my head. Perhaps that was the reason my father went so crazy after she died, because they fought and she ran off and died in the snowstorm. Or maybe, as my grandmother said, he just loved her too much. Whatever the reason, my father went a little crazy.

Before, I remember my father as a strong, gentle, darkly handsome man who used to sit down on the floor beside me and talk with me very seriously. He seldom laughed, my father, but there was a quiet calmness to his strength that made it very nice to be around him. A comfort. He was the strength, the protection; my mother was the light, the song, the laughter.

In those gray, bleak days after the funeral, I watched my father crumble. Grief furrowed his face with lines that grew deeper and longer with every passing day. The strength became a hard rigidity, the quietness an oppressive silence. His handsomeness melted away, leaving only the darkness. And he began to look at me in a way that made me afraid to be near him. Somehow he made me feel as though I were the one responsible for my mother's death. Not by what he said, for he never said anything to me. His eyes would rest on me, though, with a weight I could sense. I would look up to find his gaze so filled with pain and fury that I would run away from this man I no longer knew.

My grandmother, my father's mother, arrived in America a few days after the car accident and stayed on to look after me and my father. It was the second and last time my grandmother ever visited America. The first time was the week after I was born. Something happened then, something she would never speak of directly. Whatever it was, it embittered my grandmother both to America and to my mother's parents. Whenever she spoke of my mother's family she would always become furious.

I would lie awake in the night and listen to my grandmother talk, her voice growing shriller and louder as my father remained silent. She spoke only Italian, my grandmother, and I knew only a few words, so our conversations were limited to a hello, a pat on the head, an occasional smile. In the dark loneliness that followed my mother's death, my grandmother became the light I lived by, the rock to which I clung.

The best time for me to approach her was when she was saying her rosary. I waited until the little beads were dangling from her hand, her eyes tightly shut and her lips moving in silent intensity, and I would sense a peace descending upon me. It was the only time during those dark, lonely weeks when the pain left me, when I caught a glimmer of hope. I did not need to touch her. It was enough to simply curl up in a tight little ball at her feet and experience a calm that I did not understand, a comfort that seemed to pour from her. When she finished she would reach down with strong ancient hands and scoop me up, hold me close, murmur words in a foreign tongue. It was enough.

My return with her to Italy was never really discussed, at least not with me. One day I found her packing my things into a big trunk, and I knew with a child's intuition that I would be going with her. I was old enough to understand that my father could not look after me, but I did not want to leave my home. I was afraid of losing touch with the things that kept my mother at least a little alive in my mind. Also, I barely understood a word of what my grandmother said. But I did not want to stay alone with my father. His darkness and his grief and his silence scared me. My mother's parents were shadow figures who flitted in and out of my life at odd moments and who meant nothing to me. I knew also that my grandmother could not stay. She did not speak English, she did not fit in here, and somewhere far away another grandfather I had never met was waiting for her. So I simply accepted the fact that when my grandmother left to return to Italy, I would be going with her.

I do not remember my father ever speaking to me about my departure. He may have, but I do not recall it. I do not remember him telling me goodbye. I do not remember my father speaking to me at all after the funeral. I do not remember him holding me, or comforting me as night after night I cried myself to sleep. If anyone came to me, it was my grandmother. All my memories of the time leading up to our departure for Italy are tinged with the darkness that seemed to emanate from my father. If one emotion stood out stronger than all the rest as our plane left Detroit for Chicago and New York and London and finally Milano, I believe it must have been relief.

When my grandmother told me the following autumn that my father had moved to Germany, among my many mixed emotions was relief that he was not going to come and disturb the peace I had discovered in my grandparents' home. Fearfully I waited for them to tell me that I must go to live with him in Germany, but they never did. I wondered why at times, and I was sad about it at times, but mostly I was relieved. The little stone cottage nestled two hundred meters above the lake had become home for me. With a child's ease I was learning Italian; it was the only language I had heard since my arrival nine months earlier. I had even started school that September, gathering in the village square every morning with the other youngest students and following the nun down the steep stone steps to the tiny elementary school by the lake.

There I was taught in the Catholic tradition, with chapel every morning and prayer all the time. We prayed before class, we prayed before recess, we prayed before lunch, we prayed after lunch, we prayed before we went home. After my seventh birthday, I went to Confession and took my first Holy Communion. I went to Mass with my classmates on Wednesday, and with my grandparents on Sunday. I knelt with the others and learned all the words and did what I was told to do and felt nothing at all, save a constant anxiety. I was terrified of burning in hell. The church made fear and sin and hell so real for me, much closer than goodness or God or heaven. It was a menacing presence, a threat which shadowed me daily.

I had a lot of questions. The only time my grandmother ever lost patience with my constant inquiries was when I asked her why I had to pray to someone up in the sky that I could never see, and how I was to thank the one who had taken my mother away from me.

Once in those early years I asked my grandmother why my father had moved to Germany. Because your father hated America, she replied. He found a good job in Ann Arbor teaching Italian and German at a local high school, but he never felt comfortable with the Americans. So why did he stay there, I asked, tying one question to the next as I often did. Because your father was so crazy in love with your mother he couldn't even remember his own name, my grandmother said. He loved your mother ten times more than he hated America. Ten thousand times more. I asked, but why Germany? My grandmother's face suddenly looked very tired. She said, your father feels he needs to make a new life for himself. He needs someplace without memories. My grandmother asked if I understood. I did not, but I nodded yes. I was tired of talking about my father.

Later that same winter I asked my grandmother why my father hated me. She looked at me a long time, her eyes glittering, then replied in a very quiet voice, what a question for a son to ask. Your father doesn't hate you. I found myself suddenly shivering very hard. I did not feel any emotion, but I could not stop my trembling. My voice quivered as I said, but he never writes, he never calls, he never comes to see me. He must hate me. My grandmother was quiet a very long time. Then she said, you cannot understand how much you are like your mother. I only knew her for a short time, your mother, but I see her in everything you do. The way you talk, the way you act, the way you love music—everything.

My grandmother smiled, her eyes still glistening, and stroked the hair that was always falling in front of my eyes. Even the way you ask your questions, she said. Your father does not hate you, figlio mio. He loves you very much. But it hurts him more than he can bear to see you right now, because he cannot look at you or speak with you without seeing your mother. His wound must heal, Giovanni. It is a deep wound that pains him very much, so we must be patient and give him time to heal.

So I waited as patiently as any child of seven can wait for anything he wants very badly. Eventually I found that the ache was easing, and as more time passed I noticed it did not bother me much anymore. Then I simply stopped thinking about him entirely.

For as long as I can remember I have filled the silence in my mind with music. Anything could trigger it—the wind whispering through trees, a passing car, a dog barking, a boat chugging its way down the lake, or nothing at all. At night the tiny attic that was my room in my grandparents' cottage became the center of an orchestra. I would stand in front of the mirror dressed in my nightshirt and slippers, conducting symphonies that only I could hear.

A few months after my arrival in Italy my grandfather had started me on the accordion. At five years old my right hand was not large enough to make proper chords on the keyboard. My left hand could barely reach over to the knobby buttons on the instrument's other side. I did not have the strength to draw the bellows. I was just barely able to peek over the top of the accordion and get my nose caught in the bellows as my grandfather cranked them back and forth. The instrument's weight was enough to cut off the circulation in my legs. Still, it was a glorious machine, glittering with inlaid mother of pearl and possessing more levers and buttons and handles and gadgets than my wildest fantasy. And it was music, and one day I would play it like my grandfather did.

My grandfather could make that accordion do anything but grow legs and dance. His stubby fingers would stab and weave and slide and tremble, his great arms would heave the machine around as though it were made of feathers, and music would pour out in a torrent. He could play anything, my grandfather, but his favorites were songs from his youth, folk songs and old dance tunes that I would listen to for hours while my grandmother stomped around the cottage in a huff.

My grandmother was an educated woman, a rarity for her generation in Italy. When most older women in our village would have long since retired to black nun-like dresses and black lace-up shoes and black shawls, my grandmother continued to dress in her severe classical style. Her own father had been a pharmacist in Como. Her marriage to a simple village peasant boy had been a major scandal. But she had loved her man, and she had married him, in complete disregard of her family and centuries of tradition, and whatever second thoughts she might have had later on she had kept to herself.

My grandmother had retained something of her past, a vestige of her breeding and her attitudes that had set her apart from the other old women of the village. She had been isolated from her class by her choice of husband, and from her husband's people by her heritage. It was not until I was much older that I began to realize what a lonely life my grandmother must have led in that tiny tradition-bound Italian village on the steep-sided lake of Como.

When my grandfather brought home a miniature accordion for my sixth birthday, my grandmother was horrified. She saw it as a step backward into lower-class imprisonment, a retreat away from the struggle to ensure that her children would be properly educated. For my grandmother, a proper education was one that would give her children the opportunity to rise above the station she had chosen for herself.

My grandfather was a simple happy man, content with his ways and his village and his life. And his wife. My grandfather never tried to change my grandmother, but neither did he allow her ways to affect him. As far as my grandfather was concerned, my grandmother did what she did for a good reason. The children would make up their own minds when they were older.

My two uncles learned ambition and determination from my grandmother. Seeing they would remain frustrated and chained in Italy, they immigrated. They chose Argentina for the simple reason that a distant cousin wrote and offered to sponsor them, on the condition that they work in his restaurant for five years. Ten years later they opened their own restaurant in Buenos Aires.

My father, on the other hand, was content to live and teach in Como. He was the one more like my grandfather, my grandmother often told me, a lover of hiking and history and Italy in general. Then he met my mother, and his world was overturned as only love can do.

My grandmother did not have the heart to make a scene over my learning to play the accordion, not after seeing the joy that shone in my eyes when I held my grandfather's gift. So she adopted another strategy, and pushed me to learn a classical instrument as well.

There was no room in our tiny cottage for a piano. That would have been my grandmother's first choice. But she was afraid I would not study if she was not there to watch, so no piano. Brass and woodwinds she did not especially like. Percussion did not even enter into the picture with my grandmother. That left the strings. The cello was too big for a child. The violin was an instrument of torture in the hands of a beginner. But there happened to be a fairly famous guitarist who had retired to a villa by the lake at the edge of our village. My grandmother went to see him, then came back and asked if I would like to learn guitar.

It did not occur to me that six years old was too young to be learning two different instruments. I loved my grandparents very much, and if learning these two instruments would please them, then I would learn. I had few friends and little interest in outdoor games. My happiest moments during those years in Italy were spent with my grandmother, listening to classical music on her radio, or sitting with my grandfather by the fire as he played the accordion. I saw no conflict between the two directions. It was music. I loved it all.

My life continued on this course until my grandfather died eight years after my arrival in Italy. I was thirteen. My grandmother never said anything to me, but I knew she was very upset that my father had not come to the funeral. Once again there were angry voices in the night, but this time my grandmother was shouting over the phone, and this time I understood what she was saying. A boy needs a man in the house, she kept shouting over and over. A boy needs a father! So it came as no surprise when she told me that we were moving to the city in Germany where my father now lived—a town far, far to the north, a place called Dusseldorf.

It took my grandmother seven months to arrange her affairs. My grandfather's will and pension had required much time and many meetings with various officials. My two uncles, my father's brothers, had traveled over from Argentina for the first time in many years to be at my grandfather's funeral. Once my uncles and their families had arrived, there had been no question of our leaving Italy before they did.

Many angry telephone calls passed between my uncles and my father, especially late in the night after I had gone to bed. There were shouts and curses when he refused to join them in Como, then a second phase of angry quarreling toward the end of my uncles' stay. I followed my grandmother's example and said nothing, giving no sign that I had even heard. If she was strong enough to keep her thoughts to herself, so was I.

. . .

We took an early morning train to Dusseldorf, my grandmother and I, seven months after my grandfather's funeral. My grandmother wanted us to take the early train so we would arrive in Dusseldorf before evening. It was not a good way to start a new life, my grandmother told me, arriving in a new home after dark.

A warm May wind greeted us with the fragrance of spring when we locked the cottage and loaded our bags into the waiting taxi. Dawn had just begun to paint the faintest tinge of light above the mountains as we took the winding road along the lake to the Como train station. The lake was forty kilometers long and one of the deepest in the world. Our village was located on a steep mountainside eighteen kilometers from the city. As our taxi sped through sleeping villages, I watched the mountains across the lake take form in the growing light like jagged shadows. When we drove around outlying points of land, I could see the city up ahead, a kaleidoscope of lights reflected in the lake, shining gold and red and white.

Once we were settled in our train compartment with the baggage stored over our heads, my grandmother turned toward the window with an expression on her face that told the world she did not want to be disturbed. I sat beside her and listened to the train sounds around me. A deep basso drummed and throbbed, with little staccato beats interspersed as we passed over crossings. Doors opened and closed along the corridor outside our compartment. Voices high and low sounded through the thin wall behind my head. Two children ran past our seats; their laughter chimed in my head, their footsteps a snare drum beating time. Soon I was lost in my private world of music and memories.

I sat and listened to my music and remembered my grandfather. There was a large cafe on our village's central courtyard where my grandfather liked to go. On warm days chairs and tables were spread out amid the dusty grass and oak trees, and children would dart and squeal around the old men gathered there. The cafe itself was a raucous, smelly, voluminous hall, filled mostly with old men arguing politics and football around rickety tables, or watching the masters play *biliardo di birilli*, a form of pool where the balls are rolled by hand.

Once again I heard my grandfather's voice, and felt how he used to gather me up when I would come for him. He would point out things, his voice low and droning, the unexpressed chuckle always just below the surface. His hands were as rough as the rock he cut and shaped and formed and laid in place. His clothes were dusty and sweaty and smelly. His eyes were alight with the pure pleasure of enjoying that most special moment of his day as he sat and held me and watched the people around us.

Once I asked my grandfather the questions that my grandmother would not answer, about who this God was and why He had taken my mother away from me. I asked him how I was supposed to speak to somebody I couldn't even see, and how He could even know who I was with all the other people everywhere. I asked my silent, softly smiling grandfather with his grizzled cheeks and rough hands and shining eyes how God could love me and leave me so alone. I let him hold me in his enormously strong arms as I struggled to ask if God could find me, even after I had traveled halfway around the world to this little cottage by the lake.

My grandfather waited until I was quiet again and all the questions were over. Then he pointed with his finger to a bird singing from the nearby shrub, and he said, "Shhh, listen. Do you hear that? God doesn't hear just you, little one. He hears every bird in every tree all over the world. And look over there, do you see the little leaf falling? God sees every leaf falling from every tree, even in the darkest night in the strongest wind, when millions and millions of leaves are falling all at once, He sees every one of them. Now think for a moment, my Giovanezzo, if such a great God as this can see the littlest and greatest, how are we to understand why He does what He does? Our task is to love Him. To obey Him. To trust Him. When this life is over, then we will be able to stand before Him and ask Him why. For now, to obey is enough."

My grandfather loved people and their voices and their laughter. He would sit for hours in the cafe, talking and listening and nodding and laughing and drinking, not because he wanted to drink but because it granted him entry into the world his heart craved. He would take me in his arms when I came to call him to dinner, and he would point out people to me. "Look at the way he stands," my grandfather would say. "Look how he favors that shorter leg. I was with him the day he was caught in the landslide. I carried him down that cursed mountain on my back. And look at that one's eyes; see how they glitter when he laughs, and watch now, see how they cloud over when someone wants to quarrel. You must watch out for men who show swift emotions in their eyes, Giovanezzo, they're weak and shallow and drift with every wind. They have no base, no rock to hold on to, and they're not to be trusted. And that one there; see how he always has one eye on his dog and one on his drink. Those are the two things he lives for. Is that not a lonely life? And the old one sitting there, smiling at everyone; see how grateful he is to those who stop and say hello. He doesn't have a little Giovanni to make his days so full, does he? Do you think maybe we should go over and say hello before we leave? Do you think he would like that? Do you think your grandmother will understand why we are so late again? Come, let us say hello to the other old man."

I curled up on my seat in the gently rocking, drumming train. I sat quietly and let the music and the memories lull me, careful to hide my face in the crook of my arm so that no one in the compartment could see my tears.

The trip from Como to Dusseldorf took eleven hours. The final thirty minutes from Cologne to Dusseldorf lasted an eternity. I sat quietly in the middle seat with my grandmother between me and the window, and tried hard not to think of what would happen when we arrived.

My grandmother's face was set in hard lines as she stared bleakly out her window. Her chin jutted forward in grim determination. One hand clenched and knotted a small lace handkerchief in her lap. The other grasped her rosary, but the fingers did not move, and I felt none of the peace that usually accompanied her prayers.

She wore a gray wool dress and jacket of severe style, a suit she kept folded away for important occasions. I had seen that suit a great deal since my grandfather's funeral, and I did not like it. My grandmother was an austere woman—not tall, but shaped with the sharp chisel-strokes of determination—and the suit magnified her edges and accented the hardness of her features. Whatever softness I knew in my grandmother disappeared when she wore that suit. With her iron-gray hair pulled tightly back and held in place by a myriad of pins and clips, my grandmother looked forbidding and unapproachable.

Our compartment had two rows of three hard seats facing each other, with a glass door opening into the hallway. All of the other seats were full. I studied the people in our compartment, with their silent unsmiling faces and blank eyes busy with papers and books and knitting. No one met my gaze; I did not exist for them. I felt the void grow and grow inside me until I felt I could not breathe.

In the afternoon light there did not appear to be any sky outside our window. Smokestacks and factories jutted upward into the leaden grayness like dark silhouettes. The clouds were so solid and heavy that I could not tell how high they were. I wondered why it did not rain when the sky looked like that.

My heart was thudding loudly in my ears as we entered the city. I watched the train pass along crowded avenues and flashing lights and windows darkened in ignorance of my arrival. Up and over the city streets we rose, past soot-darkened buildings that walled us in, past the long snaking tangle of railroad tracks, slower now, and we were there. My grandmother began giving me orders about taking the luggage down, brushing my breakfast and lunch from my clothes, straightening my jacket, hauling the bags through the narrow door and down the three stairs onto the platform. Once outside I stood in the cold strange-smelling air and listened to the speaker overhead blare a message I could not understand. A gust of wet wind whipped through my clothes, robbing me of the train's warmth.

Through the silent throngs came my father. I set the luggage down, straightened myself up, and wondered what I should do. His face was scarred with deep grooves and shadows that I did not remember. He spotted my grandmother stepping out of the train, and his lips tightened into a thin, bloodless line.

I looked up at my grandmother. Her face was as tight and grim as my father's. I felt a force emanating from both of them, a hard unyielding power reflected in their strong set chins and dark eyes. I looked from one to the other and felt weak and afraid and trapped by their strength.

The struggle between them broke as my father dropped his eyes to me. He searched my face, holding me still and breathless with his gaze. Then the hardness seemed to melt away, falling like a curtain from his features to leave behind a sudden softness and pain. His eyes brimmed full of a love and longing and anguish that made him seem as helpless as I felt. His chin trembled slightly. Then my father returned his gaze to my grandmother, and I watched his face settle back into those hard lines.

"You still don't understand anything," my father said. "You never will."

"You're talking nonsense!" my grandmother snapped back. "Help us with the bags."

My father surveyed the scattered pieces of luggage and stiffened when he spotted the two at my feet. He pointed at the square black case. "What's that?"

"Enrico's accordion," my grandmother said. "The boy's playing it now."

My father glared at the other case at my feet. There was no need to say anything. Its shape could hold nothing but a guitar.

He grabbed the two bags nearest him, turned for the exit, and flung at my grandmother, "Not in my house!"

I stared in alarm at my father, then looked to my grandmother. She shook her head. Wait. Not now. I pushed back at rising fears and put my faith in her strength.

My father drove the short distance in silence. I sat in the backseat, working out what I was going to tell my grandmother as soon as we were alone. My grandmother stared blindly through a dripping window at somber buildings and crowded streets. It had finally started to rain.

My father stopped in front of a gray stucco building that stretched the entire block, with doors set at regular intervals. Three floors of small square windows faced out at the rain and the clanging streetcars and the traffic drumming by on the cobblestone street.

"Make sure you lock the doors," my father said, and got out of the car.

My grandmother opened her door and called out, "What about the luggage?"

"Leave the bags," he called back. When he arrived at the entrance and saw we were not moving, he shouted, "This isn't Italy, Mama! The bags are safe in the car."

Before my grandmother could get out of the car I said to her, "I want to go home."

"Not now," she said, standing up.

"I hate this place," I said, scrambling out. I was desperate to stop her and turn her around. "Why are we here? He doesn't want us—"

"Come on!" my father shouted from the entrance.

"Lock your door, Giovanni," my grandmother said, and started toward my father.

We followed him through the massive oak door and into the foyer. Large square ceramic tiles gave way to linoleum-covered stairs with a tall wooden banister. Set in the ceiling overhead were plain white lamps giving meager light. The hall was quiet and gray and spotlessly clean and smelled vaguely of disinfectant. Quiet murmurs came from behind various doors as we climbed to the second floor. My father opened the first door on the landing, walked in, and called for Anna.

"Sit down," he said, pointing to a doorway on his right. "I'll make us some coffee. Anna!" He walked down a short hallway and disappeared.

I followed my grandmother into a room with white unadorned walls and gray carpet. A stern sofa and two matching chairs sat facing a coffee table with plastic flowers in a small vase. A large television stood against the opposite wall. At the other side of the room sat a dining table with four chairs. A cupboard in the same reddish wood as the chairs and table rose almost to the low ceiling. Outside the two square windows the traffic rumbled.

My grandmother looked slowly around the room, sighed, walked over and sat down on the sofa. I sat down beside her.

"I want to go home," I said. "I don't—"

"I know what you want and what you don't want," my grandmother said quietly. She looked very tired. "But we have to face realities, Giovanni. I know you are young, but we cannot put this off any longer. I am seventy-three years old. Do you understand what I am saying? Seventy-three years is too old to look after a child alone. What would you do if something happened to me?"

"I can look after myself," I said, leaning so far toward her I was almost on my knees.

"No you can't, and don't talk nonsense," she said crossly. "You must have someone to help care for you, and I am too old to do it alone. Finish. Do you hear me? The time for nonsense is finished."

She took the lace handkerchief from her pocket and wiped her lips. "That leaves us two choices, Giovanni. You can go with your uncles to Buenos Aires. They have said yes, although they don't much like the idea. How could they? Their brother is still alive, he is healthy, he has a good job; why should they take his son? But they will."

She looked at me, her dark eyes deep and unblinking. "My little Giovanni, I am too old to begin a new life in South America. Germany, yes. I will be close enough to return home every now and then. But not South America. It is too far for an old woman." She paused. "Do you understand what I am saying?"

I looked at her in horror. Slowly I nodded my head.

"You have already lost one family," my grandmother said. "It is too much to ask of a child to lose a second. As long as I am able, I will be here to care for you, figlio mio, but I cannot go to South America. It is too far." Her voice was very quiet. "Now do you understand why we are in Germany?"

Before I could say anything my grandmother focused on a sound in the hallway and reset her face into rigid lines. When my father and his new wife walked into the room, my grandmother and I were sitting silently side by side on the hard square sofa, our backs to the wall.

"This is Anna," my father said gruffly, not meeting our eyes. "She doesn't understand Italian."

Anna was a sallow-faced thin woman with unkempt straw-colored hair. She looked much younger than my father. Eyes downcast, she set the coffee tray down on the table, said something to my father in German, and quietly left the room.

My grandmother patted my knee. "Go out and play, Giovanni. We must talk, your father and I."

I looked at her. "Go," she said quietly. "It is all right."

Silently I stood and walked from the room. My father did not raise his head from the cup in his hands.

I walked out of the apartment and down the stairs, listening to my steps echo loudly through the white-walled hallway. I stopped before the massive front door, wondering how I was to open it. A shadow fell over the small pane of smoked glass set in the door's center. I stepped back as a red-faced man pushed his way through the door, his arms heavily laden, and stopped to peer down at me. He said something in German.

I swallowed. "Non capisco," I said.

He looked closer, the light glinting from his glasses. He needed a shave. And a bath. I backed away.

He grunted, said something else, then walked up the stairs. I watched until he reached the first landing and turned to peer at me again.

With both hands and a shoulder I managed to wedge myself between the door and its frame. As I twisted around and freed myself, I glimpsed the man still standing there, silently watching me.

The house's exterior was of stucco, as gray and heavy as the sky. I watched the faces of people as they went by, gray and expressionless like the man on the stairs. I shivered from the cold.

From behind me a voice piped up in Italian, "The guy couldn't bother to help out, I bet."

I whirled around. "What?"

The kid was about my own age. He jerked a chin toward the apartment building. "With the door. It was too much trouble to help, right?"

I nodded. "He just stood and watched me."

The boy spat the way an Italian woman does to show contempt, without really spitting anything. "Pazzi Tedeschi." Crazy Germans. "I hit a stone on my bike the other day, fell into the street, almost got hit by a car. So there I am crawling around, trying to get my head back on straight, right? All shaky and everything because the wind was knocked outta me, and you know what? I look up and there on the sidewalk are a dozen fat Germans, all staring at me like they're hoping the next car's gonna squash me flat." He spat again. "I hate this place."

I perked up. The kid was dressed in dirty patched overalls and a ratty sweater three sizes too big, and he talked like somebody I was pretty sure my grandmother would never invite into her home. His face had a hard, pinched, hungry look to it. But he hated this place and he was Italian. He was okay, this kid.

"What's your name?"

"Giovanni di Alta," I replied.

"Okay, Gianni, you wanna candy?"

I shrugged. Nobody had ever shortened my name like that before. And I had never met anybody who seemed so urgent about everything. He talked in staccato bursts, his body in constant motion. Twisting, arching, hooking his belt, talking with hands that stayed a blur.

My shrug was all he needed. Swift as a dart he moved toward a grocery stall set in the corner of our building, a cellar shop like hundreds throughout Italy, with fruits and vegetables stacked in orderly rows along the outside walls. I did not have to look inside to know that the space would be tiny and cluttered and full from floor to ceiling with boxes and cans and bags. The kid hesitated at the point where the sidewalk descended three stone stairs to the wooden fruit stalls extending out like two overburdened arms, then jumped. He covered the distance in three strides, slid under the stalls and around the accordion-like metal doors, and disappeared into the shadow. I held my breath.

The kid emerged, racing up the steps, did a three-point turn on the sidewalk, and flew past my nose.

"Mario!" The woman's scream made me jump. Dark unkempt hair and fiery eyes stuck out of the shop. "Figlio di un diavolo! You come back in here, an' I'll chop you up in little pieces!" The head disappeared.

Mario danced across the curbstones, ignoring both me and the now-silent doorway. Feeling my eyes on him, he made a gesture to the shadows that my grandfather used to make to his cronies when he thought I was not looking. I was not sure what it meant, but I knew it was bad.

The doorway remained empty.

Mario repeated the arm movement and threw his entire body into the act. Then he strutted over, tossed me a candy bar, jerked a thumb at the grocery store, and said, "That was my mother the saint. I'd introduce you, but she's busy blessing the congregation. You heard the way she blessed me?"

I chewed and nodded. It was good candy.

"She has a special way of blessing, my mother the saint does. When she's really excited she can bless you three blocks away." Mario grinned and attacked his candy. "I knew you were Italian 'cause I heard that old lady you were with yell at that guy. He a relative?"

"My father."

"Yeah? He's the one married to the German, right?"

"Yes."

"How come I never saw you before?"

"I've been living with my grandparents in Italy."

"You gonna stay here now? Yeah? How come?"

"My grandfather died. My grandmother says we have to live here."

"Tough." He chomped on the candy. "Where you from?"

"Lago di Como. You?"

"Milano. You know Milano?"

"No."

"I'm from Porto di Ripa Ticinese; that's a section of Milano. Milano's the best city in the world. I'd go back there tomorrow if I could."

Mario tossed his head toward the doorway, now filled with three old women in black shawls, black dresses, black shoes. A touch of the old country. "My parents have their grocery store, though," he went on. "They say we gotta stay here. What for? I ask. So we can buy a nice little place for our retirement, they say. What about me, I ask, I gotta stay in this hole 'til I rot? That's when they hit me and tell me to shut my face."

A battered van pulled up in front of the store. A wiry gray-haired man got out and started unloading crates. I asked, "You live around here?"

"Up above the store. You go in that last door over there, we're on the third floor." Mario brightened. "Hey, you wanna go see my radio? I built it myself. At night I can hear Italy on it."

The wiry man caught sight of us as he hoisted a load of crates and yelled, "Mario!"

Mario's face took on the pinched look again. "My father," he said, not turning around. "He's a saint too, just like my mother. You oughtta hear them when they start blessing each other."

"Mario!"

"I gotta go," he said. "He's just back from the market."

"Okay," I said, liking him. "Maybe I'll see you after we get moved in."

"Count on it," he said, grinned, and raced off.

I watched him pick up a pile of vegetable crates almost as tall as he was and shuffle off, whistling. I walked back to my father's entrance, found the door locked, and pushed the button beside his name. A few moments later the door latch buzzed. I lunged at the door with my shoulder, braced on the frame, and worked it open far enough with my foot to slip through. I walked slowly up the stairs, scuffing and clumping my feet just to hear the echoes fill the dim and silent spaces. I shivered as the musty-smelling warmth slipped through my clothes, making me aware of how cold I had become outside.

My father's new wife was waiting for me at the apartment door. She looked at me in silence, then turned away. Resentment seemed to roll off her in waves. We had invaded her home, her silence seemed to say. We had angered her man.

As I hung up my coat I heard my father say, "All right. There is a good boarding school near here where we can send him."

"I did not bring that boy over eight hundred kilometers for you to send him off to a boarding school!" my grandmother snapped. "Are we now a family who does not care for its own young?" She lowered her voice, pleading, "He is weak. He needs the strength of a family."

"I am his father. I will decide what he needs."

"Are you? Are you? And where have you been these past eight years? Being a father?"

I entered the room and stopped at the sight of my father's expression. "It was cold outside," I said.

"It's always cold here," my father said harshly. He turned back to my grandmother, demanded, "When does your train leave?"

My grandmother's chin jutted out, her mouth set in its grim line. "I'm staying with the boy."

His face flushed. "Mai," he spat. Never.

"You talk to your mother like that?" my grandmother hissed, her voice like ice. "First you don't want the boy, then you do, then you want to keep him just to send him away?" Her voice rose to a shrill cry that hurt my ears. "Who are you to tell me what I will and will not do? You? My son?"

She arched her back, her voice bitter. "You leave a baby boy in my hands and disappear into the night. Did that not happen? I hear nothing for a year, more; then you write a letter saying the pain is too much, please keep him a few months more. Is that not correct? Does this poor old memory still serve me? Was it not this same son who writes a year later to say he has married a German girl his own parents have never even met, that he is trying to put his pain and his past behind him? Do I not recall such a letter?"

She raised her chin higher and stared coldly down her nose. "Ah, the pain, the pain, only you feel the pain, only my son suffers. Where was he when his father died? Where? By his mother's side? Helping his mother with her own burden of pain? Showing respect for all the world to see? Being the proper son? Ha!"

My father seemed turned to stone. His face was a bloodless mask. His eyes within their dark hollows remained fastened on my grandmother.

"I stay," my grandmother said with finality. "I stay until I see what kind of father this stranger is, this man who was once my son."

.   .   .

My father never again raised the issues of my going to boarding school or of my grandmother leaving. Four days after our arrival my grandmother moved into a small apartment on the floor below where Mario and his family lived. Two days after that, she returned to Italy for her household belongings. The following three nights I spent in sleepless agony, fearful that she would decide to stay in Como. Who in their right mind would return here if they did not have to? But she did return, and by the end of the second week our lives had settled into a strange routine. I slept and ate breakfast in my father's apartment, moving about the place like a shadow. The rest of my time I spent away. Anywhere else; just away.

I avoided my father and his wife as much as possible in their apartment. I remained there only because my grandmother said I must. She turned a deaf ear to my tears and pleas until once, finally losing her patience, she slapped me hard and told me that I would stop pestering her or she would leave me here alone and return to Como. I gaped at her, filled with a cold horror. My worst nightmare had suddenly flashed before me. I walked softly around my grandmother for a few days after that, dreading the moment that she might decide to leave anyway. But she never did.

One week later, on the second of May, I entered a school where foreign children learned the German language. I attended the school four hours a day, five days a week, all summer long. After lunch I would do my homework under my grandmother's watchful eye, and then play my guitar for two hours. That was all the practice my grandmother would allow me. It was summertime, she said, a boy should be outside playing with friends and growing strong.

I never played the guitar in my father's house. Once my grandmother was settled in her apartment, I moved my instruments over and left them there. My father never mentioned my music. We rarely spoke at all. We would sit together in uncomfortable silence at breakfast, the three of us, until I left for school and they for work. They worked together in the same factory, my father as a clerk and translator in the international department, and his wife as a secretary.

After school I would lunch with my grandmother, practice, then play with Mario or help in the store until someone told me to go home. Sometimes at Mario's apartment they forgot I was in the back room where Mario was building his radio set. Once his mother came back to send him to bed, and a look of surprise and sadness filled her face when she found me still there. They were always nice to me at Mario's.

My grandmother made me sit with her every evening as she covered her head with the little lace prayer shawl and said her rosary. Not every day did I feel that peace reach out and cover me, but when it did the whole world seemed to slip away. In those moments I lost all concept of time—where I was, what was troubling me. I was content to sit and listen to the music sing through my mind like a summer breeze through an open window.

On the days when the peace did not come, I would sit in silence and try not to fidget because I knew it was important to my grandmother. One evening, the week after I started the summer-long language course, she opened her eyes sooner than I expected and found me swinging my legs and staring out the front window at the building across the street.

"What are you doing, figlio mio?" she asked me. "Is this not a time to pray?"

I hesitated for a moment, but because her eyes were filled with concern rather than irritation, I spoke the truth. "Who am I supposed to pray to? A God that brought me here to a land I hate and makes me live with a man who hates me?"

My grandmother sighed softly and replied, "Your father does not hate you, Giovanni."

But I had said it and did not want to retreat. "I am afraid to pray," I said. "If I pray I feel the anger inside me, and it scares me to be so angry at God. I can't play my music and feel the anger. So I don't pray."

My grandmother looked at me in sad silence for a time, then said, "I do not want to go to Mass alone, Giovanni. Mass is too important to allow you to just give it up. If I sat in Mass alone and knew you stayed here without me, I could not pray. You will do this for me?"

"I don't mind sitting here," I said, wanting very much for her to understand. "Sometimes it feels nice, like, like . . ." I struggled to find the words, could not.

My grandmother was quiet for a while, then said very softly, "Sometimes you feel the peace, is that what you are trying to say?" I nodded, not sure if peace was the right word, but grateful that she was trying to understand something that was so important to me, especially here, especially now.

"You could find this peace within yourself, figlio mio, if only you were to learn to pray," she said. "It is not right to have another person be the bridge between yourself and our Lord Jesus."

The coldness reached up from within me. I shook my head in fear. I did not want to bring that anger any closer. Not ever.

My grandmother's expression turned immensely sad, but

all she said was, "You may come and sit with me whenever you wish, Giovanni, but I will not force you. No one can force another person to pray. It is a discipline that must come from the heart, otherwise it is not done in truth nor in spirit."

"I will come," I told her, not understanding her words, but glad just the same for having been let off so easy.

Every once in a while my grandmother would ask me to play for her at night, usually on the guitar, but six or seven times that summer she said she missed my grandfather's music. She never thought she would ever confess to such a thing, my grandmother would tell me, but why did I not play her a little on Enrico's accordion? So out would come the gaudy machine. Straps were adjusted, knobs pressed, bellows unbuckled and opened, keys punched, and suddenly the room was transported to a fire-lit cottage on a steep mountainside overlooking a broad blue lake.

I would see my grandfather perched on his stool, pipe clamped between yellowed teeth, his stubby work-worn fingers coaxing song after song from his instrument. He gave life to ancient tunes of lost loves and eternal passions, speaking of an Italy that now existed only in half-forgotten songs. I would sit beside my grandmother and play those old songs until wordlessly she would rise, sigh, pat me on the head, and go silently off to her room. I did not play the accordion unless my grandmother asked me. It was too painful.

CHAPTER

2

At the end of August, four weeks before my fourteenth birthday, I entered the German public school system.

The school was new and made of brick and glass in the shape of an H. The asphalt courtyard in front of it was filled with wandering students when I arrived. I hesitated at the sight of so many strangers. Mario grabbed the shoulder of my jacket and dragged me forward. We entered the narrow center section, and I saw through the high rear windows that the back courtyard was a little garden.

"C'mon, Gianni, we gotta find your class."

I followed Mario over to the bulletin board running down one side wall. The school years were blocked out by strips of gold ribbon, with each class list printed on a separate sheet of paper. I joined Mario by the first class and searched for my name.

Beside us at the end of the bulletin board was a full-length mirror. Staring back at me was an undersized boy who seemed to be all skin and bones and sharp angles. The face looked very pale, very sallow. Tousled black hair hung like disorderly fringe around enormous black eyes. The reflection looked lost and a little afraid.

At the age of eleven or twelve, German children were given a national examination that influenced the rest of their lives. If they did well, they could begin at a Gymnasium, an intensive high school that prepared its students for university and the higher professions. If a student did poorly, he or she was assigned to a Hauptschule. There used to be a third form of high school called a Realschule, where students who failed the national exam at eleven could prepare to take a second exam at sixteen. When I entered German school, the Realschule was slowly being phased out, and the Hauptschule was taking responsibility for helping students prepare for the later Gymnasium-Staatsexam as well.

All this came out in a discussion we had with an official of the school board. The first week in August a letter arrived telling us that I was to report to such and such a building with my parents within five days. In the end, my father, my grandmother, and I went.

The officious little man from the school board sat behind his bare desk in his white-walled room and asked a lot of questions. I translated both the questions and my father's answers for my grandmother as best as I could. When the man finally laid down his pen and closed my file, he said that now he would answer our questions. My father said nothing. My grandmother watched my father for a long moment, her expression unreadable; then she told me to ask where I would be going to school.

Because I had not taken the state exam two years ago, the man said, I would be assigned to the local Hauptschule. He explained the German system. He could see that what he said upset my grandmother, so he adopted his most professional manner and said that the German school system was the best in the world and was laid out in a precise and logical manner. My grandmother asked if I could take the state exam now. Of course not, the little man replied, I was two years too late. Ah, of course, my grandmother said.

When I was sixteen, the little man said, I could sit for the second state exam. If I passed I could enter Gymnasium then, which would still leave me with three years to prepare for the Abitur. How many students do that, my grandmother asked. The little man shuffled papers and replied, from this school, three students made the jump last year. Out of how many, my grandmother asked. The man replied, from a class of four hundred and ten.

My grandmother was silent for a time, then asked quietly,

I need to trouble this gentleman with one further question, Giovanni. Ask him about religious training in the schools. For the first time the man seemed at a loss. I don't understand the question, he replied. My grandmother said, tell him that you have been raised a good Catholic, and have been taught in a Catholic school. I need to know if this will continue. The little man showed contempt in his face and his voice. Religious training has no place in a proper school, he said. It is the task of a school to teach, not to indoctrinate. You can rest assured that no such dogmatism will be tolerated within the German school system. My grandmother sat silently through it all as I rushed to keep up. My father did not say a word. When the little man was finished, my grandmother sighed and said, I have no more questions. Thank the man for his time, Giovanni.

Wait, I said, and to the man I asked if I could take guitar lessons at my Hauptschule. He consulted another paper and replied, no, there was music appreciation twice a week, but no lessons for individual instruments. What about at the Gymnasium, I asked. He looked at me, then searched for another paper. No, not there either. But at sixteen or seventeen a student could apply to the Musikakademie. I sat and wondered dismally if my father would pay for private guitar lessons. My grandmother finally asked what I had said. When I told her she looked at me for a moment, then said quietly, thank the man, Giovanni. We have taken enough of his time.

As I stood in the hall beside Mario and searched for my name, I wondered how much private guitar lessons would cost in Germany. More than my grandmother could afford, I was fairly sure. I dreaded having to ask my father for the money, dreaded having to plead with him, dreaded being forced to go begging to my grandmother after my father said no.

"Here's your name, Gianni. Class 26-B." Mario showed disappointment. "We're in different classes this semester. Tough."

"Can't we ask them to change us?"

Mario shook his head. "They don't like switching people around."

"But I won't know anyone in my class, Mario. Who can I talk to?"

He gave me an amused look. "You'll find somebody, Gianni. The Germans aren't all cold as machines. Some of 'em are okay." He turned away. "C'mon, I'll show you where your class is. You don't wanna be late your first day."

The classroom, at the end of the building, had small windows up high on the back wall. The outer wall had tall windows covered by floor-to-ceiling curtains of green gauze. Light coming through the curtains transformed the classroom into a murky den.

Mario left me at the doorway with instructions to find him in the front hall after classes. The room was half full. I walked in and chose a desk in the far back corner.

Out of the side of my eye I watched the room fill rapidly. I kept my face turned toward the windows. Through a space in the curtain I could see the stone wall of the next building. I listened to the students laugh and chatter around me. Some of what they said I could understand, but much was slurred or shouted or distorted and meant nothing to me.

Abruptly the overhead lights went on, and into the sudden silence walked the teacher. With brisk movements she walked to the front of the class, wrote her name on the blackboard, and introduced herself as Fraulein Rohr. Twice a week we would be staying over with her for the first class, she told us, when she would teach music appreciation. The other three days we would have sports.

She was a bright, cheery woman, thin and blond, with weak blue eyes swimming behind thick lenses. Her hair fell in careless disarray around her forehead and over her shoulders. She had a nice smile, soft and tender, and she loved music. I knew that as soon as she placed the record on the turntable and closed her eyes and swayed ever so slightly to the scratchy melody.

When the piece was finished she clapped her hands and looked excitedly at the class. "Now, which one of you can tell me who composed that piece?"

It was a Mozart concerto, one of my grandmother's favorites, but I did not raise my hand. When no one else volunteered the information, she began in her brisk, excited way to describe the author, the period in which he lived, and a little about the music he wrote. She loved music, all right. I was very sorry I would see her only twice a week.

She played the first movement to another Mozart concerto and talked about it for a little while. Toward the end of the class she asked if anyone played a musical instrument.

Two girls at the front of the room raised their hands. One played piano, the other violin. I listened and watched very carefully. Fraulein Rohr gave them her soft smile, talked about how nice their instruments were, and asked how long they had been playing. Two years for the pianist, and the other had just begun. "That is wonderful," Fraulein Rohr said. "Do you have private teachers?" Both heads nodded. "And do you know about the teacher who visits this school?" I leaned forward, listening intently. The two heads nodded again. "Well," Fraulein Rohr said, "I hope you will enjoy your music very much, and study hard. Learning an instrument is never easy, but the rewards are very great; you will cherish the music all your lives."

She gave the girls another smile, looked out over the class, and asked, "Does anyone else play an instrument?"

My heart in my throat, I raised my hand.

"So, so. Someone from the back of the room finally decides to talk with me." Her smile took the sting from her words. "And what is your name?"

"Giovanni di Alta."

"What a nice name. And which instrument do you play, Giovanni?"

"Guitar," I said. I decided not to mention the accordion.

"Why, I believe we have a guitar in the common room." In a moment of sheer terror I thought she was going to ask me to play for the class, but all she said was, "You are a new student, aren't you? Yes, I see here I have a note; this is your first year in Germany." She smiled again. "I hope you enjoy it here very much."

I stammered my thanks. All the class was looking at me.

"How long have you played the guitar, Giovanni?"

"Eight years."

She showed surprise. "You started playing the guitar when you were six years old?"

I nodded.

"And who taught you?"

"A man in our village." That sounded very incomplete to me, so I added, "He taught at a conservatory before he retired."

"I see." The room was very quiet. "And so you play classical music on your guitar, is that right?"

All the attention frightened me. I dropped my eyes to my desk and nodded quickly, a short single jerk.

"And do you have a teacher here in Germany, Giovanni?" Her voice was soft, coaxing.

Again with a tiny jerk I shook my head, no.

There was a brief silence. I kept my gaze directed at my desk, but I could feel eyes on me. Fraulein Rohr said, "Perhaps you will remain after class a few minutes, Giovanni. I will give you a note for your next teacher."

The bell signaling the end of class rang. The hall outside our room erupted noisily. My classmates filed out and joined the tumult. I remained at my desk. Fraulein Rohr walked back to stand beside me.

"I saw that you were afraid when I asked you about your guitar playing. There is no need to be afraid, Giovanni. We ask every class if there is someone interested in playing an instrument because the school does not have music instruction."

I nodded. This I already knew.

"But if someone is very interested we can perhaps arrange for instructions here in the afternoon." She smiled at the sudden light in my face. "I do not know if our instructor teaches guitar; I think he does, but I'm not sure. We will have to see. He gives lessons on several instruments at all the Hauptschule in Dusseldorf. But first we need to hear you play, yes? Will you play for me now that we are alone?"

"Yes." The prospect of having a teacher overcame all my hesitations.

I followed her to the teachers' common room, which was very crowded. Fraulein Rohr led me into a small conference room off to one side, stepped out, and returned quickly with an old classical guitar.

She gave me the guitar, sat down facing me, smiled gently, and said, "Now play me something nice."

Quickly I tuned the guitar. I played a very simple melody by Mozart, one which I had studied several years ago. When I was finished I looked up to find her staring at me strangely.

"That was very nice," she said softly. "What was that called?"

I told her.

She nodded. "I thought I had heard it before. I did not know it was a piece for guitar."

"It wasn't," I said. "That was a student's rendition." I used the Italian word *riedizioni* because I did not know how to say it in German. She nodded as if she understood.

"Would you play something else?"

I would have played for her for hours. I chose another rendition, this one a bit harder, a Schubert sonata that I thought she would recognize. When I finished I looked up to find her smiling.

"That was one of my favorite pieces when I was a little girl," she said. "Was that another rendition?" She used the German word *Transkription*. "Yes? It was very nice, Giovanni. You certainly have talent. I think we should have you play for Herr Scherer. Would you like that?"

I nodded, then blurted out, "Will you be there?" I felt my face blush bright red.

Fraulein Rohr smiled in reply. "You should not be so frightened by teachers, Giovanni. We want to help you. How long have you been in Germany?"

"Six months."

"You speak German very well for only being here six months." She became serious. "It is very different here, isn't it?"

I nodded. Very, very different.

She was silent for a moment, then stood. "So. We must send you on to your next class before your teacher thinks I have kidnapped you. I will arrange for you to play for Herr Scherer. Will you play for him? Good. He is a very nice man and you don't need to be afraid of him. I will find out which afternoon he teaches here and I will let you know. Is that all right? Fine. Now let me write you your note."

As we rode the tram home from school, I told Mario about maybe having found a guitar teacher. He replied with, "I can't get over you, Gianni. I mean, the shyest guy I've ever met, playing for a teacher the first day at school."

"I was really worried about this."

"Yeah, you musta been. Hey, how about letting me hear you sometime?"

"Okay." I followed him off the tram and down toward their little store. I did not feel like practicing that day.

Mario had begun to work for his parents that summer after his older brother took a job at the American military base in Darmstadt. The store was open twelve hours a day; Mario's afternoon shift gave his mother a chance to tend to their apartment and his father time to go to the local markets.

Every cent Mario made, which was not much, went into old and battered stereo equipment. Little of it worked. Mario spent every free moment stripping and testing and repairing and reassembling. He was almost as fanatic about his mismatched pile of boxes with their flashing lights and dials and switches as I was about my music.

As soon as we entered the apartment, Mario announced the news to his mother. She clapped her hands and gave the heavens a look and a two-hand shake. I had seen the black-clad ladies of our village do that when they received good tidings. "At last," she said, "our Gianni has something to be happy about. Come, sit down. The house can wait another minute. We can celebrate with a cup of chocolate. You like chocolate? Good. You should drink more of it, you with a body like dried sticks that would blow away in a strong wind. Sit, sit, then both of you can tell me all about what happened."

So Mario told it again as if he had been in the room, making it into a feat of wonder and entertaining us both. I sat and smiled and looked about me. The apartment had a musty, damp smell that told of infrequent cleaning and airing. The kitchen was a mess. Dirty pots and pans lined the sink; peppers and onions and bits of garlic clove littered the counter by the stove. The ceramic flour crock was turned over, and flour spilled over the shelf and into the sink; around the stove were tiny spatters of grease. Mario's mother's hair was tangled in a loose knot that threatened to come undone as she leaned over me, and there was grime under her fingernails. I sat there and looked around and remembered how my grandmother would talk of women in our village who kept their houses like this.

But there was something here I could not explain, a sense of belonging. It did not matter what people might say about her housekeeping. I decided it did not matter what people thought about her at all. I was content to sit and sip my mug of hot chocolate and feel her rough hands stroke my head and listen to Mario weave his incredible story, and know that here at least was a place where I was welcome.

That evening I walked through falling mist and cold metallic air to Mass with my grandmother. She was leaning on me more heavily than usual, and had not felt at all well that afternoon. But the light in her eyes was still there, and it glowed more strongly as I told her about the possibility of guitar lessons. I watched her eyes as I spoke, standing in the misty evening, waiting for the traffic light to change. As I finished talking I realized there were only three times when I could remember the light not being there—on the train ride up to Dusseldorf, during that first argument with my father, and when my grandfather had died. There were probably other times, but I could not remember them. I watched her face and realized how much that warmth and love and light in her gaze meant to me. At times like these I could drink in the strength and the hope from her eyes.

"I am truly pleased, figlio mio. It was something which I have prayed about all summer. But I said nothing because I knew of nothing that I could do. This is not Italy."

"I know," I muttered.

"So. You have a teacher. I am very glad to see you continuing with your music." She stopped to cough into her handkerchief. "Excuse me. This cold and damp has reached into my bones today."

"This weather is making you sick," I said. "I wish we were home."

"We are home," she said sharply. "I do not have the strength to put up with your nonsense tonight. Finish."

I stood at the intersection and waited for the light to change, watching the blank faces crowding the sidewalk around me. Their skin looked gray, their eyes cold and dead as the air. There was no greenery, just steel and concrete. The traffic drummed in my ears, making me feel like a misplaced cog in a giant machine.

Because of the number of Italian families in Dusseldorf, three local churches held Wednesday and Sunday Masses in

Italian. The church on our side of town was within walking distance of our apartment. It was constructed of red brick, and looked as though it had been built to meld into the office buildings on either side. The interior was all stone and brick, so that the tiniest sound came crashing back from all sides. The windows were long thin slats filled with abstract stained glass designs. The altar was separated from the front pew by one long low step, the table and pulpit made of light-colored wood that had no adornment whatsoever. Instead of a cross, above the altar hung a figure of a man suspended by two chains reaching out from either side wall and connected to his wrists. The metal figure was thin, like a child's stick-drawing, and his face looked more asleep than in pain. The first time my grandmother entered the church, she looked around and declared, whoever built this place did not believe in God. I thought the church suited most of the people I had met in this land.

I endured the smiles and caresses of the women my grandmother had befriended, waited as quietly as I could while they gathered in clusters to adjust prayer shawls and bemoan the fates that so plagued their lives. There were few men here and almost no young people. I stood as far to the edge of the group as I could, and waited for the bell to ring and for us to enter the sanctuary.

Usually my time in Mass was spent in a dull fog. I retreated behind a veil of sleepiness to hold out what I did not want to face. But today my grandmother's words rang in my ears, and the fog would not come. This was not home for me. It never would be. I hated this place. I did not belong here. My father did not want me. To have to live with him, to see him every day and watch him turn away from me, to see the resentment in Anna's eyes whenever I entered a room, to feel their coldness toward me, was agony. It tortured me. I nodded my head slowly. Yes, I truly hated this place. I was trapped in a home and a city and a land where I did not belong and never would. I looked up at the horrid ugly sleeping figure suspended from chains across the front of the church, and I felt my anger spill out in waves. The sterile feeling of the place and the figure blanketed me with indifference. I felt trapped by forces that cared nothing for me at all.

.   .   .

Two days later I remained at school after everyone had left. Being alone and without the normal authority that regulated school life filled me with a curious sense of freedom. I walked the empty halls, listening to my footsteps echo up and down the corridors, peering into rooms that seemed so different without their normal noisy charges.

My ears led me to the classroom used by Herr Scherer. Even with the door closed the piano sounded thunderous in the empty space. I waited outside until a sullen boy a year or so older than I bounded from the room as though escaping from a dungeon. I knocked on the open door and was told to enter.

The kindness that Fraulein Rohr showed in her smile was there in Herr Scherer's eyes. They were large, gray, tired, gentle eyes. His gentle gaze softened the fatigue lines etched deeply through his face above the beard.

He nodded his head at me in greeting. "You are—" He consulted a sheet on the small table by his side. He sat in one of the teacher's straight-backed chairs next to a tired-looking piano. A battered guitar case lay near his feet. "Giovanni di Alta. Did I say that right? Can you speak German?"

"Yes."

"Come sit down." He pulled another chair over in front of his own. "You are here to show me how well you play guitar, is that right? Did you bring your guitar? No? Well, you can use mine. It is an old guitar, but it had all six strings the last time I looked, and it still plays."

I went over and sat down. He was not a tall man, but every part of him was big. His chest was broad, his face thick and seamy, his hair grayish-black and in curly disarray. He wore corduroy trousers with the knees scuffed shiny and a heavy dark hand-knitted sweater. He opened his case and held out the guitar in a strong hammer-like fist.

His voice was deep and as kind as his eyes. "Fraulein Rohr has told me that I must be careful not to bite. She says if I do you will become afraid and not play for me. Are you afraid of me, Giovanni?"

I shook my head, gave a tentative smile in reply to the one in his eyes, and took the guitar.

Herr Scherer sighed in mock relief and slapped his hands on his knees. "Ah, that's all right, then. My wife calls me a bear sometimes, but I don't remember ever eating any of my children. What would you like to play for me?"

I found my voice. "I don't know."

"Well then, why not play what you did for Fraulein Rohr? She said it was very nice, and I have always enjoyed very nice music, especially when it's played by children who don't like to be eaten."

So I played the first piece, a brief sonata. When I finished I found him looking at me very thoughtfully.

"Fraulein Rohr was correct," he said in his deep voice. "Play something else, Giovanni."

I thought a moment, then chose a piece by Rossini, simplified for students, but still retaining some of the difficult runs that were Rossini's artistic signature. I did not know anything about the pattern of Rossini and his music at that time. All I knew was that it was a difficult piece which I had mastered. I wanted to impress Herr Scherer. I wanted to become his student.

The same thoughtful look was on his face when I finished playing. Herr Scherer curled his lower lip up until it hid most of his mustache, and stared sightlessly at his guitar.

"That was very nice as well, Giovanni," Herr Scherer said. "How long have you been playing?"

"Eight years."

"Very nice," he repeated. "Do you always play without scores? Do you know that word?"

I nodded my understanding. "Once I have learned a piece I don't need to see the music."

He studied my face a moment longer, then let the smile creep back into his eyes. "Giovanni is a mouthful of a name, isn't it? I think your name would make a bigger meal than you would. What do your friends call you?"

"Gianni."

"A much easier name. You play very well, Gianni. Very well indeed. I don't think we need to stop right yet. Would you like to play something else?"

I nodded, and began retuning the guitar. I loved a piece by Barbetta where the guitar strings were tuned to a C chord. The piece had been very difficult for me to learn, because all the chord positions which I had mastered for the standard tuning no longer fit. The piece itself was melodious and not extremely difficult, but for me the swift retuning was like an announcement that I had moved into another realm of guitar. It was as though I had learned another dialect of my language.

Herr Scherer's lower lip was rolled up in thought again when I stopped. He looked at me a long time.

"So," he said, and slapped his knee again. He straightened his back from the bent-over position it had taken during my playing. His eyes smiled at me, this time a little ruefully. "I have enjoyed your performance very much, Gianni. You play very nicely. No, that is not correct. You play wonderfully."

I stammered my thanks, proud and excited and bashful at the same time.

Slowly he shook his head and tasted his mustache again. "But I cannot take you as a student."

I was crushed. "Why not?"

"Don't look at me like that, Gianni. I can't teach you a thing. You play far better than I could if I spent the rest of my years practicing guitar. No, don't laugh; it's true. I would love to have a gifted student like you, but there is nothing I can teach you. Nothing. Do you understand that?"

I nodded my head, my eyes on the floor. I felt as if I had lost a friend.

He cupped my chin in one vast hand and raised my face. "Don't feel bad, Gianni. I'm sure there is something we can work out here. It will take a few days for me to do some checking, and then we will see. Do you live with your parents?"

"With my father."

He nodded. "Can you ask your father to come talk with me one afternoon next week?" He reached for a tattered daybook on the table, thumbed the pages, squinted. "Could he come here at five o'clock next Thursday?"

I hesitated, then asked, "Can my grandmother come? She lives next door to us."

Herr Scherer looked closely at me. "Why don't you want your father to talk with me, Gianni?"

Ashamed, I looked down at the floor again. In a small voice I replied, "He doesn't like my music. He won't let me play in his house."

"Your father won't allow—" Herr Scherer cut himself off. I

looked up. His face was like stone. He asked, "Do you have somewhere to practice, Gianni?"

"At my grandmother's."

"I see." He tugged at his beard with one fist and sighed. "Well, your father must come if he is your legal guardian. Do you understand that word, guardian? I have an idea, a place where you might take your lessons, but I must first check on a few things and then speak with your father. You are very young, Gianni, so we must follow the rules very carefully. I have never tried to do this with someone so young. I have never heard of it being done. But why not? You play well enough, that's for sure. First I must talk to some other people, and then I must meet with your father. Do you think he will come talk with me?"

I thought about that. "Can my grandmother come with him?"

For the first time he smiled with his whole face and showed a mouthful of disorderly, yellowing teeth. "You think your grandmother will make him come and listen to me?"

I smiled and nodded, liking him immensely.

He laughed, a booming sound. "By all means, have your grandmother come too. I would like to meet this lady. And your father." His eyes clouded over. He sighed, turned back to his daybook, and made a note. "Five o'clock in a week from this Thursday, here in this classroom, yes?"

"Thank you."

He smiled and held out his hand. "It was nice to meet you, Gianni."

Awkwardly I extended my hand and watched as it was swallowed by his. "I am sorry that you won't be my teacher."

"So am I, Gianni, so am I. It would be nice to teach a virtuoso." He shrugged his shoulders. "But it would be a foolishness for me and a waste of time for you. Do you understand?"

I nodded, feeling slightly lightheaded. A virtuoso, he had called me.

There was a knock at the door. We both started slightly, as though caught doing something wrong. His eyes crinkled into another smile. "So. You must tell Fraulein Rohr that I thought you played very nicely too, yes? And tell her also that I was very careful and did not bite. Five o'clock Thursday after next, Gianni. With your father and your grandmother. Goodbye."

CHAPTER
3

Over the coming days my life split in two. On the one side was my music, where there was joy and a few friends and the love of my grandmother to sustain me. On the other side was everything and everyone else—a world that cared nothing for me at all, did not care whether I was even alive. The people of this world were either blind to me or wished that I was somewhere else. My father was there in this world, and his wife. So were almost all of the people in my school. I walked the halls as I walked the streets, alone in a crowd that seemed to look right through me. For most of my classmates I did not exist. When they did notice me, their hostility was a wall that held me out.

Mass and church and prayer before meals with my grandmother all fell into the world of coldness and uncaring. It never occurred to me that religion could be anything but a burden to endure. But I did not often complain. To question the existence of a God who would kill my mother and deposit me in Germany upset my grandmother very much. My thoughts and feelings about God and faith I kept to myself.

I continued to hope for the brief moments of peace during my grandmother's evening prayers. I refused to question its origin, refused to even think about what it might be. To connect it consciously to God would have threatened its presence, and the quiet times were too precious to risk losing. So I continued to sit in the evenings with my grandmother, hoping without thinking that the peace would arrive, never asking where it came from, never wanting to know. That it came was all that mattered.

In those early days I began studying the faces that surrounded me. I did not realize it at first, but with time I came to accept that I was searching. I walked the streets and looked into eyes that refused to see me. I passed silently through crowded school halls and watched faces devoid of light. Beautiful faces, ugly faces, faces framed by a rainbow of hair colors and eye shades and clothes. So few of the faces seemed to hold a light within.

I wondered sometimes if I was simply growing up and seeing something that had always been, everywhere I had lived, all the places this strange life of mine had pushed me into. Other times, especially when I was sitting with my grandmother and listening to her whispered prayers and hearing the little rosary beads click through her restless fingers, I would cling to the belief that there were places in the world where people cared. Where people saw. Where eyes showed more than just a blankness inside. Where hope and joy and light and laughter really existed. When I pushed through the heavy door of our apartment house and began another day among the blind, it helped me enormously to hold fast to this belief.

Gradually I learned to live with the coldness of my world. I wrapped myself in a blanket of lethargy, a fog that shielded me from noticing too much. There was the fog, and there was my music. I would spend hours sitting in class or walking the halls or lying in the silent darkness of my room at night, playing fantastic melodies in my mind—melodies that contained all the light and hope and joy that was absent from most of my world.

Nine days after playing for Herr Scherer, I returned to school at five o'clock with my grandmother and my father. Herr Scherer asked me to wait outside while he spoke with them. The meeting lasted over an hour. For a while, I stood in the hall and listened to the rise and fall of murmurs from behind the closed door. Then I walked up and down the empty hallway, scuffing my feet and clapping my hands, listening to the music in my head ringing with the echoes. Then I stood in the central passage looking out the tall glass windows at the back garden and wondered what they could be talking about for such a long time.

When I finally heard the door open, I raced back to stand and watch the three of them come out. My grandmother was first, and the expression on her face sent shivers up my spine. A light shone from her eyes. She stood across the hall from me and bathed me with that light.

My father's shoulders sagged as he walked slowly from the room. He wore an expression of bewildered pain. He glanced at me and swiftly turned away, and I remembered the way he had looked at me at the train station the day I had arrived from Como.

Herr Scherer was grinning broadly and showing his discolored teeth. He winked at me, then waved a sheaf of papers toward my father. "All of these have to be filled out before next Friday," he said.

My grandmother stepped over and took the papers. "Gianni, tell the gentleman I will take you myself to the academy on Friday."

I stared at her. "What academy?"

She bathed me again with that light. "The guitar professor of the Musikakademie wants you to play for him. The gentleman has told him about you. If he likes you, he will take you as a private student."

Herr Scherer asked, "Did your grandmother tell you what has happened?"

I nodded dumbly, looking back and forth from Herr Scherer's broad grin to my grandmother's shining eyes.

My father's normal grim expression returned. He turned and walked toward the end of the hall. Herr Scherer's face became blank as he watched my father's back.

"I'm sorry we took so long, Gianni," Herr Scherer said. "But your father—" He hesitated, then said simply, "Your father did not want to translate everything for your grandmother."

When my father disappeared around the corner, Herr Scherer turned to me and let the smile come back into his eyes. "If the professor decides to take you as his student, we'll enroll you at the Musikakademie," he said. "That's the only way the state will pay for your lessons."

"Tell me what he's saying," my grandmother insisted. Numb from shock, I translated about the enrollment.

She nodded her head, her shining eyes darting back and forth between me and Herr Scherer. "I understand," she said. "That is what these papers are for."

"Take the forms with you when you play for Herr Professor Doktor Schmitz," Herr Scherer said. "If he decides to take you he will present the forms to the academy board himself. You will be enrolled as a private tutorial student under Herr Professor Doktor Schmitz. Can you remember that name?"

"Herr Professor Doktor Schmitz," I repeated breathlessly.

"You address him as Herr Professor," he said. He leaned toward me and added with mock ferocity, "You will not be afraid of him, do you hear me? If you are afraid I will eat you myself. I have gone to a great deal of trouble here, Gianni. If the professor takes you, you will be the youngest student at the Musikakademie. The youngest student in the academy's history, as far as anyone knows. And if you are afraid when you meet him, I will have you with my morning toast and coffee." He pulled the edges of his mouth down. "Have I made myself clear, or should I sample a couple of toes right now, just to make sure I've got your attention?"

"I understand," I said, grinning.

"And you won't be afraid," he growled.

I shook my head. I could not believe it was really happening.

"Gianni," my grandmother pressed.

Swiftly I translated what Herr Scherer had said. She looked at him, her glance shedding the same light on him that it had on me.

"Ask the gentleman if he likes Italian food," she said. I did so.

Herr Scherer gave my grandmother a look of soulful yearning. "I love the Italian kitchen almost as much as I love my wife and children. Sometimes a little more."

"He says yes," I told my grandmother.

"Tell him that we must invite him over very soon and I will cook for him. Perhaps next week."

"And his wife," I said.

"Of course, and his wife. I did not know he was married."

Herr Scherer grinned through his unkempt beard. "Be sure

and tell me the day before, so I can prepare myself. I will skip all meals that day. And maybe do some exercise. No, that would be going too far."

"He looks forward to coming," I told my grandmother.

Herr Scherer added, "And tell her that I will try to bring the other thing we discussed to the dinner."

I translated for my grandmother and asked, "What other thing?"

"Nothing important," she said coolly. "Ask him when he wants the money."

Herr Scherer waved it aside. "First we must see if it is possible, and if he will go easy on the price." He glanced at his watch. "Do you realize we've been at it for almost two hours? My wife will roast me and serve me up for supper. Goodbye, Gianni. I am very glad this has worked out so well." He gave a little bow to my grandmother and walked down the hall, whistling a cheerful tune.

"A very fine gentleman," my grandmother said. "He has done us a great service. Come, figlio mio; it is time for us to leave as well."

My father was waiting for us at his car. When we appeared he started to say something, glanced at me, and changed his mind. He unlocked the doors and we climbed inside, my father and grandmother in front and me behind. My grandmother reached back between the front seats and took my hand. The same light and strength that I had felt from her eyes surrounded me as she squeezed my fingers in her dry, work-worn hand.

"So," she said quietly, "your son has just been praised to the very heavens by one of his teachers. Is it not a wonderful thing?"

My father did not look at either of us. I stared at the back of his head, his hair dark and neatly trimmed above his collar. "Another musician," he murmured.

"Yes," my grandmother said, as quietly as before. "Fate has brought you another one to replace the one that was taken away."

My father threw her a nervous glance and asked sharply, "What the devil are you talking about?"

"Look at your son," she said softly, her voice barely audible above the noise of the traffic. "Have you ever really looked at the boy?"

My father remained silent, his face pointed straight ahead. He started the car.

My grandmother's voice sharpened. "Look!"

As though dragged forcefully around, my father turned to me. His eyes were filled with the same expression of bewildered pain that he had shown me in the school hallway. His gaze returned to my grandmother, and then back straight ahead. He put the car in gear and pulled away from the curb.

"Can you not see it? Her spirit is alive in him; it shines in everything he does." She leaned toward my father as he drove with hands clenched tightly to the wheel. Her voice was coaxing. "Do you not see, my son? You loved her so much it almost destroyed your life to have her taken away, yet here she is again for you. A divine gift that only a gracious God could have bestowed upon you. All that He asks in return is that you give to your son the same love and devotion you would have given to her. Is that so much to ask? Is that not what your heart yearns to do? He has given you a son who looks like her, acts like her, loves music as she did. And who needs your love as she did. Your *son*."

A pain filled my chest as if a giant had wrapped his hand around me and was squeezing all the air from my body. I could not breathe. With two swift gestures of my free hand I wiped my eyes.

At the next traffic light my father turned to her, his mouth gaping slightly. He looked in agony. He then returned his gaze to the road. I sat and felt the thudding of my heart.

"She is gone," he said. The words were a groan. "And I am the cause."

My grandmother reacted as though slapped. She jerked back upright and pulled her hand from my grasp. "She is gone because you choose her to be so!" she snapped. "She is gone because you have never learned what it means to search your heart in prayer, to offer your sins and your sorrows up to the only One in heaven and earth who can heal you."

We drove the rest of the way in silence. When we pulled up in front of the house, my father got out and slammed his door. He walked hurriedly toward the entrance and disappeared.

My grandmother continued to sit there, her eyes pointed straight ahead. "So much pain," she murmured. "And for what?

Who does it help to carry this pain forever?"

"We need to get out," I said. It still hurt to breathe.

My grandmother seemed to wake up. She opened her door and stepped out. I followed her, and when I stood beside her on the sidewalk she ran one hand over my hair and down my cheek. The light was still in her eyes, but subdued now, softer.

"I am very proud of you, Giovanni," my grandmother said. "The youngest student at the Musikakademie."

"I haven't been accepted yet," I corrected.

"You will be." There was no doubt in her mind. "Very proud."

I did not know what to say, and so remained silent.

"You must search your heart and forgive your father," she went on. "It is no better for you to carry pain than it is for him to do so. Do you understand what I am saying?"

"I'm not sure," I said faintly. I did not want to talk about my father.

She sighed. "Then you must learn to pray for guidance. I am unable to heal wounds of the heart. Much as I would like to do everything for you, only our Lord in heaven can offer you this cleansing. It is a very important thing I am telling you, figlio mio. You must learn to forgive before you can know true healing."

I looked at the sidewalk and gave a slight nod, fighting down the storm of conflicting emotions that her words brought up.

"You will go practice now? Good. I will stop by the Angelettis' store for a few things, and then come up."

She patted my cheek again, the light glowing in her eyes, then walked away. I knew why she was going to the store. She and Mario's mother were becoming friends. It seemed a wonder to me, that the woman who had preferred isolation to contact with the people of her own village was now becoming friends with a woman from the slums of Milano. I thought about that as I climbed the stairs to my grandmother's apartment. I thought also about the look on my father's face, and about the light in my grandmother's eyes, and about what Herr Scherer had told me, and about the Musikakademie. But I did not think about what my grandmother had said I needed to do, to turn to the Lord in prayer. I did not want to destroy the glow of this moment with another flood of emotions I could barely control.

I let myself into my grandmother's apartment with my key.

I walked through the living room and into the windowless alcove that my grandmother called a sewing room. It was my haven, a place where both my music and I were truly welcome. It was a tiny box, less than three meters across. My grandmother had hung up and tied back heavy drapes to give the alcove an illusion of separation from the living room. Cramped as it was, the little space was my refuge from the world.

By the time I finished practicing, the pain over my father's reaction had eased. For the rest of the evening I walked on air. Mario noticed and asked about it. After I told him, he regarded me with enormous eyes. It was not the same light that had shone from my grandmother's face, but I could see he was pleased.

He slapped my shoulder. "Mio piccolo maestro," he said. "Make sure you reserve me a front-row seat for your first concert, right?"

I nodded, smiled, and started to float away when he called me back.

"Hey, Maestro, when're you gonna play something for me?"

I waved a hand vaguely toward him. "Soon," I said. It was too much trouble to plan. Soon. Right then I could see only one star on the horizon.

My promise to Herr Scherer did not help when the day finally arrived. I walked with my grandmother down the hall of the Musikakademie's second floor, reading the names beside the doors, my heart thundering in my ears. The air rang faintly from various instruments being played in practice rooms on the floor below. Beside the last door on the hall I read the name on the small brass plaque: Herr Professor Doktor Schmitz. My grandmother squeezed my shoulder, wished me luck, and said she would be waiting for me in the entrance hall downstairs and praying for my success. I stood before the door, listening to the echo of her footsteps fade away, sweating and trembling very badly.

Professor Schmitz was seated behind an oversized desk. One stick-like hand held a smoldering cigarette, the other a pen. He looked up from his papers and peered at me through wire-rimmed spectacles.

"Yes?" His voice sounded very stern.

"I-I'm Giovanni di Alta, Herr Professor, I have an—"

"Audition," Professor Schmitz finished, and dropped his head back down to his papers. He pointed two fingers and the smoldering cigarette to a door at his right.

"Wait in there," he droned, "and make yourself ready."

I walked into the adjoining room. The parquet floor was covered by a large Persian carpet. The two corner windows, heavily draped, looked out onto the park across the street. Several plaques and pictures adorned the walls. I recognized one of Segovia, signed at the bottom in an illegible scrawl. There were several armless chairs with footstools, a number of music stands, and an old filing cabinet in the corner by the door with one open drawer spilling music scores.

The floor squeaked and the walls echoed back my footsteps as I walked over and I sat down. I opened my case and began tuning my guitar. The sweat from my hand left streaks on the guitar neck. I took a cloth hanging from the back of another chair and wiped the guitar, the strings, my hands, my face.

Herr Schmitz entered the room. He was tall and seemed even taller because of his thinness. He wore dark trousers and a starched white shirt and a narrow dark tie. His skin was almost as white as his shirt. His cheeks were cavernous and his lips a thin line. The wire-rimmed spectacles glinted as he stood and regarded me before sitting down in the chair by the wall.

His voice was surprisingly deep. "Who taught you, boy?"

My mouth felt filled with cotton. I swallowed and told him the name.

"I believe I have heard of him." Herr Schmitz drew an unfiltered cigarette from the packet in his shirt pocket and lit it. I noticed the yellow stain between the first and second fingers of his left hand. I stammered that my former teacher had taught at the Bergamo conservatory before retiring.

Herr Schmitz nodded, letting the smoke out with his words. "Yes, I remember now. He must be approaching seventy." He turned and tapped the cigarette in an overflowing ashtray on a burn-marked table. "All right, boy, let me hear you play."

I had decided to start with the same Schubert sonata I had played for Fraulein Rohr. It was a simple, melodious piece, but one which translated well to the guitar. I wanted to start with something relatively easy, but something which he was fairly sure to like.

I botched it terribly.

By the last half-dozen bars, the frets were so slippery from my sweat that my trembling fingers could no longer hold down the strings. I had lost all sense of timing. I struggled grimly on to the finish, my shaking worse with each passing moment. When I stopped I hung my head, knowing I had absolutely destroyed the piece.

"Look at me, boy." Reluctantly I raised my head. "You are ashamed, yes? Of course you are. You have taken a beautiful piece of music and ripped it to shreds."

His voice had a curious lack of emotion. It was a flat deep voice, full of authority, used to giving commands. He tossed me a cloth. "Dry your hands and listen to me. It is perfectly normal to be nervous. But you have indulged yourself, and now I want you to put your nerves aside and play me some real music." He used the word *echte*. Real music. Genuine, authoritative music. Professional.

"We are going to sit here until I am satisfied I have heard you play what is real music to your ears. I am not interested in hearing you destroy good music, but if you insist on indulging yourself, I will endure it as long as necessary. Do you understand what I am saying? Good. Now I want you to try to put your nerves aside and play me something real."

My trembling was not so bad now. It helped a lot to hear that he was going to give me time to calm down.

"Close your eyes for a moment, boy. I want you to take a deep breath. That's it. Deep. Now let it out slowly. Take another one. Again. Now open your eyes and play the first thing that comes to your mind. Not what you had planned to play; something different. No, don't think about it. Play!"

I started at the sharpness of his voice, but I did as I was told. Almost before I knew what I was doing I had started the piece, a favorite of my grandfather's. It was a short composition by Rossini, and my grandfather had always said it reminded him of clean mountain air. He did not know why, he would say, but he could close his eyes and be up above the clouds, walking through a lonely mountain valley and breathing the fragrant air.

Suddenly everything was all right. My trembling and self-consciousness disappeared. Part of me was back in our cottage in Como, playing in front of the stone fireplace as my grandfather rocked and puffed on his pipe. I finished the piece and looked up, knowing I had played it well.

Professor Schmitz nodded abruptly and said in his colorless voice, "There is quite a difference when your nerves do not play the music for you."

I smiled tentatively, not sure if it was a compliment. His deep voice spoke the words like a machine.

He plucked out another cigarette, lit it, and asked, "What was to be the central piece of your audition?"

I thought about that. I had not planned one as central; I had simply chosen four pieces. I named what I considered to be the most difficult of those pieces.

He smoked and regarded me in silence from behind his glinting spectacles. "How old are you?"

"Fourteen." My birthday was in two days.

He inspected me a moment longer. "Do you think you are ready to play it for me? Yes? Good. I am ready to hear it, then. Where is the score?"

"At home. I mean, I don't need the score, Herr Professor."

There was no change in his voice or his expression. He nodded once more, a slight movement, and said, "Very well, I am ready."

I checked the guitar's tuning, adjusted one string, took a deep breath, and began.

The piece was by Frescobaldi, the first I had learned of what my old teacher called the mature pieces. It was in three movements, and was for me extremely difficult. I had spent a number of weeks on it, longer than I had taken on any other single work, spending days and days over some of the more demanding passages. I played it for Professor Schmitz better than I had ever played it in my life.

When I finished I looked up in triumph. I knew I had played well.

Professor Schmitz lit another cigarette and regarded me through the haze of smoke. "Do you know the point in the second movement where the coda is set?"

I looked at the wall, visualized the score, and found the point he was speaking of. I felt let down by the coldness in his voice. No, it was not coldness. It was a lack of any reaction whatsoever.

"Yes," I said.

"Start at that point and play for me," he ordered.

I hesitated, then bent over my guitar and began to play very carefully, trying not to think of why he was doing this. I stopped at the end of the second movement.

"So." Professor Schmitz carefully ground out the tiny stub of his cigarette, reached for his own guitar, and tuned it swiftly. "First you play like this," he said, and began.

He exaggerated the flow, making a mockery of my playing. Pauses became ridiculously long; notes were drawn into a timing totally out of sequence with the piece. It sounded alien.

When he stopped after two dozen bars I started to protest. He silenced me with an upraised hand.

"Wait," he said. "Then you tried to play it so. Mind you, I said *tried*. There is still too much flamboyance to your playing."

He began again at the coda, and played it with the precision of a Swiss watch. I listened and realized I was sitting with a master. His white fingers were so thin that the knuckles made knobs under the skin, and his head and shoulders remained in a rigid posture that would have been torture for me. But he played with the smooth exactness of one who knew the music perfectly. It sounded stilted and somewhat dead to my ears. More than that, it sounded cold, frozen into place by a total lack of feeling. The man played with the exactness of a true master, yet without any emotion whatsoever.

He played the piece to the end of the second movement, then stopped and turned to me. "Now," he said. "Do you understand?"

I nodded. I was putting an emphasis into the music that was not written. It was my way of expressing my own feelings about the piece.

"You were interpreting," he said. "You have not learned enough to begin interpretations. When you play for me, you will play exactly what is written. Nothing more, nothing less. If I ever hear another piece played as you did this one, I will throw you out on your ear. Is that clear?"

"Yes," I said, not feeling any thrill from learning that I was to be his student. His criticism of my playing with feeling was too distressing.

"Do you have the admittance papers with you? Yes, I see them here in your case. Let me have them."

I gave him the forms. I felt curiously numb, vaguely uneasy. He was clearly a great musician, and I was to begin as his private student. Why did I feel nothing?

He put down the papers after inspecting them carefully, stood, and walked to his filing cabinet.

"I want to start you with a Spanish composer of the last century, Barrios. Have you ever played any of his work? No? Good. It will make it easier for you to break with this habit of interpreting." He handed me the score. "Take the first movement only. Study it carefully. I will see you next Thursday afternoon at four o'clock."

As he stood over me the sunlight reflecting from his glasses made it impossible to see his eyes. "You will be here precisely on time," he said in his deep voice. "Not one minute late."

My grandmother was waiting for me downstairs on a bench in the entrance hall, the rosary beads clicking through her fingers. When she saw my face she stood and asked in alarm, "What is the matter?"

"Nothing. I don't know." The guitar case seemed curiously heavy. I set it down at my feet.

"Did he like you?"

I shrugged my shoulders. Did he? I truly did not know.

My grandmother demanded sharply, "Tell me what he said, Giovanni."

"I can study with him." I looked up at her in confusion. Why did I feel so threatened?

A group of students clamored through the front door, all long hair and blue jeans and laughter. They paused to shed coats and scarves and to give my grandmother and me quizzical looks. I wondered what they thought of this stern old woman in her dark gray coat and lace-up shoes standing next to a thin young boy with his ill-fitting suit and big dark eyes.

"Come, Giovanni, you can tell me about it outside." Her speaking in Italian brought more glances from the students. My grandmother ignored them. She steered me through the group and out into the cold, crisp air. For once we had sunshine.

We climbed onto our streetcar and traveled through a world transformed by sunlight. I stared out the window at a city sharpened into a clarity of lines and angles and shadows. How had I ever taken sunlight for granted? As we traveled, I did my best to explain what had happened with Professor Schmitz.

My grandmother was not sympathetic. "You play for the professor of the academy, and he likes you enough to take you as his private student. But instead of being happy, you are upset because he criticizes you. You are being a child, Giovanni."

"It's not that," I protested. It's just that he's—" I made circles in the air with my hands as I sought the words. "Like ice. His playing, the way he talks, everything. There's no fire." And I'm afraid of being trapped inside his world of ice, I wanted to say. What if he freezes my music? I yearned to say what I was afraid she would laugh at. What if he turns my heart to ice?

"He is German," my grandmother said flatly. "Do not seek to squeeze blood from a stone, figlio mio. He knows his music, yes?"

"He is a very great guitarist," I agreed. There was no question about that.

"Then you will study with him and learn as much as you can," my grandmother commanded. "And if I hear that you are failing to please your professor, I'll give you all the fire you need."

When we arrived at the apartment house, my grandmother said, "You are going to go practice? Good. I must buy a few things from Angelettis'."

She regarded me gravely and brushed the hair from my forehead. "I am very proud of you, figlio mio. You will study hard and play well for the professor, and then—" She hesitated, and gave me a brief smile. "And then we will see. You have your key, yes? Good. Go and practice, my Giovanni. I will be up soon."

. . .

Very early on I had created a routine for beginning my practice sessions. I do not remember how it had started; probably it had grown naturally from the sheer boredom of doing scales. On most days it remained as it had begun, a dance starting at the middle C tone, flowing down, flowing back, going up and up to the highest point, racing back down, changing from major to minor to seventh to ninth, an exercise that after all these countless practices brought me swiftly to a quiet state of thoughtlessness. The exercise both numbed and calmed me, stilling all the turmoil in my mind, pushing aside all awareness of a world beyond my music. When I finished the exercise I was focused, ready to begin the part of my practice that required intense effort and concentration.

But on a few days, on some very special occasions, when I reached that point of calm thoughtless flow, I was able to hear another music. A different scale. A lilting, flowing, endless pattern of notes that surged up from somewhere deep within me. It did not often happen. But on the days when it did I felt as though my heart was singing to me, telling me with crystal clarity what seemed so cloudy and confusing when I thought of it in the outside world. It sang to me of how I truly felt.

When I was happy, the scales became chimes that made my whole being vibrate. I would fly through the majors and the sevenths, following the path laid by the inner music as my guitar laughed and sang with joy. When I was sad the tune bubbled up softly like water from an underground stream, quiet and steady and all in minors and discords, and my guitar wept.

Today I heard the song, and my fingers swiftly followed it. There was no rhythm, no logic to the sequence, no line of classical development—or maybe there was, but I was so caught up in the simple pleasure of playing that I did not want to stop and think and analyze. The song had started long before I heard it, and as I followed its path I knew with utter certainty it would continue on long after it had faded from my hearing.

Today it was the song of a river, steady and sure and never-ending, a calm flow of strength, an acceptance of moving with the current of things beyond my control. For the first time since my arrival in Dusseldorf I felt a sense of rightness, of being where I was meant to be, flowing like a river through the course set out for me.

It moved like a stream of human voices, this song inside of me, sounding low and deep from waters never touched by the wind making ripples on the surface, piping staccato beats for the raindrops that made everything below the surface invisible. I followed the inner flow of harmony for as long as I could hear it, until it became a single clear note that rose higher, ever higher, climbing beyond the edge of my hearing like a bird soaring up on an unseen breeze toward the sun.

When the last whisper of inner song vanished, I started into a piece I knew very well, moving from one to the other without a pause. I did not consciously choose this piece. It simply rose up into the stillness. It was a good day, and the feeling of weightless union with my music continued on through this song as well.

When I finished the piece I looked up to find Mario standing open-mouthed beside my grandmother at the entrance to my alcove. How long had they been standing there? I had not even heard them come into the apartment.

"Madonna," Mario breathed.

My grandmother glanced at him, a faint smile touching her face. She turned back to me and said, "I want you to find a good day for the gentleman from your school, what was his name?"

"Herr Scherer," I said.

"Yes. For him and his wife to come and have dinner with us. Mario and his parents will come, too. You don't mind having your birthday a few days late, do you?"

"I can't wait 'til my mother hears you play, Gianni," Mario said.

"I don't mind," I told my grandmother.

Mario asked, "You'll play for us at the dinner, right?"

"Of course he'll play," my grandmother replied, and patted Mario on the shoulder. "Go tell your mother it is settled and I will see her tomorrow to make arrangements."

"Okay, signora," Mario said, and grinned at me. "See you, Maestro."

My grandmother remained standing there, regarding me in silence until the door closed behind Mario. Then she said, "That was not your work for the professor, was it?"

I shook my head. "That was a warm-up exercise."

"A warm-up exercise that takes half an hour?" Her face became stern. "I don't want you to avoid practicing your pieces for the professor because you think he will be hard to please. Do you hear me, figlio mio? Because he is so demanding you must practice twice as hard, and play his pieces twice as long. Do you understand?"

"Yes," I replied. She was very perceptive, my grandmother.

"Good." Her voice became brisk. "I want you to tell your father of the dinner. He must come and bring his wife. If he does not come—" She stopped, changed her mind. "He must come," she finished. "And you must work hard at your lesson for the professor. Do not ever let me hear you are shirking your lessons. Finish."

The dinner took place five days later. When I returned from school and opened the apartment house door, the aroma of rich cooking wafted around me. I raced up the stairs to my grandmother's apartment, only to find the door blocked by Mario's mother.

"Out, out! There's too much to do to have someone else underfoot today," Signora Angeletti said.

"But I need to practice."

"No practice," my grandmother called from the kitchen. "Practice has been canceled by the authorities."

"Go help Mario in the store," his mother said. "No, wait, the fool is upstairs playing with his stereo. Go upstairs and tell my youngest fool that if he comes down tonight with dirty hands, he'll sleep on his belly for a week."

My grandmother came out of the kitchen wiping her hands on her apron. Her face was flushed, and her eyes glittered. "Did you tell your father he was to be here at seven o'clock?"

"Three times," I replied.

"Stop worrying about the father," Signora Angeletti said, her eyes still on me. "Either he comes or he doesn't. Basta."

"I'm not worrying," my grandmother said. "I just want it all very clear to him when he learns—"

"He learns what he learns," Mario's mother interrupted. She and my grandmother shared a look that left me very puzzled. Signora Angeletti turned back to me and said, "Go. There's too much happening here. A piccolo maestro underfoot might find himself stepped on."

Rough hands pushed me out, and the door closed on their laughter. I stood in the gloomy hallway, astonished. I had not heard my grandmother laugh like that since before my grandfather died.

Mario let me into his apartment. "Hey, Gianni, just in time. C'mon over here, I gotta have another pair of hands."

I followed him down the long hallway. Their apartment was big—three bedrooms and a kitchen larger than my grandmother's living room. I asked, "Why aren't you in the store?"

He waved me to silence. Once we were in what now was his workroom, he said, "We gotta be quiet; my father's in bed with the flu. My brother's downstairs minding the store."

"I thought he worked for the American army."

"Yeah, he does. He's a waiter in the Officers' Club. My uncle is head of the restaurant and got him the job, you know that. But everybody's off on maneuvers or something, so Danilo's back here for a coupla weeks. C'mon, Gianni, give me a hand."

"I don't want to get electrocuted."

"What electrocute?" Mario said, sitting down in front of a work-table cluttered with coils of wire, tools, testing instruments, soldering guns, and the entrails of a very complicated-looking gadget.

"Someday I'm gonna invent me a soldering gun that lets the solder out automatically on the point where you need it," Mario said. "You press a little button and you're done. After that I'm gonna retire to the Riviera. Now you gotta hold the solder with one hand, the gun with the other, and the wire with something else, I dunno, maybe your teeth."

The room's right-hand wall supported a series of shelves made of concrete slabs and plywood boards. On it rested seven stereo components, none of them fully intact. A spaghetti of wires ran down between the back of the shelves and the wall.

"What's that thing you're playing with?"

"It's an equalizer, and I'm not playing. Are you gonna come over here or do I solder you to the wall?"

I had to be careful around Mario when he was working on his stereo. Years of quarreling with his parents over his burning obsession with electronic gadgets had left him very thin-skinned. Once during the summer I had referred to the stereo as his hobby, and for a minute I thought he was going to slug me. How would I feel if he called my guitar a hobby, he had finally shouted, just another stupid little kid's hobby.

"Hold that blue wire right there so the end touches that point," Mario said.

I did as I was told. "What does an equalizer do?"

Mario mumbled something about balancing tonal sound and told me to keep my hand still. His parents paid him slave wages for his work in the store, so all his equipment had a bandaged and battered look. I was not sure Mario minded all that much.

Every time he was finished with one gadget he would put it up on the wall and take down another, unless he had saved up enough money for something else.

He had one loudspeaker that sounded deathly ill and another that did not work at all. What was the use of buying speakers when his parents wouldn't let him turn the music up, I asked him once. So I can learn, Mario had said, chopping the words off with anger stored from answering the same question to his parents.

Soon after that headphones appeared, but they did not work either. I knew because I tried to listen to the broadcast of a guitar concert on them, but it sounded as if the audience clapped the whole time. When I said something about it Mario whipped them off my head and talked about them needing a little adjustment, that's all. I did not ask to listen again.

"There's some other guys playing music around here," Mario said. "Friday nights, right over my head."

"What?"

"Yeah, between you underneath and them on top I'm going crazy." Mario glanced up. "Just kidding, Gianni. You know I can't hear your guitar."

"Who plays upstairs, Mario?"

"Here, hold that wire just there, okay? Thanks. Some Jewish doctor, I dunno. Dr. Levisto. My mother thinks he's another prophet, the way she goes on. He's okay, I guess. You know those two skinny dark-haired twins that're always together?"

"I don't think I've seen them."

"Hey, c'mon, you've been here how long, six months? Half a year and you don't notice two kids stuck together like they were Siamese twins?"

"I'm not out on the street that much."

"Tell me something I don't already know. Okay, you can let it go now. Drop by sometime and I'll introduce you to our two shadows. Wouldn't hurt for you to get outside some, Gianni. You could meet some of my friends."

"I don't have anything to say to them," I said quietly.

Mario paused in his work to give me a look of depth far beyond his years. "There's not much in your world besides music, is there, Maestro?"

"It's my life," I said simply. "Tell me about the music upstairs."

"Yeah, if you wanna call it that." Mario turned back to his soldering. "Every Friday night about a thousand people stomp up the stairs. Sounds like those old war movies when the secret police tromp around stealing babies after everybody with any sense has gone to bed."

"The music," I pressed.

"Yeah, yeah, the music." Mario was clearly enjoying this. "I was just gonna tell you. Think you can hold that steady for me? Right. Where was I? Oh, yeah. So they get this mob of fifty thousand people upstairs, and they start moving furniture around, rolling up the rugs, and we sit downstairs with chips off the ceiling falling in our soup. They got this piano, must weigh a ton. They drag it away from the wall, pull out maybe a hundred violins, and start scraping away. My dad says all they need is a sack of tomcats and some tops off of garbage cans to whang together, and they'd be ready for television."

"Every Friday night?"

"Unfortunately."

"Think maybe I could go up, you know, and listen?"

Mario looked up again, smiling this time. "You feeling okay, Maestro?"

"I'm serious."

"You're always serious. The day you laugh is the day I fall over dead from shock." He bent back over his equalizer. "I could ask Mama. She likes you almost as much as she does Dr. Levisto. Levisto and my Maestro. Two prophets in the making. You don't believe it, just ask my mother. Sure, I'll ask her, Gianni. They'll probably let you go up. Why not? Half the city's up there already."

At six o'clock Signora Angeletti came upstairs to yell at Mario for not having taken his bath and at me for not having gone home. I ducked under her swat and scampered, followed by a dire warning of what she was going to do to me if I was late for my own party.

When I arrived at my father's apartment I found him where he always was after work, in front of the television. I heard Anna moving around in the kitchen. I started to say something to him about the party, then decided, why bother? Three times was enough.

Half an hour later, I paused outside my grandmother's door and listened to the loud talk and laughter from inside. I recognized Mario's voice, and his mother's, and my grandmother's shrill reply from the kitchen. Then I heard a deeper voice also speaking Italian. Mario's father? No, he was in bed with the flu. It had to be Mario's older brother, Danilo. It seemed very strange hearing all those voices and laughter in my grandmother's apartment. I felt awkward as I unlocked the door and walked inside.

"Hey, the birthday boy decides to show up after all." A wiry young man with Mario's pinched features and lively eyes walked over and stuck out his hand. "I'm Danilo. Nice to meet you, Gianni. I heard a lot about you. Hope you're gonna play something for us tonight."

I smiled uncertainly, feeling awkward and vaguely grown-up as I shook his hand.

The buzzer beside the door sounded. I pushed the button to release the outside door, then opened the apartment door and listened to heavy footsteps clumping up the stairs. Around the bend in the stairwell appeared Herr Scherer, who looked up at me, grinned, and waved. "I'm glad you don't live another floor higher up, Gianni. I haven't eaten all day, and I'm not sure I'd have the strength to make it."

I didn't say anything because I had spotted the woman walking up the stairs behind him. It was Fraulein Rohr.

Herr Scherer stopped in front of me, caught the direction of my gaze and grinned at my surprise. "My wife is in bed with the flu. Half of Dusseldorf is either in bed with the flu or walking around looking as if death is about to strike."

He put one arm around Fraulein Rohr's slender shoulders; in his bulky overcoat the arm looked too heavy a burden for her to bear. "So I brought my favorite music teacher instead."

"I hope that's all right," Fraulein Rohr said.

"I would have called," Herr Scherer said. "But I don't have your grandmother's number, and even if I did I couldn't tell her I've been dreaming about this meal for five days." His yellow teeth appeared through the dark scraggly beard. "Besides, my music teacher promised I could eat her pasta."

Fraulein Rohr dug him in the ribs. "No, I did not."

"It's fine," I said. It was wonderful. "Come on in."

My grandmother appeared from the kitchen. I made introductions. My grandmother said, "So this signora was the one who started it all?"

"Signorina," I corrected. "Yes."

"Tell her it is an honor to have her in my home." I did so. Then my grandmother said, "Ask the gentleman if he brought it."

"Brought what?"

"Just ask him, Gianni."

The yellow teeth appeared once more. Herr Scherer held out a guitar case I had seen but not really taken in because of my surprise over Fraulein Rohr's appearance.

I asked him, "Are you going to play tonight?"

Herr Scherer laughed. "Not unless you put something in my wine."

"Ask them for their coats, Giovanni," my grandmother said. "And let's all move into the living room."

They gave me their coats and started down the hallway. My grandmother stopped me with a hand on my arm. She asked, "Where is your father?"

"Watching television," I said.

My grandmother turned to look at Mario's mother; then she pushed me forward. "Go put their coats in the alcove and see if the guests need anything."

The living room seemed tiny, cramped, and very noisy with the seven of us milling about. I slipped into my alcove, draped their coats over a chair, heard Mario ask, "Is that it?" and his mother reply, "Shhh."

When I came back out people were finding seats, my grandmother was pouring wine into her good glasses, Mario's mother was handing it around, everybody was wearing smiles, and all eyes were on me. The guitar case Herr Scherer had brought up was sitting in the middle of the floor. My heart gave a sudden lurch.

"Happy birthday, Gianni," my grandmother said quietly.

I looked at the case, then back at her, then around at all the grinning faces. I could not move.

Numbly I walked to the case and dropped to my knees. My fingers seemed barely able to release the catches. I raised the lid and stopped breathing.

Herr Scherer said, "She's a beauty, no? A Galoya. Spanish. I told your father and grandmother about it when I met them at the school. It belonged to an old friend of mine, another crazy music teacher. Ever since his arthritis stopped him from playing he's been thinking about selling it. Trouble is, he wanted to find somebody who would appreciate it as much as he has. I told him about you, and it seems he knew Professor Schmitz, so he talked to him as well. He let it go for a song."

I scarcely heard him. The guitar seemed to glow softly. There was no mark on the neck to tell who had made it, but everything about it was artistic. Outlining the body's curves and around the central mouth was a double line of inlaid mother-of-pearl and ebony. The pattern was repeated inside the six tuning keys. Faint indentations in the middle of the first four frets spoke of age. Innumerable coats of wax buffed to a rich sheen spoke of years of loving care. I reached for the guitar and felt an energy that made my fingers tingle.

Mario asked, "Do you like it, Gianni?"

I cradled the guitar in my lap and looked up. I could scarcely see his grinning face; it seemed to swim a little before my eyes. I nodded my head, and looked back to the guitar. I could not believe it was mine.

"Fifty years old if it's a day," Herr Scherer said.

My grandmother clapped her hands. "Enough! Food is getting cold and guests are hungry. Giovanni, down with the guitar, you can play for us later. Mario, show the guests where to wash their hands. Giovanni! Put the guitar by the wall and come help me in the kitchen. It will still be there when we finish eating."

Reluctantly I set the guitar back in its case, and moved it over by the far wall. I followed my grandmother into the kitchen.

She looked at me fondly. "It is a good guitar, no?"

I stammered, "I-it's beautiful. I—"

She shoved a serving bowl full of steaming pasta into my arms and spun me around. "Wait until everyone is seated, then serve the signorina first, then the gentleman. Wait. Here." She placed two serving ladles in the bowl. "Now go. And make sure everyone has bread."

I have never seen anyone eat as Herr Scherer did that night.

Three bowls of pasta, my grandmother's hand-made tortelloni con spinaci alla panna, followed by two heaping plates of arrosto di vitello with patate al forno and a sauce made from cream and white wine and fresh porcini mushrooms. My grandmother kept glancing at him and then at me as though to say, look here, see how a man is supposed to eat. It was all lost on me. I sat between Mario and Fraulein Rohr with my new guitar directly across the room, as happy as I had ever been in my life.

"Ach du lieber," Herr Scherer groaned and dropped his fork with a clatter. "If I have one more bite I will positively explode." He stifled a belch. "I beg your pardon."

My grandmother held the platter under his nose, suggested, "Perhaps a little more veal?"

I could see he was tempted, but he shook his head. "Gianni, tell your grandmother that I would, except she'd have to use a shovel and the vacuum cleaner to get me off her carpet."

"Don't you tell her any such thing," Fraulein Rohr said sharply.

"Wait 'til you see dessert," Mario said happily.

Herr Scherer groaned and held his stomach. "Dessert! I forgot all about dessert. And it's probably something I'll just love."

My grandmother set down the platter. "What's the matter, is he sick?"

"Torta di zabaglione, with two layers of fudge and fresh whipped cream on top," Mario said, thoroughly enjoying himself. "My mother used half a liter of rum in the custard."

"Ach du lieber," Herr Scherer repeated. "I knew it. Maybe I should go jog around the block."

"Serves you right," Fraulein Rohr said crossly. "Three servings of pasta. I've never seen anyone in my life be such a pig."

"Tell me what they're saying," my grandmother insisted.

"Herr Scherer's eaten too much and doesn't have room for dessert," I said.

My grandmother gave a short harrumph and worked to keep her face straight. She looked at Mario's mother and said, "Come help me in the kitchen."

Fraulein Rohr stood along with them, ignored their demands for her to sit back down, and said to me, "Tell them if I have to sit here another minute I'm going to strangle this man for being such an imbecile."

"She said she wants to stretch her legs," I told my grandmother.

"No she didn't," Mario sang out, and translated.

My grandmother filled her arms with dishes and followed Mario's mother into the kitchen. When Fraulein Rohr joined them, I could hear the three of them in there laughing. No greater compliment could be given to an Italian mother's cooking than to have a guest ask for seconds, no greater insult than to leave the first serving unfinished. They had spotted a great eater in Herr Scherer and had taken full advantage of his lack of control without the slightest qualm. His overstuffed condition would remain their favorite topic of conversation for weeks to come.

Mario's mother returned carrying a bottle and one tiny glass. The bottle was full of clear liquid and stuffed with a tied bunch of plant stems, roots, and leaves.

"Grappa di erba," Signora Angeletti said, then in German, "Homemade. Please excuse, my German very bad. For your stomach." She smiled, exposing a mouthful of crooked teeth. She picked up the remaining dishes and returned to the kitchen.

"Yeah," Danilo said. "Grappa di erba's good stuff."

That brought a look of surprise to Mario's face. "I thought you didn't drink."

"I don't," Danilo said easily. "Not anymore, anyway. But that's just between me and my Lord."

He turned to Herr Scherer, went on, "I was pretty much on the way to becoming a full-time alcoholic. Hard thing to come to grips with—impossible so long as I tried to do it alone. But a guy down on the army base introduced me to faith, and with that gift of strength I decided drink was one of the things I was going to do without."

"Gift of strength?" Herr Scherer looked confused. "I don't understand."

"I was saved," Danilo said, his manner still easy, but a new light in his eyes. I listened carefully. This was a side to Danilo that Mario never mentioned. "I never had much to do with the church before—"

"Here comes Mama," Mario said quietly.

A sudden silence fell upon the table. Danilo looked down

and began playing with a spoon. I glanced a question at Mario, but he avoided my eyes.

"Has he tried it?" Signora Angeletti asked.

Herr Scherer understood from the direction of her eyes. He picked up the glass, sniffed, raised his eyebrows in surprise. "Smells like a meadow."

Signora Angeletti smiled her pleasure when Mario translated, then said through her son, "Every mother in northern Italy has her own secret recipe for what herbs to use and how long the grappa has to sit. Usually three or four years." She looked at me. "Gianni's grandmother has more patience than most. This has rested in her cellar for almost a decade."

Herr Scherer tossed back the glass, made his eyes even larger, and breathed out a great "hah." He shook his head. "It's like drinking liquid silk."

"The coffee will be ready in just a few minutes," my grandmother said as she reappeared. "Giovanni, ask the gentleman how he is feeling."

"Better," Herr Scherer said, pouring another small glass. "This is exceptional."

Fraulein Rohr picked up his glass and sniffed it. "Mmmm, that smells lovely."

My grandmother obviously caught her meaning, for she went back into the kitchen and swiftly returned with another small glass. As she poured out a half-measure she said, "Giovanni, tell the signorina that it is very strong."

Fraulein Rohr took a small sip and smiled at my grandmother. "That's lovely. It's homemade, isn't it?"

"Yes," I replied.

"Please tell your grandmother that it is like drinking a bouquet of wildflowers."

I did so, and watched the look that passed between them. I was glad they liked each other. Very glad.

Fraulein Rohr sipped again, and as she raised her head her eyes were caught by the cross hanging in the hallway. She stared at it as she breathed the grappa's heavy perfume, then said quietly, "I was raised a Catholic."

When I had translated, my grandmother said, "Tell her I would be honored if she would join me for Mass one day."

"I haven't been to church in, oh—" Fraulein Rohr gave a wistful smile. "Much too long."

"Our Lord is ever patient," my grandmother said, her gentle words carrying a ringing strength in the quiet room. "Ever patient and ever hopeful His children will one day return to Him."

"Amen," Danilo said, surprising us all.

The look that passed between Danilo and my grandmother was interrupted by Signora Angeletti saying, "The signora was speaking of Mass."

"She was speaking of faith," Danilo replied, his eyes never moving from my grandmother's face. "The Lord Jesus knows no boundaries, no denominations, only the hearts that are filled with His light."

"What a beautiful thought," my grandmother said.

"Maybe so," Signora Angeletti said, her voice brassy with tension. "But I'm glad his father isn't around to hear it."

I turned to find Fraulein Rohr's eyes upon me. I was saved the embarrassment of trying to translate by her saying, "You are certainly fortunate to have such a guardian, Gianni."

A guardian. I had never thought of her in those terms. But it was true. My grandmother was a guardian over my life. She was all that stood between me and the horrors of the outside world.

Fraulein Rohr turned back to my grandmother and pointed to the case. "Perhaps Gianni would like to play us something on his new guitar?"

My grandmother looked at me. "Are you ready, figlio mio?"

I swallowed and nodded, eager and afraid at the same time.

"Go and play, then," she said in her quiet, matter-of-fact way. "Make me proud."

Nervously I walked over, picked up the guitar, then went into the alcove for my stool. I was excited about playing, but at the same time very scared. I had never played in front of a group before. I sat down at the room's far end, placed the guitar on my knee, took a shaky breath, and hit the bass string.

It seemed as though an answering note was plucked deep inside me. Everything seemed to vibrate—myself, the guitar, the room, everyone watching me. Swiftly I ran up the strings. They needed only the slightest tuning. I did not know what to play. My fingers ached to touch the strings, but my mind was blank.

Play, a voice inside me commanded. Play anything. Play the first thing that comes to your mind. The words were the same as those spoken by Professor Schmitz, but here in the warmth of this room there was a sense of joy in the voice. A sense of giving. See, this still small voice was saying to me, you turn to me and I am here to guide you, to give to you, to share with you what is yours. Play with the joy of what has always been here waiting for you. I did not understand the voice, but I felt its presence deep within me. For the moment the presence was enough.

So I started with the same melody I had used in Professor Schmitz's office, the simple tune my grandfather had loved. I felt surrounded, protected, safe enough to melt and float away with the singing of this beautiful, beautiful guitar.

Without pausing I moved from that into the difficult piece I had prepared for my audition. My fingers flew over the strings as though released from shackles they never knew existed. I played the first two movements, and as I played I became two people, one who played and one who listened, and the player watched the listener flow with the music and pour out with the melody.

The guitar was a golden basin filled to the brim with sound, so full that at the slightest touch the music came cascading out like a waterfall. Never in my wildest fantasy had I ever dreamed of playing such an instrument. I could not believe it was mine.

At the end of the second movement I went immediately into another melody by Albenez, a light piece with short staccato notes that had to be timed precisely. It allowed my feelings to dance, to play joyfully as my fingers plucked the golden sounds from this sweet spring that would never run dry.

When the melody was finished and the last whisper of sound had faded, I reluctantly turned my attention from the guitar and back to the group. There was a lingering moment of silence; then everyone was clapping and shouting, "Bravo!" I felt my cheeks grow red.

"Heavens above us," Herr Scherer said. "To think that came from a fourteen-year-old boy. Outstanding."

As I walked back over and sat down, Mario grinned and punched my shoulder. He looked very pleased. "That was great, Maestro."

"Yeah," Danilo said. "That was amazing, Gianni. Mario was right. I don't know much about classical music, but I've never heard anyone play like that before."

Fraulein Rohr put her arm across my shoulders. "That was magnificent, Gianni. Do you think you could play for our class someday?"

I shook my head. The prospect was terrifying. Fraulein Rohr looked disappointed.

"Giovanni," my grandmother said. I looked at her. "Tell me what she asked you."

"She wants me to play for her class."

"Tell her yes," my grandmother commanded.

I grew very alarmed. "I can't—"

"This is the signorina who helped you, yes? We are all here because she took an interest in you, do I have that right? Tell her yes. Tell her next week would be fine. Finish." My grandmother stood. "Who wants dessert?"

Glumly I did as I was told. Fraulein Rohr was delighted. "Someday when you're famous all over the world, I will be able to say that your first public performance was in my classroom."

Herr Scherer noted my distress and said, "Look at me, Gianni. You want to make a profession of your music, yes?"

I said I hadn't much thought about it.

"Well, think about it now," he said. "If you want to play professionally, you have to get over this fear of yours. You can't hide your talent away in a box."

"But what if they don't like it?" My voice was very shrill.

"Then they don't like it." Herr Scherer shrugged. "Not everybody will appreciate your music, Gianni. You just have to be strong enough to take it in stride, you understand? Keep it in perspective of what you know about your talent, and keep on playing."

My grandmother came back in and began serving dessert. Fraulein Rohr said to me, "Gianni, perhaps you can help me eat Herr Scherer's dessert since he's so full."

Herr Scherer spooned up a bite and rolled his eyes toward heaven. "Why wasn't I born an Italian?"

Mario's brother translated for his mother, who preened. In her faulty German she said, "Old family recipe. I make special for tonight. Takes whole day."

Danilo said to me, "I've made a lot of friends down on the base, Gianni. We've got a great bunch who get together for fellowship—" He shot his mother a wary glance. "Anyway, you ought to come down and play for us sometime."

Mario complained, "I thought you told me nobody but personnel could get on the base, and that's why I couldn't go."

"Yeah," Danilo agreed. "They're pretty tough with non-Americans. I had to be vetted, that's what they call it, vetted, before I could start work. But maybe I could get one of the pastors to run interference for Gianni. I dunno; it's worth a try."

"Somebody came by to see where he lived," Signora Angeletti confirmed. "They spoke only German and English so Mario had to translate. They asked all sorts of questions."

My grandmother said quietly, "Giovanni will not have trouble getting on the base."

Danilo asked, "How's that?"

Her eyes calm and proud on me, she said, "Giovanni is American."

The whole room held its breath. I felt my face grow red again. Mario's brother said, "Huh?"

"Giovanni's mother was American, and he was born in the United States. In Michigan." My grandmother had trouble pronouncing the name. "He has a United States passport, a blue one from when he was five years old and I brought him back to Italy after his mother died."

"An American? Wow, they'll flip," Danilo said. "Hey, Gianni, you speak any English?"

I shook my head, no.

"Yes he does," my grandmother said. "He spoke only English until he was five years old." A faint smile flickered across her features. "When I came to America, my Giovanni was afraid of me because he couldn't understand what I was saying. Do you remember that, figlio mio?"

A lump grew in my throat. Keeping my eyes on my lap, I nodded my head. I remembered.

"It will be good for Giovanni to go down and meet other

Americans," my grandmother said. "And he must begin to remember his English. I cannot speak with him, but I can see to it that he reads."

"But I never learned to read English," I said.

"Then you will learn now," my grandmother ordered. "Tonight is a good time to ask the signorina if you can take English at your school."

"She teaches music, not English," I said. I was not sure I liked the idea of learning to read English. It sounded like a lot of work.

"Nonetheless, you will ask, and you will do it now. And you will tell her why. Finish." She turned back to Danilo. "Talk to your friends, young man. When they want, Giovanni will be happy to visit them."

I looked at Fraulein Rohr. She and Herr Scherer were watching the exchange with blank faces. I dropped my eyes back to the table and said, "MygrandmothersaysIgottatake-EnglishandIgottatellyouI'mAmerican."

When they didn't reply I glanced up. The pair of them stared back in shock. Fraulein Rohr managed, "I'm not sure I understood you, Gianni."

My grandmother and Mario's mother stood and began gathering plates. Mario and his brother watched me. Glumly I explained.

There was a silence when I had finished, broken finally by Fraulein Rohr's quiet voice. "Your mother was American and you were born in America? I thought you came from Italy."

My head bowed, I explained how my parents met and went to America and how I went back to Italy. I hated talking about it. Why had my grandmother made me do it? I felt as if I was tearing out something from deep inside myself and exposing it to the world.

Fraulein Rohr surprised me by running her hand down the back of my head. "I think we can put you in an English class, Gianni." I looked up to find her smiling that special way for me. "You will be the youngest student in the class, but you're used to that, aren't you? And don't worry, we won't tell anyone your secret." She looked at Herr Scherer. "Will we?"

"Not a blessed soul," Herr Scherer said, and poured himself another grappa. He looked at me over his glass and shook his head. "American." He drained the glass in one swallow.

The room was silent as everyone drank coffee. Afterward there were many goodbyes and thanks and promises to do it again very soon. Herr Scherer patted me on the head, told me gruffly to enjoy the guitar, and said he would try to be there when I played for the class. Fraulein Rohr wished me a happy birthday and kissed me on the cheek. There was something special in her look, a depth I had not seen before.

Then she was standing in front of my grandmother, the wispy blond German and the stern Italian matron, the two of them silent and staring into each other's eyes. Then they hugged each other very tightly.

I pulled Mario over to one side, asked him what his brother had been talking about earlier, this business of God and everything. Mario became uneasy.

"I dunno, Gianni. Well, maybe I do, but I'm not sure. I tell you one thing, though. All Danilo's gotta do is open his mouth about that stuff and my parents go crazy." He shook his head, looked immensely unhappy. "It's scary how mad they get, all about how he's destroying the church and talking sacrilege. I feel like running away every time it happens."

"Why do they get so mad?"

"That's just it, I don't know." Mario's pinched features nodded in the direction of my grandmother. "I heard Mama talking to her this afternoon about Danilo. Know what your grandmother said? She told Mama that maybe Danilo had a lesson there for all of us to learn. I think that's why Papa didn't come down tonight. Mama told him, and he got so mad he decided to stay in bed."

Danilo chose that moment to come over. He clapped me on the shoulder, said, "Anytime you want to come to the base, Gianni, I'll take care of everything. You're an incredible musician. My buddies'll love hearing you play."

"Thanks," I mumbled, knowing it was something I was going to avoid as long as humanly possible.

The goodbyes with the Angelettis were quickly finished. When we were alone my grandmother led me back into the living room and told me to sit. I did. She started to join me at the table, but changed her mind and remained standing, folding and unfolding a soiled napkin with nervous gestures.

"They are very nice people, your teachers. I am sorry I cannot talk directly with them, but it is clear that they are nice and that they care very much for you."

I nodded my head, wondering what was to come.

My grandmother sighed, sat, and clenched both hands together on the tabletop as though to keep them still. She sighed again, and gave me a sad look.

"I am very upset that my son chose not to join us tonight. No, not upset, that is not true. I expected nothing more." She sighed a third time, and turned away, her face looking very tired. "I wish I knew what I should do," she murmured. "I wish your grandfather—"

She turned back to me. "I cannot ask you to stay in that house any longer, figlio mio. It is not right to force you to stay if things will not improve."

She took a deep breath and began playing with the napkin again. I sat silent and still and wished there was some way I could help her with whatever it was she was trying to decide.

She thumped her hands down on the table and declared, "I will not return with you to Como. I cannot. We must stay here, in case . . . We must stay here. Do you understand?"

I nodded my head, feeling the band of emotions tightening around my chest.

"There is not much room here, but there is enough. As Danilo is so seldom at home, his mother is loaning us his bed and chest of drawers. They will fit in the alcove; we measured yesterday." She hesitated, then asked, "Is this what you want?"

"Yes," I said. I felt like singing and crying both.

She searched my face for a moment, then nodded. "You will inform your father. If there is any question, he can come talk with me." She stood, and in the movement showed her age. I stood with her. She walked around the table, held me briefly in a fierce embrace, then released me. "Go and sleep, figlio mio. It has been a busy day for us both. Bring your things over tomorrow after school, and if there are problems I will discuss them with your father."

CHAPTER
4

By the time winter set in I was struggling with music as never before in my life. My lessons with Professor Schmitz were proving to be a tremendous strain. I would leave his office after our hour together and lean against the wall, feeling as though I had just been released from a straitjacket. I could not force enough air into my lungs.

Professor Schmitz kept me on particular passages in that first piece for three months. He sought through endless repetition to break my desire to interpret and give the music a sense of emotional flow. He wanted me to become machine-like in my playing of what was there before me on the score. I resisted with an unreasoning terror, certain without knowing why that submission would mean the death of something precious.

My unspoken defense infuriated him. He seldom spoke of it directly, but I could see it clearly enough—in the angry gaze and sucked-in cheeks and clenched fingers when I allowed the music to carry me away. I strived to hold back, to lock my spirit in a frozen little cell when I was there with him. Yet at least once a lesson the love I carried for my music slipped through. I would forget Professor Schmitz, forget his cigarettes and his cold voice and his yellowed fingers and his stale smell, and I would soar away. Then I would jerk awake and cast a fearful glance toward him, and see his anger bearing down on me.

My grandmother had caught a cold that settled in her chest

and refused to budge. At night I would awaken to the sound of her coughing, and in the morning see the shadow of her night-time struggles etched upon her face. As the fever continued to sap her strength, her objections to my helping out grew weaker. After school I tried to imagine all that might need my grandmother's attention that day and did it.

Christmas came and went, and still my grandmother's health did not improve. In the mornings her eyes glittered from fever and fatigue, and her cheeks grew hollow. It began to affect my schoolwork and my practicing. Summer seemed very far away, and Como a dream from another lifetime.

I usually made something warm for dinner, but it was seldom that my grandmother had energy to eat. I learned by doing and by making mistakes and by asking Mario's mother. She would give me advice as she filled my shopping basket, and would never ask for money. My grandmother would pay her later, she always said, her dark eyes shining as she put something extra in the basket for me, a sweet or a fruit or a fresh-baked cookie. What was such a small thing among family?

If my grandmother was awake in the evenings I would sit and play for a while. That seldom occurred more than once a week. On through the cold darkness of winter these evenings together remained the light that reassured, that comforted, that spoke of hope for better days to come.

In late January I began climbing the dimly-lit stairs to the Levisto apartment. I sat silently through a number of their Friday evening concerts. The first few times they asked me to join them, but I was not interested in playing for strangers. I did not want to unearth the turmoil that surrounded my music just then. I was content to sit and sip spiced tea and smile when someone spoke to me and listen to their concerto and let them think that I was too embarrassed over the quality of my music to perform in public. The playing on those evenings was enthusiastically bad, their music hammered out with boundless energy and nailed into place with a relentless four-four beat. They were friends who met because they enjoyed playing and loved music in a simple wholehearted fashion. I returned downstairs after such evenings reeking of cheap cigar smoke and restored by the flavor of their happiness.

Mario took it upon himself to draw me out. One night in

February, after the store had closed and my grandmother was in bed, we were sitting upstairs in his workroom. Album covers littered the floor around his stereo. Mario had recently invested in an impressive pair of headphones. He handed them to me, shifted them around until he was satisfied how they rested on my ears, then lowered the turntable arm. Rock music exploded inside my head.

I sat through a couple of minutes, then took off the headphones. The room seemed incredibly still.

"How was it?"

"Loud," I said.

Mario looked pained. "That was Santana, Gianni. He's one of the best guitarists in the world."

"I don't think I like it."

Mario made a production out of raising the turntable arm and cutting off his stereo. His back to me, he said, "You haven't been around so much lately, Gianni."

"I've got a lot to do now. I have to look after my grandmother."

"It's not natural, all this time you're spending by yourself. You ought to be going out, having fun. You know, meeting people your own age."

I felt my face grow hot. "Who told you to say all that? Your mother?"

Mario looked embarrassed. "She's just worried about you, Gianni. That's all."

"I'm okay," I replied. "I just have a lot to do right now."

"A group of us are going to a concert this Friday. Chicago is playing here."

"I thought that was the name of a city."

"It is," Mario said, exasperated. "It's the name of a rock group too. They're from America. You want to come?"

"I don't think so."

"My brother was asking about you last weekend when he was here. He wants to know when you're coming to the base to play."

I stood up and made for the door. "I don't feel like it right now, Mario. I'll see you tomorrow, okay?"

Saturday mornings my father would come to visit, always dressed in a suit and tie, always strained and gray-faced and

formal. The visits had begun the week following my move to
my grandmother's apartment. I did not ask whether it was
because of something she had said. My grandmother would sit
as stiff and straight as her weakened state would allow. She
refused to speak to him of her illness. I remained in the living
room with them because my grandmother ordered me to, feeling nothing but the tide of emptiness as I sat and avoided looking at my father.

The second week of March arrived amid the worst snowstorm of the year. While I sat in the academy's basement cafe
and tried to work some warmth back into my frozen fingers, I
listened glumly to the words swirl around me. The players for
this year's guitar recital had been announced and Professor
Schmitz still had said nothing to me about it.

The professor's spring recital was on everybody's mind—
who was to play, who would not, who would do duets, who was
that year's rising star. It was one of the year's highlights for
the music academy, and from the second week of March when
the players were announced until the recital itself the performers were the school's chosen elite. That morning the entire cafe
was filled with the talk of his recital. I sat in the corner table,
ignored the occasional curious glance tossed my way, and listened to the talk swirl around me. No one said hello or asked
me to join their discussions. Why should they? I was five or six
years younger and a world apart from their long hair and blue
jeans and endless cigarettes and noisy tumult.

There was talk of the dress—black tuxedoes for male performers, black full-length gowns for the women. There was talk
of contacts made for further study, and sometimes of offers from
agents or concert masters to perform in festivals. There was
talk of pressure and fear. There was talk of the student who
had committed suicide several years ago after botching his
piece, and of the one who now played full time with the chamber
ensemble of the Berlin Philharmonic. I felt frustrated and hurt
and angry that Professor Schmitz had said nothing to me about
the recital, and knew that sitting here listening to the other
students only made matters worse.

The recital was given on the first of May. There were perhaps a dozen performers in all, six soloists and three duets. The recital always concluded with one or two pieces by the master himself. The event was held in the smaller of the two Staatstheater, which seated almost five hundred people. It was always full for the recital.

Things were not going well. I had been working on the same composition for Professor Schmitz for nine weeks. It was only the third piece he had given me since I began lessons with him in September; before that time I had seldom spent more than a few weeks on any one piece. He was also working me through a series of études. An étude was a small run or study composed for technical purposes only that forced me to hit over and over at particularly difficult aspects of playing. They were grueling lessons in discipline, void of the emotional thrill that accompanied learning a new piece. I was forced to repeat them endlessly until I heard the dull emotionless repetitions in my sleep.

The étude assigned for that week required me to hold a bar chord closed with my index finger—which meant all six strings were held tightly down with a rigid first finger—then play a rapid jouncing that alternated between the open base and the top three strings. The run concluded by forcing me to stretch my little finger out four frets while still holding the bar. I could not lunge for the note. It had to be done swiftly and cleanly so that the rapid trill of notes maintained the same beat and emphasis throughout.

In order to perform it correctly I began and ended each day with stretching exercises. I fanned out my fingers on a table so that only the four fingertips touched the wood. I then bore down hard, pushing my fingers forward across the table, so they would stretch out as far apart as possible. I pushed and stretched until I could no longer bear the pain. I refused to think of the logic of this. I was determined to do it correctly. It became an ultimate challenge thrown down by Professor Schmitz. I was going to succeed.

That lesson I played for Professor Schmitz exactly as I had intended, with an ease and flow that made it appear the most natural movement in the world. He ordered me to repeat the exercise. I did so, as cleanly as the first time. He hesitated, looked at me a long moment, then told me to play the assigned composition. I played the piece from beginning to end without pause or interruption. It was the first time this had ever occurred.

When I finished he seemed unsure of what to do; he examined me for a long moment, then nodded his head once in a brief, sharp jerk. He plucked the score from the music stand, went to his filing cabinet, searched briefly, returned, and set another score on the stand. With quick motions and a few words he pointed out the more difficult sections in the first movement.

He turned abruptly away, moved to his cigarettes on the windowsill, said, "Now you can go."

I remained very still, watching him, waiting for a word that I knew was not coming. He had not expected me to perform so well. I could see that now. It had disconcerted him. He had given me that étude thinking I would never play it correctly.

He lit a cigarette, said, "Well? Did you not hear me dismiss you?"

He was not going to mention the recital no matter what I did. It was all so clear now. What was to be gained by bringing it up? I glanced at my watch, said in a small voice, "Our lesson has lasted exactly seventeen minutes."

He filled those parchment-covered hands with other people's work. "So?" His deep voice grated with irritation and cigarette smoke. "And one piece is not enough? Your lesson lasts as long as I say it lasts, and today you do not deserve any more of my time. My time is valuable. If you want more of my time, then you must earn it, with work, with discipline."

Professor Schmitz paused to drag deeply on his cigarette. It made his cheeks even more cavernous. He eyed me through the smoke and asked, "Now do you understand?"

"Yes." I understood that I was excluded from the recital. What else was there to be said?

"So. You finally understand something. Good. You have made both our days. Now go." He turned back to his work and his cigarette.

The evening of the recital my grandmother was not feeling well. Her chest bothered her, she told me. I did not know what to say. I dreaded having to dress up in a suit and go downtown to the Staatstheater all by myself, but if I had to I would. My grandmother watched me mope around the apartment, pleading with her without saying anything out loud. Her voice took on a sharp tone and she told me to stop with the childishness. She could not go. The weather was bad and she did not feel well enough to wait by stage doors for autographs that night. All foolishness would be left for a time when she felt better.

Her remark stung me. "I'm not going to collect autographs. I want to hear the music."

She examined my face with feverish eyes. "Is that anger I hear in your voice?"

I did not back down. "I'm not interested in foolishness. Going to the recital is not foolishness. I need to hear them play."

"Ah," she said, nodding her head. "I think I understand now. Someone feels he should be up there on the stage with them. Has this old head finally seen the light?"

"It is not foolishness," I replied weakly.

She regarded me for a moment, then coughed, a racking sound that bent her almost double. It was the sound I had heard so often late at night. It sounded horrible up close.

Her breath wheezed loudly as she slowly straightened. She reached in her sleeve for the lace handkerchief that was always there, and wiped her lips. "Night air would not be good for these old bones, figlio mio. You must go alone."

I did not argue anymore. "Are you all right?"

"At my age health becomes relative, Giovanni. Yes, I am all right. This is just a cold. Sickness does not pass so quickly as when one is young and strong. It is nothing. Do not worry yourself."

"It doesn't sound like nothing. Have you seen a doctor?"

"Yes, I have seen the doctor, and I tell you not to worry. Finish. Now go get into your suit, the nice dark one you wore at Christmas. And find a clean handkerchief I can iron for your pocket." She smiled at my concern, and her voice softened. "Go, my Giovanezzo. You have a concert to attend. Your grandmother will be fine. It is just a little German cold that will pass with the coming of summer."

I arrived at the concert hall two hours before the recital was to begin. I walked across the broad pebblestone courtyard, its miniature gardens alive with spring colors. The central glass doors were open to the warm air. Inside, cleaners were polishing the marble floor. No one challenged me as I entered and walked to the smaller of the two concert chambers. I pushed through the high broad doors, entered, and sat in the corner of the back row.

Two cleaning ladies were dusting the aisles in front of the stage and talking in a language I could not understand. Only the floor lights along the empty stage were on. I sat in the shadows and watched them work, and thought. Before long they finished their cleaning and left through the side doors. The loudest sound in the room was my breathing.

The seats rose steeply up from the large stage, with two modern sculptures set with lights hanging from the high ceiling. Heavy curtains flanked the stage, with a second set opening halfway back. For this night's performance the second set would be closed, making the stage much smaller. They were open now, revealing a covered grand piano and a clutter of metal chairs and music stands.

I heard footsteps echoing in the distance. Professor Schmitz appeared from behind the curtains and stepped out onto the stage. He was dressed in his dark suit and starched white shirt and thin dark tie. In one hand he carried his guitar case and a smoldering cigarette. The other hand gripped a coat hanger holding his tuxedo.

Professor Schmitz walked to the center of the stage and set down his guitar case. I held my breath. The stage lights glinted off his steel spectacles and turned the hollows of his cheeks into dark caverns. He dragged deeply on his cigarette and let the smoke seep slowly from his nose. He stood there for several minutes, silently smoking his cigarette and regarding the empty chamber. I did not move. When the cigarette was almost burning his fingers, he picked up his case and walked briskly off the stage. His footsteps echoed down the backstage corridor. When I could no longer hear his steps, I stood and left the auditorium.

I walked out of the building, crossed the courtyard, and entered the Hofgarten, the city's central gardens. Most of the trees were just beginning to show leafy buds, but the cherry trees were in full bloom. I walked down a path strewn with white and pink petals and thought about my grandmother, about the recital, about Professor Schmitz. As the sun fell lower the air began to chill, so I crossed the six-lane road separating the gardens from the Old Town. I walked down the Altstadt's main street, which was barred to automobiles and lined with pubs and cafes. I stopped at one of the outdoor grills that served spicy meat with a lettuce and tomato topping in unleavened Arabic bread. I stood and ate and watched the people until it was time to return to the recital.

I had not anticipated that it would disturb me so badly to be in the audience and not onstage. I sat near the back of the auditorium and listened carefully to the performances and to the applause, and I felt as if a knife were being turned in my gut. Over and over I thought, I should be up there. Me. I could outplay them all. I sat and listened and felt more keenly than ever the price I was paying for disobeying Professor Schmitz's demand for cold-hearted discipline.

When the recital was over I had difficulty rising to my feet for Professor Schmitz's standing ovation. I listened to the applause and to the cries of bravo, and the hollow ache made me feel sick to my stomach. I pushed my way through the crowd and hurried from the auditorium.

I almost ran down the long hall to the outer doors and out into the courtyard. I walked through the chilly night air and wanted to laugh, to scream, to cry, to beat my fists against a wall. I should have been up there. I should be the one receiving the accolades. I sat in the tram taking me home, raging over that lost opportunity.

Yet through it all a voice inside kept saying it was my fault. I was the one who had refused to rein in my heart. I was responsible. No matter where I turned or how I raged, I kept coming back to face the fact that I was the one who had not done as Professor Schmitz had ordered. And I hated that truth most of all.

. . .

My grandparents' cottage on Lake Como was set at the end of a cobblestone path, dusty in dry weather and treacherous when wet. The path meandered between the grounds of two large villas, bordered on both sides by high stone walls almost invisible under their burdens of flowering vines. Beyond them the path curved around the mountainside that marked the border of our village. From that point there was a view straight down three hundred meters to the deep blue waters of the lake, and straight across to the Alps rising from the lake's other side.

We arrived at the cottage five weeks after the recital. The train ride down was long and very tiring. We spoke no more than a dozen words the entire trip. My grandmother sat and dozed or stared out the window of our compartment. I sat with a book in my lap and pretended to read.

The cottage was stuffy and dark when we arrived. It was also very bare, as much of the furniture and fittings were in the Dusseldorf apartment. We opened all the shutters and flung back the covers from the remaining furniture. We swept away a year's worth of accumulated dust. My grandmother worked quietly and steadily beside me, refusing to listen when I begged her to sit down and rest. I worked very hard those first few days, and as I worked I marveled at how much smaller the cottage seemed. My cubbyhole under the ceiling was so cramped that I could not move around without bending at the waist. Had I grown so much, or had I just forgotten how small it truly was?

My grandfather's presence was everywhere. The house reeked of his black pipe tobacco and echoed with the sound of his voice. I sat in his chair, closed my eyes, and was transported back to earlier days. Once again I was sitting in front of the fire and pumping the bellows of my miniature accordion. Once again I listened to his stories, played the guitar for him, felt surrounded by his silent gentle strength.

The days soon settled into a comfortable, relaxing, healing routine. Most mornings my grandmother was content to rise late and spend long hours sitting in her tiny garden with her face turned toward the sun. She was busy drawing in strength, storing it away somewhere deep inside.

For me the days were filled with exploring the new and remembering the old. Most mornings I rose with the sun and walked to my grandfather's favorite cafe for a breakfast of fresh-baked rolls and capuccino. Afterward I would take the boat-bus to Como. I walked for hours through its winding streets, or relaxed in a cafe at the lakeside, content simply to sit and watch the endless theater of Italian street life.

Afternoons I practiced. Professor Schmitz and his icy discipline were forgotten with the other shadows of that distant world. The music took on wings I thought were clipped and gone forever.

If I got back from Como in time, I accompanied my grand-mother to evening Mass. I stood outside the high church doors and watched dusk settle over the ancient village. I was content to stand and wait for my grandmother and watch the children play along cobblestone streets, or stroll among the old men gathered in the dusty piazza, or buy ice cream from the street vendors and listen to the excited chatter of the flirting teen-agers. Once in a while I entered the church with my grand-mother and sat in the cool darkness, enjoying the murmured reverberations which echoed back from the high ceilings. I did not take Communion. I did not go to Confession. I did not pray. There was only a cold hollowness within me that must have shown in my eyes when my grandmother asked me about these things, because she sighed and shook her head and turned back to her own prayers. But the soothing peace was still there for me when she prayed. I enjoyed these shared moments of calm, and did not resist when she asked me to join her inside.

The only time my grandmother and I spoke about our return was the first week in August. At dinner she asked me when school was to begin.

I hesitated, then asked, "Here or in Dusseldorf?"

My grandmother stood slowly and turned to the stove. "I think I will have a cup of tea. Would you like some?"

I said I would.

Her back to me, she continued. "I have spent much time thinking of our return, figlio mio. Many long hours I have sat in my garden and wished we could remain here all year."

"We can."

She faced me and shook her head. "No, we cannot."

"But why?"

"Giovanni, Giovanni," she sighed, her eyes somber. She walked back to the table and sat down. "Stop and think for a moment, figlio mio. Put your wishes aside and look at reality. I am old. I have been ill and close to death. Do you see? We must be where there are others to help care for you if ever something were to happen."

"But I can—"

"No you cannot," she said, not raising her voice. "Don't talk nonsense. We will go back to Dusseldorf and you will return to your studies." She laid her hands flat on the table. "Finish."

I remained silent. It seemed very clear to me at that moment, as though I had been given some superior vision that could pierce the veils of time and space, that I was called back to Germany. There was something else that needed doing, something which I had to prove. I thought of the recital and did not object further.

On the last Saturday in August, my grandmother and I returned to Dusseldorf. The following Monday I went back to school. Four days later, I faced my first lesson with Professor Schmitz.

He sat bent over papers, thin as ever. He looked up from his work, inspected me for a moment through the smoke of his eternal cigarette, then motioned me into the practice room. The same dignitaries shook his hand in the same pictures along the walls. It felt as though it had only been a week since my last lesson. I opened my case and tuned my guitar.

Professor Schmitz entered the room, crushed his cigarette out on the ashtray by the window, opened the over-stuffed filing cabinet, selected a score, came over, and placed it on the music stand. He sat down beside me and began to go over the nuances of the piece. We worked like that for three-quarters of an hour, with him explaining and me occasionally playing a passage at his command.

As I was putting away my guitar he rose, started for the door, then stopped and turned around. In his deep monotone he said, "I hope you found time to practice this summer."

"Every day," I said quietly.

He nodded, as though a minor business was now out of the way. "Until next week, then."

Friday morning between classes I went by Fraulein Rohr's classroom. I waited until the last of her students had left, then walked in.

"Gianni!" Tucking stray strands of blond hair back into place, she gave me her special smile as she walked over. "How good to see you. Did you have a nice summer?"

"Yes," I said, and rushed on, determined not to lose my nerve. "Do you still want me to play for your classes?"

The suddenness of my question put her at a loss for words.

She reached toward my forehead, but with a nervous gesture changed her mind and dropped her hand back to her side. "You certainly have grown this summer, Gianni. I will have to be careful to treat you as a young man. Yes, of course I want you to play for us."

I nodded, swallowed, asked, "When?"

She regarded me curiously. "Are you sure you want to, Gianni? No one is forcing you, I hope."

I shook my head. "I need the practice playing in front of people."

Fraulein Rohr thought a moment. "Well, I will have to arrange the times with your teachers. We have a staff meeting on Wednesday, so I can see them all at one time."

"All right." I was committed. I handed her a sheet of paper. "This is a list of my classes."

"My, you certainly have thought this out." She took the paper and looked it over. "After all this time. It's a little hard to believe you are going to play for us, Gianni."

I nodded and wiped the palms of my hands down the legs of my pants. It was hard for me, too.

"How is your grandmother?"

"Fine," I said. "We spent the summer in Como."

"How lovely." She gave me another smile. "I am certainly looking forward to this, Gianni. And I will see if Herr Scherer might like to come hear you as well." She glanced at the wall clock. "You had best run on to your next class. I will speak with you next week."

The following Wednesday Fraulein Rohr was waiting for me when I stopped by her classroom. She seemed very subdued. She asked if I would mind waiting a little longer before playing for her classes.

She looked down at her hands. "I decided to speak with the principal first. He would have to give permission for you to miss classes and play for my students." She looked up and said quietly, "He decided to call your music professor."

"I understand," I said. She did not have to say anything more.

"Your professor thinks you should perhaps wait a little longer. I told the principal that I disagreed, Gianni, and I do. I think it is nonsense. But the principal feels we should follow the wishes of your professor." She looked at me for a long moment, asked, "Is everything all right between you and your professor, Gianni?"

"Fine." What could she do?

"Well, I will not let the principal forget this matter, I promise you that." She patted my shoulder. "I am sure this will all work out very quickly, Gianni. I cannot tell you how much I am looking forward to hearing you play."

At my next lesson Professor Schmitz said he had received a call from the principal of my school.

"Yes," I said.

"He tells me you wish to play for the students. Is that true?"

I nodded my head.

"So you feel you are qualified now to give performances in public, is that it? Does your teacher have no say in the matter?"

"I need to get used to playing in front of people." I took a deep breath. "Before spring."

"I see," Professor Schmitz said slowly. He looked at me for a long time before giving an abrupt nod. "Very well. We have wasted enough time on this nonsense. Pay attention, boy, and I will explain this next passage."

I sat and listened to his droning monotone. The words began to melt and blur together. I grew increasingly angry. I kept my face calm and my eyes on the music, but the only voice I could hear clearly was the one inside my head. Wasting time? It is wasting time to conquer fear? I sat and watched his bony fingers trace the unseen notes, and over and over inside my head I asked him how preparation for my life's work could be called a waste of time.

The beginning of October arrived, and still I had not heard from Fraulein Rohr. I had stepped up my practice periods to three, sometimes four hours a day. My fingertips and hand muscles and wrists hurt so badly in the beginning that the pain kept me awake at night. But the pain soon eased, and I had begun to see my abilities climb to a new level. I had never played better.

Yet nothing seemed to satisfy Professor Schmitz. I avoided

major battles only by remaining totally silent. If he asked me a question, I answered as briefly as I could. If I added the slightest bit of flow, the minutest pause that was not written into the score, he began clapping his hands sharply to the beat and humming out the score's timing in his deep voice. At those times I felt trapped within his rigid walls of discipline, and my carefully guarded emotions threatened to boil over. I walked out of those lessons so furious I could barely see where I was going.

I hated him in those moments. I hated him and his bony discolored fingers and the stench from his cigarettes and his deep, dead voice and his flat, emotionless eyes. I hated his discipline and I hated his constant disapproval. I sat on the tram going home from those lessons and stared blindly out the window, feeling the hatred well up like some alien power within me.

Slowly, slowly, I retreated from the brink. In those moments when the anger threatened to overpower me, I saw myself entering a cold endless sleep where my music had no place. What would happen to my life if the hatred consumed me and the music died forever? I remembered the recital that previous spring, how I had sat at the back of the audience, desperately hungry to be up there on the stage. It would not happen again, I repeated over and over on those tram rides home. This spring's recital would be the door through which I would pass to my dream of becoming a professional guitarist. I sat in the tram and felt my anger slowly fade into a hardened determination.

The following Saturday morning I sat in the kitchen with my father and grandmother and looked into my father's eyes. I felt a chill of fear race down my spine. Is that what happened to him? Did some chained coldness kill the spirit within? I saw nothing but empty hopelessness, and I vowed never to let this happen to me.

The first week in November, after a particularly difficult session with Professor Schmitz, I went to the city library and checked out a book the librarian referred me to—Copland's *What To Listen For In Music*. As I held it in my hands and walked to the tram stop that cold winter afternoon, I wondered what it would be like to have such a name that I could teach others about music, write books that others might want to read, help them to feel in their heart as I did, share the joys that I felt.

After dinner that night I sat in the living room while my grandmother quietly prepared for bed. Her cough was back, and by dinnertime her energy began to fade. As soon as the table was cleared she usually went to bed. I sat and listened as she whispered her brief evening prayers, then wished her a good night.

I opened the book and began to read. I was soon engrossed; I could almost picture the man from the way he wrote—quiet, gentle, careful to choose the most precise words that would explain exactly what he intended.

And he clearly loved his music. I felt a bonding with this man as I read:

> Nineteenth century composers, primarily interested in extending the harmonic language of music, allowed their sense of rhythm to become dulled by an overdose of regularly recurring down-beats. Even the greatest of them are open to this accusation. That probably is the origin for the conception of rhythm entertained by the ordinary music teacher of the past generation, who taught that the first beat of every metrical unit is always the strong one.[1]

Not just in the last generation, I thought bleakly. I wished I had the nerve to show that passage to Professor Schmitz, but I knew I never would. I turned to the next chapter and read:

> The first essential, then, is to differentiate composers, trying to hear each separately in terms of what he wishes to communicate.[2]

Not for Professor Schmitz. His lessons dealt with the mechanics of a piece only. Not once had he ever discussed the composer's period or life or what he might be trying to say. I turned a few more pages and read:

> What we hear produces wider extremes of tension and

---

[1]Copland, *What To Listen For In Music,* McGraw-Hill, Inc., 1968. Permission of McGraw-Hill.
[2]Ibid.

release, a more vivid optimism, a grayer pessimism, climaxes of abandonment and explosive hysteria.[3]

I began flipping through the book, trying to find some passage that placed discipline and mechanics above the music's emotional content. If there was such a passage, I could not find it. I read:

> Society and culture and education and a thousand other things form the listener, and the music must appeal to what he is in order to be successful.[4]

Did Professor Schmitz allow any interpretation of the music in order to suit today's listener? Where was the emotion? Where was the attempt to understand what the composer was trying to say? Where? I turned the pages and read further:

> Always remember that a theme is, after all, only a succession of notes. Merely by changing the dynamic, that is, by playing it loudly and bravely or softly and timidly, one can transform the emotional feeling of the very same succession of notes. By a change of harmony a new poignancy may be given the theme; or by a different rhythmic treatment the same notes may result in a war dance instead of a lullaby. Every composer keeps in mind the possible metamorphosis of his succession of notes.[5]

All that week I read the book and asked myself questions. Thursday afternoon I returned to Professor Schmitz's office and prepared for my lesson, trembling at the thought of what I was planning to do.

As soon as he entered and sat down, I started. I spoke quietly, respectfully, trying to keep my voice steady. I did not wish to trouble my teacher, I said. I did not wish to argue. I wanted to learn and be as good a student as I could. But I felt that part of my study should be trying to learn what the composer was trying to communicate. I felt that attention should also be given to the music's emotional content. I spoke for what seemed a very long time. When I stopped the room was very still. I sat and returned Professor Schmitz's gaze and listened to the beating of my heart.

---

[3]Ibid.
[4]Ibid.
[5]Ibid.

Professor Schmitz took off his glasses and slowly, methodically cleaned them with his pocket handkerchief. "Listen to me, boy. You are good, very good. But you have no comprehension of who you are or what a gift you possess. Your talent is raw, untamed. It is the reason why I accepted you as a student, and why so often I wish I had not."

He put his glasses back on, reached in his shirt pocket, fingered out a cigarette, lit it. His voice droned on. "You aren't doing exercises here, boy. This is not simple schoolwork. You are playing the work of the masters, the high priests of this instrument we mortals call a guitar. To them, and to those who know their music for what it is, this music is considered sacred. In fact, many of them were indeed holy men. This work was an offering which they presented to God. Do you understand me? No, how could a fifteen-year-old boy understand this?

"Listen to me carefully, boy. That passage you slipped on last week, yes? The master may have spent months on that passage, agonizing over exactly how it would sound, what it was to signify, how it would proceed."

He took a deep drag from his cigarette, squinted at me through the smoke. "And a fifteen-year-old boy tells me that he wants to attempt an emotional interpretation of such a passage. Fine. I am sure the master would have been honored to hear of your desire."

He leaned over close to me. I could see the thin pale line of his lips, and smell the rank tobacco odor of his breath. "Now you will play this passage until you have played it perfectly, until it fits precisely into the whole. You will continue to play all pieces without comment until I tell you that you have learned the mechanics and the discipline of this instrument. Then and only then will you be ready to begin with such things as interpretation and emotional analysis. Do you understand? Yes. I see that this at least is clear. Good. Then perhaps we can finish with this waste of time and get on with our work."

.   .   .

Our final lessons before the Christmas holidays rarely lasted more than half an hour. I played what he had assigned me to study. He criticized me briefly and made me play a few passages over. When he was satisfied he would nod his head once, turn to the next assignment, explain it briefly, and dismiss me. I wondered at times if he was glad to have me leave.

In mid-January Professor Schmitz started me on a piece by Castelnuovo-Tedesco, a melodious rite of spring that begged for interpretation. It cried out to be played like the flow of a river, the steadily moving currents offset by swirls and eddies and unwritten pauses that gave life to half-hidden pools of emotion. To play it with the professor's strict sense of timing, to compress the flow into a rigid discipline, to give each note the exact same weight, was torture. I carried this burden with me through the dark weeks of winter, knowing full well what he intended. This was the challenge. If I gave in to my desire to play with flow, with interpretation, there would be no recital for me that year.

Professor Schmitz moved through the piece at a snail's pace, taking it slower and more deliberately than ever before. He was testing me, compelling me to struggle daily with my desire to run with the music's beauty. He forced me to clamp down hard on my emotions, to follow the written structure and timing, to learn discipline. I felt like a butcher.

Work on the piece continued on through February and into March. The pressure of the unmentioned recital grew on me steadily. I began to have vivid nightmares of smashing my guitar, raging through crowded streets, slashing out at unseen faces while I screamed a torrent of curses. I began to awaken in the morning feeling tired and listless. I entered the lessons with dread.

The first week in March Professor Schmitz explained the piece's final passage. He let me go after less than fifteen minutes. I understood. The ultimatum had been stated as clearly as if it had been written upon my heart.

All that week I practiced the piece, ignoring the growing tumult of my feelings, afraid to even look inside. I bound myself tighter and tighter to Professor Schmitz's rigid discipline. My exhaustion grew. I dragged myself through the days of that week.

. . .

I entered his office the following Thursday feeling nothing.

I went into the practice room, sat, opened my case, and began tuning my guitar. I saw the world through a blanket of fatigue. I set the sheet music on the stand, but I did not open it.

Professor Schmitz walked in, glanced at the closed music, nodded once, sat down. He did not need to say anything. I knew what I had to do. I ran through the strings once more, flexed my fingers, took a breath, and began.

Halfway through the first movement knife-like spasms cramped my back from holding myself too stiff. Yet I dared not relax. It was the only way I knew to hold back totally, by tensing myself and gritting my teeth and trying not to think. A trickle of sweat teased its way down my temple and cheek and jaw and neck. I did not move.

Toward the end of the second movement I faltered in my concentration, allowed a brief flash of feeling. I saw myself imprisoned and in chains, struggling in darkness and screaming at the night. But I caught myself in time. I pushed away the thought and clenched my teeth and bore down harder.

I finished the piece. I dropped my hands, too weak to set the guitar down. I felt totally drained. Every ounce of energy had been pummelled from my body and spirit by this battle I had fought within myself.

Professor Schmitz reached over and took the music from the stand. He stood and walked to his filing cabinet. He paused long enough to light a cigarette, then began searching through the cluttered top drawer. I watched him from the corner of my eye, my head still bowed over my guitar.

He walked back over, sat down, and placed a new score on the stand. "So. Today we will begin with Frescobaldi. I want you to study this first passage very carefully for next week."

I was still sweating. I could feel the moisture sticking my shirt to my body. I allowed my head to roll backward. I stared at the ceiling, sighed, shook my head very slowly. For the life of me I could not remember what had ever made this whole thing seem so important.

Professor Schmitz took a drag on his cigarette, tapped at the ashtray with nervous fingers, said with the smoke, "What do you want me to say, boy? That you played well? All right. You played well. There. Are you satisfied?"

With an effort I turned my head and looked at him. It was as though I had never really seen the man before. I had been so committed to this desire to make it, to play in his recital, to become a great classical guitarist, that I had been blind to who this man really was. What he wanted.

"I understand," I said quietly. Finally, finally, I truly understood.

"You understand nothing. You are tired and overwrought, that much I understand. Go home and rest, boy. Tomorrow look at the passage. Not tonight. Tomorrow. Study it well. It is the piece you will play in your first recital. You have seven weeks to prepare. Can you do it? I doubt it, but we will see. Now go home. I have other work to see to."

I walked out of the school, lightheaded in the early spring sunlight. *I understand,* I repeated to myself as I waited for my tram. Why had it taken so long? Why had it been so hard for me to see? The man was trying to chain me down. I had been killing myself trying to satisfy someone who could give life to nothing, not even himself. How could he impose his world of discipline and order on music? To chain it was to kill it. Did life flow to four-four time? Did the wind blow like an army march? He was *wrong.* I could play it as he wanted and create a corpse, or I could breathe life into it as I had wanted to do all along. What did I choose? Life or death?

I would not let it die. The words became a litany as I sat in the tram and stared blindly from the window. My father, Professor Schmitz, this cold-hearted land with its empty-eyed people, none of them would take it from me. This insane demand for discipline would not destroy it. Never again would I contort my music for the sake of form.

I went straight to the apartment and let myself in. I heard my grandmother in the kitchen, but I did not say anything. I did not want to talk to anyone. My fatigue and despair were gone. There was a fire burning inside me. I walked to my alcove, the tiny room where for weeks I had done battle with myself to produce a dead thing for Professor Schmitz. My grandmother called my name. I refused to hear her, to take my mind away from what was burning inside me. I took out my guitar. Professor Schmitz had taken the score, but I did not need it. All I had to do was close my eyes and the notes danced in front of me.

I began to play. I played as I had dreamed of playing. I

played with *fire*. Not with my head, not bound to a lifeless clock or stomping boots or senseless discipline. Discipline was a tool, not a prison. I knew discipline. And I knew that discipline would never rule me again.

I played the golden notes with the quiet joy of a world awakening to spring. I played the wind. I played the soft sighing of new leaves. I played and the earth came alive, rejoicing to the passage of winter's stillness. My music took on a voice of its own, a chanting soaring cadence.

When I finished and looked up, my grandmother was standing in the doorway. I sat and stared at her, seeing her anew. I saw the shadow of her illness. I saw her grim strength and determination. I saw a sadness that had built up over many years, etching itself deeply into her features, threading its gray fingers through her hair. And I saw the deep pool of calm and love that came from her prayers.

For the first time I could look and see what these prayers brought her, a foundation upon which she stood against the storms that raged about her. I saw how I had been sheltered upon that rock all my life. I did not understand her faith in someone who had allowed her to be hurt as badly as she had been. I did not see how she could turn daily to something unseen. But I could not deny the love and the wisdom that stood there beside the pain and the weight of years. I was too open, too honest with myself at that moment to deny what I was able to see.

"That was lovely, Giovanni," she said. "What do you call it?"

I told her.

"Lovely." She shook her head. "You have a great gift, figlio mio."

I nodded, thinking, she has given me so much. It is right that she be the first to hear of my awakening.

In the following weeks I came to play a dual role. With Professor Schmitz I was the dutiful student, chaining myself within his ordered boundaries of style and discipline and strict timing. After each lesson I walked out drained, my throat constricted, my chest tight.

At home I dissected my work twice, first inspecting and learning and memorizing each portion as Professor Schmitz dictated. Each note was held in bondage to its proper place, each bar played to the resounding monotony of the clock in my head. I had learned his lesson of discipline, and I would use it. My rejection of the barren limitations of the man would not force me to reject the value of his lessons. I would not reject the goodness. I simply would not stop myself there.

Hesitantly at first, then with growing assurance and strength, I released myself from these self-imposed boundaries. I experimented with timing, holding notes until the tones fell away into silence. I marveled at my daring, relished the joy of knowing that it was now my decision. I ran lines together, faster and faster and faster until the notes fell like raindrops or poured like a waterfall, cascading from the mouth of my instrument in a torrent that picked me up and rushed me away, up and away to a world where the music I played and all that I was became one.

.   .   .

One day in the middle of March Fraulein Rohr was waiting for me outside my first class. Her pale blue eyes looked very excited behind her spectacles. She asked if I was ready to play for her class.

I swallowed my surprise and the sudden lurch of fear, and replied, "Yes."

"Oh, I'm so glad." She gave me her special smile. "I was afraid it had taken so long to organize that you would have changed your mind again. Did you know we have a long weekend holiday at the end of March? Yes, of course you do. What student doesn't know about his holidays? Well, the principal has given me permission to bring my three afternoon classes together the Thursday before the holidays to hear you play. Isn't that exciting?"

"Yes," I agreed, thinking that three classes meant seventy people, maybe more. I was going to play in front of seventy strangers.

"The principal will be there too. I hope you don't mind, Gianni. I thought it would be nice to invite him."

"No, no, that's fine," I said weakly.

"He told me that if you play as well as Herr Scherer and Professor Schmitz said, he wants you to play for the school assembly before the Easter holidays."

I was not sure that I had understood her. "Professor Schmitz told the principal that I was ready to perform?"

"Well, I didn't hear their conversation, but the principal seemed very pleased when he got off the phone. He came to the teachers' lounge right after the professor called, and told me I could start arranging things."

I barely followed the remainder of the conversation as Fraulein Rohr covered timing and notes for my teachers and a number of other details. It was unbelievable. In over a year of lessons he had never done anything but criticize me. I could not understand it. Why would Professor Schmitz say nothing at all to me, and then turn around and compliment me before someone he barely knew? I said goodbye to Fraulein Rohr and walked to my next class, hurt and confused. And scared. Seventy strangers.

The two weeks leading up to my playing for the class were spent in grim preparation. The work for Professor Schmitz was completed as swiftly as possible. Afterward I turned to my pieces for Fraulein Rohr's students. Not once during those two lessons did Professor Schmitz make any reference to his conversation with the principal or speak to me about my playing at the school. I was finding it harder and harder to say anything to him at all.

I spent a great deal of time and effort deciding what to play and in what order. Most of the students would have little or no idea about classical guitar, so I decided that every other piece would be a rendition of a universally known classical composition. I would alternate these with pieces, or movements of longer works, that could be played fast and fiery to show some of the difficult lessons I had mastered. I spent several days switching pieces back and forth, until I finally gave up and forced myself to keep to the chosen order.

The classroom presentation was to be fifty-five minutes long. During the final few days I did nothing but run through the set over and over, including pauses between each piece. Each day I did the set once before school, then once again as soon as I was home, then two more times before dinner, then one final time before bed. I began to hear the pieces of that set in my dreams.

I slept in snatches the night before I was to play. I would

drift through fleeting dreams until a fear surfaced about the next day, and a sharp electric shock would hit my belly, tense my muscles, and jerk me awake. I thought morning would never come.

My grandmother watched as I toyed with my breakfast, and said, "I hope you will do well in your performance at school today."

Performance. I had not thought of it as a real performance. The knot of fear in my belly grew larger. I nodded.

"And so it begins," she said, almost to herself. Then, "Are you afraid, figlio mio?"

"Yes," I said.

"You know the music. I have heard you playing and playing the pieces, and I tell you what you refuse to admit. You know the pieces perfectly. You will find it much easier to face the day if you accept this."

I stared at her. "What if I forget?"

"You will not forget," she said flatly. She took a tiny sip of her coffee, and crumbled half of her morning roll with dry, brittle fingers. It was her way to avoid eating what she had no hunger for. She reduced her bread to crumbs that she would leave out for the birds. The birds ate more in the mornings than she did.

"I will pray for you this day, figlio mio." She raised her eyes and gave me a small smile. "I pray for you every day, but today I will say a special prayer that you perform with majesty."

"Thank you," I said, managing a little smile back. With majesty. What a beautiful thought.

"May I ask something from you in return?"

"Anything." Especially if you would promise to eat more, I thought. My grandmother seemed to sag upon her slender frame as though all the substance and the strength were slowly being drained from her body.

She nibbled at the edge of the other half of her roll, sipped her coffee, and said, "I ask that you search your mind and your heart for the answer to this question. Who gave you the gift of your music? Was it simply a matter of chance? Did it appear from thin air? Was it made out of the same dust and elements that went into the making of your body?"

As always when she spoke of these things, I was filled with

a sense of uneasiness. Vague yearnings and memories of pain seemed to conflict for my attention. I was pulled in a number of directions, all of them disturbing. I did not know what to say.

She raised her eyes from her cup and held me with a luminous gaze. "If it was indeed a God on high who gave you this magnificent gift, was it not for a purpose? And would not this purpose be to serve Him? That is my question, Giovanezzo, my beloved child. Should you not be worshiping Him with this glorious gift of musical talent which He bestowed upon you?"

I struggled for an answer and finally managed, "I will think on it."

The light faded in her eyes, but she accepted my reply with a simple nod. "That is good, figlio mio. Now go and play with the majesty He has given you."

After a lunch I did not touch, I followed Fraulein Rohr to her classroom. The desks had been pushed tightly together in the center of the room. Folding chairs were set down both sides and along the back. Her desk was pushed over to the window, and the long worktable was gone. At the front of the room rested one lonely chair and a tiny footstool.

"It is going to be very cramped, but all seventy-six of us will be able to sit down." She sounded breathless. "I think they will listen much better if they are seated."

I nodded my head, thinking that the rows of chairs seemed to stretch out endlessly.

"You have all this period to practice; I'll leave you here by yourself. When the next bell rings, put your guitar behind my desk. It will be safe there, don't you think? Come and meet me in the teachers' lounge. You can wait there until everyone is settled; then I will bring you in."

She patted me gently on the shoulder. "I'm sure you will do just fine, Gianni." She turned and left the room.

I sat in the chair at the front of the room with my guitar in my lap. I could not think of anything to play. My mind was a blank. I could not remember the pieces I had chosen, much less the order I had placed them in. I sat listening to my heart and wondering, why am I here? Did all of the recital students go to this trouble to prepare? Did anyone else feel this terror of playing in front of people? Was this something I would have to live with for the rest of my life?

I looked at the clock beside the door, and was shocked to find that I had been sitting there for almost twenty minutes. I wiped my hands on the towel I had packed in my guitar case and carefully tuned the strings. The notes echoed loudly in the empty room. I liked the sound. The linoleum floor and concrete walls seemed to amplify the guitar's power. I played a simple practice run, a tonal exercise that ran up and down one octave from middle C. I listened to the sound bouncing back at me, enjoying the way the echo melted the notes together.

I played the run again, much faster this time, and the edges of the notes seemed to blur with the reverberation. I did the run in minor and then in seventh, then slapped the strings silent with the palm of my hand. The air vibrated from the music that was no longer there.

I felt the world stop to catch its breath. I saw myself back in my living room, sitting quietly and listening to the rosary beads click through my grandmother's fingers. I felt the peace settle upon my mind and heart, and knew without needing to question it that she was praying for me. And there, faintly, barely audible, straining to be heard through the ringing silence, was my lilting inner melody.

I held my breath and tentatively began to play. It seemed so faint, so fragile that it might fade away at any moment. But it did not. As I followed its lyrical course on my guitar, I felt the peace and calming joy continue to build.

The bell ending class rang, and the inner melody faded away. Yet the peace remained. I was certain that my grandmother was seated in her favorite chair, a Bible open in her lap, her eyes closed, her lips moving in whispered prayer. I felt her calm strength and knew that somehow I was shielded from my fear.

I walked to the teachers' lounge. Fraulein Rohr was standing outside the door with a portly woman I did not know. She smiled when she saw me.

"This is Frau Holz, Gianni. She will walk down with you in a few minutes." She was very excited. "Are you nervous?"

"A little," I said. I felt calm and yet nervous. Very afraid, yet not afraid at all. How was that possible?

"You go on to class," Frau Holz said. "It will be a zoo in there with all those students."

"Herr Scherer should be helping out, if he was able to get away on time."

Frau Holz laughed. "Herr Scherer will be the worst of the lot. Go. We will be just fine."

Fraulein Rohr smiled at me. "I'll see you in a few minutes, Gianni." Then she was gone.

"Would you like something to drink? I believe I might find us a nice cup of cocoa if you are thirsty."

I told Frau Holz that cocoa would be fine and followed her into the lounge. Teachers glanced my way as I entered and gave little smiles. They all seemed to know who I was. I found an empty chair in the corner and sat down. Gradually attention in the room turned away from me. Frau Holz returned and handed me a steaming mug. She sat down in the seat beside me and told me how her dog had just had puppies, and how she was afraid she would have five little monsters tearing up her garden that next summer instead of just one. I sat and took tiny sips from my cocoa and listened to her describe a dog that could eat roses without getting stuck by the thorns.

Frau Holz glanced at her watch and asked if I was ready to go. I said yes and gave her my mug. She carried it back into the kitchen and did not say anything about how little I had drunk. As we walked down the hall she told me she had a free period, and asked if I would mind if she stayed to listen. I said no. She asked if I was nervous. A little, I repeated.

"You're just like my husband," she said, stopping at the door to Fraulein Rohr's class and knocking. "You'd never know he was scared about anything. Cool as ice, at least on the outside."

Fraulein Rohr opened the door. She looked strangely flushed. She gave us a nervous smile and held open the door.

I walked in, the calming power shielding me from the sight. The class looked entirely different now, much larger and much, much fuller. Every seat was taken and two teachers I did not know stood in the back corner beside the window. The principal was there, in the front row next to the door. From the chair beside him Herr Scherer gave me a yellow-toothed grin and a wink.

I walked over to Fraulein Rohr's desk and fumbled with the catches to my guitar case. My fingers trembled slightly, but the calm within remained the stronger force. I was pulled in two directions, one shaking with fear and the other sheltered in an oasis of peace.

I wiped my hands thoroughly on the towel before picking up the guitar, and listened to Fraulein Rohr tell the class who I was and how I had come from Italy and that I was now the youngest student at the Musikakademie. I carried my guitar and the towel over and sat down. I rubbed my hands again, then the guitar's neck, and kept my eyes turned away from that cramped gathering. Fraulein Rohr laid her hand on my shoulder as she finished her introduction. When she stopped talking Herr Scherer started clapping and the class joined in.

"All right, Gianni," Fraulein Rohr said. She gave me another little smile and sat down beside Herr Scherer.

I took a deep breath, flexed my fingers, plucked each string to check the tuning, made one adjustment, took another breath, and began.

There were some stirrings and whispers as I started playing. My fingers were still trembling. I did not make mistakes, but I played the first bars awkwardly and had no feel for the strings. But the calm remained, a welling up from the very center of my chest, a quiet message of strength. Before I reached the midpoint of the piece the trembling had passed, and the room had become very still.

When I finished, the applause was loud, pressing at the room's confines. It both embarrassed and excited me. I wiped my hands on the towel and was glad to see that they were steady. I did not look at the people. As soon as the applause died down I started the second piece. It was a fast arpeggio, the first of the difficult pieces and the shortest. I played it very well, very fast. The ending started low on the bass string and flew up to a light trilling on the top fret of the highest string, fading away before the speed of the run could register. There was a moment's silence at the end, then applause and excited laughter. I looked up, and saw Fraulein Rohr clapping hard, smiling with her eyes and biting her lower lip. Herr Scherer called out a loud bravo and winked at me again. I could not help grinning.

Soon it was all over. Too soon. The audience clapped loud and long, and I wished there was time to play some more.

The principal stood up while the class reverberated to the applause, shook my hand with both of his, then turned to the class and raised his hands for silence. He was a short, chubby man with eyes that did not smile with the rest of his face. When he raised his arms his coat lifted to reveal a protruding belly.

"I am sure you all want to join me in thanking Giovanni di Alta for his performance," he said. He let the applause go on for a moment, then stopped it, saying, "I am very happy to say that Giovanni has agreed to play for the school assembly before the Easter break, so we will all be able to enjoy his music again." There was some excited talk and people started moving about.

"Class dismissed," he said, and the class erupted. As the students laughed and talked and tumbled from their cramped rows, I went to Fraulein Rohr's desk and packed away my guitar. A couple of students I knew vaguely called out to me; I looked up and smiled in reply. The principal came over and shook my hand again. He was joined by Herr Scherer and Fraulein Rohr.

"That was outstanding," the principal said. "Have you ever heard anything like that before?"

"He captivated the room," Herr Scherer said. "Nine-tenths of them wouldn't know Mozart from mozzarella, but for a whole blessed hour you could have heard a pin drop."

"I'm very proud of you, Gianni," Fraulein Rohr said, her eyes shining.

"Young man, I hope you'll excuse me for announcing that you would play for the assembly before asking you officially. Fraulein Rohr said you were willing."

I told the principal it was fine.

"Excellent. Now, let's see—" The principal's ruddy features creased in thought. "We have the two speakers, they will take perhaps twenty minutes. Then there's the skit by the dramatics class, another twenty. Would you care to play for twenty minutes between the speeches and the play?"

I said that whatever he wanted would be all right.

"That's settled then. I must be getting back to work." Briskly he shook my hand a third time and departed.

"I don't know what to say." Fraulein Rohr's eyes flickered back and forth between me and Herr Scherer. "I'm honestly at a loss for words."

"Then I'll say it for you." Herr Scherer laid a hand on my

shoulder and said solemnly, "Gianni, you have the makings of a world-class guitarist. For every thousand people who can play the right notes, only one will be able to reach out and capture their listeners. Maybe only one in ten thousand. Before today I thought you might have this power. Today I am sure. You held this circus absolutely spellbound for an hour. I was listening for it, and even so there were moments when I forgot where I was. Do you understand what I am saying? You are a magnificent guitarist. Keep it up. I am very proud of you.

"There." He dropped his hand and looked at Fraulein Rohr. "Was that all right?"

"Perfect," she said, her voice a little shaky. She blinked her eyes very rapidly and repeated, "That was perfect."

. . .

One afternoon as we were returning from school together, Mario told me, "The whole school is talking about you, Gianni."

"What are they saying?"

"How you're the youngest in the whole history of the Musikakademie, you know, stuff like that." Mario swept his hair back and gave a satisfied grin. "Some of the students are talking about how there's this young Italian kid studying at the academy, and that there's never been a German his age to do it. Really gets their backs up, Maestro."

The previous summer and autumn Mario had been busy turning some invisible corner. Now when we met after school, it seemed that he was speaking some alien language. His caustic humor had become a cynical, all-knowing bitterness. He had let his hair grow out very long, and had taken to wearing black. He was always getting into fights. At least once a week I went home alone because he was held after school for one problem or another. The battles he had with his parents were becoming the stuff of legends around the neighborhood.

The discussions we did have revolved around three things. Girls and what they did or did not do were described in the most graphic detail. Mario was an endless source of knowledge about the rock music scene, traveling almost every weekend to some city or another for a concert. And his pleasure in street-fighting knew no bounds.

Earlier that autumn, German television had broadcast a

series of programs, about four villages in southern Germany where the population of foreigners was larger than that of Germans. Following that, a couple of the weekly magazines had dedicated entire issues to the theme of foreign cultures infiltrating Germany. There were pictures of mosques and smoke-filled cafes and kerchief-covered women and swarthy-skinned street cleaners and restaurants with menus only in Turkish or Greek or Portuguese.

The backlash was swift and smoldering. Swastikas appeared on numerous buildings. Neo-Nazi and other extreme right-wing groups became both vocal and abusive in their appeal for the foreigners to go home. At night, cars filled with foul-mouthed men began patrolling neighborhoods where the majority of inhabitants were foreign, looking for trouble. A multitude of discussions and spokesmen and advertisements called for calm and pointed out that without immigrant workers, the prosperous German industrial machine would grind to a halt.

In the school, skinhead gangs vandalized the walls with words like Kanake, Neger, Spaghetti-Fresser. All ended with *Raus*, the German command for "out." The Turks and the Italians and the Greeks formed their own gangs, and violence was a constant threat. Mario hung around a group of toughs who spoke of battles as something to yearn for.

Mario stretched his legs under the tram seat in front of us and said casually, "I'm quitting school in the spring, Maestro. Had about all I can stand."

"So?" It did not really surprise me. "Have you told your parents yet?"

"Gonna do it tonight. You and the old lady might wanna take a walk after dinner. A long one."

I nodded. Several times a week their voices made our walls shake. "What are you going to do?"

"Got a job working in a Frankfurt recording studio. My brother helped set it up. Said at least then he'd be able to keep an eye on me, since it's only an hour from where he works at the Darmstadt base. I'll be going to school nights; there's a special place there to study sound engineering. Best place in Europe, so I've heard. The studio's kinda mickey mouse, but there's another one here in Dusseldorf I've been talking to that's promised me a job when I finish the course. The one here does a lot of the big rock groups."

"That's great, Mario," I said, thinking how much I would miss him.

"You gotta come down and visit us, Gianni. Danilo still wants you to come play for his friends."

I put him off with, "Let me get through this recital, Mario. That's about as far ahead as I can see right now."

. . .

As Easter approached, teachers began to stop their conversations and stare at me as I walked by. They would smile as I looked their way. Students I didn't know said hello in the halls. The attention both flustered and pleased me.

I had decided to give myself one simple piece at the beginning of the assembly to relax and get used to being on stage, and then spend the remaining time on three very difficult pieces. I no longer felt a need to play familiar tunes to draw them in.

The morning of my performance, my grandmother was strangely quiet. As I rose from the breakfast table I asked her if everything was all right.

"You are playing for the school today, is that correct?"

"Yes." I did not understand the question. We had talked about it several times, most recently the night before as she ironed my suit.

She nodded her head slowly, her eyes on her coffee cup. "Do you perhaps recall the promise you made before your last performance, figlio mio? Does that busy head of yours have time to remember promises made to an old woman?"

I heaved a silent sigh as I placed my dishes in the sink. Why did she have to hit on me about such things just as I was preparing for a performance? A door that normally remained locked deep within me threatened to spring open, revealing all the pain and anger and memories that I kept so carefully buried.

I pushed the thoughts aside. "I remember."

"And have you come to any conclusion about this? Has there been any answer within your heart?"

I stood there behind her, looking down on the disheveled

gray curls. Do not force these things on me, I wanted to tell her. You don't know what it does to me when you talk about all this. But the words would not come. I remained standing there, silent and angry.

"I cannot stop praying for you, Giovanni," she said finally. "I would rather stop breathing. But my first prayer is for the salvation of your eternal soul. There is nothing more important than this. Nothing."

She swiveled around, raised her face, and held me with her eyes. "There are two things you must remember at all times, Giovanni. Are you listening to me?"

"Yes."

"Very well, then. First, whatever part of your life you do not dedicate to the Lord's service becomes a barrier to knowing Him. There is always the danger, figlio mio, that He may destroy this barrier in order to draw you closer to Him."

Her eyes were solemn, her voice stronger than I had heard it in months. "Do you wish for this to happen to your music? Do you wish to make it into some defense of your selfish nature that you use to keep your Lord and Maker out of your life?"

I shook my head. A storm of confusion rose around me as thoughts swirled and pushed at me. Yet there was an answering chord to her words that struck somewhere deep inside. And this troubled me most of all.

"No, of course you do not. This is why you must open your eyes, Giovanni. Learn what it means to pray, to seek your Lord."

She lowered her eyes to the table. With careful motions she folded her napkin along precise lines, gathering herself. She went on, "And here is the second thing, figlio mio. You will never know a purpose, never find a reason great enough to satisfy your endless hunger to play and perform, until you learn what it means to live with a deep and abiding faith in your Savior. All else is sham. All else is the ultimate lie, a lie you tell both to yourself and to Christ."

As the assembly was about to begin, I stood backstage and watched through a space in the curtain as the students filed in. It felt exhilarating to be free of all the normal school restrictions, to stand and observe several hundred students file in and keep quiet and sit where they were told. I spotted Mario up near the front of the hall and suppressed an impulse to wave. Behind me the two dramatics teachers were busy herding their students together into a relatively silent group along the side wall. My guitar was in a back cubbyhole, one with a door that shut so I could practice during the speeches. But I didn't feel the need to rehearse anymore.

The calm was not there that morning, but I tried hard not to think about it, or about my grandmother's words. Confusion and inner turmoil were the last things I needed then. I was a little nervous; a cool tingling in my belly made everything stand out sharp and clear as though I had been tuned to a higher level. My hands were steady and not sweating too badly. I could barely wait to walk out there and show them that I was more than just the youngest kid at the academy. I wanted them to smile and say hello because of *me*.

I stood and watched the principal give a few opening re-marks, then listened to the first speaker without really hearing what he was saying. When the second speaker started talking I walked back to my alcove. As I passed the gaggle of students in their costumes and garish make-up, they and the teachers gave excited smiles and wished me luck.

I closed the door to my closet-sized room, sat, tuned my gui-tar, and spent the few remaining minutes doing little études to keep myself warm. When it was time, I stood and opened the door.

I felt a flutter of real fear as I edged back up to the stage corner in time to hear the applause for the second speaker die away. As the principal stood and began to introduce me, all of my doubts and insecurities flooded back in a wave. What if I made a mistake? What if I forgot the music? Was I going to make a fool of myself out there? Look at all those *people*.

In a pang of anxiety, I missed the calm of my grandmother's prayers with the pain of a broken heart. I regretted never hav-ing told her of the peace she had given me, the closeness I felt between us in those moments before my first performance. It was a mistake not to have told her about it, I realized with painful certainty, and realized at the same moment that I had said nothing because I wanted to share the credit for my success with no one.

It was a terrifying realization, made worse because I caught a glimpse of another truth behind it. It was just a heartbeat of awareness, come and gone so quickly that I had no time to put it into words. There was simply an echo of emptiness, a vision of a greater need hidden behind this one. It shook me to my core, but passed so swiftly that I could easily deny it. I fastened my attention upon the principal.

The principal was saying, "As most of you already know, Giovanni di Alta is a student under Herr Professor Doktor Schmitz at the Dusseldorf Musikakademie, the youngest student in the academy's history. His professor speaks very highly of Giovanni's progress."

Not to me, I thought. In the wash of anger that followed, all my fear vanished. It was a second revelation, one that lifted me away from the shock and isolation of the moment before. I had found another barrier, one called anger. I needed nothing else. If they refused to accept me for what I was, it was their problem. I was good. And I was going to show them.

As I waited for the principal's signal, I decided that I no longer needed the first warm-up piece. I was angry and I was ready. I wanted to walk out there and hit them as powerfully and quickly as I could.

There was light applause from the audience as I walked out, adjusted the chair and footstool, and sat down. The principal walked to the side of the stage and sat beside the two speakers. As I waited for the talk and murmurs and rustling to die down I ran through the strings. The tuning was fine. I placed myself in position, fingers poised, left foot on the tiny stool, back straight, head angled toward the guitar's neck, and I waited. The assembly grew still. I waited through the silence for a moment more, drawing it out. Then I began.

I flamed through the first piece. It was a series of runs tied together by a very simple melody, and should have taken a bit over six minutes to play. I did it in less than four. I realized that most of these people did not know classical guitar music. I did as the Copland book suggested, and played to the audience. I did not make it precisely correct in timing and emphasis. I played to impress and excite. I played as fast and fiery as I could, running up the speed until my fingers were a blur, hitting the final chords with my whole body in motion, flinging my hand up and away to signal the end of the piece.

The assembly erupted. I held up my right hand, the one I had flung out on the last chord, and if anything the applause grew louder. I could not help smiling. My whole body drank in the clamor. It was meant for me, Giovanni di Alta. For *me*. When the applause faded I could not begin the next piece because of the excited talk and laughter. There was a chorus of shushes and shouts for quiet. I went back into the preparatory position, and held it in perfect stillness. I felt in total control. There was no fear, just a tingling of nerves as though I were breathing champagne. When there was total silence, I started the second piece.

This was a counterpoint between a bass melody played on the low string with the thumb, and a series of light trilling runs played by almost feathering the top strings. I wanted to emphasize how the bass notes acted like pillars to hold up the airy high notes, so each time I played the bass string I struck downward with my head and shoulders. Pam. Pam. Pam. Bobbing and striking the bass with more force than was called for, but drawing the audience's attention to how both flowed together in a contrasting balance.

My guitar trembled with the force of the applause. I sat and grinned and looked out over the sea of faces.

The third and last piece started out slowly and mournfully. It built up both speed and force, and ended with a series of runs punctuated by sharp loud chords. These chords were strummed by flinging down all four fingers in cadence, then slamming the sound off with a hand-blade across the strings. I could hear the reverberation off the hall's back wall as I began each new scale. The echo punctuated and blended in, becoming an unexpected part of the song, as I made each chord sharper and louder than the previous one. The climax was a furious chord strumming that I held through four full beats, then slapped off with my hand just behind the guitar's mouth, so that the final force boomed and echoed over the audience.

As I stood and bowed to the applause, I discovered that I was breathing hard and perspiring. I wiped my forehead, then held the hand up to the audience. For some reason that made them even more excited. The principal came over and shook my hand, and said something I could not understand over the applause. I turned back to the students, still grinning, wishing the moment would go on forever.

. . .

As the recital date grew near, the distance between what I learned for Professor Schmitz and what I played for myself widened into a vast chasm. I wondered at this ability to hide what I considered my true work and my real intentions from my teacher. In his presence I played what he wanted to hear. He continued to work through the piece passage by passage. The recital drew steadily closer.

The week before the recital I went to the Staatstheater. It was the first time I had been there since the preceding May. Posters announcing the recital adorned all the marquees. I let myself into the hall, walked down the steeply sloping steps, and climbed up on stage.

I stood there a long time, looking out over the empty seats. I felt a little apprehensive, a little nervous, a little scared—but not much. A chasm had grown up between me and everything that had to do with Professor Schmitz. As I walked around the empty stage I remembered cowering in my seat the year before, watching Professor Schmitz stand where I was now. Yes, I was scared. But I was ready. I knew what I was going to do. I could not see beyond the recital, but that did not matter so much at the moment. I had decided. I would remain true to my music.

The night of the recital my grandmother came into my alcove as I was dressing. She stood beside the opened curtains watching me struggle with the little black studs that were used instead of buttons on my dress shirt. She came over, brushed away my hands, and began doing up the studs with quick little motions.

"Your grandfather used to wear shirts with studs every Sunday," she told me. Up close her breathing sounded hoarse and strained to my ears. "He never was able to do them himself."

When the shirt front and both sleeves were done she fastened my bow tie in place. By then a sheen of moisture had gathered on her forehead. "I've always enjoyed men's dress clothes. They are so classic. Every little piece just so."

I watched her face with growing concern. "Is your fever back again?"

"It is nothing for you to concern yourself with tonight, figlio mio." Though scratchy, her voice carried a note of calm serenity. "I had a bad night, that's all. I have rested this afternoon and will go straight to bed after the performance. Tomorrow I will be fine."

She helped me on with the dark jacket with its satin stripe on the lapel, matching the ones running down both pant legs. She showed me how to adjust the shirt's cuffs, then stepped back. Her eyes were shining brightly.

"My boy has become a man," she said softly. "Come. I want you to see yourself."

My alcove did not have a mirror. I followed my grandmother down the hall to her bedroom. When we were inside she closed the door in order to expose the full-length mirror on the back.

"Che bell' ometto," my grandmother murmured. "What a handsome young man. I'm so proud of you."

My dark curls entirely covered my ears, but the sloppy distracted air was gone. The formal clothes were so severe and conservative that my hair could have been done like this intentionally to offset them. I was a study in black. Black tuxedo, black bow tie, curly black hair tumbling onto the shoulders of my coat, black eyes. The darkness of my clothes made my eyes look huge. I had never thought of myself as attractive; I had never given much thought to my appearance at all. I could not believe what I was seeing in the mirror.

"So proud," my grandmother repeated. "I wish your mother and grandfather—"

She turned away. I saw her shoulders tremble before her iron control returned. Her back straightened. She turned to me, asked, "Would you please do something for me, figlio mio?"

"Yes."

Her voice was very soft as she said, "I would like for you to pray with me before we leave for your concert." Her eyes took on an aching appeal. "Please, Giovanni. This is very important to me."

I nodded, not trusting my voice.

She led me to her bedside, smiled with a shy joy. "I cannot tell you how often I have thought and dreamed of this, figlio mio. So many nights, speaking to the blessed Father before I lay down my head, hoping that someday you would be here beside me in prayer."

Stiffly I knelt beside her. On the wall opposite her bed was an ancient painting of Jesus' face. To have something to focus on, I concentrated on it, seeing the fatigue and the pain as the blood flowed down from His crown of thorns. Draped around the painting was the rosary of my grandmother's mother, the little wooden cross dangling like a solitary beacon. The painting and the rosary had been on the wall above my grandparents' bed for as long as I could remember.

I copied her movements as she folded her hands before her face and bowed her head, feeling enormously uncomfortable, wondering why I had agreed.

"Our blessed Father," she said, and stopped. I heard my grandmother swallow heavily, take a ragged breath, and begin once more. "Beloved Lord of all, we kneel before you and give our deepest praise. It is you who granted my Giovanni his talent, and we thank you for this gift. I ask you please to bless him with your guidance and your protection. May you always be with him."

Guidance and protection. I felt the power of truth in her words, recalled the rage and the frustration of that past winter, saw in an instant of clarity how much of it had come because I had felt so utterly, totally alone.

"Help my Giovanni to find you. Show him what it means to walk in faith all his days. Teach him to love you. Give him that special meaning to his life that is found only in you."

My grandmother became silent. I felt my body trembling, but it was not from fear. Half of me wanted to speak; the other half fought and struggled and cried that there was no one to hear me. I yearned and I felt the fool. I opened my mouth, but before the first word came I felt a tide of emotion so strong that I choked back the sobs. Why did I want to cry? Why had I allowed myself to be forced into doing this? Why must I be pushed into this turmoil time after time? I buried my face in the bedcover. I had nothing to say.

After a moment's stillness, I heard my grandmother's gentle amen. She laid a hand upon my shoulder, and for some reason the gesture made the burning in my chest become stronger. I gritted my teeth and pressed hard with my forehead on the bed. I was embarrassed to have her see this reaction.

I felt the mattress press down as she leaned upon it and rose stiffly to her feet. She patted my shoulder, said gently, "I will go and make myself ready, figlio mio. Thank you for this gift."

My grandmother and I arrived at the Staatstheater an hour before the program was to begin. While she waited by the stage door, I entered the watchman's office and left my guitar. I heard loud, nervous voices farther along the hallway, but I had no desire to join them.

Together we walked around the front to the wide semicircular band of colonnaded doors. The usher, an old man with stooped shoulders and a receding hairline, took my grandmother's ticket and reached for mine.

"I'm performing tonight."

He looked me over. "What's your name, kid?"

"Giovanni di Alta."

He pulled a program from his coat pocket, opened it with shaky hands. "Alta, Alta, yeah, here you are." Rheumy eyes turned to inspect me once more. "How old are you, kid?"

"Old enough," I said, and led my grandmother inside.

The central foyer was split by a sweeping staircase that rose in graceful curves to the second floor balcony. I walked with her up the stairs, pausing halfway for her to admire the vast crystal chandelier and to catch her breath. We took one of the tables at the balcony's edge so she could watch the people parade around below her in all their finery. I asked her if she wanted something to drink.

"I believe I will have one of those little bottles of champagne tonight. What do they call them?"

"A split."

"Yes. I have not drunk champagne in years. On such a night I should indulge myself a little, don't you think?"

I went to the bar at the back wall, and brought back a split of champagne for her and a soda for me.

She poured a small glass for herself and watched the bubbles fade. She lifted the glass toward me, said, "To your success tonight, figlio mio."

I smiled and drank my soda.

"Look at how calm you are. Don't you feel the least bit nervous?"

"A little," I admitted. I spotted a program resting on an empty table. I walked over and picked it up. "They forgot to give you one," I said, holding it out.

She motioned for me to keep it. "Tell me what it says."

It was printed on heavy white paper with embossed edges. The heading was in large Gothic print, and read: *Fifteenth Annual Evening of Classical Guitar.* Underneath in smaller type it said: *Recital by Professor Doktor Wolfgang Schmitz and Selected Students of the Dusseldorf Musikakademie.*

I opened the program and felt the world lurch slightly. My name was at the top of the page. My grandmother noticed and asked me what was the matter.

"I play first," I said faintly.

"I do not understand," my grandmother said.

"The first and final slots are reserved for his star pupils." I had simply assumed I would be somewhere near the middle.

Her face shone. "This is truly a wonderful thing, Giovanni. He must have great confidence in you, your professor."

I looked out over the filling hall. Women wore elegantly piled coiffures and long dresses and many jewels. The men looked straight and stiff and proud in their evening clothes. I did not want to tell my grandmother how shocked I was by this. First performer for the recital. Professor Schmitz had not even mentioned it. After announcing that I was to play, he had not spoken of the recital at all.

"Gianni!"

I stood as Fraulein Rohr reached the top of the stairs. Her face was alive with excitement. I thought she looked vaguely alien in the dark velvet gown, with her hair all pinned into place.

"Let me stop and catch my breath. Goodness, you look very handsome tonight. Yes, thank you, I'd love to sit down. Herr Scherer is still looking for a parking space. I saw Mario with his mother downstairs somewhere; they said that they would be up soon. My, look at all the people. Are you nervous?"

I nodded. "I'm playing first tonight."

Her eyes became very round behind her glasses. "Gianni! That's wonderful! What an honor. Wait until Herr Scherer hears of this."

She looked at my grandmother. "Please say to her that she must be very proud of her grandson."

I translated, and my grandmother nodded and said quietly,

"It all comes from the simple kindness that she and the gentleman showed to you. Please tell her how very grateful I am, how indebted."

When I translated, Fraulein Rohr became much more like her normal self, slightly flustered and reaching for the wayward strands of hair that tonight were not there. She looked at me with an expression of awe. "A student of mine is to be first performer in the great professor's recital. I'm so excited I don't know what to do with myself."

My grandmother said, "Ask the signorina if she would care for a taste of my champagne. I would find the moment so much nicer if I could share this."

I did so, then said to my grandmother, "I have to go."

"I know." She reached over, grasped my hand with surprising strength. "You will go up on the stage and you will play beautifully. Of that I am perfectly sure."

I looked into her eyes, saw the utter serenity that not even two winters of ill health could remove. For a moment I wanted to stop and sit and tell her everything, how I had been forced to do what I was going to do.

"I am so happy for you," she said, basking me in the glow from her eyes. "There is only one thing in this entire world which could make me happier, figlio mio."

She paused and gave my hand another squeeze. "But this is not the time to speak of such things. Now go and make me proud."

A chill damp wind reached inside my clothes as I left the lighted foyer and entered the darkness. I hunched my shoulders and hustled around the building to the stage entrance. I retrieved my guitar from the watchman, signed his entry book, and walked down the hall. I turned a corner and climbed a flight of narrow stairs. Ceiling lights were set in metal mesh baskets. The walls were painted pale yellow. Everywhere there was ordered clutter—bunches of music stands, boxes with scribbled labels, folding chairs, stacks of printed notices for upcoming events. Voices from the audience echoed down the hallway like the murmur of a distant sea.

I turned a corner and faced a group of young people in evening dress. They were all at least four or five years older than I. The taller boy, a blond-haired giant of twenty-two or twenty-three with aristocratic features, looked down his nose at me. "What do you want?"

"I'm Giovanni di Alta. I'm playing tonight."

"You're di Alta?"

"Yes. Is there—"

"We'd heard Schmitz had taken a middle schooler," said a very pretty girl with auburn hair. "Nobody believed it."

"Di Alta," the tall young man said, unable to grasp it. "You're the one playing first?"

"How old are you, kid?"

"Fifteen. Is there a practice room I can use?"

The girl pointed down a side hall. "Use any that's free."

I could feel their eyes follow me down the hall. I entered an empty room, set down the guitar, heard one say, "Fifteen years old; can you believe it?"

"And first on the recital."

"Have you ever heard him play?"

"Heard him? I've never even *seen* him before."

I closed the door on their voices. I opened my case, took out the guitar and the little towel. Carefully I tuned the strings, polished the neck and face, ran through a few practice scales. I did the opening bars of my piece, then one more practice scale, and stopped. I was ready. I knew what I was going to do. I would give him the precision he demanded. I would play with all the discipline I had.

But I would also give him *fire*.

Professor Schmitz stood by the dark curtain that separated the wings from the lighted stage. As the first performer, I stood beside him, waiting for his signal. He made no opening remarks at his recitals. One went out, one played, one bowed, one returned.

At five minutes past the hour he turned and looked at me for the first time. His face was rigid. The ever-present cigarette sent lazy tendrils floating up between us.

"It is time," he said. "You are ready?"

"Yes." For whatever came, I was ready.

He did not let me go. For a moment more he stared at me,

then said in his deep monotone, "You will play as I have taught you, boy, or—"

He searched my face as though seeking a flicker of rebellion. He finished with, "You will play as I have instructed. Do you understand?"

"I understand you," I said. Perhaps for the first time, I thought. You and your gifts. And your limitations.

He hesitated a moment longer, then stepped aside. "Very well," he said. "Go and play."

I stepped past him and walked out on stage.

The applause was polite and lasted as long as it took me to walk to the chair at center stage and bow. I straightened and stared outward. The lights ringing the stage floor left the audience in shadows, but I could see their faces. I felt little fear.

I sat down, adjusted the tiny footstool, set the guitar in place, ran up the strings, adjusted one slightly, did it again, took a breath, flexed my fingers, and began.

The piece had three movements. The first I played as Professor Schmitz dictated, with disciplined precision. This was my gift to the professor. This much I owed him. It was an announcement, both to him and to the world, that I had studied his lesson of discipline and I had learned it well. Each note was measured and laid in place with the precision of a master bricklayer. It was music as he wanted it, my professor. It was music bound firmly to the precise dictates of the written score.

I finished the movement and paused the required moment. The audience was very still. I began the second movement.

This was the movement of questioning. There was no outright rebellion. It was a time of asking, what if? What if I were to relax the discipline here and allow the notes to flow? Was something destroyed, or rather was something gained? And what would happen if I held this note just the slightest breath longer than dictated by strict timing? Did that not also add a new dimension, a subtle hint of something deeper, something I would have lost had I held rigidly to notes chained to the page?

The second movement ended. The audience remained still, almost nonexistent. I held the moment longer than was necessary, flexing my fingers, hunching over the guitar, wanting to show very clearly that a statement was about to be made. Then I began.

The third and final movement was a declaration. This is how it should be, I said—moving beyond discipline to a freedom of emotional interpretation; giving of my heart as well as of my head and fingers; marrying my own emotions to those of the composer. It was not a slurring of difficult passages, but a creating of emotional flow. I stopped for a span long enough to make the heart pause. I flowed lyrically through a passage that begged to be played as one continuous idea. I hesitated over a note that was both pinnacle and climax, then moved reluctantly onward. Onward, ever onward, to the sadly whispered end.

"Bravo!"

It was shouted from the back and caught by a dozen other voices before I could rise to my feet. I bowed and felt the applause wash over me. I raised my head and held out my arms, still grasping the guitar in my left hand. All I could think was, it is over. Whatever happens now, this phase of my life has ended. I stood and shared this moment of ending with the loudly clapping audience, then turned and walked from the stage.

Professor Schmitz stood in his place by the back curtain. When I approached, he turned away from me and spoke to the next performer. I did not break stride.

I walked to my case, packed my guitar away, stood and murmured thanks to the congratulations from other performers. As I walked toward the exit I felt eyes upon me. I turned to see Professor Schmitz looking my way. I stopped and faced him fully. He said nothing.

Then I turned and left the hall.

CHAPTER
5

It was not until midmorning that I emerged from my little alcove. I found my grandmother in the kitchen. Her chair was turned so that her face caught the sunlight streaming in through the back window. Her eyes were closed. Her features looked very drawn, very pale. Her little radio on the kitchen cabinet was playing a Verdi opera. I pulled out a chair as quietly as I could, and set it where I could see both her face and the blue sky outside the window. I sat like that for over an hour, feeling the banked-up fatigue wash over me in waves, watching her face, remembering.

When the second act was completed she opened her eyes with a long, soft sigh. She stood slowly, turned the music down to a faint background whisper, sat again, and wished me a good morning.

"I was thinking of your grandfather," she said. "And of Como."

"So was I."

"Are you hungry?"

I shook my head. "Maybe in a little while."

She did not object. "He hated opera, your grandfather. He was such a good-natured gentleman about most things, but he simply could not abide this music." Her eyes looked into the past, and a faint smile pulled at the edges of her mouth. "He said a herd of cows late for milking could sing better."

"He always made us listen to it in the kitchen with the door closed," I recalled.

"Yes," she sighed. "Those days with our young Giovanni learning opera with me in the kitchen and folk music with his grandfather by the fire. I have found myself thinking a great deal about those days."

"They were the happiest days of my life," I said.

"For me as well, figlio mio. Your grandfather used to call you his last ray of summer sun. Can you remember that?"

I nodded my head.

"He told me once—" With an unsteady hand she ran a thumb and forefinger down either side of her head. "He told me that he must have done something very good to have his winter days graced with such a gift as you. I told your grandfather it was because he had put up with me all those years."

It felt as though he were there in the kitchen with us. A bright pinprick of longing opened in my heart and spread until my whole chest was filled with its hollow ache.

"He was much quieter in his faith than I am, but he believed in God," my grandmother said. "Sometimes late at night he would ask me to read to him from the Book. But I never thought it was in the Word that he knew his Lord. He did it because he knew it was important to me, just like going with me to Mass. You know he never learned to read or write very well."

I nodded. It had never seemed very important to me, just one of the traits that made my grandfather who he was.

"I once asked him what he said in his prayers. He smiled and said, when he could hear the voices in the wind and the voice in his heart, he knew that whatever he wanted to ask was already heard." She looked at me. "He would have been so proud of you, figlio mio. So very proud."

I took an unsteady breath. "I have to quit my lessons with the professor."

She was not surprised. "I have known things were not well. I have seen it in your face for months. And last night when you told me that you were to play first, I saw it again. You did not know your professor had given you the position of honor?"

"No." As briefly as I could I told her of the battle between us. I described the dilemma, the conflict, the growing frustration. And my decision. She listened in silence, her eyes watch-

ing with calm understanding, her face impassive. When I finished she continued to regard me for a time. I was glad to have
it all out in the open, very glad.

"I look at you, and I see a young man where before I saw a
child. Where did the child disappear to, figlio mio? How did the
child become a man so quickly?" She gazed at me, giving her
head a tiny shake. "Will you accept the advice of an old
woman?"

"Always."

"It is hard for a man to find his way in this world. There are
so many decisions, so many choices to make. And now that you
are a young man you must begin to make these choices on your
own. Where you will go, how you will play, whom you will obey,
what you will and will not accept as instruction from your
teachers. Do you see? So many choices, so many difficult passages to overcome.

"A man needs guidance, Giovanni. A man needs someone
he can turn to and ask for help. Someone who sees beyond the
veil of time and understands where these paths are truly leading. Someone who sees the dangers before they arise and leads
us away from life's many pitfalls. There is only one Lord who
can offer you this safety, figlio mio. Only one. And He stands
with open arms waiting for you to invite Him in."

With both hands gripping the arms of her chair she pushed
herself erect, walked to the sink, and began filling the coffeepot
with water. "But man yearns for independence. A young man
especially. He is strong and he is able to make his own decisions
about his life. To ask for guidance from his Maker is to admit
to weakness. Yet we are weak, Giovanni. All of us. Weak and
self-centered and blind to all but our own selfish desires. I am
speaking to you as a grown man, figlio mio. This is the essential
nature of us all. We desire to be independent and to run alone
and unguided toward our death."

She spooned in the coffee, patted it down, closed the lid, set
it on the stove. Her back still to me, she asked, "Now that it is
over, Giovanni, how do you feel? About the concert and the
difficulties with your professor."

I thought it over. "Numb and tired."

She placed the bread basket on the table before me. "Yes.
You have won your battle, and yet there is no sense of accom-

plishment. Do you wonder why that is? Do you ask yourself how you could strive toward this goal, and then once it is achieved, you feel nothing? How could it be?"

My grandmother walked over to her chair and steadied herself by leaning on the back. "Goals sought for themselves bring nothing. This is a truth that you will find repeated in your life so long as you continue to walk the path alone. That which you do for yourself will never satisfy. You will achieve it and you will immediately begin seeking something else to go after. Always an endless cycle of want and need and endless hunger, until you finally realize that there is only one thing which will ever satisfy you, which will ever fill the void in your life."

The child is still here, I thought to myself. And he is very frightened by this rushing of events, carrying him forward into the unknown. I did not know what to tell my grandmother.

She brought cup and saucer over, poured in a thimbleful of coffee and filled it to the brim with milk. I had been drinking this at breakfast for as long as I could remember. Slowly my grandmother lowered herself down to the seat across from mine. She drew the handkerchief from her sleeve, wiped the moisture from her forehead.

"I have some news for you as well, figlio mio." My grandmother knotted the handkerchief into a tight little ball. "I finally did as you requested and visited the doctor again. He is concerned about my condition. He says that a cold should not last as long as this one has. He wants to run some tests."

The chill that spread through my belly did not leave room for any appetite. I stared across the table at her and waited.

She refused to meet my eyes. "I was supposed to enter the hospital last week, but I requested a delay. I am very glad I was there to hear you perform, figlio mio. Very glad."

I found my voice, managed, "How long?"

"How long do I stay in the hospital? I do not know. A few days, probably." She forced a smile. "Long enough for a little rest, and for the doctors to prod these old bones."

I found myself unable to take it in. "When are you to go?"

"This afternoon. Now that your recital is over, I want to go quickly so that I may return. Hospitals are an unpleasantness. I do not feel comfortable having an unpleasantness to look forward to. I prefer to go now so that it will be behind me as soon as possible."

She pushed herself to her feet, walked around the table, and laid a hand on my shoulder. "I will not tell you not to worry because that would be foolishness. I will tell you to be strong. And if you cannot be strong, Giovanni, remember there is someone there who will be strong for you, if you let Him."

"I wish you had told me," I said weakly.

"So that you could have one more thing to worry about before your performance? That is nonsense, and we have too much else to do this morning than discuss nonsense. Finish."

She remained standing behind me, her hand on my shoulder. In a calmer voice she went on. "I want you to do one thing for me while I am away, Giovanni. This is very important to me. Are you listening to what I am saying?"

I nodded. I was listening.

She took a breath. "Go see your father. Talk to him. Tell him of your life and your decisions. If you can, make peace with him. If not, at least tell him what you will do with your life. I have informed him of my visit to the hospital, so you shall be spared that. He is still your father, Giovanni. Show him this respect. Please. For me."

. . .

My grandmother would not permit me to accompany her to the hospital. Signora Angeletti ignored the appeal in my eyes and agreed. "There are times when a woman needs a woman's help," Signora Angeletti said. "You will go tomorrow once she is settled. I will come by this evening and tell you where her room is located. You will eat with us tonight, of course. Good. And where will you sleep? Here? You would not be too lonely? Well, perhaps it is better."

I called a cab and walked slowly down the stairs with my grandmother leaning heavily on my arm. I stood and watched them drive away. When I returned upstairs the apartment seemed a hollow cavern.

For the first time in years I was tempted to lie to my grandmother, tell her I had seen my father, avoid the whole thing. But I was afraid my grandmother would look deeply and search out the truth. That more than anything else kept me from lying. I feared my grandmother's piercing gaze and the shame of being caught in a lie. If I was going, I knew it was something that I could not put off. If I delayed it, I would continue to do so and then have to lie. So that afternoon I left the empty apartment and walked next door.

I rang the buzzer to my father's apartment. As I climbed the stairs Anna stood waiting in the doorway. She showed no reaction at all to my arrival. I asked if my father was there. In the living room, she said. I walked down the hallway, following the sounds of the television, willing my heart to quieten.

My father was watching television from one of the rigid upholstered chairs flanking the coffee table. The same vase of plastic flowers sat in the center of the otherwise bare table. I walked over and sat down on the sofa, its frame as hard and unyielding as it had been the day I had begged my grandmother to take us back to Como.

With his remote control my father turned the sound off. The pictures continued to flicker and jump. The life seemed to be fading steadily from his face. His hair was turning gray, the lines on his face becoming deeper, his dark eyes dull and receding farther into their sockets. The thin set of his mouth had eased from grim determination to sagging resignation. His face was as gray as his hair.

I found it easier to watch the television than my father. "I am leaving the Musikakademie," I said. "There are problems. My professor and I are not getting along. I do not know what will happen, even if I will return to school next year." He said nothing.

"I came by to pay my respects," I told the television, barely aware of what I was saying. "My respects, yes. And to tell you what I will do with my life. If the difficulties of this past winter have taught me anything, it is that I want to become a professional musician. I do not know how. I do not even know if I will remain with classical music. But that is the direction I am headed."

"A musician," he said dully. He passed a limp hand over his face. "You're going to be a musician."

I rose to my feet. It felt difficult to draw breath in the room. I wish you well, I said, my eyes on the floor, the empty walls, the flickering television, the door, anywhere but on my father. I began inching myself from the room. My respects, yes, I said. My respects to both you and Anna. I hope—I had to search frantically for something to say as I moved toward the hallway. I hope you will be well, I said. And happy. Yes, and happy. And I leave you my respects.

The door slammed loudly behind me, echoing up and down the empty stairwell. I raced down the stairs and out the door and down the sidewalk, taking great gulps of air as I struggled to escape the desperation I had glimpsed in my father's eyes.

That night my fears took on vague forms and whispered to me in half-heard voices. I woke up cold and sweaty, and walked down the hallway to the bathroom. On the way back I stopped and looked at my grandmother's empty bed. I had folded down the covers so they would be ready for her when she came home. In the lonely dark hours I stood in the doorway and felt the sick fear and allowed myself to wonder if she was ever coming back.

The next morning I took the tram to the hospital. I walked along the high iron fence until I came to the guardhouse and the barred entrance. No one asked who I was or why I was there. I simply joined the rush of people and walked onto the hospital grounds.

The buildings were separated by thin strips of grass and shrubs where patients in bathrobes and pajamas walked slowly back and forth. I entered the middle building, the oldest one, built of gray granite and mortar. The mortar had darkened with time and ran like thick black veins all over the building. Inside, the walls were high and bright yellow. The entrance hall, tiled in flagstone and lined with soft chairs, was filled with people in quiet conversation. It was well-lit and warm and rich with the smells of coffee from the corner restaurant and of flowers from the tiny florist.

Upstairs in my grandmother's hall the building's age was more visible. The walls reached up very high. The lighting was distant and not so strong. The windows at the hall's ends were set in granite almost two feet thick. Noises echoed up and down the hallway, as though the voices of patients long since gone were trapped and held there forever. The corridors were lined with empty beds and metal stands and bulletin boards and long wooden benches where Turkish women in bright head-kerchiefs fed crying babies from greasy paper bags.

I stopped at the room number Signora Angeletti had written down for me. Gently I knocked on the door and entered. There were four beds in the room, separated by thin metal cupboards and night tables. All of the beds were occupied by old women locked in their own silent struggles. My grandmother's was the one nearest the far wall, set beneath a grimy window.

Her eyes watched me walk toward her, but her head did not rise from the pillow. She looked very tired. I sat in the metal-backed chair and grasped her hand. I did not know what to say.

She eyed the book in my jacket pocket, asked, "What are you reading?"

I lifted the book and showed her the cover. I was rereading Copland's *What To Listen For In Music.*

"Is that English? Yes?" She looked pleased. "What is it about?"

I told her.

"Music. Of course." She gave her slight smile. "It is good that you are keeping up with your English, figlio mio."

She turned her head back toward the ceiling. The skin on her chin and neck settled into wrinkled folds. "It would be good to hear your music again." She closed her eyes. "Perhaps some-day you could bring your guitar and play for me here."

"Tomorrow," I said.

The faint smile returned. "Be sure and speak with the sister first. Now read your book, Giovanni. I think I will rest a mo-ment."

The hall nurse looked at me curiously when I asked her, but she said it would be all right if I came with my guitar, provided I did not play for too long. Yes, tomorrow would be fine, she said, the curious expression still on her face.

The following day was Sunday. The halls were more crowded with visitors on Sunday mornings than on any other day of the week. The hospital was very strict about visiting hours, espe-cially in the public wards—one and a half hours before lunch and another hour in the late afternoon on Saturdays and Sun-days. I tried not to think about the other people as I carried my guitar through the hospital corridors, but I could feel their eyes on me, and I felt my face grow hot.

When my grandmother smiled her approval at my arrival, I knew I had done the right thing. "What a nice Sunday gift. I hope you asked the sister."

"I did." Her voice sounded very dry and hoarse, and I knew her rest had been disturbed by all the visitors. There were people crowded around all the other beds in her room. "What do you want me to play?"

"Something nice." She turned her head and coughed, a deep racking wheeze that brought perspiration out on her forehead. When the coughing stopped she dropped her head back to the pillow and breathed hoarsely.

"Are you all right?" The sound of that cough left me cold. My chest hurt for her. "Should I call a nurse?"

Weakly she waved a hand in dismissal. "The doctor has given me something to make me cough. He says I must begin to clear my lungs."

"It sounds terrible."

"He says it is necessary. Now, sit down and play me something nice." She settled back on her pillow. "I will close my eyes and rest for a moment."

I opened my case, took out the guitar, and sat with my back to the window. I faced the room and the people. The group of visitors slowly turned my way. I would have preferred to sit so I could not see them, but I wanted my grandmother to be able to open her eyes and look my way and feel that we were alone. I fought down my nervousness, quickly tuned the guitar, and began to play.

My movements were awkward, almost forced. I stayed with simple melodies and played slowly, carefully. Play something nice, my grandmother had said. I played my guitar and tried to draw light into this room with my music, tried to build a shield of light around my grandmother's bed, a shield that would hold and protect and heal her until it was time for her to come home.

After I had played several melodies I looked up and saw that my grandmother had turned her head slightly and was watching me. "That was very nice, Giovanni," she whispered.

"Bravo," said a louder voice from beside one of the other beds. "Do you speak German?"

Reluctantly I raised my eyes. Most of the people were looking at me and smiling. A doctor and one of the nurses stood in the doorway.

"Yes," I replied.

"How old are you?"

"Fifteen."

"Fifteen? You play like that at fifteen? Where did you learn?"

"Here and in Italy." I looked back to my grandmother, willing the man to leave us alone.

My grandmother asked, "They like your music, no?"

I nodded.

"Bene, I am glad." Her gaze became piercing. "There are others here who perhaps need the music as much as I do, no?"

"Yes," I said, feeling vaguely ashamed.

"Good, figlio mio. I am glad you understand. A gift from God should be given to all who are in need." She turned back toward the ceiling and the strength seemed to drain from her face, leaving it empty and fragile. "Play us a little more then, Giovanni. I will close my eyes a moment. Suddenly I feel very tired."

I played a few more pieces, and when I finished she was asleep. I packed up my guitar and walked past the other beds, returning the smiles and nods and goodbyes and trying not to feel embarrassed. I walked down the stairs and through the flagstone entrance hall and out into the warm spring air.

That night I lay in my windowless alcove with the drapes closed to give me an illusion of privacy. I looked up into darkness and recalled how fragile and vulnerable she had appeared. When the fear rose up like a specter I sought frantically for something that would keep it at bay, and once again heard her voice. A gift from God. It was as though I had never heard the idea before. The words seemed to illuminate my room.

The next morning I arrived at the hospital a few minutes late. I hurried up the stairs and down the long corridors, said hello to the head nurse, opened the door to my grandmother's room, and came to a halt.

Seated at the table beneath the window were my father and my grandmother. They both looked toward me. I felt glued to the spot.

"Come and sit down, Giovanni," my grandmother said.

A coldness started to well up inside me. "I'll just be outside," I said. I backed out and shut the door.

I was trembling as I walked over and sat down on one of the

hard wooden benches. The door to my grandmother's room opened. My father came out. His face looked white and drawn.

"She wants you to come back inside."

I shook my head. "I'll wait here," I said.

My father stood there a moment, looking at me, saying nothing. Eventually he turned and went back into the room.

I don't know how long I sat there. I remained in my place at one end of the hard wooden bench, watching the world of the hospital swirl around me, surrounded by my own inner coldness.

Finally my father came out. He looked very grim as he shrugged on his jacket and walked away. He did not look my way.

I hesitated, then stood and walked into my grandmother's room. The air was still charged with my father's presence. My grandmother sat at the table and stared unblinkingly out the window. The light from outside seemed to magnify her fragility, her fatigue. I walked over to her.

"You should be lying down," I said.

She turned around. It seemed to take a moment before she was able to focus on me. "The doctor said I should get out of bed for a few moments every day."

"How do you feel?"

"Tired." She held out an arm. "Help me back to bed, figlio mio."

I supported most of her weight as she shuffled the brief distance, sat, and eased herself gingerly under the covers. I adjusted things as best I could.

With a limp hand she pointed toward her nightstand. "Take the Bible from the drawer, Giovanni."

Metal grated upon metal as I pulled the drawer open. Awkwardly I lifted out the big Book, its cover limp and softened by use. I held it out to her.

"Sit, sit, I do not wish to look up to you." When I had drawn up a chair, she said, "Why did you not come in and sit with your father, Giovanni?"

I shook my head, feeling the coldness well up again.

"I asked you a question."

Again I shook my head. I was afraid of what I might say.

My grandmother looked at me a long time before saying,

"Perhaps I should have sent you to your uncles in South America after all."

"No!" I shouted the word, pushing at her in alarm.

"What a tone to use!" she said, her eyes sparking.

"I'm not leaving you."

She turned her face to the ceiling. "Being close to death makes one see such things more clearly."

"You're not going to die," I said, fighting down panic. "Why are you talking like this? I hate you talking this nonsense."

Her eyes remained directed upward. "The day of my passing is for the Lord to decide. Whether it comes today or tomorrow or in twenty years is not for us to say. But I have passed close to death with this illness. I lie here and feel it watching me. And I know that sometime, as the Lord wills, it shall come for me again."

Weakly she waved my unspoken protests aside. "That is unimportant. What is important—listen carefully to me, Giovanni. What is important is that you do not let yourself be consumed by this hatred of yours."

I sat in silence. Was that what this coldness was, this feeling of almost everything inside me being asleep? I did not understand.

She turned and searched my face. Her eyes were luminous. "To be consumed by hatred is worse than to be consumed by grief, figlio mio. Do you hear what I am saying? Tell me if you understand."

"Yes," I answered, my voice very small. I was filled with coldness, a cold like death. Was that what hatred was—a little death?

"I am not sure you fully understand." She paused a moment, then said, "Open the Book to Ephesians, and read to me the last part of chapter four. No, Giovanni, turn farther toward the back. After Corinthians comes Galatians and then Ephesians."

Awkwardly I turned the pages, trying to recall the last time I had read from the Bible. Not since my school days in Como, I decided. I read:

"And grieve not the holy Spirit of God, whereby ye are sealed unto the day of redemption. Let all bitterness, and wrath, and anger, and clamor, and evil speaking, be put away from you, with all malice. And be ye kind one to another, forgiving one another, even as God for Christ's sake hath forgiven you."

"God knows that it is hard for us to forgive," my grandmother said. "But in His Son we find the strength to forgive all who wrong us, all who hurt us, all who do not answer our needs as we would wish."

With visible effort she raised herself up on one arm. She leaned toward me, saying with great intensity, "But before you can have His help to forgive, Giovanni, you must ask Him into your life. Do you see? If you fail to ask God's assistance, how can He give you the strength? How can He keep you from walking ever further into the darkness of anger? I do not say that you have no reason to feel this way. I say that no reason is reason enough. *No* reason, figlio mio. Nothing is so great as to be worth the walk in darkness that results from not forgiving."

She eased herself back to her pillow, keeping her eyes on me all the time. I sat still, held by that dark burning gaze, but I looked inward as well as outward. Her coal-black eyes were a mirror, showing me what I did not wish to see within myself. I saw the pain and the hurt and the anger I had so carefully hidden away. I saw the memories of a father who was not there, who never called, who did not care. And I felt what the coldness had kept hidden from me. Oh yes, I hated him. The strength of that icy hatred frightened me, and my music was balanced with this hatred. Whichever won would destroy the other. And I was scared of losing either.

My grandmother's voice brought me back. "You must find for yourself the strength of Christ. When you are weak, He will be strong for you. Always, always remember that." She turned away and shut her eyes.

. . . .

When I arrived on Tuesday the head nurse came out from behind her glassed-in desk and gave me a brisk hello. "Your grandmother had a bad night last night," she said. "I'm not sure it's such a good idea for you to go in right now."

I felt fear gripping my gut. "Is she all right?"

The sister's voice became clipped. "A bad night means a bad night, nothing more. She did not sleep well, and finally she is resting. She is suffering from severe congestion in both lungs.

Do you understand those words?"

"Yes."

"She has a pulmonary disorder; the doctors are not sure how serious it is. Nights like these are to be expected." She paused, and brought out the professional smile. "I suppose it is all right for you to go in as long as you sit quietly and do not disturb her."

I showed her my book. "I will just sit and read."

"Fine. And what is your book, may I see?" She bent closer and read the title. She looked back at me. "You read English?"

"Yes. It's hard, though."

"And you speak German and Italian, I've heard both of those. Your German is quite good, by the way. Can you read in those languages, too?"

"Yes."

She looked at me a moment longer, then said, "Not too long today, young man. And be as quiet as you can."

I thanked her and walked to my grandmother's room. Crossing to her bed I felt the same empty dread rising that I lived with through the dark lonely nights. She lay motionless on her back, a grayish pallor to her skin. I nodded a greeting to the woman in the next bed, silently set the chair down beside my grandmother, and pretended to read. I could not concentrate on the words, but I kept the book open on my lap as I sat and looked at my grandmother, and willed her to get well.

Two tubes connected her left arm to plastic globes hung from a thin metal stand. Colored wires passed from her chest back to a machine that lit up and beeped softly in time to her pulse. Another set of tubes projected from her nostrils. A clear plastic tube was connected to the side of her mouth.

She did not open her eyes the entire time I was there. She only moved twice, to lean away from me and cough those deep, racking wheezes that left her face covered with a sheen of perspiration. Then she would lie back and breathe hoarsely.

When I reentered the corridor the head nurse came out to greet me. "Would you like a cup of tea, young man?"

"No, thank you." The thought of swallowing anything made me ill.

She studied my face, then became very stern. "Now you listen to me, young man. I will not have any such nonsense from you. I get enough from my patients. Your grandmother is an old woman, and she is very ill, but she is strong. She needs your strength, not your worries. Do you understand?"

I could barely manage a nod.

"For a woman of her age such things are to be expected. The doctors are doing everything possible for her. You must be patient and hope that she will improve."

I wandered the streets in a blind, unseeing panic for hours before finally making my way home. I walked into the Angelettis' little store, and was vastly relieved to find the signora there alone. Before I had finished my story she was moving, swiftly lifting the apron over her head, dialing the phone and ordering her husband downstairs, patting her hair into place, rubbing work-grimed hands on a little cloth, reaching into the register for money. I stood and allowed the storm to swirl around me, and gave in to the emptiness.

She led me outside and into a waiting taxi. She had me repeat my story on the way to the hospital, made me eat bits of an orange that she peeled as I talked. When I faltered she barked at me sharply. Hold on, she said again and again. Be strong. Your grandmother needs your strength.

When we arrived at the hospital, Signora Angeletti insisted on stopping by the florist before going upstairs, and then rushed into the bathroom to wash her hands and pin back her hair. We walked up the stairs in silence. I felt my legs were made of lead.

My grandmother's hall was very still. Visiting hours were long since over. A breathless hush followed us down the corridor. Soft tatters of conversation behind closed doors and the squeaking of nurses' shoes down side-corridors only intensified the quiet.

When the head nurse saw us she started to come out from her cubicle, hesitated, then reached for the phone. She cupped a hand to the mouthpiece, hiding her lips from view as she said a few brief words and then set the receiver down. Her eyes stayed steady on us.

There was no smile of greeting for me this time. "I have asked the doctor to come speak with you."

"The signora, she is all right?" Signora Angeletti held the

flowers so tightly the little blossoms quivered.

"Why don't we wait—ah, here he comes now." She moved back in evident relief. "This is Dr. Walthers."

I turned to face a bearded man in a white coat with a stethoscope and several other instruments stuffed in his pockets. His eyes were gray and rimmed with dark circles. "Are you relatives of the patient?"

"This is the woman's grandson, Doctor."

"Ah. Well. Shall we sit here?" He motioned toward the wooden bench. "Bring me the forms, please, Sister."

Signora Angeletti seated herself. I stood beside her and let her take my hand. She clenched it with a strength that grated my bones together.

"Do you understand German?" He sounded very weary.

"Yes." My heart was pounding so hard I could scarcely get out the word.

"I'm afraid your grandmother has passed away. I'm sorry. We did all we could to save her, but she waited too long to come in. Her lungs were too weak to support her." He crossed limp arms and leaned against the opposite wall. His voice was as dull as his eyes. "She surprised us, I'm afraid. She had a bad moment last night, but she survived it all right. We did not expect another attack so soon."

The sister gave him a stack of papers attached to a metal clipboard. He fastened his eyes upon them and continued to talk of fluid and breathing problems and heart failure. Signora Angeletti bowed her head and began to weep softly. I felt the chasm open at my feet and swallow me whole.

It took a moment to realize that the doctor had asked me something. Forms were being held out for my signature. I looked at him, saw his mouth move, but could not make sense of the noise. I looked helplessly at Signora Angeletti.

"You must sign them, Gianni," she whispered. "They are for your grandmother."

I nodded slowly, but could not raise my hand to take the pen. I looked up at the doctor and said, "I want to take her home."

PART TWO

*I will lead the blind by ways they have not known,
along unfamiliar paths I will guide them; I will turn
the darkness into light before them and make the
rough places smooth. These are the things I will do; I
will not forsake them.*

ISAIAH 42:16

CHAPTER
6

When I awoke the sun was high above the eastern hills, the ones which rose behind my cottage and rimmed that side of Lake Como. My bedroom was already warm enough to be stuffy. I threw back the covers, immensely relieved to find no rumpled little music fan beside me. Some days it was harder than others to include a stranger in my morning routine.

The wooden shutters were barred three-quarters closed. Even so, approaching the window was painful. I squinted and shuffled and opened first the window then the shutters. I stood there in the faint breeze and breathed the sweet mountain air.

"Not much that can beat a pretty springtime mornin'," a deep voice rumbled. I pulled my head back into the shadows, opened my eyes a bit, recognized the big black man from the club the night before. Jake. His name was Jake. And his wife with the incredible voice was called Amy.

"For a while there I thought maybe you were gonna sleep all day." He was dressed in faded jeans, skin-tight T-shirt, and slip-on leather boots. He looked more solid than the garden wall he leaned against. "You alone in there?"

"Far as I can tell," I replied. "What are you doing up here?"

"Mario dropped me off 'bout an hour ago. He wanted to stick around but I thought maybe we oughtta talk just the two of us." Jake swivelled around, looked out over the two hundred-meter drop to the lake and the mountains beyond. "Man, this sure is some view."

"Hang on a second," I said, and backed away from the window. I found some pants, tossed on a shirt, slid into loafers old and broken-down enough to need no socks. I stopped by the bathroom to wash my face. The cold water didn't reach the tingling ache at the back of my eyeballs, or cleanse the stuffiness from my head, so I swallowed several aspirin before heading for the kitchen.

Sunlight streamed through the kitchen's back windows, turning everything to aching brightness and impenetrable shadows. The rising sun provided strong morning light to the kitchen and the tiny back garden. By early afternoon the back would be lost in shadows and the lake below would sparkle like a liquid jewel. I was high enough up the hillside to watch sunsets turn the distant snow-capped Alps to burnished gold.

I filled the coffeepot at the old stone sink, lit the stove, set the pot in place. The refrigerator was the only new appliance in the kitchen; the only other addition to the cottage was a massive stereo. Everything else was as it had been for as long as I could remember. I slept in my grandparents' bed, ate at their battered kitchen table, spent my free evenings in my grandfather's rocker, felt their silent presence surround me.

As I stood and waited for the water to boil I wondered why I did not feel upset over Jake interrupting my routine. The village tradespeople had long since learned never to approach my cottage before early afternoon. I unlocked the cottage's front door that opened off the kitchen pantry. Outside the door a waist-high stone wall curved around the garden's perimeter, beyond which rose the tops of pines growing from the cliffs below. Through the trees the lake and distant mountains were clearly visible.

I normally took my coffee here on the pantry bench, where my grandfather used to sit after work to take off his heavy boots and the woolen socks my grandmother had knitted for him. If he was especially tired that day, my grandmother would fill an enamel washbasin with hot water and pour in a liberal dose of healing salts. He would sit as I did now, puffing on his pipe, wiping his face with an old towel, and watching the sun set behind the Alps on the lake's other side. As I sipped my coffee and looked out over the gathering day, I often thought of him, and how I had tried never to bother him until that first pipe had been tamped down and refilled.

Today I leaned out the doorway, called, "You want coffee?"

Jake rounded the corner of the house. "No thanks, man. You go right ahead."

"Amy has a beautiful voice," I said, returning to the kitchen. I pulled bread from the old wooden bin and cut myself a slice. "You hungry?"

"Just fine, thanks. Yeah, the lady's got a lotta talent. She wanted to call you this morning, say how much she liked singin' with you. Mario said this place don't have no phone, though."

"I like the privacy. Anybody who wants to talk to me can come by the club."

"Yeah, a man needs time to himself," Jake agreed. He leaned his massive form against the stone border-wall, picked at a flake of granite on a block that had been set down by my great-grandfather. "This is some place you got here."

"Thanks," I said, and pointed out over the lake to where the white-topped peaks rose in gentle glory. "On a clear day like this you can see the old passes. That hump to the right is Bernadino. In the summer, pilgrims from all over northern Europe came down through there, oh, twelve hundred years ago."

Jake squinted against the morning glare, said to the horizon, "Bet you been wonderin' why I've been after you like this."

"It crossed my mind," I agreed, glad to have it out in the open. "Sure you won't take coffee?"

"No thanks, I'm all set." Jake straightened from the wall, rubbed the knuckles of one hand. "Yeah, if I was in your place I'd think the guy had to be crazy, comin' after me like that."

I turned back to the kitchen, lifted the pot from the stove, poured coffee into the waiting cup. "I like it here, Jake. It doesn't have anything to do with not wanting to play with you and your group."

"I know what you got and I know what you think you got. It ain't the same, man. I know it and deep down inside so do you. Don't you think you been lyin' to yourself long enough?"

I took my cup with me to the front doorstep. "What are you talking about?"

Jake's gaze had gone cold. "It's the fire, man. Go look in the mirror. The fire's goin' out."

"You're talking crazy."

"Go take a look at yourself," he repeated. His voice carried a lazy power, as if he were flexing his muscles. "You been wonderin' how the music don't carry the same weight anymore. Sure you have. You're a smart man. Ain't so easy, is it, tryin' to make it connect like it used to. Used to be, all you had to do was hold the music inside you, and you were alive. Now it takes a little smoke, a touch of the powder, a sip of wine. Don't feel the same, does it?"

"I—"

"Easiest thing in the world, runnin' away. All you gotta do is turn around and there they are, a thousand ways to flee. That's what you're doin', man. You're runnin' away." Jake turned so that he stood flat to the wall, his head lifted up toward a distant sky. "Spent half my life runnin' away in hate. I'm talkin' big time, Gianni. Yeah, lotta hate. Lotta good reasons. Just lookin' to see how far I could get lost in the darkness. Pretty far, man, I tell you."

He dropped his gaze to me. "That's why I can talk to you like this, on account of havin' visited there myself."

I sipped at the coffee I could not taste. It was hard to stand there, yet it felt as though a nail had been pounded through a hollow point in my chest and on into the door behind me. I couldn't leave. I couldn't.

"Be true to yourself, Gianni," Jake said. His eyes turned into dark wells. "All you gotta do is ask Him. Such a heavy burden, man, all those memories, all that pain. Don't you ever wish you could lay it down, rest a spell? He's standin' there with His arms out, just waitin' for you to turn around and call to Him."

He lifted himself up and onto the wall. "I don't know myself what I'm doin' here. Make a lot more sense to find a strong Christian, somebody who wouldn't make trouble. Always thought we had to have people in the band who lived by the Word. Still do."

Part of me said it didn't matter what Jake thought of me. But a louder voice cried out in wordless yearning, a voice I had not heard in a long while. All I said was, "I've made a profession out of never making trouble for the bands who hired me."

He ignored my explanation. "But the Lord spoke to me. I can't tell you how because I can't put it into words. Only words that make a lotta sense to me these days are in the Bible, and they say don't mix my affairs with sinners. But the Lord spoke to my heart, and He said that you're ready to be saved."

I reached toward the pantry bench and set down my cup; I found I could not control the trembling of my fingers. I hid my hands by crossing my arms across my chest and leaned back against the doorjamb. "Is that what you want from me?" I asked. "You want me to be saved, whatever that is?"

"If you want to stay with the band it'll have to happen, my man. Have to. I'm not askin' that now, though. Can't ask what I know you can't give. But you're gonna have to agree to come and listen when we talk Bible, and you're gonna have to pray with us."

"Even though I don't believe there's anybody up there listening to what you have to say?"

"Even though," Jake agreed. "You gotta try. Gotta give the Lord a chance to speak to you. That's part of the bargain."

I feigned a lack of concern. "I'll think about it."

"Yeah, you do that." Jake gave me a look like the ones I had come to know from Mario, full of ancient wisdom and the ability to see much deeper than I liked. His gaze had the power of a mirror, and the longer I looked the more I felt the barrier crumble. I saw the life I led as a shield of lies, constructed with painstaking care to hide me from the truth. I stood and met his eyes with a false calmness and felt torn in two. Part of me wished to use this newfound truth and search within; part of me screamed silently to turn and flee.

"There's one more thing," Jake said, breaking the silence.

"What's that?"

"You gotta give up the drugs. All of 'em. The booze, too."

I shrugged nonchalantly. "No problem."

He smiled at that. "I ain't talkin' just about when you're up playin' with us, Gianni. I mean full time. Gotta clean up your act."

I felt my face grow red. "I don't see how I live in Como has anything to do with my playing in Germany. Seems to me I'd be doing you a favor to help out for a while."

"I know it does," Jake said, easing himself down off the wall. "Never thought I'd be talkin' to somebody in the band about this stuff."

"Then don't."

"I can't tell you not to do it because the Bible says it's wrong, not when you don't much care what the Bible says about anything." Jake bowed his head, rubbed one hand against the other. "You ever heard of cortisone, Gianni?"

"Sure."

"Had a buddy once, his adrenal gland started actin' up, so the doctors started givin' him shots of cortisone. Problem was, that adrenal gland caught wind of this new stuff, see, and just shut down all the way. Last I heard this guy was doin' three, sometimes four shots of the stuff every day. Had to, to stay alive. Hooked on it for the rest of his life."

Jake raised his eyes and pinned me to the cottage wall. "Souls do that too, my man. You put these drugs into your body, keep lookin' for that American dream in the bowl of your hash pipe or in that pretty silver spoon, know what happens? Your soul just plain stops tryin'. Stops talkin' to you. Stops makin' your days shine with wonder. So you gotta take more and more stuff to plug up all that emptiness, to give you some kind of fire for your music.

"The trouble with this new fire is, sooner or later it's gonna eat you up. You hear what I'm sayin', Gianni? Eat you alive, suck you dry, leave you lost. Lost and dead, because one day you're gonna wake up and find out the music ain't there any more. The fire's gone out. When that happens, it won't make any difference whether that body of yours keeps on clickin' or not. Soon as the fire's out and the music stops, you're dead."

He started for the gate, a massive black mountain which moved with incredible grace. Where he had been standing was now only empty space, and suddenly I was more afraid than I'd been since those first days after my grandmother's death.

I followed him down the gravel path. At the garden's edge he stopped and turned back, his face set as though carved in eternal granite.

"You gotta decide before it's too late." His voice rolled like distant thunder. "You go on like you're doin' right now, and you'll just keep on down that tunnel 'til the fire's gone out and there ain't nothing 'round you but the blackest, evilest, most hopeless darkness there is. Either that, or you turn around and ask for help and start searchin' for the *real* light."

Jake reached down for the garden gate, swung it open, walked out, latched it shut behind him. He gave me one more penetrating glance. "This ain't no game, Gianni. Life or death is all it is."

. . .

That evening I waited until the last possible moment to arrive at the club. Jake's presence remained with me throughout the day, along with a jumble of conflicting emotions that crowded and shoved and jostled for position. One would win out, and I would suddenly be confronted with an image and a brief snatch of words. I thought of a thousand excellent answers intended to cut him down to size. None of them helped; none of them quieted my mind.

Bruno was busy on the pipe when I arrived. He looked up, offered the smoke, and said in greeting, "Alessandro's been in half a dozen times looking for you."

I pushed the pipe aside, set down my guitar, shrugged off my jacket. "I better go see what he wants."

"He said to look for him at the bar. There or the office."

The bar, separated from the dining tables by a brass railing, marble statues, and a lot of leafy fronds, was constructed to meld with the walls. It was constructed of raw mountain stone so tightly fitted as to require only a smudge of mortar, and was topped by long slabs of varnished hardwood. The only other change Alessandro had made to the courtyard itself was to hang multicolored velvet drapes at intervals around the perimeter. They hid various storerooms and doors to the kitchen and to the office, and acted as baffles against reverberated sound. The floor was polished flagstone, flayed and chipped and weathered by six centuries of use. Alessandro had filled in the holes and replaced all that was beyond repair, then ordered tables with adjustable legs so that they would not wobble on the uneven surface.

The bar was softly lit by candles on nearby tables and by dusk-light filtering through the glass far above our heads. The place was about half-full, a good crowd for that early at night.

Alessandro stood by the wall between the bar and the entrance, directing waiters and greeting guests and chatting with all who stopped by.

He spotted me and motioned with his head toward the reservation desk. I waited while he smiled and laughed and bowed his graceful bulk past a few newcomers, then watched his face fall as he approached me.

"You didn't stop by for dinner tonight."

"I got held up," I replied.

"Better go in and at least have a bite to eat. It's bad to start a long night on an empty stomach."

"You didn't keep coming by my room all evening to talk about food."

"No." Alessandro smoothed his beard with a downward swipe of his hand. "I've got some bad news and some terrible news. Which do you want first?"

"Let's step into it gradually," I said. "I've had a rough day."

"Tell me about it. Okay. Your agent called. Antonio says Giorgio Coppa's put off starting his album for a while. The guy wants to rework a couple of songs. 'Tonio asks if you want to go down to Rome for a couple of weeks. He's got some new guy down there looking for a lead guitarist. Says the guy's using somebody now who plays with a hammer and a pair of heavy gloves."

Traveling back and forth to Rome would be out of the question if I intended to continue playing in the club. "What are you telling me?"

"C'mon over here, Maestro. Want you to see something."

Alessandro walked to a velvet baffle hanging midway down the left-hand wall. With a nervous glance toward the bar, he pulled the heavy cloth over to one side.

"Take a look, Gianni. My lady's gotten sick."

A crack started at the floor and snaked right up the wall as far as I could see. At the thickest point it was perhaps two handspans wide and just as deep.

I leaned close, looked up, asked, "Is the wall bulging up there?"

"I had the engineers in today. And yesterday, and the day before. Guys from Milano specializing in old structures. Told me the weight of the glass is causing the wall to shift."

"So what happens now?"

"They gotta shore up the wall with a couple of support girders. They say when it's finished, you won't be able to tell where they are."

"The girders have to be on the inside of the wall?"

"One does. Another one or two outside."

"You're going to have to close down, aren't you." It was not a question. I thought about my conversation with Jake. "How long?"

Alessandro let the curtain drop back. "They told me a week."

We shared a laugh over that. Italian builders made promises that would cause even the most hard-hearted Riviera Romeo to blush with shame. They would say anything, promise anything, to win a contract. Anything. Once the paper was signed, the words vanished like smoke in the wind.

I asked again, "How long?"

"A month, maybe six weeks. I figure we can reopen as soon as this inside girder is set in place. They'll do that first. I'm paying them to work 'round the clock until that one's in place."

"So when do they start?"

"Week after next, Maestro. I've spent all day calling around, postponing reservations. I couldn't get in touch with you since your cottage doesn't have a phone."

I shook my head. Despite my attempt at calm, I was shaken by the timing of it all.

Alessandro misunderstood, was suddenly all concern. "The contract for you and the boys still stands, Gianni. I can't afford to pay you guys full rate while we're closed, but you'll be taken care of. You got money problems, caro, we'll work something out."

"It's not the money, Alessandro, but thanks," I said, trying to put real gratitude behind the words. "You told the others?"

"You mean the band? No, I figured you'd want to do that once you decided about the studio work." He forced a smile, but the worry didn't leave his eyes. "Rome in springtime is a magic place, Maestro. Maybe you oughtta take Antonio's offer."

"Maybe. I'll think it over." I could not get over how it had all come together. Jake would no doubt say that an invisible hand was guiding me along an unseen path. I wasn't sure I liked being moved around like a pawn on a chessboard. "I better go tell the guys."

Bruno and Claudio were arranging white powder in thin lines on the mirror when I arrived. "Alessandro's got to close up for emergency repairs," I told them.

"We heard." Bruno planted the little pipe in his nose, bent over, did two lines, leaned back, sniffed hard, blinked his eyes.

Claudio took the tube. "Some of the staff are talking about renting a place at Portofino. You want to go?"

"I don't know. Maybe. Antonio may have work for us in Rome."

That brought a light to Bruno's eyes. "Rome is an incredible place this time of year, Maestro."

"So I hear." I searched for words, said, "I've been thinking about maybe taking an offer in Germany."

"You'd go to Germany over Rome?" Claudio looked shocked. "What for?"

"This got something to do with your friend Mario?" Bruno offered me the pipe. "Want a hit?"

"Not right now, thanks." No drugs, Jake had said. He had made it sound like some mission impossible. "It'd just be for a week or so, until they find a new lead guitarist."

They shared a glance. "You're a good friend, Maestro," Claudio said.

"I can't believe you'd go back to Germany for them." Bruno knew the faintest sketches of my early years in Dusseldorf.

"Neither can I."

The room turned very close, the air heavy with its load of smoke. I grabbed my guitar, decided the first set could be done in my street clothes. "I've got some things I need to talk over with Alessandro," I said. "See you after the set."

A velvet rope barred the entrance, and almost all the tables were full. I dropped my guitar in the shadow of the stage and eased myself down to the main floor. Waiters paused to ask where I'd been; had I heard; was I coming to Portofino? Alessandro moved like a graceful bear, flitting from tables to bar to kitchen to entrance. He had a smile and a kind word for everyone.

Alessandro spotted me and exaggerated his surprise with wide eyes and slack jaw. I never came out front before playing. Voices called to me from various tables. I stopped here and there to shake offered hands, declined invitations to sit and share a glass of wine. Now that I was out there, I had no idea why I had come.

The bar was as crowded as Alessandro would permit during dinnertime. The prices were very high; bars to either side of us offered the same drinks at less than half the cost. Yet every night Alessandro turned away more people than he allowed in.

The only guests guaranteed nightly entrance were beautiful girls without escorts. The bar had become known as a relatively safe gathering place for models and actresses up from Milan, or girls who aspired to that game, or ones who simply wished they could. Local businessmen would have given their right arms for Alessandro's address book. He limited male entry to the super-rich, the big names, the fortunate, and a few friends. According to Alessandro, a friend was somebody who would be there when the roof fell in, and those he could count on the thumbs of one hand.

The bearded bear glided up beside me. "Don't let the action at the bar spoil your concentration tonight, Maestro."

"A lot of young lovelies around," I agreed.

"The Count's back with a new granddaughter; see them there under the dead palm?"

"Amazing she can lift her fork with all that weight on her wrist."

A dark-haired beauty detached herself from the bar crowd, walked to the fern border, smiled and beckoned me over. Because Alessandro was expecting it, I asked, "You remember her name?"

"Francesca something. Girl must have been in some all-time hurry to get over here. Looks to me like she forgot to put on anything under that dress." He looked at me. "You decided what you're going to do?"

I nodded. "Mario's band lost their lead guitarist a couple of weeks ago. I thought maybe I'd go help out until they find a replacement."

"Mario's a good kid. Kinda crazy over this religion thing, though." He patted me on the back. "Nice of you to help out a friend like this, Maestro. Says a lot about you."

I felt shamed by his praise. "I think maybe I'll go say hello to Francesca something before I start the set."

"Real nice of you to come out front tonight, Maestro," Alessandro said, resting a heavy hand on my shoulder. "Know how much you hate it before you play. Means a lot. Especially tonight."

I nodded, felt my face grow hot. "Are you going to make an announcement?"

"Before your first late-night set. Everyone is being told as they come in, but I thought I'd just say a little something extra then, open up a few bottles on the house. Better go see to the girl, Maestro. It's about time for you to go on."

Francesca wore a form-fitting black knit dress that ended a long way above her knees. Her hair was an auburn frame encircling a beautiful face and eager eyes. The teeth that shone at my approach were small and perfect and touched by the tip of a little pink tongue.

She pouted and said in greeting, "You haven't called me in weeks, Gianni. Do you forget girls so easy?"

"Not you," I replied. I reached over heads to shake the bartender's hand, declined his offer of a glass of wine, asked for a club soda instead.

She trailed one finger down the edge of her champagne glass and eyed me over the rim. "You will play that special song for me tonight, Gianni?"

"Of course," I said, and had to search frantically before remembering. She was a George Benson fan, and loved his rendition of "Masquerade." "Are you going to come up and dance with us if we play it?"

"Up on stage?" Her eyes opened wide. "You mean it, Gianni? You want me to come up and dance?"

I regretted the invitation as soon as the words were out. "Maybe later, okay? It's kind of a special night tonight."

"Yeah, I heard. Too bad the place has to close for a while." Her expression changed to one I could feel in my gut. She asked softly, "Maybe I could come dance for you after you've finished playing. Would you like that, Gianni?"

This time, besides the desire that swept up like a hungry flame came a sense of *knowing*. I looked at the beautiful face, saw the girl who would wake up beside me the next morning, and felt the dusty emptiness. She yearned for more than just a single night of flashing passion, yet knew that to ask for it would break the unspoken rule of my independence. She would be unhappy and I would sense it, although nothing would be said. I would spend my morning waiting impatiently for her to leave. I wanted her, yet I felt some silent whisper pressing me to see beyond the want. Beyond the moment. Beyond the physical desire.

A tap on the shoulder saved me from having to reply. "Hate to disturb you, Maestro, but it's time to go on."

I smiled at Francesca. "Maybe we can talk later."

She smiled back. "Just talk?"

Weaving my way through the tables, I lifted myself onto the stage, brought guitar and stool toward the front, plugged in, waved and smiled to the scattered applause, and without preamble began.

It was different playing without the barrier of a high. Very different. The music seemed to come out mechanically, without real challenge or meaning. I brought up the image of a smiling Francesca and the invitation in her eyes, but found no answering desire within myself. I let the image slide away, and did something that I had never done before. I stopped at the end of the first song and looked out over the audience.

As long as the dinner crowd dominated the room, the lights remained on, soft and unfocused. When Mario had helped Alessandro with the sound system, he had also rigged a series of low-powered floorlights that rimmed the stage; they offered a sort of electric candle-glow to my early set. I could look out over the entire room, if I wanted to, which I never did. Until now.

No barrier separated me from the people now, no high enclosed me within the cocoon of my music. And I could hear no answering music within my heart. I looked out over the applauding people at their food-laden tables and out to the smiling bar-crowd. I searched within, and I found nothing. With no acknowledgment of the applause, I turned back to my guitar.

I stayed on classical pieces throughout the entire set, playing with the same unfeeling precision that I had fled from in Germany. I could not believe I was really thinking of returning, even for a few days. I had spent years struggling to erase every memory of that place.

Yet the truth of Jake's words lay before me, a stark reminder of what I had failed to see for myself. I looked out over the crowd, saw the shallowness of it all. What would happen if I disappeared tomorrow? Would any of the smiling bar girls remember me, miss me, wonder what had happened to the musician? Which of them felt what I was trying to give? The question made me look inside, yet the view there was no better. What could I give from such an emptiness? If I had so little within, what was there to fuel the music, the giving? My pain at Jake's words returned, and I decided to cut the set short. I was afraid of the desolate wind whispering through me.

. . . .

For the first time in years I left after the last show as sober as I had arrived. I walked the streets, felt the brisk nighttime breeze whisk the cigarette smoke from my clothes and hair. I followed the cobblestone street back to the Piazza Duomo, fronted by shops and restaurants on one side and by the the central Como cathedral on the other. I had passed the structure several times a day for the better part of my life, and never thought of it as more than a majestic building, a monument to Como's earlier days. Like all local schoolchildren, I had toured the massive place in the company of several nuns. I had been ordered to bow and make the sign of the cross before the altar, and had looked up in awe at the distant bowed ceiling with its intricate layering of gold. Tonight I stood in the silent plaza, my collar turned up against the chill, and stared at the cross upon the higher dome, a black form etched distinctly upon the star-flecked heavens.

I turned down the narrow way which connected the cathedral's plaza with the one which fronted the lake. The Piazza Cavour was a massive affair, a full two hundred paces across. Three sides contained banks and cafes and exclusive shops and four-star hotels. The vast middle section held carefully tended flower beds crisscrossed by miniature paths and lines of heavy wooden benches. In the daylight hours the young people swarmed here. They filled the air with excited chatter and smoke from their "motos," miniature two-stroke motorcycles permitted to anyone over the age of fourteen. Ice cream vans plied their trade, acting as gathering points for various cliques.

Old men and tourists filled the sidewalk cafes, spending hours over tiny cups of coffee and idle chatter, eyeing the beautiful young people and wishing they could recapture what was lost and gone forever.

At four-thirty in the morning, the Piazza Cavour was dark and empty. A line of taxis stood outside the city's largest hotel, while the drivers dozed and waited for a last call. I knew most of them by name. Tonight I walked in front of them, exchanged subdued hellos with the only driver still awake, and crossed the plaza.

The plaza's fourth side fronted the lake. Piers for the city's boat-buses jutted from the shoreline, the ancient vessels looking clean and new and stately in the vague lighting. A chain of faint yellow globes hung above the lakefront and continued down the road. Occasionally a car would downshift and barrel around the snaking curves, flicker into view, and just as swiftly roar away. The drivers swept through the nighttime vacuum oblivious to all but the momentary freedom of speed. Their fleeting presence amplified my own aloneness.

I crossed the road and walked out to the end of the long breakwater pier. The night breeze blew off the lake, carrying with it the biting chill of distant mountains. From across the waters shimmered the lights of Cernobbio, the second main village upon the lake. Sparkling yellow pinpoints of illumination beckoned, lifting the eye as they climbed the hillside. Beyond the lakeside hills rose the silent shadows of the Alps, a jagged line carved across the horizon.

I jammed my fists into my coat pockets, took deep draughts of the sweet biting air, and realized when I had known this feeling before. It was on the Thursday boat-trips into Como after four days off the smoke. It was the emptiness I hated to confront and which I usually pushed away in anticipation of the coming high. But there was no high to look forward to tonight, no drugged dullness to blank out my awareness. I was surrounded by beauty on all sides, and I felt nothing.

As long as I was busy, as long as the world crowded in with noises and sights and smells and people and action, I could remain blind to what was inside me. But the night's silent beauty was a mirror. I looked out and searched inward at the same time, seeking an answering chord of beauty in my heart.

Yet there was nothing—only the aching emptiness, the pain harbored over years and years, the memories I had spent my entire adult life running from. They were all there. I had never escaped.

I had everything I had always wanted. I was a professional musician, a celebrity known by almost everyone in the city. Heads turned wherever I went. I fielded at least one offer a week for an album, a radio spot, a television interview. I ate the finest food, drank the finest wine. I knew the black sticky hash of Afghanistan, the pungent odor of fresh Thai sticks, the Nigerian elephant weed, the crumbly blond Lebanese hashish. My four guitars were the finest that money could buy. Beautiful women were available for me whenever I felt the faintest hint of desire. I had more money than I could ever want to spend. I lived where I wanted, in a cottage fashioned by the hands of my grandfather's father's father. I had it all.

I huddled down deeper inside my jacket, wiped a sleeve across tears drawn out by the wind. There was no escape here. I stood exposed. The cold seemed to blow straight through me, revealing the hollowness within. All the barriers and blockades I had spent years constructing were exposed for the lies they were. All the dreams, all the achievements, all the possessions, all the careful protections were meaningless. I was utterly naked, defenseless, empty.

There had to be more. This couldn't be all there was to life. I was terrified by the thought of joining Mario and Jake and Amy, but I knew no one else who offered an answer, who said they knew a better way. I stood and shivered and watched dawn slowly erase the stars from a cloudless sky, and endured the pain that this new-found honesty had revealed.

I was going back to Germany. I could not explain it or find any logic to justify this decision. But I felt drawn there by answers to questions which I could not even express.

There had to be a better way.

CHAPTER
7

From Mainz to Koblenz the train journeyed directly beside the Rhine. I sat and watched an ancient landscape pass outside my window. Castles dotted hilltops, overlooking medieval villages and sculpted acres of vineyards. Under cloudy skies the river ran strong and sullen. Nothing in the towns moved—no cars, no people, no sign of life. The scene held a timeless air.

What was I doing here, I asked myself repeatedly. For me, Germany remained a place to flee from, and yet here I was, risking a dream-like lifestyle to come and play with a group I did not know. What was drawing me here? I gazed at my reflection in the window and condemned myself roundly for ever coming back.

As the train rolled into the Dusseldorf station later that afternoon, I decided I would return to Como before the weekend was over.

The air was wet and warm as I opened the train's door. Jake was there to greet me. I handed him the four guitars one at a time, grabbed my satchel, stepped to the ground, let my hand be engulfed by one of his. He wore gray flannel trousers tucked into leather boots that looked very soft, very comfortable. His leather jacket was form-fitted to broad shoulders and a relatively small waist. The zipper was open far enough to show muscles straining at the fabric of a thin silk T-shirt. His face was a black stone mask, his eyes hidden behind wrap-around shades. Passengers leaving or boarding the train skirted far around him and commented to one another about his size.

"Mario's just finishing up a session at the studio where he works," Jake said. "He'll be meeting us at the place."

I nodded as though I understood. "Does it ever bother you, people staring like that?"

"Not anymore," he replied, reaching for one of my cases. "You been working on those songs I sent?"

"Every day."

"Good man." He pointed with his jaw. "Car's out back. What say we take the side exit down there."

Every other day I had received a cassette from Jake, each painstakingly labelled "Set One—Intro and Lead-In," "Set Two—Hard Rock," and so on. The more I listened to his songs, the easier it became to set aside the disturbing emotions brought up by the lyrics and concentrate on the music. I had spent the past eleven days playing out the final nights in the club, memorizing my parts from the cassette, and fighting with myself over this decision to come to Germany. Most nights I had gone to bed trying to make up excuses to free myself from this promise and still let me keep Mario as my friend. By the time the train had left Como I was down to just one reason for going—because I said I would.

"Our place is about ten blocks from here," Jake said. His van was a new Mercedes MB–10, with a back area tall enough for me to stand up in. The floors, walls and ceiling were padded with multicolored layers of old packing quilts.

"You've got to be real careful to get receipts for everything to do with the band," Jake instructed. "At the end of each month give everything to Hans, our man on horns. He keeps the books."

As we drove, places and buildings rose from my memory like shadows in a dream. Jake left the main road and began winding his way past a series of factories and tumble-down warehouses. "Mario is sound engineer. Man's responsible for all sound checks, settin' up and tearin' down. Lights too. Everybody follows his orders before and after each concert."

Jake stopped in front of an old warehouse covered in soot and decorated with letters so faded they could not be read. The sidewalk was cracked and pitted, the street threaded by rusting rail-lines and clumps of weeds. He pushed open a metal door imbedded in a larger garage door and we went inside.

High overhead burned a string of industrial lights, and above them loomed girders and dark shapes. The floor was dotted with old oil stains, but it was clean. The temperature was much cooler than outside. The back third of the warehouse was sectioned off by a wall of fiberboard with two doors set thirty feet apart. From behind the left-hand door came muffled noises.

"Shoulda seen this place when we started," Jake said, and pointed toward the right-hand entrance. "Let's take a look in there first."

He opened the cheap prefab door, said, "Our practice room. We've sweated blood over this place."

The floor was covered with layer upon layer of old carpet. The top layer was a dozen oriental rugs, replete with holes and raveled edges. It was a wondrous bazaar of colors.

"Took almost every cent we had," Jake said. "Like to see this extra warehouse space someday be a little Bible study classroom or maybe a small gathering place for young people. All that's gonna have to wait. Can't afford much else right now."

Two great stacks of speakers stood like sentinels in each corner of the playing area. Fronting them was a collection of wind instruments, each on a little silver stand—three saxophones of various sizes, a flute, a clarinet, a trumpet, a flugelhorn, and a trombone. Behind them, to the right of the drums, stood double congas almost four feet high. A slender metal stand sprouted beside the congas, holding a dozen pencil-thin tubular bells. Against the wall rose shelves holding every imaginable percussion instrument. The drums just seemed to go on and on, a vast array of cymbals and silver-plated shapes. To their left stood an upright piano facing the back wall. In front of it were four keyboards stationed on a special A-frame that stacked them like hi-tech steps.

The whole arena was encircled by a ring of microphones. In front of the mike stands squatted four odd-angled playbacks, the speaker boxes used to direct music toward the stage so the musicians could hear it. Two sets of professional lights and a third stand for the dual spots were stacked over to one side.

"Some of the places where we play don't have their own lighting," Jake said. "We got these for free. Bought the PA system from a rental agency that was upgrading. We took some time looking at the mixing board, so they finally said if we went for the whole deal they'd throw in the lights."

Next to the spotlights, near the back wall and facing the playing area, were the sound and light mixing boards. A multitude of jacks sprouted from the sound board's back, leading into a trunk of cables that snaked along the floor toward the instruments. For each jack there were several slide bars and an array of tuner knobs.

Jake ran a hand along the board's face. "Like Mario says, this baby'll make a sneeze sound like the Hallelujah Chorus."

The outer door clanged open and quiet voices echoed in the distance. A couple of men entered the playing room. The elder was almost bald and had streaks of gray in his carefully tended beard. He wore a flannel workshirt, dungarees, and sneakers. His hazel eyes wore a look of gentle inquiry. The younger was tall and lanky, with curly blond hair and the enormous blue eyes of an eternal innocent.

"These are our horn players," Jake said. "Karl and Hans. Guys, like you to meet Gianni."

"Nice to meet you, kid," Karl, the bearded one, said.

The blond gave a shy smile, shook hands, said nothing.

"Hans is our token mute," Jake said. "Only time he talks is when he's singin' or talkin' about the Gospel."

"Same thing," Hans said, smiling again in that quiet way.

"Hans is studyin' religion at the local university. Don't ask me why. Don't never say enough to make a halfway preacher. Karl's a social worker in real life. Works with handicapped kids."

Karl asked, "You speak German?"

"Not in almost ten years."

"Mario's told us a lot about you. I'm looking forward to hearing you play."

"C'mon, Gianni," Jake said. "Want you to meet the others."

He led me around the mixing boards, back through another prefab door. We entered a second room, this one lit by old table lamps with tattered shades and lined with comfortable-looking furniture. One back corner had a small kitchenette; the second held a sleeping alcove with curtains drawn around wall bunks. The floor was carpeted as the practice room, the walls decorated with posters announcing revivals and concerts by groups I had never heard of. Shelves held books and videos and CD's and albums. Musical instruments and sheet music were strewn everywhere. A large television flickered against the left wall; beside it was a very impressive stereo set.

Mario was lounging at one end of the sofa dressed in a tattered T-shirt and sweat-stained jeans. "Salve, Maestro." He looked very tired. "I'd get up but I think maybe if I did I'd fall over. Spent the whole night at the studio working on a remix."

The man next to Mario had rust-colored hair clamped to his head in kinky curls. He sprawled on the sofa with arms and legs stretched out at unlikely angles. It reminded me of the way a rag doll looks after being tossed aside. I had never seen anybody so relaxed.

His attention remained glued to the television. He said to no one in particular, "Something's waiting just around the corner."

"Limp dude with the busted fingers there is Pipo," Jake rumbled. "Percussion. Late of Miami, Rio, Dallas, and New York."

"Don't forget Los Angeles, man," Pipo said, his eyes still fixed on the screen. "Land of the midnight breakfast. Home to every idol on earth. Only place in the world where if it snowed people'd be out waving hundred dollar bills at the sky."

"Pipo's hooked on thrillers," Mario said to me. "Especially the old black-and-white ones."

"What's his problem?" Pipo complained. "I mean, he oughtta know some serious business is coming down."

"How come?" Mario winked at me, played the straight man. "The girl just said she was gonna marry him."

"That don't mean diddle." Pipo waved a hand with three heavily bandaged fingers at the screen. "Listen to the music. Anybody with sense is gonna know when they start playing that heavy music it's time for the ax. That dude must be a fool. How come he's just walking straight into the mess is what I want to know."

Jake asked, "Think maybe you could say hello to your new lead guitarist?"

"Yep, there it is," Pipo replied. "Major trouble. Dude's gonna catch it now."

Jake said to me, "Man likes to think he's our problem child."

Pipo stretched elaborately tattooed arms over his head, gave me a bored once-over. "You really hot stuff like they say?"

I shook my head. "I just play a little guitar, is all."

He dropped his arms like a puppet whose strings were cut, turned his attention back to the television. "At least you don't blow your own horn."

Jake shook his head, gave a little, mmm-hmm. He said, "That's some greetin' for a new band member."

Mario gave a drawn-out groan and pushed himself erect. He smiled tiredly at me, said, "You about ready to warm up, Maestro?"

Once we were back in the practice room, Jake said, "Our lead guitarist wasn't always an easy dude to be around."

"What Jake is saying," Mario explained, "is that he can't tell you what he thinks of that guy and still face himself in the mirror."

"Set a lotta people's teeth on edge. Used it as a shield, 'cause he just didn't have the talent of the rest of the group."

"Amy said if he put half as much energy into being a better musician as he did in being difficult, we'd have had a superstar on our hands," Mario said.

"Couldn't keep up with the rest of the band on a lot of things," Jake said.

"Pipo called him our divine brake," Mario said. "The guy just loved that."

"Heat was up pretty high for a while," Jake said. "Especially for Pipo."

"Give them a chance to get to know you, Maestro," Mario said, flipping switches and adjusting knobs on the mixing board. "They'll come around."

"I've got a little something planned," Jake said, a hint of a smile touching his eyes. "That is, if you don't mind sort of an initiation."

"I don't mind."

Mario introduced me to Lothar, their keyboard player from Bern. He was a tangle-haired study in denim—trousers, shirt, jacket, and blue denim sneakers. His eyes were all over the room, wandering and touching everywhere, never staying anywhere for long. Lothar worked with him sometimes in the studio, Mario told me. That was where the group had first come together. The man nodded, shook my hand, said nothing.

One by one they all came in and took their positions. I set up beside Lothar as Jake directed. Amy arrived and came over to greet me with a warm hug. "How've you been, Gianni?"

"Okay," I said, glad to see her again. "This room is great. Very professional."

"Just another sweatshop, kid," Pipo said, tightening the heads on his congas. "Whips and chains are outside."

She grasped me by the elbow and led me to the drums. "Gianni, I want you to meet Sameh."

I took in the Egyptian's toffee-colored skin, the dark eyes and hair, the murmured hello, the calm power, the swift handshake. He turned back to pulling the mike-booms down into position around his drums.

Pipo clapped a hand down hard, and the room reverberated to the conga's thunder. "Mario, you found out how to work that thing yet?"

"My gear's working fine," Mario said, not looking up. "Give me something, Pipo."

"Blow you away, baby." Pipo began to beat out a steady salsa rhythm. As he played, the muscles and veins on his arms and neck stood out distinctly. The tattered bandages on the first three fingers of each hand marked the point that struck the congas.

Mario fiddled with various switches until the power of Pipo's congas started thumping through the PA and into my chest.

"Okay, Hans," Mario called.

The blond young man walked over, picked up the trumpet, approached his mike, began to play in time to Pipo's beat. He ran up the scale, drawing out his high notes, fell down so low the music became a sputter, slid back into his run. He was very good. Mario worked with both hands; the trumpet's sound welled up and up, filling the chamber. It was fresh, authentic, powerful.

"Your turn, Karl," Mario yelled.

Karl picked up the alto sax, quickly checked the tuning, and swung into the melody played by Hans. Without a pause, without a false note, he just blended in, melded with the trumpet, then soared off on a road of his own. Mario drew his sound up until it matched and blended.

Dancing in place behind his board, Mario lifted both hands over his head and hooked pointed fingers down toward the drums.

Sameh drove through a rapid-fire trill that started on the snare and took him over all the drums within the space of a dozen heartbeats. His beat was solid, sure, tremendously powerful. The cymbals crashed and chimed, the bass danced a staccato beat; his sticks were a solid blur.

Mario called over, "You wanna hook up, Gianni?"

"Naw, wait a minute," Jake said loudly from the doorway.

The music ended sharply. I liked that. It was the surest signal of a professional group. No jockeying for power, no running solos on after the others had stopped, no getting lost in the thrill of being the center of attention. When the leader said stop, they stopped. Sharp and clean, without dissention.

Jake looked at me. "You been practicin' hard?"

"Yes." I ignored the attention that turned my way.

"You learned all the cassettes I sent you?"

I nodded.

Jake looked around, made sure the room was listening. "How well?"

I thought about that. "I can play all the songs on the cassettes in order. And I know all the solos."

"Just the guitar solos, or for all the other instruments, too?"

"All the solos." There was no need to say the only reason I had learned them was boredom. With the album work postponed, there had been nothing else to fill the time.

"Okay, lemme ask you something," Jake said. "You know the songs well enough to change the key and still play them exactly the same?"

"Yes." Of course.

"Well," Jake said. "What if I wanted to change the tempo—maybe take a love song and make it into rhythm and blues?"

Amy walked over, her smile a shield against all the eyes focused on me. "What Daddy Jake is asking is whether you can help fit a song around my voice."

"I'd like to try," I said. "It's a pretty standard studio technique."

"Maybe for you," Pipo muttered.

"Plug in your guitar, Gianni," Jake said. "I think it's time to show 'em what we got here."

"Use the cord there by Lothar, Maestro," Mario said.

I selected the Stratocaster. It sounded like Jake was after power. I plugged myself in, tuned to Lothar's keyboard, heard Mario draw me up and out of the PA.

Jake asked, "What is the first song on the Set Two tape?"

I shook my head. "I don't know any of the titles."

"That's right, I forgot," Jake drawled, and casually raked the room with his gaze. "You never heard any of this music before, have you?"

"No." I took a long time tuning, tried a couple of brief runs, listened to the way the room echoed and absorbed the sound, tried to tell myself it was just like working in a new studio. Just proving myself again. Nothing more.

Jake turned to Pipo. In that lazy rumble he said, "Tell you what, man. Why don't you just take that song, change the tempo to a Latin or salsa or something and really jazz it up, you know? Take the basic tune and just do whatever you want to it."

Pipo shot a glance my way, shrugged. "Why not?"

Lothar asked, "What about the key?"

"Yeah, the key." Jake's eyes glimmered humor as he glanced toward Amy. "Don't matter much about no key, does it? You just play whichever key you want, however you please. Think you can handle that?"

Lothar thought it over, leaned over the keyboard, started playing two steps above the key on the cassette. I would have no problem changing over.

Lothar stopped, asked, "How's that?"

"All right by me," Jake said. "You got any problems with that, Gianni?"

I shook my head, understanding what he wanted.

Jake turned to Pipo, nodded. "All right, my man. Hit it."

"But I haven't told him the key yet," Lothar said.

Jake didn't turn around. "Hit it, Pipo."

Pipo raised his eyes to the ceiling, made patterns in the air above his congas as he listened to the music in his head, lowered his hands, and pounded out a strong rock salsa.

Jake gave Sameh the nod, and he swung in on drums. It was tight, polished, high-powered.

Jake turned to me, mouthed, *Hit it*. I did as he said, adding the dischords to match the way Lothar had played. I began putting in half notes to accent the salsa beat, forgetting all about the novelty of the place, the eyes of the people.

Jake's booming laugh brought me around. I looked over. Pipo had stopped playing and was watching me with hard, careful eyes. I turned toward him and swung into the solo, keeping more or less to the way it had been structured on the tape, but with tempo and chord changes to match the salsa.

Pipo gave me a nod, little more than a jerk of his head, but the message was clear. He began following the beat line on the higher conga. I added runs within runs, doubling and tripling the notes, playing fast for the simple thrill of it.

He ran off a little trill; I made my own notes fit his beat. He shouted a laugh, hit a blur on both congas. I followed with another run. Boom, boom, the two congas together, followed by a blinding flurry. I hit the next chords full on, then slid down a run as fast as I could play.

Jake held up a clenched fist, and I followed the others down a quick run and ended. Pipo rewarded me with an enormous grin, said, "You're okay, man!" He turned, grinning, to Jake. "I think maybe we oughtta keep this one."

"Long as you approve," Jake said, looking at Amy.

Pipo let me go with a pat on the back. "Yeah, the kid's all right. And he's little enough, he gives us any problems we all just sit on him."

"Okay." Jake moved toward the back of the room, motioned for the others to join him. "Prayer time. Everybody over here."

I put down my guitar, followed the others over to the mixing board, allowed my hands to be taken by Hans on one side and Amy on the other. I raised my head, looked straight at Mario. His headphones were draped around his neck, the skin around his eyes smudged with fatigue. But his gaze held a calm joy and a strength that made a mockery of my need for barriers. I looked into the eyes of my oldest friend, really looked, and yearned for what he had found for himself.

"Welcome to Natural Light," Jake said. "Let's turn it over to the Father and get to work."

．　　．　　．

"The band used to be just a weekend deal for everybody," Amy explained to me as we sat in a restaurant that evening. "It started off just as a way of ministering through music, you know, a way of putting our faith to work. But it started growing faster than any of us expected." She reached over and squeezed her husband's massive arm. "Any of us, that is, except Daddy Jake. He never doubted it for a moment."

"Things are finally catchin' fire," Jake agreed.

The three of us were seated in a Kneipe, a sort of neighborhood restaurant found all over Germany, located not far from Jake and Amy's apartment. The Kneipe generally served good but simple food, and beer from one of Germany's three hundred breweries. Because Mario's apartment was so small, Jake and Amy had offered to let me stay with them; after practice Mario had pleaded exhaustion and left me in their care.

"We all had our regular jobs, still do," Amy went on. "But we're beginning to ask if maybe we need to start looking at things differently."

"People gotta ask some tough questions," Jake said. "Hans is tryin' to finish up at seminary, Karl is a full-on social worker specializin' in handicapped children. Sameh and Pipo are doin' big-time studio work."

"You too," Amy said quietly. "Me too, for that matter."

"Yeah, but it's different for them. That's been their life, you know? Hard for a man to give up what he thought was his life's work. There's a fork in the road, though, right up ahead. Gotta spend some time on their knees, I told 'em, find out which way the Lord wants them to go."

We had stopped by their apartment before coming to the restaurant so I could drop off my bags. It was very different from what I expected, very much in contrast to the building's worn and dusky exterior. The living room walls were covered with framed and autographed posters from past European tours. Polished wood floors were covered with large Turkish rugs, bright swatches of color topped by brass and wood octagonal tables. Around the tables were comfortable-looking chairs with wooden arms and leather cushions. Tall brass urns adorned several corners, filled with the feathered fronds of dried plants. The dining space was separated from the living room proper by an enormous stereo flanked by bookshelves. One side was filled with large illustrated volumes. The other side, all six shelves, was jammed full of albums and CD's.

Jake said to me, "Those were some hot licks you played there today."

"I thought so too," Amy agreed. "You really are a fine guitarist."

"Mario told us you'd show up ready to roll," Jake said. "He was right. Good thing too, what with our next gig on Wednesday."

"We've got a gig in five days?" It was the first I had heard of it.

"Didn't want to say anything about it unless we were sure you'd be with us," Jake said. "We got one more practice on Tuesday, but you and me, we'll be pushin' it hard between now and then."

When our meal arrived Amy thanked the waiter in flawless German. I asked her where she had learned to speak like that.

"Here," she replied in English. "Where else?"

"You've lived in Dusseldorf for a long time?"

She shook her head. "Darmstadt. South of Frankfurt. It's where we're playing next week, as a matter of fact. Do you know it?"

"I know where it is, I've never been there. The only place I've really been in Germany is Dusseldorf." I turned away from that topic by asking Jake, "Do you speak German too?"

"Never could get my mouth to fit around those sounds," he replied. "I speak enough to find my way around, but any real conversation is taken care of by the lady here."

"What languages do you speak, Gianni?" Amy asked.

"Italian, English and German."

"Mario told us you're American, is that right?"

I nodded, said, "I haven't lived there since I was five."

"Yes, Mario told us. Maybe that's why you have such an incredible accent. It doesn't sound really Italian, though. Kind of a mish-mash. Almost British sometimes."

"They teach British English in the German schools," I explained.

"That's right, they do," Amy said. "I forgot. It never affected me like that, since we were always around my father and all his American buddies."

"You studied in Germany?"

"Gymnasium for six years," she replied. "Then I decided to go full time with my music."

"I thought you were American."

"I am. Or half, anyway. But the only real time I've ever spent in the States were summers with my grandmama in St. Louis. It was always hot and muggy and it rained a lot, I remember that much. My daddy was a full-time army man. When his last tour of duty ended, he got us a house near the Darmstadt base and went to work as a civilian in the PX."

Amy's dark hair was cut long and full, cascading around an oval face with strong features and full lips. High cheekbones framed black shining eyes. Her skin was flawless, a beautiful canvas for the emotions that shone from her as she spoke. Beside Jake she looked petite. When she looked up to his face, she talked in a low husky burr that sent shivers up my spine.

They had their own way of talking, those two. It made me feel very alone to watch the way they moved in such fluid tandem. Amy dominated the conversation, but only because Jake held her aloft. She was the dark beauty that the world gaped at, he the unyielding pedestal that raised her up.

Jake was content to let Amy speak for them both, adding a few deep-spoken words from time to time more in emphasis than in any need to be noticed. She spoke with a performer's desire to be the center of attention, casting her words out with heart-snaring honesty.

I asked her where she had developed such an amazing stage presence. Not to mention such a beautiful voice. I had seldom seen the two qualities so well matched in a performer, and never in one who did not need an entourage on hand to help carry their ego. Amy glanced at Jake before answering, a question in her eyes. Jake looked down at her for a long moment, and the granite facade of his face yielded to reveal a deeper, different man. He nodded to her, a simple motion that for some reason brought a look of pure love to her eyes.

She turned back to me and began, "I've been singing in nightclubs and hotel bars since I was seventeen years old. Had a backup on keyboards who programed our drum machine. You make good money touring the big hotels in Europe, but it's a nowhere kind of job. I started drinking more than was good for me, didn't find anything wrong with a little toot now and then. Got to be on friendly terms with some of the big spenders, and when some halfway decent old boy put the moves on me, I'd think, why not? Only I was smart enough not to do it for free."

"Smart," Jake rumbled, nodding his head slowly. "Real smart."

She took a tiny sip from her drink, set it down, said, "I'd just gotten back from a long weekend with some guy at an exclusive resort. Only thing I can remember about him is he drove one of those fancy Italian cars. Isn't that something? Spend three days with a man and I can't remember his name, his face, nothing at all except he drove too fast. Gave me a sapphire bracelet with rocks the size of peanuts. I think I lost it, I don't remember. Money didn't have any more meaning for me than life."

The waiter came over to clear our plates. Amy sat in silence, her eyes fixed on the table by her hands. I did not know what to do, what to say, how to react. Her openness overwhelmed me.

Jake leaned across the table, said to me, "The lady's just plantin' seeds, Gianni. God willin', you'll understand that in time."

When the waiter departed she went on. "My father met Jake at a jazz joint and dragged him home. It was one of those rare occasions when I was on speaking terms with my family. I was the youngest daughter, the best looking, and the most trouble. My father met my mother while he was stationed in Japan after World War Two. My mother was trying to support half a dozen relatives by dancing in a GI bar. When she started seeing my father, things got a lot easier for her family. Suddenly there was meat on the table every night, cigarettes, and other goods they could trade.

"Her family was smart enough not to ask where the stuff was coming from, and she was smart enough to keep quiet about having fallen for a foreigner, and a black American to boot. Mama finally told her father the day they were married, which was the day before the army shipped my father off to Germany. Mama sent her family a check for fifty dollars a month every month for the next ten years. That's not an easy thing to do when you're trying to raise a family of four girls on an NCO's pay. The checks were always cashed, too. Every single one. But you know what? My mama never heard from her family again. Not a peep."

"Every place on earth's got its share of people determined to live without love and forgiveness," Jake said. "They say there ain't no need for the Lord in their lives, then turn around and just keep on showin' how bitter is the harvest for a man walkin' on his own."

Amy looked up at him, asked quietly, "Am I doing this right?"

"I hear a fine-lookin' woman talkin' from the Spirit," Jake said. "Tellin' her version of the most beautiful story on earth. She don't need to ask me if it's right. Go ahead, sister. The man's waitin'."

She turned back to me. "Pop is a very serious, straight-laced type, but plays a pretty mean blues piano. The night he brought Jake home, I sat downstairs and listened to them jam. Jake was strumming along on this guitar my sister had tried to learn on years before, doing all these fancy moves and running all over that music."

"Just playin' a little twelve-bar blues, is all," Jake said.

"Those two played and talked until dawn. Every time the music stopped, Jake would start in about the salvation of Jesus Christ. He never looked my way, not one time. But I felt all the words were meant for me. I could tell my father didn't like what Jake had to say, but he was liking the music too much to quit. That was the first night I could ever remember sitting with Pop for more than fifteen minutes without us fighting."

"The Holy Spirit was talkin' to two hungry souls," Jake said. "Didn't neither one of them have time for anger."

"Jake just sat there, quoting Scriptures and making all the sense in the world. I felt as if somebody had tied me to the chair; I didn't have any strength to move. Then all of a sudden I was crying, sobbing so hard I couldn't breathe. It felt as if something inside of me was breaking up and washing away, like I was dying.

"It was what Jake had been waiting for. He came over to me and asked my father if he could take me into the kitchen. Pop was so shocked, I could barely see him through my tears but I still remember his expression. Here was the tough little girl that nothing could touch, not anger or slaps or the meanest words he could find, crying so hard she couldn't stand up straight. Jake took me back into the kitchen, sat me down, took my hands, and asked me if I'd like to pray with him."

Jake touched her hand gently. "The waiter's standin' over there givin' us the eye, must be a dozen people at the door waitin' for tables. Time to pay up and get out, we can carry this story home with us."

"I sure will," Amy said, sliding from the booth. "This is one story that's inscribed on my heart for the rest of my life."

That night, as I lay in my bed and listened to the dull whispers and vague sounds of a home I did not know in a city where I did not belong, I could not leave the story of Amy's coming to faith behind. I painted the darkness above my head with the visions that her words brought forth, and I felt such a bonding with her sorrow that I ached for her and for myself at the same time.

The scenes that danced before my eyes were from the life that had been my own. I ached for the little Mario who swooped from his parents' store armed with gifts for his newest friend, for the feel of my grandfather's beard, for the love of my stern and giving grandmother, for the mother who was no more than a shadow-encrusted memory. I recalled these scenes as Amy had, telling them to my own mind and heart, fashioning them into a story to be told to the stranger I had become.

Yet there was a difference between Amy's story and the one I told myself. Amy's story had an ending, while mine seemed to go nowhere at all. I lay sleepless in the dark of that unsettling night and wondered what gave them the strength to believe so strongly in something unseen.

.　.　.

Early Wednesday afternoon we set off for Darmstadt. Jake and Amy led the way in the tightly packed van. I rode in the second car with Mario and another full load of equipment. Somewhere between Mainz and Frankfurt I fell asleep. A couple of hours later Mario shook me awake in time to see us pull into Darmstadt. New buildings beside ancient structures told of wartime destruction, giving the town a confused look—half modern and faceless, half old and gracious. Every few moments a low-flying jet sliced the air above our heads and screamed away.

We followed the signs to the American military base and joined the line of cars inching toward the main gates. The sun was beginning to peek through the clouds, splashing brightly on wet streets. Just before the gates, Jake pulled the van over to one side and stopped. A man who looked vaguely familiar walked over; not until Mario had hopped from the car and embraced him did I recognize Danilo, Mario's older brother. I had not seen him since my fourteenth birthday.

Jake climbed from the van, accepted Danilo's embrace with stone-faced ease. Amy bounced down and smothered him. I looked across the street, saw soldiers eyeing us strangely and talking among themselves. Jake waited for a break in the line of cars, walked over, accepted an uncertain salute with a solemn nod.

"Anybody that big, they gotta either shoot or salute," Danilo said to me, and stuck out his hand. "How you been, Maestro?"

"Not bad. Good to see you again, Danilo."

"How long has it been? Seven, eight years?"

"More like eleven."

"Yeah? Who'd ever have thought that night that we'd be getting together now to spread the Word?" Danilo reached out, snagged his brother's neck with one elbow. "Or that my baby brother'd have come to see the light?"

Beyond us lines of two-story apartment buildings stood like sentries behind a tall wire mesh fence. The street before the gatehouse was lined with small grocery trucks, their backs and sides opened to reveal fruits and vegetables and meats and canned goods. Many of the men and women who stood chatting and shopping were dressed in camouflage uniforms.

Danilo led Mario and me across the street and up to the gatehouse. The broad entrance gate was marked by a flagpole, several large signs, barriers, and a dozen armed men. Six wore mottled green; the others had dark blue uniforms, polished black boots laced with white strings, and berets cocked jauntily down on one side. One of them came over, gave Danilo a mock salute.

"How's it goin', Dago?"

"Not bad, not bad," Danilo replied. "You remember my brother, Mario."

The man grinned, offered his hand. "Sure, the Dago Junior. Still making 'em roar, kid?"

"Every chance I get," Mario replied.

The man jerked a thumb toward the gatehouse, where Jake seemed barely contained by the cramped quarters. "Those guys sure take their time with your buddy. Guess they think he'd be better off in a cage."

"He's probably talking Bible and handing out tracts," Danilo replied. "This is Gianni, the guy I told you about. Gianni, this is Al Williams, a brother in the Lord."

Al offered his hand. "You really a genius like he says?"

"You gotta hear him play," Danilo said proudly.

"Maybe later. I got duty for another four hours. Steve told me to call so he could come down and walk you past the duty officer. That is, unless your buddy decides to eat the lieutenant. How much does that guy weigh, any idea?"

"Jake?" Danilo shrugged. "Fill a seven-foot sack with concrete and weigh it. That should give you an idea."

"Park around back and wait for Steve to come down. No terrorists in your van, right?"

"Not today."

"Be sure to come back out through this gate, okay?" The soldier waved at us. "Nice to meet you guys."

Jake returned to the van just as a young man in a starched green uniform and heavy black-framed glasses came walking over. He smiled at Danilo. "What's up, Dago?"

"Guys, this is Reverend Steve Hawkins," Danilo said. "He's the chaplain here and the on-base coordinator for the Navigators. Steve, I'd like you to meet the band Natural Light."

Amy was standing beside me; I asked her who they were, these Navigators. She replied, "They're a group of Christians who minister mostly on military bases and college campuses."

Steve Hawkins cupped a hand over his eyes, leaned back and stared up at Jake. "They bring you along in case we're invaded?"

"This is Jake Templer, the band leader," Danilo said. "He'll be leading the prayer group today."

"How you doin', Reverend?"

Steve drew back in mock horror and grinned. "If I give you my hand, do you promise to give it back?"

"This is Amy, the lead singer. And here's the new kid I was telling you about, Giovanni di Alta. Call him Gianni."

"Or Maestro—did I say that right? Dago's built you up to be another Segovia."

"Wait 'til you hear him."

"Yeah, well, I look forward to that." He turned back to Jake. "We decided to hold the prayer meeting in the barracks. It looks like there's gonna be quite a few guys there who don't have much more than a nodding acquaintance with the Lord, if that. We thought it would help them relax if it wasn't held in the church."

"Fine with us," Jake said. "The room big enough for everybody?"

"This barracks has a nice commons room, and we've reserved it for—" Steve lowered his head and glanced at his watch. I could see the skin under his short-cropped blond hair. "Five minutes ago. We better get a move on. Dago, you want to help me sign them in?"

The buildings on the central street were three-story squat white cinderblock squares. Through the trees I spotted a couple of newer structures, bigger and set with larger windows. Enormous signs on the carefully trimmed lawns in front of each building were all printed in English. Some of the longer buildings had big signs hung over the front doors decorated with shields and initials that I did not understand.

The mottled green uniforms—fatigues, Danilo called them—were everywhere. Even the trucks were painted in camouflage. We stopped at an intersection to let a squad of troops march by in front of us; many of the soldiers were women. Danilo pulled into a large parking lot that ran along the outer fence. As we headed for the front of the building, I asked Danilo about the nickname everyone was calling him.

Danilo laughed. "Dago's a bad name for a Latino in America. Only I didn't know that when I first started working here. Some of the guys in the kitchen used to call me that, and I liked the sound of it. So I started introducing myself as Dago Angeletti. When I found out what it meant, it was too late."

We paused to let a group of loud-voiced men in fatigues and

crew cuts enter the building before us. Most of them looked twice my size.

Steve led us up the stairs and through the entrance. He stopped in front of a bored-looking man seated behind a battered desk just inside the double doors.

"You remember Dago, Harry," Steve said.

"Yeah, sure."

"We're getting together with some of the guys in the back room. You oughtta come join us."

"Can't." The guy leaned back to reveal a massive belly. The chair creaked dangerously under his weight. "Captain's put me on extra duty all weekend."

"Tough," Danilo offered.

"You ain't lyin'."

"This is the group that's playing for us tonight. Okay if we all go on through?"

"Yeah, sure." The bored eyes glanced over us. "Dago says you guys are pretty hot."

"They are," Danilo said.

"Yeah, well, if the captain don't decide to hang me I'll try and stop by tonight."

Steve bent over the clipboard. "Okay if I just say Dago and friends?"

"Not on your life. Somebody put down Attila and Co. yesterday. That's what got me in this mess. Captain gave me nineteen kinds of grief. Write out all their names."

Steve laboriously signed us in, then led us across the hall, through a set of swinging doors, and into a room lined on one side with windows and on the other with vending machines. Folding metal chairs were formed into a circle in the center of the room. About thirty people wearing everything from jeans and sweatsuits to full uniforms watched us come in.

"Sorry we're late," Steve said briskly. "I'd like to introduce you to the band Natural Light."

We sat down and shook hands with the people nearest us, bowed our heads and let Steve lead us in an opening prayer. When we finished Jake cleared his throat, opened his Bible, and leaned over it for another moment of silence.

There was a special quality to the waiting, a sense of awe over Jake's size. I saw glances exchanged as he hunkered over his Bible, unconsciously flexing shoulders that seemed acres across. I studied the faces in the little circle.

I saw cropped hair and coiled strength and erect posture and watchful eyes. About half the group were women, and they too showed a toughness, an edge of hard-won confidence. I looked back at Jake and realized he was one of them. He could talk to them because he had been there, seen it, lived through it, survived.

"Always had a good feelin' about Paul," Jake rumbled. "Man was a soldier. We don't know how many Christians he murdered, or helped to imprison and torture, but we know he was after all he could find. Thought he was followin' the Law, living right 'cause he was fightin' the good fight."

Jake set one massive hand on his knee. "Known guys all my life who lost themselves in that lie. Yeah, figured all they had to do was follow orders. Men so blind with anger all they can do is hold it in 'til somebody tells 'em which way to point and shoot."

His eyes took on a look of ancient exhaustion. "We got all kinda ways to justify rage. We make it up all formal, with orders and books and officers who gotta take the responsibility for what we're gonna do. Paul did that, too. He was a Pharisee, a Roman citizen, man from the tribe of Benjamin. Had all the rank and all the right moves. Had every right reason to hate and hunt and kill.

"The Bible don't tell us what the man thought before he was saved. Don't have to, far as I'm concerned. Don't have to tell me what I've seen for myself." He leaned forward and raked the circle with his gaze. "I'll tell you one thing for sure, right now, right here. One thing Paul didn't have was hope.

"Rage and hope can't live in the same heart. You got rage, you've burned up every hope you ever had. Man's got a thousand reasons to hate. I'll give you just one for why you gotta get rid of it, only reason that's ever meant anything to me. Hope, found through faith in Christ. Man who's lived without it knows how much it means, how empty life is without it."

I glanced at the others in the room. A few sat with arms crossed, faces totally blank, masks of stone reflecting hearts that were not moved. Some held open Bibles and nodded their heads, recognizing something they'd already found out for themselves. A few others, hard faces touched by aching vulnerability, were locked in introspection. Their eyes cried out with unspoken pain.

"Paul was walkin' down the Damascus Road. It was hot, real hot. Hot and dry and dusty. Man was sweatin' hard and the dust was caked all over him. Probably dressed in battle fatigues, sandals and some kinda belt to hold his gear and keep things from swingin' around when he was fightin'. Shield maybe slung over one shoulder, maybe had a knife strapped to his shin. Lotta guys still do that, keep it around for the hand-to-hand. Big sword. I've always seen Paul as a big man. Strong. Carried a lotta steel. Liked the feel of that handle. Yeah. Probably walked with his sword hand wrapped around the hilt. Man's worn that sword so long it's a part of him. Keeps it oiled with a little leather cloth he's got stowed in his kit. Probably gotta a coupla dark stains on it, though. Awful hard to get old bloodstains off that steel.

"Then he sees this light in front of him. Light so strong it blinds the man. Light powerful enough to outshine a desert sun. I spent a lotta time thinkin' about that light. Wondered what it musta been like, strong enough to turn that old soldier's knees to jelly."

Jake looked over the group, asked, "Anybody know what Jesus said to the soldier?"

A voice replied from the circle, " 'Saul, Saul, why do you persecute me?' "

"Not persecute my men," Jake said. "Not kill my believers. No, the Lord says, persecute *me*. This was *personal*. The Lord lived in the hearts of His believers, and when one of them was hurt, so was the King."

He started turning pages, said, "How 'bout somebody readin' from Colossians, chapter one, verses twenty-five through twenty-seven."

After a moment another voice read,

> I have become its servant by the commission God gave me to present to you the word of God in its fullness—the mystery that has been kept hidden for ages and generations, but now is disclosed to the saints. To them God has chosen to make known among the gentiles the glorious riches of this mystery, which is Christ in you, the hope of glory.

"You gotta remember, now," Jake went on. "This was written by the old soldier himself. Cleansed by the light that blinded him back there on the Damascus Road. It came into that empty place deep inside him. Behind the veil of his hate. And it gave his soul an anchor of hope."

Jake leaned back in his chair, went on, "I was your basic angry young man. Born on a mean little farm in North Carolina, didn't hardly raise nothin' but a lotta dust. Learned to stay mad all the time. I was angry at who I was, how trapped the system kept me, what they'd done to my family, what they were gonna do to me if they could. Hated 'most everybody."

From her seat beside him, Amy slid a hand down his arm, let it rest on his thigh. The look she gave him brimmed with the bonding of shared pain.

"Older I got, the more I learned to control it, let it out when I needed it most. Found I could get what I wanted just holdin' all that hate inside, lookin' at somebody and lettin' them see they were playin' with fire, messin' with the *man*. Wouldn't listen to nobody, nossir. Too much chance they was just out to play with my head.

"Only reason I could stay in school was 'cause I was the football team's shinin' star; yeah, couldn't let no color or no hate get in the way of all those touchdowns. Coach took care of my teachers. That man had his hands full, I tell you. They either wanted to patronize me or dominate me, and I wasn't havin' none of that stuff. Naw. They'd start off with their little games, sayin' one thing with their mouths and another with their eyes, and I'd just let the hate show through. Stand up real close to those ofays, yeah, right up so's they gotta lift up their chins to see me, and bombard 'em with all the hate I had inside.

"Busted my knee that last year, fightin' after a ball game someplace in the middle of nowhere. That was the excuse they all been waitin' for. Didn't even give me time to clear out my locker. Came and told me in the hospital." Jake twisted his head over to one side, rounded out the words. "We don't see as how we can let you come back, Mr. Templer. 'Fraid you're just not a positive influence on the other students."

I searched his face for a trace of the anger he spoke of, found only the same focused power that was always in his eyes. It felt as though the room itself were holding its breath, listening with

an intensity that went far beyond any desire to hear just the
words.

"Joined up just as soon as my leg was straightened out.
Looked like the only way left for me to escape bein' broken by
the farm. Spent eleven years in our man's army. Made my sergeant's stripes the beginnin' of year two. Spent another year
hearin' 'nigger' every time a white man said 'sergeant.' Then I
met a man who showed me how to turn the burden over to Jesus.
Big white boy, thirty-year man, master sergeant from the
Bronx. Taught me it wasn't the strong man who held out on his
own. Greatest sign of courage a man could have was to give it
up, turn it over, trust in the Lord Jesus. Hard lesson, man, I
fought it like a tiger. Hard to fight the truth, though. Means
shuttin' your ears to the voice of your heart.

"It's like . . ." Jake raised two strong black hands in front
of his face, molded the air with a force that bunched the muscles
in his arms. "Man, it's like my whole life was just clay, didn't
make no sense at all long as I was tryin' to put it together
myself. Then I turned it over to the Lord, and what happens?
He takes the whole mess and makes it into something beautiful.
Gives it meanin'. Turns it from somethin' ugly and angry and
full of hate, and makes it a glory to His name. And the more I
learn to turn it over to Him, the more beautiful it becomes.

"All the trouble in this world, all the sorrow, seems to me a
Christian's the only person on earth who's got a reason to sing.
When Jesus saves you, man, He puts a song in your heart. You
don't need drugs or sex or anger to push you to sing. You're not
scrapin' the bottom of the barrel anymore. Naw, the barrel's so
full now you've *got* to sing. Sing praises to the name of the One
who saved us, taught us what hope and joy and peace really
mean."

He flipped the pages of his Bible, asked, "Somebody want to
read Colossians for us again? Chapter one, verses twenty-five
through twenty-seven."

Fingers searched the pages, then a voice read:

> "I have become its servant by the commission God
> gave me to present to you the word of God in its fullness—
> the mystery that has been kept hidden for ages and gen-
> erations, but is now disclosed to the saints. To them God
> has chosen to make known among the Gentiles the glo-

rious riches of this mystery, which is Christ in you, the hope of glory."

Jake let the silence hold long enough to look around the circle of faces. "The old soldier sure did change, didn't he? So full of hope he's got to share it with the world. Spends his life talkin' about love and light and the gift of hope. The riches of this mystery, how a man so bitter and full of hate can be cleansed. Totally cleansed, totally free. And then filled with the hope of glory."

He bowed his head, said, "Let us pray."

. . .

It bothered me that there was no backstage room for the musicians. It bothered me even more that the hall was almost empty.

Our own lights were set up to either side of a stage clearly designed for theatrical performances. Heavy velvet curtains were bound out of the way of our PA stack. The stage floor was polished wood. Up front were cueing boxes that we used as backdrops for our playback speakers. Mario had balanced the sound as best he could, considering the hall's high ceiling and stark concrete walls and wood floor. He would handle both lights and music mixing that night, since the military chapel's budget was too tight to afford a professional lighting job. Pipo predicted that Mario would be busier than a monkey trying to hold three bananas and a tree limb during a hurricane.

We were standing in the cramped hallway behind the stage, trying not to get in each other's way, waiting for the cue from Reverend Steve Hawkins to go onstage. There was no need to check the crowd. Scattered voices rang through the hall's empty spaces. The place sounded cavernous.

Amy came over. "It's not exactly what you're used to, is it, Gianni?"

"Not exactly," I agreed glumly.

"And it doesn't help for me to tell you that the numbers don't matter, so long as we're doing the Lord's work."

"Not a lot," I agreed.

"Leaving a beautiful club in a beautiful city to come and play with people you don't know. And then what happens? You get yourself stuck in this big drafty hall with only about thirty people out there wanting to hear your music."

I nodded and studied the floor at my feet. I did not want to tell Amy that this was only the latest in a series of problems I had faced since my return to Germany. The entire week had been full of painful solitude. Between practice sessions with Jake I had walked streets crowded with memories I had sought for years to bury. Returning to this cold, bleak land had only resurrected my loneliness and pain. I struggled with a constant desire to flee, yet a return to Como held the same emptiness that had driven me north. I stood in the back hallway and listened to snatches of conversation echo through the empty auditorium, and wondered if I would ever find answers. Or peace.

Amy asked, "Have you ever heard the story of Gideon, Gianni?"

The name was familiar, but I could not remember the story. I shook my head.

"He was called by the Lord to free his land from oppressors. He gathered this enormous army, and do you know what the Lord told him to do? Send all but a handful home, God said. I want to make sure that when victory comes, all the people of this nation will know that it comes through me, and not from some effort of their own."

Amy settled a gentle hand on my shoulder. "Maybe that's what he's doing here for you, Gianni. Maybe He has something special He wants to show you, and He doesn't want you to think afterward that it came because there was a great crowd or a beautiful hall. I can't tell you why it's like this. All I can say is that *everything* works to the good for those who love the Lord and seek to do His will."

I gazed into dark eyes full of loving concern. "I feel deep in my being that you are here for a special purpose," she said softly. "Trust in Him."

"I don't even know who He is," I replied.

She nodded, understanding. "Just give Him time, Gianni. Seek Him with all your heart and mind. He will answer you."

"You people sound so sure," I said. "We've got an empty hall out there and all you can do is praise God like He's done you some enormous favor."

"He has," Amy replied softly.

Reverend Hawkins appeared on the stairs leading up to the stage and gave Jake the high sign.

"Okay," Jake signaled to the band. "Gather 'round, everybody. Let's have a prayer and get to it."

Once again I allowed my hands to be grasped by these strangers, bowed my head, and listened to words spoken to a being whose existence I did not believe in. Afterward, as Jake climbed the stairs beside me, he said, "Heard you talking to the lady back there. You know what Christ said about tryin' to live alone? 'Without me you can do nothing.'"

My shoulders bounced in a humorless laugh. "I've been playing music all my life without your God."

Jake shook his head. "Wasn't talkin' about your music."

"So what are we talking about?"

"Your life," Jake replied. "Won't ever know the ultimate 'til you know Jesus Christ. Won't ever understand what it means to live with a purpose."

I entered the stage behind him. The applause was faint and scattered. Jake walked to the front of the stage, raised a mallet-sized fist and outstretched finger into the spotlight, called, "Praise the Lord!"

There was an awkward silence in reply. I felt thoroughly embarrassed for the man. Jake walked back to his position, as stone-faced as ever. He nodded to us. "Hit it hard."

Sameh clicked us off and we swung into our first song, a hard-rock form of White Heart's "He Is Returning." I looked around at the others, saw six bodies moving in time to the punching sound, spotted the makings of a grin on Jake's hard features, watched a heavy-lidded satisfaction show on Sameh's bobbing head, saw Pipo dance behind his congas. They appeared oblivious to the almost-empty hall.

Finishing the first song, we swung immediately into the second, "Long Ago" by Jon Gibson. It was a reggae funk, a strong beat that gave Pipo the chance to run wild. Karl sang lead, we all swung in behind him on the chorus. I spotted people gathering at the hall's two back entrances. Others appeared behind them, and began pushing the first ones forward. Steve Hawkins went over to shake hands and gesture them toward chairs. Those down front were dancing in their seats, smiling up at us. I found myself smiling back.

"Inside Out," a song by Bryan Duncan, was next. It was my turn to shine, drawing a tension of sound between Sameh, Pipo and me. Karl's voice reached out over our rolling funk, but could not dominate. He was a good singer, but not a drawing card. He lacked the magic a lead singer required. I thought I could sing better than he did, but I did not offer. I was not ready to sing the words that Karl was belting out.

The cheers were loud and long, especially considering the size of the crowd. As more people spilled through the open doors, Jake waved a hand in thanks, kept it up high, turned around and pulled the fist down for Sameh to count us out.

The next song was a surprise favorite of mine, "The Lord Came Through" by Russ Taff. It had a fifties rock-and-roll swing, and set the crowd moving. Hans was all over the stage with his horn, the quiet little man transformed to a bouncing bundle of energy. There had been no hint of this change in our practice sessions, yet there he was, spinning and dancing and bending backward on the high notes so far that his head nearly reached the floor. I looked toward Sameh. The placid mask was gone, replaced by an enormous grin. The sphinx played like one possessed.

"Fallen World" by David Mullen, the final song before Amy's entry, required my shifting to the steel-string hollow-body Ibanez. When I was strapped on and plugged in, I turned to Sameh. He counted with silent lips, then began hitting a fluid tattoo on the side of his snare. I replied with rapid licks to fit his timing. His eyes burned like black diamonds.

I felt myself caught up in something totally new, a magnetic force that drew me toward the others on the stage. I returned Sameh's grin, found myself laughing in reply to Pipo's whooping shout. The power was electric. Karl sang the words, help me live and help me love in a fallen world; they took on a meaning that was never there in the practice sessions. It was a truth, a cry, a plea that tugged at my heart. Something was happening up here. The open doors, the milling bodies, the sounds reverberating back toward us from the almost-empty hall; it all drew away into the distance. A joining was taking place, touching all of us. Help me live and help me love in a

---

¹David Mullen, "Fallen World," copyright © 1989, Word Music/ASCAP.

fallen world, Karl cried, and I wanted to cry too.

Pipo picked up bell and drumstick, raised them up over his head, and came dancing out from behind his congas. I switched over to the guitar's second pick-up and powered into my solo. Pipo weaved his way around Jake, stopped in front of me, dropped the stick and bell down to either side of his body, then swooped them up and over his head to beat the time in thunderclaps. On the chorus, we faced each other and sang into the same mike. Help me live and help me love in a fallen world. I swung back to Jake and Sameh, clipped the heavy rock beat as Karl sang out the final line, and finished.

I didn't know so few people could make so much noise.

Pipo flung a sweaty arm across my shoulders and yelled over the applause, "Think maybe we're gonna have to keep you."

"Gianni di Alta on lead guitar," Jake called, waited for the applause and the whistles to die down, then finished, "Gianni's playin' his first gig with us tonight. Nice to see the Lord do His work through such a talented man."

When the break arrived—we were only doing two sets that night—I was too charged up to stop. The hall had continued to fill throughout the set; at least a hundred people milled about. I had never seen so many easy smiles at a concert, so much laughter, so little cigarette smoke.

I walked over to where Jake was chatting softly with Amy and toweling his arms and face. "Would it be all right if I did a classical piece?"

A look passed between them; then Amy moved over and slid an arm around my waist. "Is my Giovanezzo still caught up in the Spirit?"

I disengaged. "Where did you hear that?"

"Giovanezzo? Why, did I say it wrong?"

"You said it perfect. I just haven't heard it in a long time, is all." Ten years, to be exact.

"Mario told me your grandmother used to call you that sometimes." Her look was soft, very concerned. "Did I say something wrong, Gianni?"

"No, it's fine. It just startled me."

"I won't use it again if you don't like it."

"It doesn't matter, I guess." It amazed me how natural it

had sounded in her mouth. "You have a very nice Italian accent."

She preened. "Think maybe I should try out for the opera?"

"Seems to me the lady's right where she's meant to be," Jake murmured.

"I think so too," I said. Giovanezzo. Little Giovanni.

"You want to do a solo, go ahead," Jake told me. "Like me to give you an intro?"

"No, that's all right." I smiled at Amy, said again, "It was nice what you said. Really."

She smiled back. "Knock 'em dead, Maestro."

I went over and asked Mario if he'd mind putting me through the PA. He gave me one of his knowing looks. All he said was, "You want a spot?"

"No, I'd rather play out in the open."

Mario nodded as though expecting nothing less. "It really makes a difference when the Spirit is there, doesn't it, Maestro?"

I shrugged. "I just want to play a little on the hollow-body."

"Sure, Maestro," Mario said, his gaze steady. "That's all it is."

I walked up on stage, picked up the Chet Atkins, plugged it in, raised it to the crowd as they greeted me with scattered applause. The conversation and laughter faltered, but picked up again when the lights remained on. I didn't mind at all. I brought Lothar's stool out from behind the keyboards, set it where I could use one of the playback speakers as a footstool, sat down, did a quick tuning, adjusted the volume, and began.

I decided to play a Spanish piece I had learned several years ago during one of my brief forays back into classical. It was a piece full of fire and fury, one that captured the wild spirit of flamenco. I did not even try to tame it. I allowed the music to run free, and played to an audience that was probably hearing classical guitar for the first time.

I caressed the strings as the piece moved through a passage of lost love and heavy hearts, then struck with all my might as the explosive Latino passion screamed out the frustration and hunger of unquenched desire. The power of those hotly strummed sequences roared from the PA and leaped back at me from the rear wall. I felt myself being carried away as the crescendo approached, playing faster and faster as the last runs shattered the air, striking the chords with a flurry of blows, smashing out their glorious sound like a madman.

The last note seemed to ring out into infinity. When the final breath of sound whispered away, I looked up and drank it in.

The hall was bedlam. People shouted, whistled, clapped, stamped their feet. Behind the mixing board Mario was waving two fists over his head and shouting something that I could not hear.

Jake appeared from the side entrance, walked up, shook my hand and patted me on the shoulder. He bent toward the nearest mike. "Giovanni di Alta, ladies and gentlemen."

The audience roared its approval. I smiled and waved, then turned to accept a hug from Amy. Jake strapped on his bass, returned to the mike, asked the crowd, "Y'all mind if we try a little jam?"

I thought Mario was going to leap over his boards.

Jake turned to me. "Wanna try a Judgment Day Blues?"

Amy laughed. "Perfect."

"Soft and slow," Jake said, strapping on his bass. "Just take it and play it any way you want, Gianni. We'll work around your lead."

I nodded and bent over my guitar. "Judgment Day Blues" was a song by Mark Farner,[2] straight R&B. I thought it over. "Let's keep to the original timing."

Jake nodded, asked, "Want me to start?"

"You and Amy," I said. "I'll work in around her voice."

He turned to her, asked, "That sound all right to you?"

Her eyes remained on me. "Whatever Giovanezzo wants is fine by me."

Jake began to hit a simple three-note melody, hammering the sound with his thumb, chopping off the sound with the side of his palm. It added a sharp beat to the music, both drumbeat and deep-throated melody. He repeated the notes, adding little runs, filling in the spaces. Amy pulled her mike free, flipped the cord out, did a little swaying dance in front of Jake, began to hum softly to his solo.

I played the opening chord, then slid my third finger up and ran through the singer's opening line, Well, there's a great day a'comin', then drifted down a minor run to blend in with Jake and hit the chord again.

"Sweet, Giovanezzo, oooh, sweet," Amy murmured, her mike at her side.

Lord gave me a message, have you heard the news, my guitar sang, and ran off into the distance for a moment, then drifted back for the chords. Amy began humming again. The crowd was totally silent.

Amy lilted through the first verse, singing light and clean, holding back on the strength, pouring honey over the words. Lord gave me a message, have you heard the news.

With the chorus she rose up to her full height, turned to the audience, lifted her chin and the mike together, and let it rip. Some folks don't even know they've got it, she cried. Naw, they don't even know. But they'll be cryin' when they find out they've got the Judgment Day Blues.

Jake pumped his upper body in time to the thumping bass. He was the anchor for both of us, holding us to earth and binding us together. His whole world was set around those simple chords. They told a story which Amy's words brought out and explained. The deep-throated music did not reach my mind; it went deeper, beyond the realm of words.

I hit a note once, twice, a third time, bouncing in time to the steady rhythm. Then I halved the time between notes for the space of one bar. A third halving. And on the fourth, when my notes were a rapid-fire staccato and my fingers a blur, I danced a tiny circle, up a half octave, back, down the same distance, holding the strings and plucking that first note. Another rapid reaching, and I soared a full two octaves in the space of a heartbeat. I slowed and climbed at a steady pace, starting from the low point of the first string, up and up, hovering around a point in harmony to Amy's voice, changing direction without conscious thought, riding the music like an eagle on unseen gusts of wind. Higher and higher I moved, trilling a song to the empty spaces between Jake's beat.

Pipo bounced up the side stairs to the stage, said as he passed me, "You think I'm gonna miss this, you're whacko."

"Count me in too," Sameh said, and climbed in behind his drums.

As the two of them powered in, I unstrapped the hollow-body and changed to the Stratocaster. I listened as Amy started lashing out the second verse. I held back, played the chords, heard her cry to the audience. It's a vast epidemic, she sang. People all over the world been tryin' to work it out. Pipo played the wooden block a while, then picked up the second stick and offered Sameh an alternate rhythm on the open snare—dancing all the while, grinning like an idiot. Sameh and Jake remained fixed in their expressions, their eyes reflecting an inner light.

At the end of the second chorus Amy pointed at me. "Raise it up, Gianni!"

I powered my way up a steep incline, pausing now and then to chord a reminder of just where we were. She raised her mike and soared alongside me. The solo verse ended, and there was no longer any need for either of us to touch earth. She went back to singing the words, but the tune was something of her own creation, something pulled from the very deepest part of her. I listened and followed—a run here, a swoop and dive there, playing to the path her spirit traveled.

When we stopped, we all stopped together. There was no need for words or signals. The song finished and rose into the breathless silence of the room. I stood there for the space of a heartbeat, marveling at what we had just done; then we all broke out laughing.

Amy wrapped her arms around me, drew me over so she could hold Jake and me both. Pipo raced around, pounded us on the back, laughed into my ear.

"We did it, baby!" he shouted. "We just broke loose and flew away."

CHAPTER
8

The sound of soft laughter drew me from bed the next morning. I slipped on a pair of trousers, stopped by the bathroom to wash my face, and entered the kitchen to find Amy wearing a simple cream-colored dress and Jake a coat and tie.

"Good morning, sleepyhead," Amy said. "You've got just enough time for a cup of coffee before we head out for church."

"Can't keep the Lord waitin'," Jake said. "Not on His day."

Although the morning still held a springtime chill, sunlight poured from a cloudless sky. We traveled through silent tree-lined streets, the other cars moving at a lazy Sunday-morning pace. Amy sat in the front seat beside Jake, stroking languid fingers along the back of his neck and humming brief snatches of songs.

There was no church anywhere in sight when we pulled into a crowded parking lot and stopped. Families moving toward a set of open glass doors turned, smiled, and waved in the van's direction.

"Where are we?"

"International School of Dusseldorf," Jake replied. "Least-ways, that's what it is during the week. Sundays it belongs to the Lord."

"It's for children from first grade right up through high school," Amy said. "Almost all the classes are in English."

"Big hit with the expense-account crowd," Jake said.

"They're 'bout the only ones who can afford it."

"Tuition is over fifteen thousand dollars a year," Amy said. "Executives with big multinational companies send their children here."

"Congregation's been looking for a permanent home," Jake said. "But 'til we find what we need, this'll do all right."

"A prayer group used to meet near here eight or nine years ago," Amy said. "They wrote the Southern Baptist Foreign Mission Board and asked them to send a missionary-preacher. A year or so later they sent over Reverend Bill DeLay from Atlanta, Georgia. Since he arrived, the church has grown from a dozen couples to over four hundred people."

We entered a noisy, unprepossessing hall, its walls constructed of unadorned concrete, the balcony railings and ceiling of steel siding. Light filtered in through a filthy skylight, augmented by rows of naked bulbs with metal shades. Creaky folding chairs were being scraped across the floor and set into place. I allowed Amy and Jake to lead me toward the front, then slid into the indicated seat, enormously embarrassed to be there. I could not help but compare this to the church in Como, or even the one in my little village. I felt embarrassed for them all, to be forced to endure such conditions and call it a church.

The altar was a small rickety table covered by a simple white cloth; it held an open Bible, an old wooden cross, and two unlit candles in wooden holders. The minister's podium was a battered music stand with a matchbook jammed under one leg to keep it level. Behind the minister's place rose a makeshift stage; the stage-curtains were strips of old sheets sewn together with multicolored thread, drawn back and held open with masking tape. The backdrop was a crude painting, obviously done by very young children, of a man on a horse.

It was a poor excuse for a church. Yet as I looked around the room, I was struck by the simple joy on most people's faces. They did not seem to notice the surroundings at all.

The congregation was a rainbow of races. Directly in front of me sat three blacks in African garb. Amy stood and greeted an incoming family with a bow and a few words in Japanese; their joy at her words was a pleasure to behold. I rose at Jake's gesture to shake hands with a diminutive group of young people from the Philippines. I caught words in German and several languages I had never heard before. And all around me floated the drawling laughter of Americans.

The minister appeared, a distinguished bearded man dressed in a conservative suit and gold-rimmed glasses. I watched him stop to shake hands and nod; he seemed to know everyone by first name.

In his opening remarks the minister took time to greet many people specifically—a woman back after a long illness; a family returned from three months in America; a man whose wife had just given birth to their second child; a visitor back for a third time.

Then he turned to Jake and asked him to introduce his guest. At Amy's urging I rose with the towering giant, heard him say, "Like to introduce our new lead guitarist, Giovanni di Alta. Gianni's from Como, that's a city in northern Italy. He's one of the most talented musicians I've ever heard."

"Amen," intoned Amy.

"We're certainly happy to have you with us today, Gianni," the minister told me. "We hope this will be the first of many worship services you share with us."

I mumbled my thanks and sat down, more nervous than I had been since my first performance in front of Fraulein Rohr's class.

The minister then turned the service over to a young blond woman who approached the battered upright piano set to one side of the stage. She greeted the congregation and invited them to stand and join in worshiping the Lord in song. I watched as with the first lyrics a few people raised their hands and began clapping in time to the music. I kept my hands by my sides, listened to the joyful noise, watched Amy's long fingers make little dancing circles in the air between claps, felt enormously out of place.

When the congregation was again seated the minister returned to the podium and invited everyone to join him in prayer. I listened as he began to name people and their specific needs. This family has a daughter who was rushed to the hospital last night and the doctors still cannot explain why she is having trouble with her breathing, except to say that she has had an allergic reaction. Please pray for them. This man's wife left last week for America after receiving word that her sister had delivered triplets. Please pray for them. This woman has been laid off, and is busy looking for work. Please pray for her. This young man, a friend to many of us, is a political refugee from Ghana; he has just received a telegram from his mother saying that his brother has died. No further information was given, he cannot get a telephone line through to his home town, and he cannot return. Please pray for him and his family. Pray for them. Pray.

When the prayer was finished he asked people to open their Bibles to Psalm 40, then waited until the pages stopped rustling. Amy swiveled around so that I could read with her. Someone from the congregation approached the podium and began reading the passage. I watched him, watched the others following along in their own Bibles. Some took out pens and marked the passage. I turned back to the Bible that Amy was holding out for me, scanned the page, and froze.

Words on the opposite page reached out and held me fast. From the thirty-eighth psalm, I read:

> I am like a deaf man who cannot hear,
> Like a mute, who cannot open his mouth;
> I have become like a man who does not hear,
> Whose mouth can offer no reply. . . .
> For I am about to fall,
> And my pain is ever with me.
> I confess my iniquity;
> I am troubled by my sin. . . .
> O Lord, do not forsake me;
> Be not far from me, O my God.
> Come quickly to help me,
> O Lord my Savior.

I do not know how long my eyes were fixed on the page. Again and again I read the words, felt their power echo deep within me. My pain is ever with me. I fight and struggle to hold on to the joy of my music, but I need the push of drugs to find that surging inspiration, that force to lift me above the pains and memories that weigh me down. I am like a mute who cannot open his mouth.

I felt a gentle hand on my back and lifted my head to find Amy looking at me with concern. She mouthed the words, are you all right? I nodded, turned my head toward the front, felt the words continue to ring in my head. My pain is ever with me.

"The fortieth psalm is David's public testimony," the minister was explaining. " 'I've got something to share with you,' he is saying. 'I've got some good news. The Lord has treated me like a loving father would treat his child. He has succored me, and I have begun to heal. He has lifted me from my pain and sorrow and darkness.' "

Hastily I turned back to the Bible, located Psalm 40, and read:

> I waited patiently for the Lord;
> He turned to me and heard my cry.
> He lifted me out of the slimy pit,
> Out of the mud and mire;
> He set my feet on a rock
> And gave me a firm place to stand.
> He put a new song in my mouth,
> A hymn of praise to our God.
> Many will see and fear
> And put their trust in the Lord.

"What better way is there to describe our troubles than a slimy pit?" The minister paused as the congregation murmured agreement, then went on. "Trouble is like quicksand. Once we get in, it is almost impossible to get out. The harder we struggle, the deeper we sink.

"In the midst of depression, what happens to us? We lose the ability to laugh. To sing. To hope. The empty void within us reaches out with dark eager hands and envelopes our lives. We become trapped in the dark pit of hopelessness, and we feel there is no chance of our ever escaping."

I felt as if I were listening to a concerned friend who was speaking directly to me. There was no longer any awareness of the surroundings, of the other people, of anything but this message. There was no room in me for anything else.

"Yet not only did the Lord rescue David; He lifted David from the pit of his despair and placed him upon a rock, gave him a firm foundation upon which to stand and live his life. And what is more, God put a song in David's heart. A *new* song.

And what kind of song is it? What does the psalm tell us?

"First, it is a song of *deliverance*. It describes how God has rescued him. He brought David out of the horrible turmoil of his earlier life. There is a deliverer, David is telling us. And what He did for David He will do for us if only we will let Him.

"Second, it is a song of *security*. 'He placed my feet upon a rock. He established my life upon a firm foundation.' The Lord can handle life's troubles, and so can we, once we learn to keep our eyes upon Him, to seek His guidance in all things.

"Third, it is a song of *gratitude*. The remainder of this psalm speaks of how grateful David is to the Lord for His salvation.

"Isn't it something, how this wealthy society of ours is so ungrateful for what it has? Life is reduced to a constant hunt after more of the same—more goods, a better home, nicer clothes, more money; never taking time to give thanks for what we already have. It strikes me as both funny and tragic, how people never seem to realize that they are so ungrateful because what they have has no true value."

He adjusted his glasses and looked down at his podium. "Fourth, this is a song of *experience*. We must personally experience what the Lord can do in our lives in order to understand His divine majesty. No one can put this power into words, no one can live this lesson for us. We must surrender to His guidance in order to understand. All that anyone else can do is follow David's example and witness. Look at the lives the Lord has changed; hear the song; be filled with awe and respect; put your trust in God Almighty."

The minister paused and looked out over the group assembled in the dingy auditorium. "What kind of song are you singing?" he asked. "Everyone sings in one way or another; all of us give a testimony to others through how we lead our lives. The question is, what message do you give to others? What do you hold dearest in your own heart? What song does the world hear through the witnessing of your life?"

His voice carried the strength of utter certainty as he said, "It is only when you have turned it over to the Lord and asked Him for a cleansing of sin and a directing of your footsteps that you will know a true and lasting peace. It is only when you know His peace that you can sing as David has, sing of new joy and hope."

. . .

That evening I went over to Mario's for dinner. His apartment was one fair-sized room with a tiny bathroom and a kitchen too small for two people to stand in together. Pipo sat on the sofa bed and I in one of the canvas-backed chairs and listened to Mario sing snatches of songs in three languages as he prepared dinner.

"Mario took me for a walk this afternoon down that shopping street, you know, the fancy one, what's it called?"

"Koenigsallee," Mario called from the kitchen. "Yeah, that's some street. Every idol money can buy."

"They got this window, nothing in it but watches," Pipo said. "One of 'em, a Rolex I think it was, cost fourteen thousand dollars. You hear what I'm saying? Man, if I could afford a fourteen thousand dollar watch, I could afford to be late."

I asked, "You live in Cologne, right?"

"Used to, yeah. My girlfriend's with a mission project down there. We're getting married in three months and we're gonna live up here. Things are looking good for the band. Time to find a place closer to the heat."

"Pipo's lived all over the place," Mario's voice drifted unseen from the kitchen. "If he doesn't pick up and find another home every two or three months, he starts getting antsy."

"I lived in L.A. for a while before I met the Lord," Pipo said. "Los Angeles, yeah, that's some city."

"Pipo was one of the best-known percussionists on the West Coast," Mario said, appearing in the doorway, looking at his friend with quiet pride. "Then the Lord reached down and called him to His service."

"More like, Jesus reached down into the gutter and fished me out," Pipo said. "I tell you, man, I took so much acid in that place I thought Picasso was a photographer."

"Pipo decided it was time to leave a few bad habits behind," Mario said, winking at me.

"I was living on mushroom omelets and girls who specialized in permanent damage," Pipo said. "I was a dedicated disciple of the John Lennon school, you know? Artistically talented pessimists. I had this big poster over my bed, this nasty-looking mama in fish-net stockings and a see-through outfit.

Underneath, it said, 'So what do I get for being a good little girl?' Real healthy California attitude."

Mario came back in with an enormous bowl of salad and set it down in the middle of his glass-and-chrome table. "Pull up a chair, Pipo; soup's on."

Pipo stood, stretched, did a boneless slide into the chair opposite mine. "I've done just about everything you'd expect a pop musician to do. Stuffed enough powder up my nose to buy Colombia, went through traveling companions like there was a revolving door beside my bed. All the time, man, I kept up this major fairy tale in my head. You know how it is, right? If all you do is smoke weed, you keep telling yourself how much better you are than the guy who's heavy on pills. You get into acid, you got the guys sticking needles in their veins to look down on. And all the time, you keep telling yourself how you got everything under control. What a joke."

Mario came in and set down steaming plates piled high with pasta. He sat down and asked Pipo for the blessing.

Pipo bent over his plate and said, "Father, thanks for not turning my brain to burned toast. Amen."

Mario watched him a moment. "That's it?"

"Sounded pretty profound to me, man."

Mario lowered his head again. "Heavenly Father, we are truly grateful for this time of sharing and friendship. Please bless this food to our bodies, and all our many gifts to the doing of your blessed will. In Christ's holy name, amen."

Pipo raised his head. "You think maybe next time I should bring a script?"

"You gotta learn to read before it'd do any good," Mario said, and to me, "Buon appetito, Maestro."

We ate in the companionable silence of friends who did not need unnecessary conversation. The pasta was great. Mario beamed over our compliments, confessed that it came from a little Italian grocery around the corner.

"Like the ones your parents used to have?" I asked, remembering.

"Maestro, the first time I went in there, I felt like I was coming home. Say, that reminds me. Mama told me to tell you hello."

"How are they?"

"They finally bought their little place down in the Piemonte countryside, but I think they're about ready to die of boredom. Papa never had the chance to learn how to slow down. They can't get over how both their boys have grown up into religious derelicts either. That's Papa's description. Mama calls us her untamed monks."

He stood, gathered plates, told me to stay where I was. I felt a sudden urge to tell them about the experience in church that morning, but could not bring myself to talk about it. Instead I asked Pipo how he had made the big change.

"Coupla big things, lotta little ones. I got involved on this album with some real wild men, spent six months going a thousand miles an hour inside. You gotta understand, beat was king for me, the only god I knew. Man, there wasn't nothing that'd make me happier than playing hot tunes. Nothing. I used to get outta ten, twelve hours in the studio, go down to a place in L.A. called Westwood. Real Yuppie heaven, man. Lotsa little ritzy restaurants, no place to park, all these really cute girlies with their expense-account guys walking around. So I'd show up after twelve hours in the studio, still in my tank top and cutoffs, smelling like a bear fresh outta hibernation. A bunch of Rastafarians used to get down there about sunset, smoke a little reefer, play some heavy beats on their congas. I was just about crazy enough to fit in."

Mario called from the kitchen, "He asked you how you got saved."

"Yeah, yeah, I was just getting to that. Anyway, so we got the album finished, and the next day I woke up and for the life of me could not remember who this chick was in bed with me. Or where she'd come from. Or how I'd gotten there. So I went into the kitchen, and started thinking it over, and you know what? Man, I'd been stoned for thirty solid weeks. I don't mean once in a while for thirty weeks, no way. Stoned solid. Pills or grass or booze or something. Dropped acid two, sometimes three times a week. And all the time, I kept telling myself, this is cool, yeah, I can handle it. I'm in total control.

"So I drove down to the beach, and just walked up and down all day long. First time in six months I wasn't doing something. And all of a sudden I found myself just crying out at the sky, 'Help me, God. You gotta get me outta this mess, 'cause I'll never be able to do it myself.' "

Pipo always gave off an air of barely controlled energy. Even when he was relaxed into his rag-doll state, he somehow appeared to be in motion. When he talked, he went into a repertoire of hand and wrist gestures. A quick scratch on the arm, an idle fingering of the bandages around three fingers on each hand, a brief hunching of his shoulder muscles, a rapid-fire signalling to stress a point—all swiftly brought back under control, cut off before they really started. Even the simple movements were enough to show the energy that made him such a powerful percussionist.

"I didn't know who Jesus was, not then. And I was too weak to stick with it, so I just kept falling. I was still having that love affair with the gutter. But I started feeling this change. There wasn't anything I could do for myself, no way. I think even then I knew it was a gift from someone outside myself. I started staying straight longer and longer between highs. Started preferring my own company more. Started avoiding the man-eaters in high heels.

"Then when I fell, you know, got high and started playing the little games with the chicks that hung out around the studios, it was hard to ignore that little voice inside my head. And coming down just kept getting worse. Man, I'd feel so *empty*. Even when I was high that emptiness'd stay right there inside me. The drugs didn't make it go away, not ever. They just kind of painted over it for a while. I started dreading those next mornings even before I got high.

"So I started praying, once in a while at first, then every day, then like every time I thought of it. I discovered that the days were a lot better when I prayed, and I was stronger, and I could resist temptation a little better.

"By then I was looking for my own answers. Started reading the Bible, found some passages that really spoke to my heart. The first one was from Joshua, chapter twenty-four, verse fifteen: 'Choose this day whom you will serve.' I wrote it up in big letters and stuck it where that girl used to be, over my bed. By that time I'd just about decided this grace was the best thing going, and I just wasn't strong enough to stay around L.A. and keep from falling again. I was beginning to see a lot more clearly what my idols were, and I wanted to put as much distance between them and me as I could. So I went to Europe.

Worked in London for a while, then got this offer for a studio gig in Germany, and met our man Mario here. He introduced me to Jake, and Jake told me about Christian music. Blew me away, man. Before that, I thought all there was to Christian music was hymns and funeral marches."

Mario came in carrying two cups of freshly brewed espresso, set them down, patted me on the shoulder, and left the room without speaking. I watched him return to the kitchen, waited until I heard the clatter of dishes before saying to Pipo, "I think I can understand what you're driving at. But I feel like I've got to know more before I do anything."

"Hey, you know what, this is really great." Pipo stretched out, set both feet on the sofa, sprawled as only he could do. "I mean, it's nice you trust me enough to talk like this. The problem is, if I say something there's a chance you're gonna think I'm pushing. And I don't want that."

I tried to ape his relaxed posture but could not get rid of the tension. "Go ahead and push."

"So you can push back, right?" Pipo grinned. "What is it Mario calls you, that name in Italian?"

"Maestro."

"I like it. Maestro. Yeah, the more I hear you play the better it fits. Maestro, there's never any way that you're gonna know Jesus until you ask Him into your life. This is one lesson you'll never find in a book or through talking to others. Long as you play that game, all you're doing is holding Him out. Deep down inside you know it, too. You feel that emptiness, that hunger down in your gut, so you stick around and play the game, talking to me and Amy and listening to Jake in the prayer group, right? Always the outsider. You keep telling yourself you're still learning, gotta know more before you can take the big step. That's a lotta baloney, Maestro."

"I'm just not ready yet," I protested.

"Tell me another one. What, you need a little more emptiness and futility in your life, is that it? Gotta walk a little farther down that dark path? Gianni, the Bible says that *now* is the day of salvation. Says you gotta take it when it's offered, when the Lord is there for you to seek."

"You guys talk about the Bible like it was some kind of all-powerful answer for everything. I've looked at it a couple of times. All that blood and killing and stuff. It's just a book."

"That's right, it is. And it'll stay just a book as long as you're on the outside looking in. That's how it is, Gianni. You can't have it both ways. If you want to see the Lord's wisdom in His work, you gotta ask Him to show it to you himself. God works from the inside out. The biggest changes that He brings to your life are the ones down deep, where only you and He can ever find them."

Out of the corner of my eye I caught sight of Mario leaning against the doorjamb, watching us in utter stillness. I asked in Italian, "You want to come over and take a couple of slugs at me too?"

He pushed himself erect, walked over, said in English, "Sounds to me like Pipo's doing just fine, Maestro."

Pipo slithered upright to make room for Mario. His eyes didn't leave my face. "You think maybe you'd like to pray with us, Gianni?"

"I don't know what to say." It sounded feeble even to me. "I don't even know if God exists."

"Only way you'll ever know is if you let God show you," Mario said. "And you've got to let Him in for that to happen."

"Why don't you just tell Him that?" Pipo suggested easily. "Just say what you did to me. If God's there, He'll let you know."

" 'Behold,' " Mario said quietly, " 'I stand at the door and knock: If any man hear my voice, and open the door, I will come in to him, and will sup with him, and he with me.' "

"What do you say, Gianni?" Pipo's eyes seemed alight with their own fire.

I did not know what to say, so I just nodded. All right.

Pipo slid his feet to the floor, bowed over, waited as Mario folded his hands and lowered his head. Pipo said, "I'll just start; then you say whatever comes to your mind and heart.

"Oh, Lord of all the universe, we thank you for this gift of your Son, Jesus Christ. We were lost and wandering in darkness, and you sent your Son to lead us home. It's such a miracle, Father. Times like this, I can hardly believe how lucky I am to know your love. I'd just like to say thank you, God. Thank you for caring about somebody like me.

"There's another brother here with us today, Lord. He's a good man, and he's looking as hard as he knows how. We pray that your Spirit will fill him, Lord. Show him that you truly are the All in All, the one true light leading us home. Bless Gianni with your presence in his life. Call him by name, Father."

The old pressure returned, pushing with a strength that brought a lump to my throat. I opened my mouth, searched for words, found nothing. Then I heard it. I opened my eyes, saw Mario sitting there on the sofa, his head bowed, the scar over his eye a dark shadow, his black hair oiled and bound back tightly into the silver clasp, tears streaming down his face. I sat and fought down the surging power in my chest and watched him cry quietly.

Reluctantly I bowed my head again, closed my eyes, clenched one hand with the other and fought for control. I squeezed my eyelids tightly shut, searched for words.

"I don't know if you exist," I said, my voice shaking from the effort. "I don't know who I'm praying to. But if you're really there, then I want to know you. I know I've made mistakes, and a lot of the time I don't even know what I want. So if you're there, then I need to know you."

"In Christ's holy name we pray," Pipo whispered. "Amen."

CHAPTER
9

That night the dream came. Vague forms whispered through the fog of my slumber. I awoke several hours later, bathed in sweat and breathing hard. I climbed out of bed, changed my damp T-shirt and shorts, tried to recall what the dream had been about. It scared me, that dream, yet a curtain had fallen inside my mind, and now I could not remember what I had seen.

I walked through the quiet, sunlit apartment to the bathroom. On the way back to my bedroom I stopped outside Jake and Amy's bedroom door. I stood there a moment, wondering what gave them such strength and sureness. I had prayed as they wanted, yet I felt nothing. Was I just fooling myself? Did they really have something given to them from a higher power? Or were they simply stronger than I, and had found within themselves the will to overcome their problems?

At practice the next day, I was relieved that no one made a fuss about my having prayed. Amy gave me a very long hug. Jake laid a heavy hand on my shoulder and said, be sure and keep the flame alive.

There were three concerts over the next seven days. Two were at military bases near Mainz and Nurnberg, and before each there was a prayer meeting—one led by Jake, the other by Amy. Natural Light had performed at both bases before, and the crowds were very large, very noisy. Jake began each performance with an outstretched forefinger and the words, Praise the Lord.

The third concert was in Hagen, a city to the north of Dusseldorf, where we would be the lead-in band for several visiting Christian acts from America. It had the others very excited, as the extra publicity would be useful. Much time was spent in carefully selecting songs that would fit the following acts in tone and power, yet not originate from the artists with whom we would perform.

Each night I had the dream again. Each time I awoke to the sound of my hammering heart, my bedclothes damp and clammy. I could not remember the dream. I returned to sleep with the nagging thought that there was something I was neglecting to do.

I watched those performances from a very great distance, observing the others, wondering if they truly had something to offer me, asking myself over and over if I really belonged.

Amy noticed my silence, and after our part of the Hagen concert, approached me in the hall's parking lot and asked if everything was all right. I hesitated for a moment, drawn by her concern to share how troubled I was by my doubts. But something held me back, something that I was unable to put my finger on. The answer was tied to my dreams, and the prospect of confronting those vague shadows terrified me.

I searched for something else to say, came up with, "You're a lot more talented than some of these others here tonight."

She did not deny it. "But it's their music, Gianni, their songs. That's what separates the men from the boys. Jake's been writing some lyrics, but he needs to have somebody else help him with the songs themselves."

"That's what you are hoping I'll do, isn't it?" It seemed so simple now, almost as though this was what I had been expecting to hear.

"Only if you feel the Lord leading you in that direction," she replied.

"It's incredible how you people could be so patient," I said. "You make it sound like you could wait a thousand years."

"As long as we need to," she said. "As long as it takes."

"My grandmother could do that," I said, remembering. "There always was this part of her that nothing could touch.

Not bad news or sickness or problems—nothing."

"She sounds like a wonderful woman, Gianni."

"She was," I said. "She would have liked you."

"What a nice thing to say." She graced me with a smile. "Yes, we hoped you would help us compose our own songs. We all knew you had the talent for it that very first practice. Jake and I were sure of it after we first heard you in Como. Mario has been telling us that all along, but Jake was right when he said that it can't happen until you accept the Lord Jesus into your life."

I started walking across the darkened lot. "I've prayed."

"Yes, you have, and it is a wonderful start," she agreed. "Truly a great beginning, Gianni."

Amy walked up close beside me, grasped my arm, led me over to the lone streetlight marking the parking lot entrance. "I have something here that might help you."

She reached into her purse, brought out a pocket Bible, searched the pages, handed it over. "This is from the Book of Hebrews, Gianni. Read here, chapter eleven, verse six."

I looked where her finger was pointed, though it still made me uncomfortable to pick up the Book. I read, " 'And without faith it is impossible to please God, because anyone who comes to him must believe that he exists and that he rewards those who earnestly seek him.' "

"It's not enough to just say the words," she told me. "It's not enough just to sit around and wait for Him to give you the gift of salvation. You've got to believe."

I liked her too much to put her off with lies. "I don't see how I'm supposed to believe in something I can't see. Or should I just believe because if I don't I'm doomed?"

Amy shook her head. "No, Gianni. If you make a decision based on fear, you're moving away from God."

"Then how?"

"I pray that God will show himself to you in a way that will leave no doubt in your mind or heart of His existence." Her eyes were luminous in the half-light, her face serious, her voice soft. "But you must be ready to listen to His voice, Gianni, in whatever way He chooses to speak to you. You have to *want* to hear Him. The Bible is full of criticism for people who refuse to heed God's call. Don't let that happen to you, please. Study the Bible whenever you can. Pray that God will speak to you, and pray that you will be able to hear His voice. And I will pray for you with all my heart."

Two days later we had a return performance in Darmstadt. I traveled down in the car with Sameh, Hans, and Karl. They remained perpetually silent, at peace with their own lack of words. In the midst of my own internal struggles I found their presence comforting. Being around the others would have required making conversation. There was nothing for me to say at the moment, nothing that I knew how to put into words.

I had continued trying to pray, standing in the circles before each practice and performance, listening to the peaceful fervor in their voices, yearning for their strength, feeling defeated by my own doubts. Amy's words echoed in my mind and heart, *have faith*. I longed for the peace their faith brought, hungered for something to fill the emptiness, yet did not know where or how to search. My prayers echoed the emptiness of my heart. And the dreams returned every night. I awoke each morning feeling unrested and disturbed, haunted by half-seen forms that frightened me too much to seek out and identify.

That trip, sharing the peaceful silence with those three, was welcome relief. I knew them only through what Mario had told me, for they rarely spoke about themselves. Sameh was a Coptic Christian from Alexandria, Egypt. His father and mother had emigrated to Dusseldorf when Sameh was still a baby. He had come to the realization at the ripe old age of sixteen that his family's faith was all show and no substance, and went looking for his own answers. He found them in an evangelical organization in the heart of Dusseldorf known as *Das Jesus Haus*. When music was shown to be his calling, he played for several years in the house's gospel band, and eventually did several albums and television shows with them. That was where Jake found him.

Karl worked with severely handicapped children when not busy with the band. Mario said he had visited the home once and could not bring himself to go again. The children were all orphans, all suffering from physical or mental handicaps, all unable to look after themselves, all abandoned by their families. And Karl loved them. Mario told me that he really believed Karl did not see their twisted little bodies and mishapen heads at all. His love was too great. It blinded him to all but their need for affection, and he gave with a fullness that shone from his eyes like the sun.

Hans was the quietest of them all, a silent ghost who rarely raised his eyes to mine except to smile in greeting. He was a divinity student in his final year at the Protestant seminary near Cologne. Once that week I asked him why he was studying to be a minister when he clearly didn't like to talk. Hans raised the flute he had been polishing, said, this and my horn are all the voice I need.

There were a lot of smiles this time in Darmstadt, as well as a warm greeting from the Reverend Steve Hawkins and a prayer group so large a second circle formed around the room's perimeter. Danilo, Mario's brother, was there. Three of his friends who worked with the Navigators at other bases were up with vans full of people. They were expecting a capacity crowd, we were told over and over during the sound check. They were clearly excited to have us back.

We made a McDonald's run after the sound check. As we entered, Pipo spotted an American magazine on an empty table and brightened visibly. He spread his food out in a semicircle around the magazine—two quarter-pounders, two orders of french fries, a large Coke, and a large coffee—then proceeded to peel off the extra bread and squeeze the two hamburgers together, letting the juice run down over his fries.

"That is just about the sickest thing I have ever seen," Mario declared.

"What you've got here are a musician's two essential food groups," Pipo said, not looking up from his magazine. "Grease and caffeine."

Amy was sitting beside him. She was not eating. She lifted the magazine to reveal the Cosmopolitan logo, gave a humorless laugh. "That ol' Cosmo mentality," Amy said. "It doesn't matter what you do, just so long as you look good doing it."

"This is about the silliest stuff I've ever seen," Pipo agreed.

"And money," Amy said. "That's one thing a Cosmo girl can't *ever* get enough of. You can never be too thin or too rich."

"You know what?" Pipo tossed the magazine aside. "I think

I could live without wasting time on this stuff ever again."

"Don't forget the Cosmo Bedside Astrologer," Amy went on. "It's the only way on earth a girl is gonna know her sexual compatibility with all those men she's picking up. Girl needs all the help she can get."

There was a bitter cast to Amy's face, a sharp edge to her voice that I had never heard before. I looked around the table and saw that the others had stopped eating and were watching her closely.

"Half the pop-psychology articles are on how to find Mister Right, and the other half are how to get rid of Mister Wrong." Her eyes focused on no one at the table; her voice was metallic. "A lot about beauty, a lot about cheating on your man. And every other issue, they give you this Cosmo make-over. The poor little girl is called a 'mouseburger' before they start on her, and a 'vixen' when they finish. Lots of cosmetics, dangly earrings, over-fluffed hair. Gives all those girls who didn't get blessed with an all-star face and body a ray of hope."

"Seems to me like maybe I've met a couple of those Cosmo girls somewhere along the way," Pipo said quietly.

"Me too," Mario agreed.

"Shallow, shallow, shallow," Amy said. She was clearly angry and talking loud enough to attract attention from other tables. "Feeding on a lot of girls' weakest point, their insecurity. Teaching them that it's okay to be loose, to be immoral, to have nothing to live for except a nice dress and pretty make-up and lots of money and a good-looking man in their bed."

There was an awkward pause; then Pipo asked if she was all right.

"Not at all." She slid from her seat, refusing to meet anyone's eyes. "I'll see you back at the van."

Jake watched her go, did not make any move to follow. "That reverend fellow who met us at the gate mentioned that he'd met Amy's dad the other night," he said, his eyes on the doors. "Thought it right and proper to invite the man to join us for the show. Gonna need a special prayer tonight for Amy; she's got a special challenge in front of her."

Amy was shy during the first couple of songs, her voice very quiet. She stood front and center on the stage, a white double-breasted jacket buttoned up over her dress, her fingers laced together in front of her jacket. The only time she touched the mike was to adjust it.

After the second song Pipo started to say something to her, but Jake frowned and shook his head. Jake looked at Amy, said, "Doin' just fine, sister."

"Could I have something to drink?" She refused to look at anyone directly, raised her head only to shift the hair from her face. It was the only time I had seen her not respond to the audience's applause with a smile.

Jake was all concern. "Sure you can. What you want?"

She looked at him, her eyes wide as saucers. "Am I gonna mess it up, Jake?"

"Naw, naw, baby, everything's gonna be just fine." Jake almost crooned the words. "Gotta give yourself time to get used to it, that's all."

"We're all praying for you," Pipo called.

"That's right," Hans said, his voice so soft I barely heard it.

"Just let the Holy Spirit fill you," Jake said. "Now what you wanna drink?"

"I don't know. Coke, I guess."

Pipo was out from behind the congas before Jake could turn his way. In an instant he was back up the backstage stairs, cup in hand. "Here you go, Amy."

"Thanks." She avoided his eyes.

"You're doing just great. No, really. I think this soft start-up really has class."

She gave Jake a doubtful glance; he nodded his agreement. "Time to be movin' on. The people are waitin'."

I don't know what the audience thought of our interlude. The seats stretched back into the shadows caused by our stage lights; all four hundred tickets had sold out a week ago. I searched as far back into the well-behaved, smiling, chatting crowd as the lights permitted. There were numerous black faces, but none which struck me as Amy's father.

The third song was "The Wonder of Your World" by Rich Mullins. I played the Ibanez hollow-body for it, strumming with a feather-light pick. I thought I heard some of the old Amy showing through. Jake heard it too. He watched her with a look of pure relief. A few of the fans in the front-row began to clap along in time to the beat.

At the song's end Amy waved to the sustained applause, turned and walked back to us. She patted her face with the towel, took a long drink, asked, "Was that all right?"

"You're doin' fine, baby," Jake told her. "Just fine."

"Okay." She set down her drink and said to no one in particular, "Time to turn up the heat."

As she walked back out to the microphone Amy flipped up the collar of her jacket, not bothering to adjust her dishevelled hair. She pulled her sleeves up above her elbows, raising her arms above her head as she did so. She planted her feet to either side of the microphone stand, gave the crowd a double thumbs up. Jake showed brilliant teeth as he turned and gave Sameh the nod.

The next song, "You Turn Me" by Vickie Winans[1], was a hard-driving gutsy song, and once it was well under way Amy plucked out the mike and began her strut. Grins spread among the band, and the sound opened up. Two-thirds of the way through the song there was a duel of voices. Jake, Lothar and I sang against Karl, Hans, and Pipo, with Amy keeping score way up high above us all. Turn me, we cried over and over, turn me to grace. When we ended, the audience shouted back their approval.

Amy moved to the back of the stage, patted her face, and asked Jake, "That sounded all right, didn't it?"

"Dynamite. Pure dynamite."

"You sure?"

"Look at the crowd, baby. This place is packed with happy people."

During the remainder of the set, Amy gave everything she had for each song, and afterward came back to Jake and begged to know if it was okay. Jake encouraged her the best he could; then she went back up front and sang her heart out all over again.

When the set ended, Amy gave the crowd a final bow and smile and promise to return soon. As we were walking down

---

[1]Vickie Winans, "You Turn Me," from the album "Be Encouraged," copyright © Lexicon Music Inc.

the backstage stairs the Reverend Hawkins came up followed by a stranger. He was a light-skinned older black man, very handsome in a hard-edged way. His hair was salt-and-pepper gray, his sharp-cornered face unlined. He stood very erect, very rigid, very straight and polished. He wore his clothes like a uniform; his shirt was sparkling white, his striped tie set with a tiny diamond stud, his shoes so shiny they reflected the overhead lights.

Jake walked forward with Amy a tiny half step behind him, both her hands intertwined with one of his. The man shook Jake's hand briskly, gave Amy a brief nod. Amy was clearly willing to let her husband speak for her. Jake and the man exchanged a few words; then with a nod to them and the chaplain, the man pivoted around and walked off.

As soon as the chaplain had followed the man back down the hallway, Amy turned to Jake and said, "I'm going outside for a while."

"Ain't you gonna eat something? They're fixin' us a table back in the chaplain's room."

"I'm not hungry and I want some air. Can I have your Bible, please? Mine's back somewhere in my things."

Reluctantly Jake pulled the tattered volume from his back pocket. "Sure you don't want me to come with you?"

"I'll be all right. Can I have the keys to the van too, please?"

Jake watched her leave with a helpless look on his strong features. When she was gone he noticed me standing beside him. "Girl ain't never had nothin' but trouble with that man. The Lord's got His work cut out for Him, helpin' her carry that load."

He turned and left for the chaplain's room, too disturbed to notice the effect his words had on me. I hesitated, then followed Amy out into the night.

I found her seated behind the wheel of the van, the interior light shining on the Bible propped on the steering wheel. She rolled the window down when she saw me coming. "Did Jake tell you to come out here?"

"No." Now that I was there, I was not sure why I had come. "I wanted to ask you something, but I can do it later."

In reply Amy opened the door and slid over, careful to keep her place in the Book. I climbed in and shut the door. "What are you reading?"

"Oh, I did what I always do when life is pressing in on me. I said a little prayer, asked Him to guide me, and opened the Book. I saw it was Revelation and started to close it, thinking I had made a mistake. But the Lord knew what He was doing."

She raised the Book and read, " 'The kingdom of the world has become the kingdom of our Lord and of his Christ, and he will reign for ever and ever.'

"This doesn't mean now, Gianni. This is what's going to happen after the Tribulation, when Christ comes to reign on earth. I must have read these words a hundred times, but they never had a meaning for me like they do now. All the things that trouble us, all our pains and angers and worries and doubts, they are all going to pass. Every one of them. All we have to do is keep our eyes on the Lord."

She lowered the Bible to her lap, spread her hands out to cover the pages. "Until that time, we still have a friend who will never fail us in our times of need. We just need to learn how to turn whatever is bothering us over to Him."

Amy looked out over the darkened parking lot. "When Jake said he wanted you to come live with us, I was really afraid. He said that it would be the only way you would ever understand what it meant to accept the Lord Jesus into your life, by seeing an example of a living faith in other people. I told him that was why I was so afraid. I mean, it's one thing to have somebody come in for a performance, see us up on stage and go away feeling filled with the Spirit. It's totally different, though, when somebody comes in and sees you when you're tired, or down, or hurting. My faith isn't perfect, Gianni. It's a long way from it. I was afraid of making mistakes in front of you. Like now."

"I don't think you've made mistakes," I replied.

She chose not to hear me. "All I ever wanted to do was sing. It was the only time I ever felt alive, whole, free from all the mess that we had at home. The rest of life was just something to try and put up with. When I was sixteen I got a job singing with a local band, and did some studio gigs and advertising jingles. It drove my father around the bend. I spent the next two years getting yelled at and being slapped around. He called my singing the devil's work. Strange thing to hear from a man I never saw pray or go to church. He'd drop us off every week, come by and pick us up after it was over, but he never set foot inside the church himself. He didn't have a thing against my singing, long as I was in the church choir. But soon as I started with that band, he wouldn't leave it alone."

She screwed up her face, lowered her voice, said to the front window, " 'No 'count white boys. Druggies and hippies and trash, that's all they are. I won't let no girl of mine be seen with no-good white trash, nossir. None of my girls'll wind up a whore-lady with a road show.' "

Amy closed the Bible and cradled it to her chest. "What really bothered him wasn't the music, though. It was what other folks'd think. He lived for the army. I used to wish my Pop'd love me just half as much as he loved his job.

"My father demanded perfection from us. All of us, Mama included. He had to have the best—the finest soldiers, the sharpest unit, the prettiest wife, the cleanest home. My sisters and I had to be the best students, the best dressers, show the world we were Pop's little angels.

"I studied because I loved learning. I proved to myself that I was smart, that I could do just as well as anybody else. Then I'd go in and blow the tests. It was the only way I could get his attention, see, when he bawled me out. I was Pop's big disap-pointment, and I got back at him every way I could, just looking for ways to hurt him and upset him. All the time, though, deep down I kept wishing he'd love me."

She cleared her cheeks with two backhand swipes. "I finally decided I just had to get a little tougher. You know. Tough enough to take it, to live without my father's love. I started going out with boys who were hurting as bad as I was, hiding behind masks of good looks and money. I was better than them, though. I knew it and I showed it. They had all of these *things*—the right car and the great pad and the good dope and the perfect clothes. But they were all show. Just a big show.

"They looked at me like they looked at everything else, just what they could see on the outside. The nice legs, the nice body, that's all they ever saw. But I knew there was something more, and I looked down on them because they never could reach it. I was the most condescending little snit you ever saw. I could cut a man up one side and down the other without flicking an eyebrow. They hated it, but they loved it too. It took me a long time to understand that. I finally saw that they kept after me because I was always a little unattainable."

Amy turned to me with eyes as deep as wells. "You know what happened then."

"Jake," I said softly, hurting for her.

"After I met him I fought like mad. It still pains me to remember what a fool I was. I did everything I could think of to make that man hate me. I even brought one of those silly little playboys to a restaurant where I was supposed to be meeting Jake. The man didn't even bat an eye. He told the guy about the rich man meeting Jesus on the road, asked if he wanted to pray with us. It blew the guy's mind. Then Jake stood up and said he must have been mistaken, he thought he was going to be meeting a sister in the Lord for an evening of sharing in the Word. Can you imagine how I felt? An evening of sharing in the Word.

"It took me a while, but I finally came to realize that Jake was somebody who saw *inside* me. He saw the emptiness and the pain and the anger, and all he wanted was to show me how to fill that space with something better. He never talked about his own love. He never seemed the slightest bit interested in my beauty. That shocked me cold, I tell you. He never talked about loving me himself, never laid a hand on me. He only seemed interested in my heart. I wish there was some way I could describe how much that meant to me. He made all the games seem so silly, such dirty little lies. That's why I was able to keep listening to him talk about the Lord, because he never talked to the outside Amy, the girl the rest of the world saw. He talked to my heart. He kept talking about the Lord and His love. A Lord that loved me for what I truly was, beyond all the lies and the barriers I had spent a lifetime putting together."

Amy turned back toward the front windshield, let out a long sigh. "I made peace with my Pop, the best peace I could. And the Lord keeps pushing me a little further along every time He thinks I'm ready. This is the first time my father's ever come to hear me sing, though. The very first time in my whole life."

I thought back to that talk with Jake outside my little cottage, remembered the problems I had with my own father. We were quiet a long time, sitting side by side, staring out the front windshield at the silent parking lot, both lost in our own thoughts. I yearned for a way to tell her what I was thinking, but the words would not come.

Finally Amy said, "Thank you for letting me share all this with you, Gianni."

"I learned a lot. Really."

"That's the power of sharing, I suppose. You can learn from the pain of others if you're only willing to listen. It helps to know someone's been down there too."

"And made it back up again," I added.

She looked deep into my eyes. "It's so wonderful to see you open yourself up to Him, Gianni. His healing power is there for you, just as it is for me. Unconditional love. He's just waiting to share it with you."

The pressure in my heart was too intense for me to speak. I sat and searched her face and struggled with my conflicting inner voices.

Amy patted my hand, gave me her gentle smile. "Think maybe we ought to check in with the others? I imagine Daddy Jake's just about borderline frantic."

I returned to the hall feeling split in two. There were answers here to questions I did not even know I had. I could not grasp them, could not see how I could face up to it. I was afraid to listen too closely to the voices inside my mind.

I felt so utterly filled with doubt. What if they were wrong? What if all they were basing their lives on was nothing more than their own imaginations, seeking to fill the void in their lives with a myth? I was terrified of making a mistake, of being fooled, of being forced to confront the shadows in my mind and heart.

The dream was waiting for me when I went to sleep that night. I closed my eyes and drifted away, and the next instant all the veils were down, all the blinders torn away. I slept, and dreamed a dream as real as the world I had left behind.

I stood at the edge of a clearing made dark and gloomy by a misting rain. The limbs of the trees surrounding the clearing were bowed and motionless under the rain's silent weight.

I watched as four cowled figures slowly entered the clearing. They droned in deep voices words I could not understand. Their robes slid across the ground, making them seem to float as they walked. They were carrying a casket. They began to lower the casket from their shoulders, and I saw that it had no lid, and that it was empty.

I peered at the figures, but their heavy cowls were drawn down so that I could not see their faces. The figures dropped the casket, and it floated down into a shallow grave that opened at their feet, landing with the sound of thunder.

One by one, three of the figures fell into the grave. They lay in haphazard confusion, their limbs intertwined, their cowls thrown back. I saw their faces at last. It was my mother, my grandfather, and my grandmother.

The remaining cowled figure started shoveling in dirt. I wanted to scream, but the earth was falling into my mouth as well as into the grave.

My mother opened her eyes and looked straight at me. I spat out dirt and tried to run to her, but the sod was falling faster now, piling up around me and holding me tight. It filled my mouth and made it hard to breathe.

The hooded figure kept shoveling in dirt until the grave was full. He brought up an enormous wooden stave, and shoved the sharply pointed end into the mound of earth. Then he began to grow taller and taller until he towered over me and the grave. He picked up a giant hammer and raised it high over his head.

A hand broke out of the ground. It reached toward me, pleading. I struggled to break out of the mountain of earth that held me fast, but I could not move. The hammer fell and struck the stave with the boom of a cannon. Again it fell. The third time, the cowl dropped back. It was my father.

I awoke with a cry and sat up rigid in bed, gasping for breath. My bedclothes were soaking wet. On trembling legs I got out of bed, undressed and dressed again. Then I began to pack.

It was impossible to forgive my father. How could I forgive someone whom I hated so much that I had spent a decade trying to forget his very name? Where had this search for God brought me except back to the point of confronting my hatred? I had not found God: I had only rediscovered an old pain. I closed my carry-bag, silently opened the bedroom door, picked up the case holding my classical guitar, reached for my bag and shoes, and padded across the wooden floor on bare feet. At the entrance to the apartment I hesitated long enough to make sure I had keys to the warehouse so that I could pick up my other guitars. I was not coming back.

PART THREE

Every story of conversion is the story of a blessed defeat.

C. S. LEWIS

CHAPTER
10

The train pulled into Como just after dark. I felt strangely empty. I shrugged it off as a change in climate, as Como was already well into springtime warmth. I caught a taxi directly to the restaurant. Now that I was back, I felt reluctant to go home to my cottage.

Alessandro was too tired to show me much enthusiasm. "You're seven weeks too early," he said in greeting.

I unloaded my bag and guitar cases from the taxi, and looked around. The tables and chairs were piled into a gigantic jumble against the far wall and covered with paint-spattered tarpaulins. Masonry equipment and stone-cutting machines were set up around the center of the restaurant. Wheelbarrows and portable concrete mixers and spades were backed up against the waiter's station. Scaffolding grew up the side wall, surrounding a new metal girder which was still colored a raw red. At its base were dabs of gray paint where the workmen were attempting to match the color of the wall. Dust was everywhere.

In the midst of this chaos was one table littered with papers. A sweat-streaked Alessandro was seated with two equally dirty men whom I did not know. A bottle and glasses were set in front of them.

Alessandro waved a weary hand toward the pile, said, "Fish yourself out a chair and join us, Maestro."

"Thanks, I've been sitting in a train all day."

He nodded. "These are the heads of the construction crew," Alessandro said, and to them, "Giovanni di Alta is the star musician of our show."

We exchanged greetings. Alessandro offered me his glass, apologized for not having the energy to go back to the kitchen for another one. I took a sip out of politeness, realized it was the first alcohol I had tasted in over two weeks, asked him how it was going.

"The fiend you see leaning against my wall here has been a mean one to deal with." He leaned back on two legs, and the chair groaned dangerously. "You would not believe what that rogue has put us through."

I gave the steel pillar another look, asked, "If it's up why will it take so long to reopen?"

"Because the second one has to go inside too," offered one of the construction men, draining his glass in one tired motion.

"The wall is leaning inward. The main support has to be on this side," Alessandro explained. "I think maybe I'm gonna take a month's vacation, let them put this one in without me."

"It won't be so bad," the other man spoke up. He had a voice that spoke of grappa and late nights and thousands of unfiltered cigarettes. "We've learned how to do it now."

Alessandro made a weary suggestion as to what the man could do with such nonsense, then said to me, "Antonio has been calling here from Milan two, three times a day looking for you. He asked me this morning if I knew of any detectives in Germany that spoke Italian."

"He's got a job for me," I guessed.

Alessandro nodded, dropped his chair to four legs, leaned forward and filled his glass. "Coppa's decided to go in and do his first two songs. He's got one they want to use as a single, Antonio says, and the record company is screaming for something to release. They started the day before yesterday."

The prospect of working on a major album was much more appealing than having to face the isolation of my little cottage. "I think maybe I'll go on down tonight, check into a hotel."

"Why not?" Alessandro drained his glass, lumbered to his feet. "Sure isn't anything for you to do around here, unless you're looking for blisters and a sore back."

.   .   .

Coppa normally used a studio very near Milan's Piazza Duomo, the city's central square. The next morning I arrived to find the place jammed by the hangers-on with whom Giorgio Coppa always surrounded himself. Studio work with Coppa was usually a twenty-four hour party. That was one reason why his albums always took so long to record.

He was successful enough to demand and receive whatever he wanted. There was something about working in the studio that always excited girls—that is, until the boredom of repeated takes set in. For this reason, the girls Coppa brought with him usually changed every few days.

I knew enough of the crew to receive a hero's welcome when I walked in. There were a lot of grins, several voices shouting thanks toward the ceiling, many looks of open curiosity from girls I didn't recognize. I was led straight through to the live room, where Coppa was smoking a cigarette between takes.

"Maestro, salve." Coppa moved off his stool, glided over toward the door, offered me his hand and a glad smile. "We were beginning to worry."

Coppa was a man in his late twenties who was going prematurely gray. Beneath the close-cropped curls his face was unlined. It was a handsome face, like a well-tanned full-lipped David. His concerts were mobbed by teenage girls who rushed the stage and sang his lyrics back to him, reaching up to touch his legs as he danced. He sang of physical love in scarcely veiled lyrics, and liked to have a beautiful girl watching through the studio window as he recorded. He said it helped put him in the right mood.

"I got this idea for a song," he told me. "It burned through me like a fire. I had to record it, and I need you to do the acoustic."

He took me by the shoulder, said, "The guys are all over in the lounge. Have Ricki play the tracks, try it out, and come tell me what you think."

I nodded agreement, said, "Somebody better call Antonio before he decides to drive to Germany after me."

Coppa turned around, not letting me go, said to someone behind us, "See to it." And to me, "Great you could come, Maestro. I think we've got us a hit here."

I walked down the long hallway that ran beside the control room. I waved to the sound engineer through the triple-paned windows, wondered why I didn't feel any pleasure over being back.

The lounge was a typical Coppa mixture of laid-back musicians and beautiful girls. A television with the sound cut off was showing a quiet car chase. The stereo that climbed the back wall was cut down low and played tracks from the Rolling Stones' new album. Someone called a greeting. I walked over, said a hello to those I knew. I found Ricki, the group's road manager, shook hands, endured the pats and the questions and the demands for where I had been hiding myself. He led me into the practice room, closed the door against the noise, held up the cassette with a flourish.

"I think we got ourselves a winner here." He slid it into the slot of a portable stereo, closed it, hit the Play switch.

The song was without lyrics, so I could follow the musical flow without interruption. It was the base upon which the words would be laid, and needed to be listened to by itself to be dissected. I had often heard musicians say they could tell they had a hit if the music was strong enough to stand alone.

It was a fairly typical Coppa beat, slow and languid with a hint of Latin spice. I could hear the lyrics already. He would describe a meeting, a talk, a touch, a night of love. It was good music. I nodded my approval to Ricki, pushed hard at the emptiness that was welling up inside. I picked up the battered hollow-body that was leaning against the wall, started strumming along. I sought the only way I knew how to ease this sense of distance between myself and the world, through my music.

The door opened to admit Coppa. With him came the bass guitarist whom I knew vaguely. Two copper-colored heads peaked out from behind the two men. The prettier of the two girls smiled me a welcome.

Ricki told them to shut the door, pulled a joint from the same pocket that had held the cassette, said, "Moroccan keef, Maestro. Righteous stuff."

"Knock your head off," the bass guitarist agreed.

The hunger hit me like a clenched fist to the gut. I wanted to smoke as much as I had wanted anything in my life. I tried to remember when I had gone so long without smoking, could not. I *wanted* it.

Yet there was something that held me back. It was like a gentle tug at my heart, a yearning for something else, a reminder of the night on the Como pier. And the thought came and rested in my mind like a brilliant light.

I don't belong here.

Yet the desire was stronger than the voice. I took the joint, accepted a light, took a long, long hit. Nodded the approval they were waiting for.

The flood of emptiness swelled out from my heart to encompass my entire being, the room, the people, my music. I didn't feel the beginnings of a new high. All I felt was a dull throbbing surge of hopelessness. What was I doing here? Something had changed. I didn't belong.

I handed the joint back, waved my hand against the offer of more, said I had not been feeling well. I endured their expressions of concern. I told Coppa I liked the song, asked how he wanted it played. I forced myself to concentrate. All the while my heart toned to the aching bell of emptiness. I didn't belong.

The takes went on forever. The clock hands crept around, signaling hour after hour of work without meaning. Coppa seemed dissatisfied with everything I did. I listened to his comments, tried to follow his lead, played like a machine.

I was taking a break in the late afternoon, staring at a sound-baffled wall I didn't see, when I was struck by the memory of another time. I saw myself back in the high-ceilinged room of Professor Schmitz, playing once again that tortuous rite of spring. I wiped at the memory with a sweat stained towel, when the thought came unbidden and unwanted. I have spent over a decade running from the thing I hated most, and where has it taken me? Right back to the same place. I have gone nowhere at all. Nowhere.

When the session finally finished I changed clothes, refused their invitations, and left on my own. I walked the four blocks to my favorite restaurant in Milan, Alla Collina Pistoiese. I accepted the owner's bow and handshake, was shown to my regular table, ordered without really thinking. Now that I was here I wished I hadn't come. I wasn't really hungry, didn't want to be around people, didn't know what I wanted. I ate food I couldn't taste, sipped at wine that seemed bland. I paid the bill and left as soon as I could.

I walked around the corner and entered the miniature Piazza St. Alessandro. Rising from the other side was a monolithic cathedral that dwarfed the surrounding buildings and the cars that drummed over the old cobblestones. I found my footsteps leading across the plaza and up the many broad steps to the cathedral's main entrance. I pushed against the massive oak doors, was surprised to find them locked. I checked my watch. Evening mass should have just ended. I set my shoulder and pushed again, harder this time. The doors did not budge. I could just as well have been pushing against a stone wall.

For a reason I could not explain, a wave of panic swept through me. I leapt against the door, hammering it with my body. It did not give. I did not know why it was suddenly so important to get inside, but I had to enter. I *had* to.

The thought was like a cry in the darkness. What if faith is like this? Again I thrust my shoulder at the door, and tore my shirt. The thought rode on a wave of fear. What if I had waited too long? I turned and leaned against the door, my chest heaving. What if I had refused the invitation, and the invitation had been taken away from me? What would I do? Where would I go?

I pushed myself off the door and stumbled into the night.

.   .   .

I felt a mixture of relief and shame upon arriving at the studio the next morning to find Mario waiting for me. I paid off the taxi, hesitated, walked across the street to where he slouched against the wall.

I asked in greeting, "Did they tell you to bring your knife for this trip?"

With his shoulder he pushed himself erect, said, "I won't say that everybody is real pleased, Maestro. But you'd be surprised how much they understand."

"I wish they'd explain it to me, then." I stood and looked at him a long moment, said, "If you'd have shown up yesterday I wouldn't have talked to you."

Mario nodded thoughtfully, as though it made all the sense in the world. He grasped my arm, propelled me down the street, said, "Let's go down to the Piazza and watch the world go by."

It was a three-block walk to the Piazza Duomo, dominated by Milan's central cathedral. The church had recently been cleaned for the first time in three hundred years, and now the stonework gleamed brightly in the midmorning sun. It rose up over one hundred meters. The central doors were so broad and high that a knight in full armor could ride in on horseback, as was common during the Duomo early years.

Leading off one of the streets that fronted the piazza was

the most famous covered promenade in all Italy, the site of legendary court intrigues and romantic trysts for six centuries. The arched ceiling was a full five stories above the marble-laced walkway. Its broad avenues were lined with cafes, restaurants, and stores that charged prices sufficiently high to afford the staggering rents.

Mario waved us toward a table in the corner cafe. It granted us a view of the cathedral, the plaza, the branching promenade, and the multitudes of nationalities who walked by. He ordered a capuccino and a freshly squeezed orange juice; I asked for the same.

"So, Maestro," Mario said, giving me his gentle smile. "You wanna tell me why we're talking today?"

"You mean, why we're talking here in Milan, or what happened yesterday so that we're talking here now?"

He laced his fingers behind his head, told me, "Why don't you just start at the beginning. I can't think of anything else that's very pressing right now."

It felt wonderful to have someone to whom I could talk, who would understand and not criticize. He sat and watched me with his look of quiet wisdom as I described the dream, relived the panic of my departure from Dusseldorf. He seemed to hold his breath as I described my return and the feeling inside the studio and my even worse panic when I found the church doors closed to me. The outside clamor and swirling throngs became a floating cloud without meaning or substance. We were bound together, Mario and I, by his power to listen with a quiet mind.

I finished with, "I can see I don't belong here. I can't lie to myself about that anymore. The problem is, I don't know where to go. I don't feel like I belong anywhere anymore."

Mario leaned forward, said, "You don't know how important a discovery you've just made, Gianni. Listen to me, brother. *Nobody belongs.* It's one of the great myths the world spins to hold us fast. Nobody belongs. Our home is elsewhere."

He reached into his back pocket, came up with a well-worn Bible. I told him, "You guys draw those things out like gunslingers."

"More like shields," he replied, not looking up as he riffled through the pages. "You really ought to study this Book, Maestro. It's God's word, given to each and every one of us. Some singer, I don't remember who, once called it a love letter showing us the way home."

He handed it over, pointed at a place on the page, said, "Read this."

It was from Jonah, chapter 2, verse 8. I read, " 'Those who cling to worthless idols forfeit the grace that could be theirs.' "

"It looks to me like the Lord is making your way straight, Gianni," he told me. "He's showing you that the idols you used to hold have to be given up. The old ways have to be abandoned, to make room for the new."

He took the Bible, turned pages, handed it back, said, "Read verse fifteen."

It was from 1 John, chapter 2. I read, " 'Do not love the world or anything in the world. If anyone loves the world, the love of the Father is not in him.' "

"One more, Maestro, and I'm through," Mario said, searching the pages once again. He handed it back, said, "Second Corinthians, chapter five, right there under my finger. Read verses seventeen and eighteen."

I did so. " 'Therefore, if anyone is in Christ, he is a new creation; the old has gone, the new has come! All this is from God, who reconciled us to himself through Christ and gave us the ministry of reconciliation: that God was reconciling the world to himself in Christ, not counting men's sins against them.' "

"There's your answer, Gianni," Mario told me, taking the Bible back and slipping it into his pocket. "You can die to this world by allowing Christ into your heart, accepting Him as your personal Savior, and letting Him carry the load of your sins for you."

I did not have anything to say. There was such simple truth there, such an appealing force that my mind's vague stirrings of disquiet meant nothing. Something was tugging at my heart, pushing me forward. For the first time I was beginning to really feel that the answer might lie here. Not with the people. With the *message*.

"Amy said to tell you that they are all praying for you," Mario told me. "And Jake said to tell you the same thing he told me, back when he found me up in Hamburg. It's a couple of passages from the fourth and fifth chapters of Ephesians. I've looked at it enough, I don't think I need the Book for this one."

Mario leaned back in his chair, closed his eyes, recited from memory:

With regard to your former way of life, put off your old self, which is being corrupted by its deceitful desires; to be made new in the attitude of your minds; and to put on the new self, created to be like God in true righteousness and holiness.

For you were once darkness, but now you are light in the Lord. Live as children of light (for the fruit of the light consists in all goodness, righteousness and truth) and find out what pleases the Lord. Have nothing to do with the fruitless deeds of darkness, but rather expose them. For it is shameful even to mention what the disobedient do in secret.

Be very careful, then, how you live—not as unwise but as wise, making the most of every opportunity.

I spent a long moment mulling over the words and bringing the world back into focus. Finally I turned to Mario, asked, "So what do I have to do?"

"Open your heart and mind to the Lord Jesus in prayer. Ask Him to enter in, to fill you with His Holy Spirit, and to grant you His eternal salvation and forgiveness. And study the Bible. I can't stress this enough, Gianni. Every answer you need is right there waiting for you."

I pushed myself to my feet, signaled the waiter, said, "Let's go get started before I lose my nerve."

Mario gave me a brilliant smile, followed me up, said, "Sounds good to me, Maestro."

When I started off across the street toward the cathedral, Mario stopped me with a hand on my arm. "I'd rather we chose someplace a little more private. Where's your hotel?"

"Three, maybe four blocks away."

"It's a pretty day, why don't we walk?"

As we strolled down sunlit streets, I asked him, "Did they ask you to come down?"

He shook his head. "It was my idea. I told them you might need a little help saying goodbye to your old life."

I stumbled under the weight of his perception. "I just wish my faith was stronger."

He laughed at that. "Don't we all."

"That's a joke. You guys don't ever doubt anything."

"Don't think that for a minute, Maestro. We all have doubts. Especially in the bad times. It's something, though, how once the bad times are over we can see how clearly the Lord's guiding hand has been there to see us through."

We walked on in silence. I took my key from the hotel concierge, climbed the stairs, let myself into the cramped little room. My hand hesitated over the light switch. Mario stood in the entrance behind me and waited.

I said, "Now that I'm here I don't know what to do."

"Turn to Jesus," Mario said.

His eyes shone in the half-light streaking through the shuttered window. He said, "That's all you have to do, Gianni. God'll take care of the rest. Surrender your will to Him and ask Him to put you upon the Way."

Following his lead I lowered myself to my knees on the worn carpet. I bowed my head, closed my eyes so tight my eyelids trembled, clenched my hands together. I need help, I prayed.

"Help me, God," I said. "Help me see where I belong. Help me leave behind these things that have never brought me lasting happiness. Help me find something that will fill the emptiness."

I had to stop. The flame in my chest was overwhelming, pushing a lump into my throat and tears from my eyes. Help me, I prayed.

"Show me the salvation of Jesus Christ," I went on, my voice very hoarse. I felt Mario's gentle hand come to rest upon my shoulder, and I had to stop again. I took a very deep, very shaky breath, went on. "I know now I can't find the way myself. I need your help. Help me turn to you. Help me see what it is you want me to do."

With the softness of a mother's caress I felt the peace descend upon me. My expanding heart echoed a sensation of overpowering love. An idea came to me, a final plea to be made. *Help me heal.*

I said the words, and felt enfolded within an embrace of love. It was a door opening within me, a gift from somewhere beyond myself. And with its gift came understanding. Help was here. I no longer needed to carry these burdens on my own. Help was here.

I heard Mario whisper the words, "In Christ's holy name we pray." I repeated the words, and felt the presence of love—calm and brilliant and peaceful. Help was here.

After a long while I raised my head, found Mario watching me with joy-filled eyes. He dropped his hand from my shoulder, said simply, "Praise the Lord."

CHAPTER

11

I carried feelings of both shame and defiance into the practice room upon my return to Dusseldorf. They wouldn't say anything outright, I imagined, but it would be clear in their eyes. They had been forced to cancel a performance because of my disappearance, Mario told me. They would wonder if I could be trusted; they would be thinking of finding someone else. I braced myself for the sideways looks and veiled hostility, especially from Pipo. He would take it all very personally, I was sure. I followed Mario into the warehouse and wondered where I would go when they no longer wanted me in the band.

Instead, Jake started us right off on a new song, Margaret Becker's "Stay Close to Me." We began on a ragged note, everyone a little slow at getting back into the music. But try as I might, I could find no hostility in their greetings. Even Lothar and Hans came over to welcome me back.

The song was a good one, a simple melody that moved back and forth between us as Amy pleaded for the Lord to stay close to her. The beat was slow and solid, matching the thunder that rumbled in the distance. The longer we played, the closer the thunderstorm came to our shelter.

Jake called a break, and we stopped and sprawled on the sofas and chairs and carpeted floor. The storm arrived with thunder rolling overhead in a deep rumbling basso. Rain began to drum softly on the metal roof. Little tinkling cymbals sounded outside the small windows as drops fell on the panes. We shared a contented silence and listened to the storm, and I felt a sense of tranquility I had never before known.

Without a word, Hans walked over, picked up his trumpet, and started to play; it was straight improvisation. The shy young man who almost never spoke had found enough safety in that moment to play for us. The notes fell in bell-like purity from his instrument, a softly chanted song of praise.

Jake carried one of the metal-backed chairs over to the stand of instruments. He sat down again, plugged in his bass, bent over, and began to play. There was no hesitation, no question, no misplaced notes. He knew exactly what Hans wanted to say.

Pipo was next, then Sameh, then Lothar, then me. Karl and Amy sat for a long time on the sofa, laughing softly. Then they got up and joined in the song of praise, Karl on alto sax and Amy drifting through a hummed melody with eyes closed and hands lifted over her head.

When it was over we all stood around and laughed. No need for words. We knew.

Amy walked over, draped her arms around my neck. "Welcome back, brother."

The feeling was still with us when we packed our gear the next afternoon. I had seldom seen so many smiles, heard so much laughter—even from Jake.

We were going to a mountain village between Cologne and the former East German border, a place called Gummersbach. A group of evangelical organizations spread throughout the region had rented a Schutzhalle, a public hall owned by the local hunt club. Karl told us on the way up that in medieval times these hunt clubs were the civil defense leagues of the small city-states. Unless the city-state became incorporated within a principality or kingdom large enough to afford its own army, the hunt clubs were their only source of protection. There were no police.

The autobahn took us through forested valleys before the exit for Gummersbach. The city was built upon a series of hills that dominated the surrounding valleys. Near the top of the highest peak stood the Schutzhalle. The hall was eighty meters long and thirty meters wide with a hand-laid floor of polished wood. The ceiling was open-raftered, its massive timbers streaked with dark smoky stains from centuries of oil-burning lamps. The stage was one of the biggest we had ever used, with theater lights hung among the rafters.

The manager was there to greet us, along with the head of the largest local evangelical Gemeinde. "Six hundred people coming tonight, from as far away as Cologne and Olpe. You folks really pack them in."

Jake nodded, shook hands and made introductions, then pulled us off to one side. To Hans he said, "What say we start with your song tonight?"

Hans took on the look of a hunted animal. He set down the mike stands he was carrying. "I don't know."

Amy was there beside him. "Nobody's pushing you, remember that."

"Just an idea," Jake said. "Start off with you alone on stage, single spotlight, play your piece awhile. We come out one by one, have them keep the light just on you 'til everybody's out and playing. We all swing through it one time together, then stop, four clicks from Sameh, and hit it with 'Part Of Me.' "

Hans kept scanning the floor, the ceiling, anywhere but Jake's face. Amy said to him, "This is totally up to you, Hans. But if you want my advice, I think it sounds like a great idea."

Karl stepped around in front of them. "So do I."

Hans nodded once. "Okay."

"Nobody's pushing you," Amy said again.

"I'll do it," Hans said, louder this time.

"You change your mind," Jake said, "just let me know and we'll drop it. Right up to the last minute. No problem, you hear?"

The trumpet caught a glint of light in the darkened hall as Hans lifted it to his mouth. The whistles and cheers that had greeted the dimming of the lights became louder. From backstage I could see Hans hesitate and pull the trumpet back from his mouth.

We had decided to let him start in total darkness, then raise the single spotlight very, very slowly. The noise continued and

270

still Hans hesitated. Then a single note sounded from the loud-speakers, a long tremulous call that lifted a step, swayed back down, fled around the scale like a frightened child seeking his way. I willed myself outward, desperately wanting him to succeed.

The notes took on a greater strength, the faltering steps became steadier, the crowd began to quiet down. By the time the spotlight's first glow picked him out, Hans's playing was strong, his eyes closed, his body swaying slightly. His music was crisp and soaring. I felt a lump grow in my throat, and looked at Amy. She was biting her lip and watching him with shining eyes.

After a few moments we slipped out onto the stage, careful to stay away from the spotlight. The crowd had no chance to catch its breath at the song's end. A moment of silence, and we jumped headfirst into "Part Of Me" from Donna McElroy. When we finished, Jake raised the solitary forefinger and shouted his "Praise the Lord!" The crowd roared back at us with a force I felt in my chest.

When we were packing to leave, Jake walked over and handed me a crumpled sheet of paper. I opened it along creases softened from repeated folding. Across the top of the page was written, "Love Enough to Share." I looked at Jake. He refused to meet my eyes.

"Been carryin' this around for over a month," he told the side wall. "Finished workin' on it a couple of days before you arrived. Think maybe you'd like to put some music to it?"

"I've never written a song," I replied.

"Don't matter. How many albums you worked on, Gianni?"

"I don't know, twenty-five, maybe thirty. I can't remember."

He nodded, his face somber. "How many songs you figure you reworked to fit that little group down there in Como?"

"Hundreds. More."

"So you know what makes a good song work, right? You know how to work in a solid beat to fit the lyrics. You know how to play the hook line, build up that simple catchy refrain or bridge that'll drill a hole in their hearts and come poppin' back up hours after they've heard the tune."

"Why don't you do the music? It's your song."

"Tried to, but it didn't work. Man's gotta know where his limitations are. Spent all my life workin' the beat. Ain't got no problems fittin' words around a solid rhythm. But I can't get the music. No way. That's gotta be somebody else's job."

I looked down at the words. It was a simple lyric, almost a chant. Over and over came the message, through knowing Christ the heart was refilled. Knowing His love, we have too much love for us alone. We can give from all that He gave us. They were good lyrics. I decided a funk would probably fit well.

"Think maybe you can make it work?"

"I don't know, Jake. I'll try," I said, not looking up from the sheet. Perhaps a slight touch of rock for the bridge.

"Well, see what you can do with it," he said gruffly, and walked away.

That week I went to work on it in earnest, carrying the song with me to gigs, curling up in the backseat of whichever car I traveled in, hearing various beats in my head, trying to fit them to the lyrics. Nothing seemed to work. I began to doubt my ability, and questioned whether Jake had made a mistake in pinning his hopes on someone who could not produce.

One evening at home I voiced my frustrations. Jake was not the least bit sympathetic. "Man wants to build an album in a day," he said to Amy.

"It's not that at all. I just can't get anywhere. The song is a good one, I can feel it. But nothing I come up with seems to fit."

Jake gave me his stony-eyed look. "Maybe that's your problem."

"What are you talking about?"

"Sounds to me like you're tryin' to do this on your own. Gotta learn to take it to the Lord, Gianni. Ask the Man himself to guide your work."

"You really think God is going to take some kind of personal interest in a song?"

"He takes an interest in everything," Jake replied flatly. "No exceptions, no ways around it. Do it yourself, and you're not doin' His will."

"The moment you rely totally on faith, it all becomes clear," Amy said. "Sometimes it's a giant step, and sometimes there's a tremendous amount of fear over the move. But so long as you hold back and try to keep control for yourself, you'll never know the Lord's direction."

"Study the Bible and pray," Jake added. "You gotta pray about it loud and long and every day. Keep the line open 'til He puts the missin' pieces in place."

Once they were in bed, I sat at the dining room table leafing through the Bible. I didn't even know what I was looking for until I found it. The words came from the thirty-seventh psalm, and their simple majesty rang in me as if I were a bell and they a hammer.

> Delight yourself in the Lord
> And he will give you the desires of your heart.
> Commit your way to the Lord;
> Trust in him and he will do this:
> He will make your righteousness shine like the dawn,
> The justice of your cause like the noonday sun.

I would write this for Him, I realized. It would be a dance of joy, of gratitude. Delight in the Lord. Such a simple idea. How long had I seen it as a burden, something to avoid at all cost? And He had replied with gentle guidance and an offer of total forgiveness. Yes. Delight in the Lord. It fit perfectly.

Dawn was lighting the street outside the kitchen window by the time I had worked out the song. Almost all of it came from the thoughts and ideas I had run through in the previous week. But now there was a difference. Now there was an emotional theme with which I could bind the musical score together. Now there was both direction and purpose. A purpose. That was what Jake had said I would find.

Too full of creative energy to go to bed, I flipped through the albums, selected one from White Heart, searched out the cut entitled "GTO." It fit my mood perfectly. I turned on the stereo, fitted the headphones on snugly, swung the volume control up a long way, and let the needle drop. I danced around the room as far as the headphone cord would allow, fingered the chords and reared back so far I could see an upside-down Jake stumble owl-eyed out of his bedroom.

I straightened up, slid off the headphones, was shocked and embarrassed to hear the music pouring full blast from the speakers. I fumbled for the switch and plunged the room into silence.

"I thought I had the speakers off. Sorry."

"For a minute there I thought maybe I was back in basic training." Jake rubbed a sleep-creased cheek. "Mind telling me what's going on?"

My face flushed, I replied, "I think I've just worked out the song."

"Mm-hmmm." Jake walked back into the bedroom, saying as he closed the door, "You ever do that again, we're gonna be talkin' serious trouble."

I returned to the dining room table to gather my papers, heard Amy's sleepy murmur and Jake's answering rumble through the bedroom door. Then there was laughter, high and chiming from Amy, a deep-throated chuckle from Jake, and I smiled in return. It was time for bed.

. . .

"Gianni wrote us a song" were the first words Jake said as we entered the practice room.

Pipo did a trill on his conga. "Got some fancy footwork in there for me, I hope."

I pulled out the papers and spread them on the top of the mixing board. Mario reached across, thumped my shoulder, gave me a grin. I replied with a nervous smile. It was suddenly very important that they like the song.

I handed out sheets to Karl, Hans, and Amy. Pipo came around and craned over Hans's shoulder. "Are those scores?"

"They sure are," Karl said, examining his page.

Pipo gave me a round-eyed look and asked, "You did scores for everybody?"

"Naw, man didn't have time to get down all those little jitters for the drums," Jake replied. "Had to make do with just Karl, Amy, and Hans."

"Can you read a score and hear the music in your head?" Pipo asked.

I nodded and turned to Lothar. "I didn't make one up for you. I thought we could just go through the chord changes together, is that all right?"

"What are you gonna do for your next act?" Pipo demanded. "Sprout wings and fly away?"

"Naw, naw, man's got a ways to go yet before he takes off for his mansion in the sky," Jake said. "C'mon, let's try this tune on for size."

Amy was to begin the melody with a strong, clear, simple tone; this was natural for her as she tended to start all songs very simply and save her soaring for the end. Hans was to play a slightly more intricate line on the trumpet. Karl would then jazz it up even more on the sax while Hans lingered as long as he could on his final note. Then Karl would hold his final high note while Amy started back with the next melody line. Until the solo, Lothar and I would play a simple chording backup. I hoped that Hans and Karl would add a complexity that complemented the purity of Amy's opening words, and show a promise of what was yet to come. But I wasn't sure of anything. It had sounded good in my head. Now I was very afraid of how it would sound when we all played it together.

It was rough going at first. Amy couldn't find a comfortable range, and we had to switch the key twice. This meant Karl and Hans had to transpose what was written for them, which was very difficult while playing music they had never heard before. Jake was all gentle patience, and steadied us mightily.

For three hours we worked with each instrument in turn, playing it over and over, watching each person take the song and work it until the sounds came naturally. Then without warning it all came together; Amy picked up the melody and sang it with crystal clarity, Hans fitted to her in smooth precision, Karl followed, Pipo and Jake and Sameh molded perfectly into the beat. But before we were halfway through Amy was waving us to a halt with the microphone down at her side.

Jake walked up to her, shifted his bass out of the way. "What's the matter?"

"I can't sing this," she muffled, not looking at anyone. "It's too good. I've got a lump in my throat the size of a grapefruit."

Jake rubbed a soft circle on her back. "Just take a couple of deep breaths, everything's gonna be fine."

"How would you like it if I got up there on stage and burst into tears? Would I look like a fool or what?"

Jake worked to keep the smile off his face, kept the hand

busy on her back, looked at me and nodded. He had felt it too.

The song was going to work. The melody started out simply, built up as it passed from hand to hand, and burst upward, first with a duet between me and Lothar and then with Amy's leaping finale. Yes. It was really going to work.

Pipo shook his head and looked at me. "Man, what took you so long?"

Karl walked over, gave me his gentle smile, said he liked it very much. From his place by the side wall, Hans looked over and nodded agreement. Mario gave me a double thumbs-up. Amy wrapped her arms around Jake, told us she was going to have to find some kind of anti-cry pill before she ever did that one on the stage.

The lack of sleep came down heavy on me. I was drained, yet very happy. I had taken Jake's words and given them the emotional power of a melody that made the idea live. I accepted the congratulations, grinned in reply to Jake's nod, knew the song had come from somewhere far beyond me. I felt lifted beyond myself, granted a gift of creativity that was more than I could have ever known by myself. For the first time I wanted to be alone, wanted to pray, wanted to thank the Creator who had worked His wonder through me.

We had a concert in Liege, Belgium, the next night. The audience was enlarged by two church groups that had driven over from Aachen, the nearest major German city. People came up, told us proudly how they had been to all of our concerts in the area, how far they had driven, how much they enjoyed hearing the songs, asked us to play a particular favorite. Jake and Amy played official ambassadors and treated them all as very special guests.

Before we went on, Amy said she would sing "Love Enough to Share" if we could fit it in between a couple of old standards and not tell the audience a thing. Just swing into it and out of it, moving from song to song without giving her time to think that she was performing an original. Jake nodded as though it was the most reasonable request in the world, and put it into the first set. She refused to meet our eyes after the number was finished, but I could tell from the smiles on everyone else's face and the audience's reaction that they shared my opinion. The song was a good one.

The next day, after a brief practice crammed into the only afternoon that week when we would not be traveling, Jake handed me another sheet with that same frozen-faced embarrassment. "See what you can do with it," he said, and started to walk off.

I grasped an arm that felt solid as a tree trunk and asked, "How many songs do you have completed?"

"Don't never finish a song," Jake replied, refusing to meet my eyes. "Just get to the point where I can give one up."

"Well," I persisted, "how many half-finished songs do you have?"

"Never counted," he said. "Been writing lyrics ever since I came to know the Lord. Thing is, I want to make sure what I give you is good enough for the band."

I looked at the sheet in my hand. "I'm sure it is, Jake," I said, and let him go.

The weeks moved by in a constant whirl of activity. I allowed myself to be swept along, content for the moment to live from day to day. I spent what free time was left between practices and travel and concerts working on new songs and studying the Bible. I was not yet comfortable with this new life of faith; I still felt that it was a flickering candle whose flame constantly threatened to go out. I stayed close to the group, feeding off their strength, reassured by their belief. It was not necessary to talk with them about my doubts and my weaknesses. Being among them was enough.

The third song that Jake gave me was entitled "If Only You Could Know." The lyrics were simple, the wording meant for a lighthearted pop. It was an appeal to those who wandered alone, telling them that the salvation offered by Jesus Christ was the world's one hope.

Before practice the next day Amy came up, hovered a moment in uncertainty, and said, "Jake told me you've finished the song."

"Just about." It had been the easiest one thus far, almost as though the chords had been set down above the words, playing back in my head as I had read the sheet. All that was left was the solo, and I had decided to let Lothar and Hans handle that themselves.

"What do you think?" She sounded very anxious.

"I like it." It had a good cadence, and the message really struck home with me.

She was clearly pleased. "I'd like to do a couple of extra verses after the solo. Will there be a solo?"

"Probably."

She took a breath. "I want to do it in Japanese."

I stared at her.

"And French. And maybe German, too, if Jake doesn't mind me cutting his lyrics down to just one verse in English." She hurried on, as though afraid I would turn her down. "Then, see, I could show the universality of Christ's message in a different way, by singing it in different languages. You know I speak them, Gianni. I want to try it. Will you help me?"

"Sure." I could not help grinning. She sounded like a little girl.

"Can we do it this afternoon?"

"Do you have the words ready?"

"Right here." She fanned the air with a couple of sheets of paper. "I hardly slept a wink, kept turning on the light and writing it all down. I finally got up and went into the bathroom. I sat there so long my legs fell asleep, and I walked back to bed with pincushions under both feet. Can we try it, please?"

"Sure we can, Amy."

She gave me a fierce hug. "Wait 'til you hear it, Gianni. You'll love it."

She was right. Amy's voice fluttered and soared over the strange sounding words. The cadence and voice movement dictated a substantial change in how the notes flowed, and this bolstered the song tremendously. After each verse she returned to English and sang the bridge alone, then had the message of universality bolstered by all of us powering in on backup vocals for the refrains. After each refrain she began again, alone and fragile, calling in four different languages for all the world to come and hear.

When we finally worked it all the way through the only one who was not smiling was Jake. He stood and pulled at his lower lip and examined the floor at his feet.

Amy asked anxiously, "Didn't you like it?"

"It's different from how I thought it would be," Jake said. "Most times Gianni gives me back something like what I was hearin' in my head, but not this time. This is real different."

"He's changed it a lot to fit the extra verses," Amy agreed.

Jake turned to me. "What do you think of it?"

It was the first time he had asked me outright about a song. I did not need to think it over. "I like the change. It strengthens the song a lot."

He nodded. "Maybe so."

Amy watched him. "Are you mad at me for changing your song?"

"Ain't my song anymore," he said. "It's everyone's. If I'm doing this for Him and not for myself, I oughtta be big enough to accept whatever you think might help it grow."

The week that followed was a big push—three concerts and another two songs completed, practices on every free day as well as during the sound checks. In two weeks we were scheduled to play a series of concerts with two well-known American bands over for a tour of Holland and Germany. Jake wanted to use it as a chance to introduce an entire set of our own music.

I spent my meager free moments reading the Gospel of John. Amy had made it a special request, saying it was time I moved into a more careful study of the Word. She urged me not to read to finish the section, but rather to seek out a special meaning in each passage. Start with prayer and end with prayer, she advised me. This is a special message sent from Him to you. Let God be the one to show you what you need to find there.

The concerts with the American gospel groups went extremely well—so well, in fact, that they invited Jake to bring our music to Nashville and meet with executives at the Christian record labels. It took several invitations before Jake allowed himself to believe that the offer was real and not just words on the wind.

I had never seen Jake so excited as on the night he told us he had decided to go to Nashville. "Gonna rock the town," he said. "Gonna see my day dawn."

Pipo, Mario, Amy and I were watching him pack, enjoying the excitement and the joy that radiated from his normally immovable features. Pipo asked Jake if he'd learned to play as a kid.

"I played back then, sure. Most everybody I knew played or sang. We had this little band, played a hot soul beat, lotta down-home blues, little R&B, little early funk. We were pretty good. Didn't really get started with music 'til the military, though."

"You never tried to get any songs recorded back then?" Pipo asked.

Jake laughed at Pipo, a booming sound. "Man, you think some big-time agent's gonna come down, check out the talent in Oakes, North Carolina? Hike down some dusty tobacco road, walk into a converted barn sellin' moonshine and needle beer, listen to the bloods play? Naw, naw."

He moved back to his packing, went on, "I'll tell you what it was like. One time I was workin' out in the fields with my daddy, we'd stopped for a water break. Used to have this old mule, Jehoshaphat my daddy'd named him. That mule could drink more water than ten men. Got my first muscles carryin' water out to the fields for my daddy and that mule. My daddy told me that day, son, don't you ever let me see you bein' what people *expect* you to be. Gotta be just a little bit tougher, little bit stronger, little bit meaner. Don't ever let 'em get you down. They do, son, they'll never let you get up again. Not ever.

"My daddy was a good man, too good to take what the world loaded on his heart. Lost himself in drink and sayings. Had a saying for everything. Still wake up at night sometimes, hear his voice heavy with moonshine moanin' through the walls. Can't never trust the white man, yeah, my daddy said that one a lot. Don't matter how hard I work, I can't never get ahead without gettin' out. Sunk my whole life croppin' the white man's tobacco, ain't got nothin' to show for it but blisters and a bad back. He'd sit in there for hours tellin' my momma stuff like that, never knowin' there was this little fella lyin' there awake on the other side of that flimsy wall, just takin' it all in. Took me a long time to get rid of that anger my daddy left me, learn there might be a better way. *Long* time."

Jake paused, straightened from his case, said, "Been car-ryin' this dream with me ever since I was able to set that anger down. Never thought of it 'til now that maybe the Lord had to get rid of the anger to make room in my heart for a *new* dream."

Amy smiled for the joy that lit his face. "Dreams really do come true, don't they?"

"Don't know whether to laugh or cry," Jake replied. "I wanted this so bad I didn't dare hope."

"And now it's here," Amy said, loving him with her gaze.

"Gotta go now," he said. "Gotta strike while the iron's hot and the people still remember my name."

"Good thing we've got this five-day break," Amy agreed.

"I'm gone," Jake said. "I'm there. This is one done deal."

CHAPTER
12

Jake returned through the Dusseldorf airport gate a drained and beaten man. Amy ran to him; he accepted her embrace as a man might endure a sudden rain, hunched over against what he could not avoid. He flinched at something she said, shook his head slowly like a very old man.

A noisy crowd had seen Jake off to Nashville. Speculation had been rife during the days after his departure, the excitement infecting us all. Then he had called to say he was coming home a day early, and for Amy to pick him up. That was all. No reason was given, no explanation made.

I walked over, stopped when I was close enough to see the pain in his eyes. "Welcome back."

"I couldn't make it happen," he told me, his voice devoid of strength. "Tried everything I knew how but sell myself on the street, and just couldn't get anybody to hear what I was tryin' to say."

"It's all right, baby," Amy crooned, her arms still wrapped around him. "C'mon, let's get your bags and go home."

"Never knew a man could feel so right about something and not get anywhere at all," Jake said, looking around as though he was not sure where he was or how he got there. "Never knew a body could hurt this bad."

He allowed me to take his luggage without comment, let Amy point him around to the passenger seat. He slid into the car, closed his door, leaned back on the headrest with a long sigh.

"Didn't make any difference how high up the ladder I started," Jake told the roof of the car. "To all those dudes I was just another unknown. All those questions, man oh man. I never knew there were so many questions about my own music that I didn't know the answers to."

Amy closed her door and put the key in the ignition, but did not start the car. "Like what?"

"Like how are they supposed to build on popularity we got six thousand miles away," Jake said, his voice dull with defeat. "Like how are they supposed to know if our music'll go over with Americans."

"So who on earth do they think we've been playing to on all these military bases?"

"Hybrids." Jake rolled his head over to view her through half-closed eyes. "Didn't you know that? All these people here in the military, they're nothing but hybrids. They stick around 'cause we're the only American band in town."

"But what about our music, Jake?" Amy pleaded. "Didn't they have anything to say about our music?"

Jake scrubbed his face hard with two hands. "Depends on who you talk to. One man says we're too black, so we go to a gospel label, and they say we're too white. One dude says the sound's too hard, the next says we got too many songs that aren't hard enough. And then the next one doesn't say a thing. He just opens this drawer to his desk, shows me cassettes from a couple hundred other bands beggin' to be heard."

Amy stared at him a moment longer, then turned on the ignition and said, "We're going to get you home to bed, Jake. Everything will look a lot better after you've had some rest."

"Didn't matter who took me in, didn't matter who we met. Didn't matter how big they smiled, or how loud they made their hellos. Wasn't nothin' in their eyes but a big stone wall."

"Everything's gonna be all right," Amy said, reaching over to stroke his leg. "You're just tired, is all."

"They got too many people hittin' on them all the time to want to listen to anybody new. What they're really lookin' for is a band that's already got a following. A band they can bank on."

"Everything's just fine, honey," Amy said, giving Jake a worried glance. "You'll see."

"Guess maybe they've been burned too many times to trust their own ears anymore," Jake said. He turned his face toward the side window, closed his eyes once more. "Spent four days looking for a trustin' soul and an open heart. Reminded me of my old man lookin' for a banker with an open hand when he was down and out."

Jake was out of the van and stumbling toward the apartment house entrance before Amy had the motor turned off. She signaled for me to bring in the bags, rushed around to support her man with one slender arm around his waist.

Once inside the apartment Jake hesitated, looked around in bewilderment. "What am I doin' here? I didn't get what I was after, how come I'm back?"

"So you can rest up and try again," Amy said. "Now go on in and get some sleep, Jake. You're just tired."

"I'm beat is what I am," he said. "Guess my daddy was right. You want something bad enough, the man's gonna use it like a handle to hold you down."

Amy put her hands on her hips and said, "You just go get yourself in bed before somebody gives you what you been asking for ever since you got off that plane, sir!"

He wiped his face with one tired hand. "Woman, what are you talkin' about now?"

"When you're worn out you get a little short, no matter how tall you are." Amy pointed toward the door. "Now go in there and stop playing superman. Nobody ever said you had to carry this load by yourself. But sure to goodness you're not going to hear any answers 'til you've gotten yourself some rest."

"I can't rest," he complained. "Got too much to do, all this stuff to figure out. Can't go rest now."

Anger gave Amy the strength to turn Jake's bulk around and propel him into the bedroom. "Good *night*, Mister Templer."

She followed him into the bedroom. I stood in the living room and listened to their voices murmur through the closed door. Jake's voice rumbled like distant thunder; Amy's replies were short and rising in cadence. I dropped the bags by the front door and walked into the kitchen.

When Amy reappeared she wore a strained expression.

"That poor man is absolutely exhausted."

"You look like you could use a rest, too."

"It always wears me out to quarrel with Jake." She wrapped her arms around her waist and hugged herself. "It costs more than it's worth. If I have a temper fit with Jake I can't talk to God 'til we're back in working order again."

I felt the numbness that had set in upon meeting Jake at the airport begin to recede, leaving in its place a hollow ache of disappointment. "So what do we do now?"

"About the music?" Amy gave her head a weary shake. "I don't know. Jake was putting so much store into that trip. And into all those promises people made him. The thing he forgot was that none of them make the deals or own the companies."

"I guess we all forgot that," I agreed.

"It's always easier to see these things once they're over." She looked toward the bedroom door, whispered to herself, "The biggest tree always falls the hardest, doesn't it?"

Jake moved through the next few days like a silent shadow. He would sit down for meals, toy with his food, stand and leave without a word. He walked the streets around their apartment house for hours, disappeared into their darkened bedroom and closed the door on Amy's pleas to let her in, let her help, talk with her. Jake never even acknowledged that he heard her.

One afternoon after practice, I suggested that it was time for me to move out. Amy showed real fear, pulled me over to one side, said quietly, "Leave just when I need you most? You even think about it again and I'll toss in the towel."

I looked over to where Jake was seated on the sofa staring at nothing. "He acts like he's mortally wounded."

"The tougher they come, the harder they fall," Amy said, her eyes on Jake. His hands rested numbly on his guitar, as though waiting for someone to come over and order him to unstrap. "God wasn't finished breaking him down, I guess."

"I don't understand."

"I'm not sure I do either, Gianni. I can only tell you what it appears the Lord is showing me in my prayers and studies. My man grew up fighting for dignity and purpose. That fight is still going on inside him. Sometimes Jake has trouble being able to turn that fight over, to surrender, and to win through surrendering."

"I hate seeing him like this," I told her. "It makes me mad and I don't know why. I feel like shouting at him, taking him by the shoulders and shaking him awake."

"We all rely on Jake's strength so much we feel cheated when it's not there," Amy agreed. "He's a strong man, and the strong have the weakness of wanting to rely on their own strength rather than the Lord's. So God still had to do some crushing, I suppose. And He chose the time when Jake was surest of his own strength."

"I wish there was something I could do."

"There is," Amy said, giving me a warm, sad-happy smile. "Have faith in the Lord's goodness, Giovanezzo. And pray for us, will you please? We both need your prayers just now."

That week we had four concerts scheduled. Kaiserslautern and Wiesbaden were followed by an outdoor concert in Basel, Switzerland, and another show at Karlsruhe. Jake's silent half-presence weighed heavily on all of us, adding to the strain of travel and strange beds and sound checks and hurried meals and long nights.

Throughout this difficult period, Pipo continued to fill the void with cheer. As the travel and the back-to-back concerts and Jake's brooding silence took their toll on everyone else, his confidence remained unshakable. You tell me one person in this whole world who doesn't go through a rough patch every once in a while, he told us time and again; Jake'll pull himself out of it, wait and see. Pipo did all he could to lift us from the gloom. His antics were perpetual, his grin seldom slipping. We leaned on him, and responded with grateful smiles to the worst of his jokes. And prayed for Jake's recovery. His sorrow left the whole band crippled. All, that is, save Pipo.

The travel allowed me to do some internal inspection, hard as it was at times to face up to what I found. Part of me ached for Jake, yet another side was angry with him. Furious. At times I could not look at him without wanting to shout in his face. He was being weak when we all needed him. He had led me to this thing called faith with such utter strength and sureness, only to let me down. I did not realize how much I had come to rely on his leadership until it was no longer there.

I had no place to turn except to the Bible, no one to speak to except God. In the midst of those hectic days I found the link between myself and Christ growing stronger, and turning to prayer progressively easier. I recalled Amy once saying that all things worked together for the good of those who love the Lord and sought to do His will. I searched out the passage in the Bible, copied it out on a card, and taped it to the inside of my guitar case. I found myself drawing considerable strength and comfort from those words.

We had a two-day hiatus between Basel and Karlsruhe, long enough for us to return home for the first time that week. I asked Amy to give me another song from Jake's file. She didn't want to; that was something for him to decide, she said.

"Just give me the one on top," I replied. "I don't want to trouble him about it, but I need something to work on. I need to find something to do, something constructive. I have to keep trying."

Amy looked at me a long time. "That is exactly what I told Jake last night."

The title of the song she brought me was "For Those Who Give In Your Name." I scanned the lyrics and felt a strong power in the words. Jake had written the song to all those who had helped him find his way, the beacons who had lit his early steps. I liked it very much, and could identify with it more than any other song he had given me. The characters were different, but the story was the same in my own life. I was eager to start on the melody.

I held back until Jake and Amy were in bed, not wanting to risk any interruption. Once the apartment was quiet I opened the Bible, knowing that here was the foundation upon which I would work. I left the Book open at the passage from 1 John that read, "Dear children, let us not love with words or tongue but with actions and in truth."

I moved the Bible to the center of the table and pushed aside all conflicting thoughts about Jake's problems and my own pains and doubts. Many voices clamored to be heard that night, many who had shown me the love and the light and the Way. This would be their song. My grandmother and my grandfather and my mother—each had comforted and succored me. I would write their melodies, and write it for the Father who granted me this healing and rebirth.

My mother's melody was the easiest. Hers was the high, lilting melody of the flute, the wordless lullaby sung to a sleepy child. It was a simple tune, a trill of notes played on the verge of night, meant to drift with the dreamer into love-filled slumber.

My grandfather was the song's foundation, the underlying chords and bass and gentle percussion, the hint of a force so sure of its power that it did not need to be loud. The power was not in his strength but in gentleness. It was such an underlying murmur that if one did not know to listen for it, it would go unnoticed. Yes. That was my grandfather's way. He needed nothing from others, least of all recognition in their eyes. His acclaim came from a greater source.

I spent hours on my grandmother's song—the faith that defied all odds, the glory sung even unto death. Her melody was thanks for the love and the light and the direction, an answer to her most fervent prayer.

When the three melodies were completed, I went to the bathroom to wash my face. I entered the living room and stopped, standing outside the dining table's circle of light, looking down on the scattered pages and the Bible in their midst. The song would be too jerky, too unstable, with three different melodies. Hadn't they really shared the same melody, all shown me the same love? Yes. That was it. Each had given me the same, but each in a different way. Yes. So what I needed was to meld the three together, to allow each to complement the other. I sat down and went back to work.

There had to be a counter-balancing melody, a song that lay hauntingly in the background until each stanza ended, some response from my side that welled up between the verses to link them together. Yes. My own emotion would link the melodies. The sax would play for me, lilting through the higher limits to mirror the flute's shadow-song.

As soon as the melodies were completed, I began the joining, a thanks to the Father who granted me the freedom to know this joy. It was a shout of liberation from the chains of memories and of pain. It was a chorus of healing, a joining of all voices into one.

Jake lumbered heavily into the kitchen as I was finishing the main score. Bleary-eyed, he peered over my shoulder. "Been up all night again?"

I did not reply. I watched him walk over and pour himself a cup of coffee, feeling sympathy for him, caring for him without the anger and the frustration and the worry of previous days. I had felt the Spirit move through me that night, using me and filling me with a power to create far beyond anything I could have done on my own. In the midst of all the turmoil and unsolved problems and unanswered doubts, I had known a complete and uninterrupted peace. It was still with me now, as I sat and watched Jake stare blindly out the kitchen window.

Jake looked at me, sipped his coffee. "Amy said you had a message I needed to hear. Seein' you sit there and work all night is a lot clearer than anything you could say to me in words."

I did not answer him. I was too busy reveling in this sense of knowing the invisible, partaking of something that comforted me in the face of so much that I did not understand.

Jake nodded, as though I had given him the answer he expected. "Better get on to bed, Gianni. We leave for Karlsruhe in less than six hours."

. . .

We gathered for a hurried dinner before the Karlsruhe concert. As soon as the orders were given and the menus collected, Pipo started in. We leaned forward, thankful for anything to ease the silent burden that Jake pressed upon us.

Pipo went on, "There was this grandmother, see, older than Father Time, all skin and bones and just shriveled up to nothing. Then she got real sick, and the word went out to all the family, her time's coming. Everybody dropped everything and came running. All the children and grandchildren and cousins, man, that house was a zoo.

"So there they are, all crowded around the bed and everything, and her son's down on his knees with his face right up close to hers. And he goes, 'Momma, Momma, is there anything we can do for you?'

"You know how old ladies are when they don't have their teeth in. She kinda chews on her cheeks for a second, and wheezes out, 'I'd like a glass of milk.'

"So her son jumps up like a bolt of lightning's struck his head and turns to whoever's right behind him and says, 'You heard the lady. Go get her some milk and right smart. And don't get it outta the refrigerator. Go take the bucket and milk old Bessie. This might be the last glass of milk Granny drinks, and it's gotta be fresh.'

"It turns out, though, the guy standing right behind him is his nephew Fred. Fred's got his own way of doing things, see. Not bad, just different. So Fred goes out back and milks Bessie, then comes back in and when he's getting out the glass he spots a bottle of vodka there on the shelf. Fred decides maybe a little joy-juice won't hurt old Granny, so he opens up the bottle and pours a little in. Then he decides in for a penny in for a pound, so he dumps in a whole lot more. Then he puts on his most innocent expression and takes the glass in to Granny.

"So Granny picks up the glass with this hand that looks like it's made outta twigs and takes this real tiny sip. She lies there a minute real quiet, then she reaches over and takes another sip, a bigger one this time. Then she picks up the glass a third time and drains it. When she puts her head back down after that she's got the first smile on her face anybody can remember seeing in months.

"So her son leans back over the bed, asks, 'Granny, is there anything else we can do for you?'

"Granny just lies there with her eyes closed and that smile on her old face, and says, 'Don't sell that cow.'"

Jake spoke up for the first time in what seemed like weeks. "That joke's as old as I am."

While the rest of us sorted through our astonishment Pipo shrugged easily, said, "You got a better one?"

Jake stared at him a long moment, said quietly, "Not right now."

"This mean you're back in the land of the living?"

"Maybe." Jake nodded his thanks to the waiter as his plate was set down, turned his attention to his food.

Pipo watched him, a little smile flickering over his features, then said to the group, "There's this guy, claims he's got a talking dog. So his buddy bets him ten dollars he can't get the dog to talk, okay? The guy turns to his dog, says, what's on top of that building? The dog goes, roof! The guy asks, and how're the roads? The dog goes, rough! The guy asks, who hit the most home runs? The dog goes, Ruth! His buddy gets disgusted and refuses to pay up. So the dog looks up at his owner, says, what's the matter, was it Mickey Mantle?"

Amy reached across me to wrap an arm around his neck. "You know what? You're the most special nut I know."

"Haven't you heard? You gotta be a little crazy to be a musician. It's written up in the articles of confederation. No sane people allowed. Isn't that right, Jake?"

Without lifting his eyes from his plate he responded, "If it ain't, it oughtta be."

The rest of us shared a look around the table and turned to our food with lightened hearts.

The concert in Karlsruhe went well. For the first time since his return from America, Jake greeted the crowd with a forefinger directed skyward and a strong, Praise the Lord! We watched him speak with Amy from time to time, nod a response to her touch on his arm, signal to Sameh the beginning of each song.

We were packing up after the concert, listening to our voices echo back from an empty hall, when a trio appeared at the stage door. The older man was dressed in a blue sports coat that failed to hide the slight bulge spilling over his belt. He had short-cropped white hair and a thin smile that looked pasted on. He was flanked by a pair of young men wearing jeans and sweatshirts and very embarrassed expressions.

Pipo tripped down the stairs carrying one of the congas and whistling a cheery tune. The man stepped forward, asked in English, "Sir, are you with the band?"

"That's right." Pipo set the conga down. "Can I do something for you?"

"Well, I wanted to speak to your band leader, if you could point him out to me."

Pipo caught himself before his head was halfway around. I avoided looking back to where Jake was seated on Sameh's drum stool, slowly taping a tear in his guitar case.

"I guess I'll do as good as anybody," Pipo said, pitching his voice loud enough so that Jake could hear and take over if he wanted to. "What you need, man?"

"I'm an elder in the Trinity Baptist Church, which serves all the bases around Nurnberg. These two young men and a number of their friends have been after us for some time to have an evening worship based around music like yours. I drove up for this concert so that I could see for myself."

One of the young men said, "I just became a Christian a couple of years ago. Christian rock's really meant a lot to me."

"Me too," his friend added. "Your concert was great, by the way."

"I'm not so sure about that," the older man interjected. "I've tried to keep an open mind about all this, but I'm not convinced this is a good thing. No sir, I have to say that I'm not convinced at all."

Pipo's smile didn't slip an inch. "You know how it is, man. Everybody's got their own taste in music."

"My taste has nothing to do with it." The man's eyes were sky blue and very clear. He looked immensely concerned about what he was saying, and politely determined. "I came to this concert hoping for I don't know what, but whatever it was, I didn't find it. I couldn't tell the difference between your music and MTV."

"The difference is in the message," Pipo said, the smile no longer in his eyes.

"Yes, that's exactly what my friends here told me. But I couldn't make head nor tail of many of the songs, and the others—" He shook his head. "What I heard you do to some of the old hymns and psalms really put my teeth on edge."

The whole band was listening now. Amy glided over, placed a reassuring hand on Pipo's shoulder. "Why was that, sir?"

The man began jingling coins in his pocket. He looked increasingly worried and very much out of place. "I kept asking myself, 'Why should we use the devil's music to get the truth across?' I felt tainted. Yes, ma'am, that's exactly how I felt as I sat and watched you prance around. Tainted."

"Larry Norman did a song about that a while back," Pipo said, his voice flat. "He called it 'Why Should the Devil Have All the Good Music?' Little rock-and-roll piece. Maybe you ought to hear what he has to say."

"What about all the others?" Amy gestured toward the empty hall. "We had over five hundred people out there tonight. Shouldn't they be able to praise Him as they choose?"

"Praise who, ma'am?" The man's gaze was direct and penetrating. "I just wonder if we're on the same side of the street."

Amy remained unruffled. "I tried to make that message as clear as I knew how, both in the lyrics and in what I said between the songs."

The man turned and gazed out over the empty hall. "I sat there tonight and watched those kids dance up and down the aisles, and I listened to all the applause, and I kept asking myself how on earth people like you could become successful and still have a true Christian testimony."

"Because we don't do it for ourselves," Pipo replied.

"Fame carries a great risk," Amy agreed. "But there are hundreds of evangelists—Billy Graham is a perfect example—who have taken the message of Christ all over the world, and still held on to their humility and their faith."

"Well, I'll certainly think on what you said," he told them. "But I've got to tell you that I'm not convinced. Not for one instant am I the least little bit convinced this is true service."

He nodded to them and briskly walked from the hall. The two young men turned and followed, their faces bearing expressions of defeat. Pipo watched their departure, said to no one in particular, "You know how it is, man. The old wooden flute just packed up a while back, and I never could get the hang of playing a lyre."

"Our Lord didn't work with a choir when He walked this earth," Amy said. "And I don't recall ever seeing anything in the Scriptures about contemporary music being an instrument of darkness. Music is music. It can all be used for praise; the key is reaching a person's heart. Just because he didn't care for our music doesn't mean it's wrong for the next person."

"You never can tell," Pipo said. "Maybe the guy thinks he's got some direct line to the hereafter, some special call on everybody else's taste in music."

"No, he was too sincere for that. He just hasn't seen that other people's spiritual needs aren't met in the exact same form as his own." She shook her head. "I feel so sorry for those kids. How many people do we exclude from salvation with attitudes like this? Isn't it our responsibility to convey the message in a way that fits the need?"

"You said it, sister," Jake said, rising from his stool.

Amy turned to where he stood on the stage. Her look softened. "You all right, honey?"

"I'm tired," he said. "Deep-down tired. Gotta find some way of setting this burden down. Think maybe we can take time for a prayer?"

She nodded, gave him her quiet smile, and said, "I'll get the others."

"I tell you what it's like," Jake said, when we were gathered and settled in a circle. "It's like my best just ain't good enough. It's more than a disappointment. It's like everything inside me has been denied. And what hurts most of all is how I let everybody down."

"You haven't let anybody down, Jake," Amy said, reaching for his hand. "You did all you could."

Around us spread the remnants of what had not yet been packed away. Pipo sat on the wooden box that held his percussion instruments and wrapped new tape around bruised fingers. Hans and Karl leaned against the last PA box. Sameh rested on a seat of cymbal cases. Lothar was long gone. Mario settled himself down next to me, stretched his legs out over the coiled cables with a tired sigh.

"You give it everything you got," Jake went on, refusing to acknowledge her words. "Not just what you wanted to give, but *everything*. The deepest part of who I am went into makin' that contract real. And it still wasn't enough. Man, that is *failure*."

I waited for somebody to object, to try to push the talk on to something that was not so painful. No one spoke. I looked around the circle, as surprised by their silence as I was pained by Jake's words. They were taking it in, allowing him to unburden himself. There were no complaints, no objections, no false attempts to lessen the importance of what he was saying. They listened, and they shared with him the load and the pain.

"Anger came back to me then," Jake said, his gaze resting on the floor. "Not anger at those people in Nashville. Naw. I learned to handle the meanness folks showed each other a long time ago. Anger at *me*. Anger at *God*. If I'd let myself, I'd have hated Him too much right then to ever make it back.

"Thought I'd left that hate and anger behind me for good. But just when I was goin' for the big one, the dream I've been holdin' on to all my life, there it was. Just waitin' to destroy me once and for all. And for the first time in years I didn't have no place to turn.

"God knew what my limits were. But He still had me take all those dreams and all those hopes and carry them off across the ocean, then stand there and watch them get turned to dust. It hurt, man, hurt worse than anything I've ever known."

The circle sat and rested in silence, all eyes on Jake's bowed head. With her free hand Amy reached over, made beckoning fingers for Karl to join up. One by one we grasped each other's hands.

Pipo reached over for Jake's other hand. "You're on, big man."

Jake let loose a broken-winded sigh that went on and on. Then, "God, you know me and still you made me do it. You put this inside me, Father. You gave me this dream. And then you told me what to do with it. All I did was what you said for me to do. I did my part. And it still wasn't enough.

"You made me a man, Lord. But you don't treat me like no man. You let them laugh at me. You let them heap scorn on my head. They wouldn't come out and say it, but I could hear their thoughts clear as day, and they were sayin', the man just ain't good enough.

"What hurts me most of all is that you say I'm not good enough too, Lord. By not bein' there when I really needed you, you said it plain as day. So what's a man supposed to do, Lord? Where's a man supposed to turn?"

A long silence stretched out before Amy finally spoke, her quiet voice weighed down by Jake's pain. "Heavenly Father, your ways are so difficult for us to understand at times. I see the pain of my beloved husband, and I must ask too, Father, why it must be so. I ask for him because he cannot find the words to ask you himself right now. Show us what the purpose is here, Father. You know the innermost needs of our hearts, and you can hear the plea in Jake's heart. Heal him, Father. Ease his pain. Show him how much we need him, how much we all rely on his strength. Help him to see what a good and great man he truly is. And help him to understand why he had to suffer as he did. Grant him the wisdom of understanding. Give him the miracle of your divine healing."

. . .

Up close the Reverend Bill DeLay held the same calm power

that he radiated from the podium. His wife Cathy was a motherly mixture of softness and understanding and strength. Where Bill was quiet and reserved, Cathy was outgoing and sympathetic. She greeted us with warm, genuine hugs. There was no false gushiness about either of them. All that they gave came straight from the heart.

Amy had called them the morning after our return from Karlsruhe. When I walked into the room she looked over and said, it came to me during the prayer last night. Now I don't know why it took me so long to think of it. What are you doing, I asked. She cradled the phone to her ear, said, calling in some reinforcements.

The DeLays had their own individual ways of dealing with Jake's pain. Cathy listened with silent commiseration, feeling for him. I watched the sorrow in Bill's eyes grow ever deeper; then he shifted his attention to something without meaning—the table, a magazine on the nearby stand, the kitchen door, anything that held none of Jake's agony. Once the pain diminished, he would turn back for another dose. It was a remarkable show of strength, this willingness to hear Jake through to the end.

Jake finished with, "Seemed to me that God wasn't there for me. Felt like I was lookin' for Him as much as I was a recordin' contract. Why'd He send me there if it wasn't to get started on an album? I ain't lyin'. Nashville was the first time in years I felt like the Lord wasn't there when I needed Him."

"He was there," Amy said, holding one of his hands with both of hers.

"Of course He was," Cathy DeLay agreed. "But it does seem as if He's sometimes hard of hearing, doesn't it?"

Bill DeLay spoke for the first time since the meal had begun. " 'Awake, O Lord! Why do you sleep?' "

"That's from Psalms, isn't it?" Amy asked.

"The forty-fourth," Cathy confirmed.

Bill DeLay seemed to read off the wall behind my head:

Awake, O Lord! Why do you sleep?
Rouse yourself! Do not reject us forever.
Why do you hide your face
And forget our misery and oppression?
We are brought down to the dust;
Our bodies cling to the ground.

Rise up and help us;
Redeem us because of your unfailing love.

"That about sums it up," Jake said, not lifting his eyes from his plate.

"David's army had just suffered a tremendous defeat when he wrote that," Bill said. "He was asking his Lord why it had happened, why they had to suffer the distress and scorn and shame of it all. They were His chosen people, His blessed children. The only thing David could use to describe the feeling was that the Lord had slept through David's hour of great need."

"Left David to suffer alone," Jake said. "Don't make no sense at all. Right when you need Him the most, He ain't around."

"The Bible says God is Spirit and must be worshiped in spirit and in truth," Bill replied. "We must seek Him through the presence of His Spirit in us."

"Sometimes in moments of great trial our distress robs us of the ability to find Him," Cathy agreed. "We must be strong in those times, Jake. We must remember the Lord we serve, and have faith."

"Who knows what His divine plan might have been here?" Bill took off his glasses and rubbed tired eyes. "We know from Acts that Paul was called by the Lord's messenger to go to Rome. But right after the message arrives, his ship is hammered by a storm that blows them a thousand miles off course, and they become shipwrecked on Malta. There they are, wretched and tired and starving, and then to top it all off as they were trying to get a fire started Paul gets bitten by a poisonous snake. Who could ever have thought that the Lord had a hand in this? Yet because of this seemingly random series of events, Paul was able to convert the entire island nation. He established an enclave of Christianity that a thousand years later became a front-line bastion against the spread of Islam."

The minister put his glasses on again and leaned across the table toward Jake. "In times like these, you have to seek His will. You have to hunger after His guidance. You must hold fast to hope. You must be patient and wait upon the Lord."

"And know He will answer you," Amy said quietly.

Bill slowly nodded his head. "That most of all."

CHAPTER
13

The day Alessandro called, Jake had taped a hand-printed sheet to the bathroom mirror. He caught me looking at it and said, "Lead singer of the Rez Band, dude by the name of Glenn Kaiser, put it together. Found it in their magazine yesterday. It really touched deep, thought maybe I'd keep it up for a while."

I peered at the mirror and read:

The Christian Musician Must Be:

1. More concerned with relationships than musicianship (God, family and church)
2. Desiring the fruit of the Spirit more than the fruit of one's artistic labors (Gal. 5:22–24)
3. Desiring God's approval more than man's acclaim
4. More active in prayer than in trying to get one's songs recorded[1]

I felt his pain, felt a need to give him back what I had received. "You're one of the most godly men I've ever met, Jake."

"Always room to improve," he replied. "Always something else inside I've gotta learn to turn over to the Father. Always one more dream, one more ambition, one more hope I'm tryin' to keep all to myself."

I kept my eyes fastened on the paper. "I've received a call

---

[1]"Christian Musician Must Be," adapted from an article by Glenn Kaiser of the Rez Band as published in *Crossroads (Jesus People U.S.A.)*.

from Como. The club's opening back up late next week. And Giorgio Coppa, this singer I've been working with, wants to start work on his album in Turin three days from now."

"And?"

"I don't know what to do. I feel like I have to go, but I don't know if I want to."

"You don't know if you're strong enough to hang on to what you've found," Jake corrected.

"That too," I admitted. "But I promised Alessandro I'd be there when he reopened. And I signed a contract to perform on Coppa's album."

"Then you gotta go," Jake said. "Ain't no other way. When do you leave?"

"After tomorrow's performance."

"Not bad timin'," Jake said. "Band's got a three-week break. Shame you won't be gettin' any time off. You figure three weeks'll be enough?"

I shrugged. "How can you be so sure I need to do this?"

"Don't take it so hard, man. You gotta remember there's a lesson in everything." Jake's words seemed directed more toward himself than to me. "Sometimes you don't know what it is 'til it's over, and sometimes it's only so's you learn to lean heavy on the Lord's strength. That's what you gotta remember while you're down there, my man. You can't resist it, but He can. Use this time to learn how to seek Him out."

"Is it all right if I take some of the songs to work on while I'm gone?"

I regretted saying it as soon as the words were out. A shadow of pain flickered across Jake's features, a stab that bit deep. He pulled the stone mask back into place, said, "Ain't no reason why you shouldn't. Take any you want."

Mario was just as firm when I told him about it. "We learn a lot of big lessons through the tough times, Gianni. Maybe you oughtta see this as a testing."

I muttered something about not being so sure I was ready for any such testing just yet.

"You're ready," he replied. "If He's given this to you, it's for a reason."

But what happens if I don't make it, I asked myself, sensing a familiar gut-level hunger at the thought of all that was waiting for me. "That's easy for you to say."

"What, you think you're the only one who gets tempted? You think the Lord's laid some special burden on poor little Gianni?"

"Take it easy, Mario. I didn't mean it like that."

"Wise up, Maestro. The world hits us all, every way it can. You gotta learn to stand strong in the Lord, turn from temptation when it beckons. See it for what it really is. You can't hide behind the band for the rest of your life. If He calls you to go out in the world, then go. Just remember to be *in* the world, but not *of* it."

Two days later I flew from Dusseldorf to Turin. It was the first time I had been on a plane since my return from America as a child. I sat and watched the clouds flow by beneath me and tried to remember that other voyage. So much had happened to that lonely little child. So very much.

Turin—along with Milan, Rome, Naples, and Verona—was a major center for the Italian recording industry. Although I had spent enough time there to know my way around, I had never felt comfortable in Turin. There were too many people, too much dust and noise, too strong a sense of living inside an industrial prison. The people I knew within the Turin recording business wore thick skins and blinders; they carefully filtered everything they saw and heard and experienced.

The city was ringed by hills and filled with the companies that supplied the Fiat fortress. In the dry summer months the air remained still and stagnant, its load of smog and dust growing daily heavier. By early June, when I arrived, streetlights glowed at night with soft silver halos. On the worst days pedestrians hid red-rimmed eyes behind dark glasses. They breathed and sweated through scarves held to their faces, and dreamed of escaping on weekends to the overcrowded beaches along the Italian Riviera.

At night men dominated the city. They gathered in the piazzas and punctuated the dry dusty air with their voices and gestures. They strolled and talked and filled the cafes with their smoke. In the quarters where the Southerners lived, the Nopolitans and the Calebresi and the Pugliese and the Sicilians imported to staff the industrial might of Fiat, the men carried rosaries or worry beads and clicked the baubles in time to their speech.

Few women appeared on the streets after dark, and those who did remained close to their husbands—not necessarily with them, but close. Trios of men walked and talked and smoked and fanned the air with their hands, while their women followed three paces behind, equally involved in their own world of gossip. At night the women did not sling their purses over their shoulders; they grasped them in the hand not needed for speech and pressed them close to their chests. No matter how involved their own discussions might become, one eye was always fixed on the man up ahead.

Giorgio Coppa was operating from a Turin studio because it was the only one available at such short notice. Coppa usually waited for the flame of inspiration to ignite, then moved heaven and earth to record while the emotions were still fresh. The result was a panic-driven effort by all involved to gather at his beck and call. Studio time and recording costs were doubled by his tendency to arrive with half-finished songs, then doubled again by working with studio musicians who, having never heard the songs, practiced in sound rooms costing seven hundred dollars a day. Added to this was Coppa's love of a good time. The record companies endured him because his albums sold, and sold well.

As usual, I stayed in a small guesthouse on a quiet tree-lined back street. It was four blocks from the noisy chaos of Turin's Porta Nuova train station and was surrounded by private villas and carefully tended rose gardens. My daily guitar practice was a delight to the old signora who ran the place. She invited me to use her rooftop terrace; for two hours each day I shared the morning with the birds and the awakening city.

Instead of joining Coppa and his band upon arrival, I called from the guesthouse and asked when I was to play. His road manager was clearly pleased to hear from me, but very concerned when I refused to come join the revelry. Come on over and hear the songs, he urged. I would listen to them before I was to play, I responded, very afraid of my own weaknesses. When was I scheduled to be recorded, I asked. There was a long pause on the other end, then the reply, we'll have to get back to you.

That evening Giorgio Coppa himself came over to talk with me. With him was a young girl who scarcely took her eyes off him long enough to say hello, a young record company executive I did not know, and Ricki, Coppa's road manager.

"We were worried about you, Maestro," Coppa told me. His voice was warm, gentle, concerned, like his songs—all soft romance and barely veiled desire.

I held up the sheet of Jake's lyrics I had been working on when the signora had called me to the door. "I've got work to do, that's all."

But Coppa wasn't satisfied. "You know it means a lot to me, to all of us, that you've always been a part of our group when we record. Not just some musician off the street in for a few takes, grab the money and *ciao ragazzi*. That's not how you're feeling about it now, is it, Maestro?"

"Not at all."

"So why don't you come join us? Bring your work if you like, but come over, spend some time." His expression was like his voice, all concerned coaxing. "You know I like to have your advice on the songs. We've got some nice people over there, good times for everybody."

Ricki, the road manager, made a circle with thumb and forefinger behind Giorgio's shoulder and gave me a lewd grin.

Giorgio pressed it home. "Why don't you come on over, Maestro? We don't mind you working around there, right, Ricki?"

"Not at all."

"We just want you around when we need that special input you can give. You can understand that, as much a professional as you are. We can find you a little space where you can get off by yourself and work on your songs all you like."

"*Assolutamente*," the record company representative agreed, the gleam of avarice clear in his eyes. "If Giovanni di Alta is finally doing songs of his own, we want to work with him right from the start."

I could feel it all closing in, feel the rising tide of desire. Eager forces tugged at me to return. The young girl idly stroking Coppa's arm looked fantastic. If I didn't have her I could easily have another, I told myself, and knew it was true. Appetite surged into a gnawing hunger. All those things I had left behind suddenly looked more attractive than anything I had found. In that moment they also looked much more real.

Yet the voice of my heart's yearnings had gathered strength

over the past few weeks. Prayer was there waiting when I resisted the hunger in my body. I said the silent words, and felt stairs rise out of the darkness. I clung to what seemed a feeble strength and prayed for help. I'm falling, Father, I prayed. The words were a gift that came from somewhere beyond my own desire-fuddled brain. All I needed was to hesitate, to listen to the deeper yearning. Help me, Father. Save me from myself.

Coppa leaned forward and patted my shoulder. "You've just come in today, isn't that right? You must be very tired."

The temptations and the prayer did battle for my allegiance. I managed a nod.

"Why don't we leave you to rest, and perhaps you'll come join us tomorrow, yes?" He took my silence for assent and graced me with his smile. "Sleep well, Maestro. We need you and your talents on our side."

It was not an easy night. I tossed and turned and dozed in fits. There were so many good reasons for giving in to the desire. So *many*. Toward dawn I made my fifth or sixth trip down the hall to the bathroom, and was halted in my tracks by the sensation of standing at the mouth of a chasm. In the hallway's gloomy depths I saw the maw open at my feet, wider and wider, while I stood with one foot to either side. I returned to bed, remembering the last time I had sensed such a powerful impression, sitting in Professor Schmitz's practice room, chaining the music and myself to his inhuman discipline. There was something that needed doing, I realized as I pulled the covers back over me. It was not just that I needed to resist this temptation. I needed to take some definite step.

Eventually I fell into a restless sleep and awoke to a blade of sunshine that had worked its way through the curtains and fallen across my face. The instant my feet touched the floor, I knew what it was I had to do.

I did not even wait until after my morning coffee to call Alessandro. I feared that if I hesitated I would not have the strength to go through with it. As I dialed his number, pinpricks of fear laced through me. What if I was losing something that I would truly value only once it was gone? Twice I put the phone down, then picked it up and dialed again. By the time the line clicked and hummed and began to ring, perspiration was beading on my forehead.

His reaction was surprisingly calm. "Bad news comes in storms, Maestro. It's the way of the world."

"I'll be back when you open," I pleaded, panic-stricken with the risk I was taking.

"Doesn't matter how long it's for," he replied. "If you're leaving, it's going to be a blow."

"Bruno and Claudio will stay on. As popular as the place is now, you could get anybody you like."

"Anybody but you, right, Maestro?"

The hand that held the phone was shaking. "I just feel like it's time to make a move."

Alessandro sighed long and deep. "You're going to stay up in Germany and play with Mario's band?"

"Yes."

"Aren't they some kind of religious group or something?"

"Christian, yes, that's right."

"So what can I say? It's not money. How can I argue against this religious stuff?" Alessandro moaned a curse.

A thought struck me with the power of a lightning flash. "How would you like us to come down and play your club for a week or so?"

There was silence on the other end of the phone, then, "Your whole group? With that singer you had here back before the sky fell?"

"Amy, yes. The group's called Natural Light."

"The crowd really loved her," Alessandro mused out loud. "How about three weeks, six nights a week, a reopening special?"

"I don't know, that's a long time. The band's on a break right now, but I'm not sure what's already planned on the other side."

"Three weeks, Maestro." A touch of the old strength returned. "It's the least you can do for me."

"I'll ask. I don't handle the bookings, you understand. But I'll try."

"Do more than try," he said. "Gotta go, Maestro. We've been friends too long for me to tell you what I'm thinking right now. See you and your group in eight days. Ciao."

Less than half an hour later Amy called. "How's the world treating you, my Giovanezzo?"

"Hard," I said. I wished for some way to tell her what a

comfort it was to hear her voice just then.

"Would it help any if Mario and I were to come down?"

I was tempted, but decided, "No, you stay and enjoy your vacation."

"Some vacation. Daddy Jake left on one of his mystery tours this morning, said he had a man in Holland who might hold the key. You have any idea what he's talking about?"

"No."

"Neither do I. He left a message for you, though. Said if you had time, go meet the people at ICM there in Turin. Italian Christian Media. You got a pen handy?"

"Right here."

She gave me the address. "He didn't say what it was about. He was in too much of an all-fired hurry to say more than that we should pray for him. As if I've been doing anything else. He must have thought it was important that you call these people, though. Spent more time on it than he did on telling me good-bye."

I told her of the request from Alessandro. Amy was doubtful. "Three weeks is a long time for us to be booked anywhere right now, Gianni. Especially on such short notice."

"I know. But he really put the pressure on me. I feel like if the band can't do it, maybe I'll have to stay down that long by myself. He's been a good friend, and I need to help him get started back again."

She thought it over. "Jake's got our calendar with him. Why don't you just leave it with me and let's see what he says. No need to worry until we're sure there's a problem."

Armed with a genuine need to be elsewhere, I called the studio and told Ricki, the band manager, that I would not be coming in until it was time for me to record. The news did not go over well. Didn't I understand how much Coppa wanted me there throughout the recording? Yes, I said, please give him my apologies but I have other things that need seeing to. Ricki was not sympathetic. What else could be more important than making this album a success? I didn't say it was more important, I replied, I just have to do it.

Ricki's lack of response left me sensing that my days on the project were numbered. I was somewhat surprised at how little I seemed to mind. There was already a distance opening up between me and the flames I had felt the night before.

The ICM address was for a street near the Porta Suza train station, an area of town best known for high-rise tenements, neighborhoods structured like imported Sicilian and Calebresi villages, and crime. The taxi driver circled the block twice before dropping me off with a shrug at an angular building with an unmarked doorway. Just inside the entrance was a small sign pointing toward the basement. I walked down concrete stairs and stopped before what appeared to be an open jail-cell door. Beyond this was yet another door of solid steel, this one closed. I hesitated, then rang the buzzer.

Inside everything was white and clean and fresh-smelling and intensely friendly. The three women staffing the reception and back office, two Italians and one American, all looked calmly busy. All had time to listen attentively as they moved about, their hands filled with other work.

The American introduced herself as Bea Custer and seemed not at all disturbed that I did not know why I was there. "You're with a gospel group, is that right?"

It seemed very strange to have our music labeled gospel, but I agreed. "In Germany."

"But you're Italian; isn't that an Italian accent I'm hearing? Is all your group Italian?"

"Just me and the sound engineer. The rest are German, Swiss, and American."

Bea was a gray-haired matron of indeterminate years with a calm, take-charge attitude. She met my gaze with firm directness and drew me out with patient strength. I decided that I liked this Bea Custer very much.

"I was called by one of the band members this morning who said I should stop by and introduce myself."

"Well, all bookings for non-Italian groups are managed by Denny Hurst." She turned and walked to a door leading off the back of the reception area and said to someone I could not see, "There's a gentleman here with a German gospel group." She turned back to me. "What was it called again, young man?"

"Natural Light."

"Hey, that was fast." A young man in a T-shirt and jeans popped through the doorway and walked toward me with a smile and outstretched hand. "I just heard about you guys last week. I'm Denny Hurst."

"Giovanni di Alta."

"That's right, they told me there was an Italian with the group." He was American to the bone, this young man, judging from his voice and his friendly openness and the relaxed way he slouched on the wall. "You play guitar, right? Yeah, they say you're pretty hot."

Bea leaned against the reception desk and listened with frank curiosity. "Did you come all the way down here just to speak with us, young man?"

I shook my head. "I'm working on an album right now. We're using a studio here in Turin."

Denny asked, "Anybody I know?"

"Giorgio Coppa."

The two Italian ladies looked up from their work. Bea and Denny exchanged glances. Denny said, "Sure, I've heard of him. He's really big around here. Seems strange he'd be using a Christian artist, you know, with the kind of music he makes."

I did not want to try to explain my own background, so I kept silent.

Bea answered for me. "This young man must have what it takes."

"Yeah, I guess so." Denny eyed me speculatively. "We're putting together a group of concerts here in Turin for two Italian Christian artists, Albino Montisci and Luca Genta. Ever heard of them?"

"I don't think so."

"Albino's getting very well known, he's done a couple of pretty successful albums. He tours Germany, Holland, Switzerland, even did a concert and television gig in Los Angeles last year. Anyway, we were looking for one other band to play with them, and I heard about you guys at a conference I went to last week in Munich. It was a gathering of the Christian booking agents in Europe, you know, to talk about our problems. And this guy who books a lot of the military bases told me about you. Said you guys were hot."

"Maybe we could play on the fact that he's working with some of the major artists like Coppa," Bea suggested.

"Absolutely." Denny asked me, "You played with anybody else we might have heard about?"

I named a few of the other albums I had worked on and

watched their astonishment grow.

"This is great." Denny was clearly picking up speed. "Maybe we could book you guys in as a solo act too. You got a sample cassette on you?"

I shook my head. "I didn't know I was going to be coming by. To tell the truth, I'm still not even sure what ICM is."

They laughed at that, the easy laughter of people with nothing to hide. "Sometimes we're not so sure either," Bea told me.

"Hang on a second," Denny said, moving around the desk. "Let me see if Domenico is free."

"We only began in 1987," Bea told me. "And we suffered through a couple of false starts after that. Domenico Manolio is our president. He wanted it to be a nonprofit trust, but the Italians put every barrier you could think of and then some in his way, so he turned it into a private corporation and tried again. They didn't have any problem with that. There's never been this separation between business and church in Italy. Look at Banco San Paulo. Basically all it does is handle the finances of the Catholic church."

I nodded as though I understood. "So you're a booking agency?"

A voice from behind me said, "Among other things."

I turned to face the speaker, a middle-aged man with thinning hair and a smooth unlined face. From behind spectacles his tired eyes wore an expression of perpetual surprise. He extended his hand, introduced himself as Domenico. Just that. For an Italian to be so nonchalant, especially the president of a commercial concern, was unheard of. He was dressed in an open-necked shirt, dark pants void of their once sharp creases, and scuffed loafers. Despite the man's casual air, he gave off a sense of barely suppressed power. It was like standing next to a quietly humming dynamo.

"I was just telling him what we did," Bea said.

"Too much to give us time to sleep," he said in English, then switched to Italian. "It's the same story with any new company. Too much to do and not enough of anything. Where are you from?"

"Lago di Como."

"But you work with a German gospel band?"

"It has German members, but all of our songs are in English, and the lead singer is American."

"And you've worked on all the albums Denny just told me about? So how did you get involved with this Christian band?"

I hesitated, decided on, "It's a long story."

He nodded as though satisfied, and said to Denny, "You're right, there's a lot we can work on here."

Domenico extended his hand to me. "When can you get Denny a tape of your music?"

"Tomorrow, I hope."

He gave the room a brief smile and returned to his office. The atmosphere remained charged with his presence.

"That's the reason why we're here," Bea said.

"The man never stops," Denny agreed.

"ICM is his baby," Bea told me. "It imports American Christian music to Italy, and has its own distribution system throughout the country."

"And record club," Denny added. "And monthly magazine."

"The only one of its kind in Italy," Bea said.

"Did you mention the radio station?" Denny asked.

"Not yet."

"Eighteen thousand watts, FM-stereo," Denny said. "And thirteen feeder stations across northern Italy. Strictly Christian programming."

"All in four years," Bea said once more. "All because of that one man and the Lord he serves."

I called Mario upon my return to the guesthouse and told him of my visit. He excitedly agreed to send the cassette down by courier. "It's a day for good news," he told me over the phone. "Amy talked to Jake, and the man sounded happy." I was not sure I had heard him right. "Happy," Mario repeated. "Said he would be back in a couple of days, hopefully with some good news."

"What news?"

"I'm afraid to guess," Mario said, "but if it's enough to make Jake sound happy, it's gotta be something big."

It surprised me, the way Denny listened to our music. There

was none of the cynical superiority that characterized the secular recording and booking industries. So many of the people with whom I had worked tried constantly to impress everyone around them with just how indispensable they were. Power was an elusive prey to be trapped and held with exclusivity. Denny could not have been more different.

He took me into a radio sound room that was not in use, then waited patiently for Bea and the two Italian women and three men I did not know to jam their way in and around the open door. The six songs—four of our own and two renditions— were greeted with smiles and praise. His own attitude was one of having already made up his mind and being pleased to have it confirmed by reality.

"A couple of those harder numbers won't get by some of the local ministers," Denny warned. "Think maybe you could structure a couple of sets around mostly pop and slow tunes?"

He was asking me to fit my playing to the audience. I had been doing that all my life. "I'll have to ask the others, but I think it'll be okay."

"There are fifty-four evangelical churches in the area surrounding Turin," Bea said from her place by the console. "If we want this to be successful, we're going to need some of the larger ones to help spread the word. Some won't do it if they know you'll be playing hard rock. We're having a tough time showing them that it's the message that counts, mostly because gospel rock is an American phenomenon, and most of them don't speak any English."

"Chameleon music, Ray Bevan calls it," Denny said. "He's a Welsh singer who's built up a big following around here. He waits and plays all his harder tunes once the reverends are tucked away in bed."

"The church leaders will want to meet you," Bea added. "They believe personal contact is the best way to make sure the group is really going to preach the Word of God with their music."

"Probably want you to lead a prayer group too," Denny predicted.

"And we'll want to tape an interview," Bea said.

I waited for the group to disperse before cornering Denny and telling him I couldn't lead the prayer meetings or do the interviews. He studied me carefully before asking why not.

I felt thoroughly ashamed, as though caught in a lie. "I've only been, well, praying for a little while."

The outrage I expected did not arrive. "How long have you been saved?"

"A couple of weeks," I said, my eyes on the floor.

He shocked me with a hard slap on the shoulder. "Praise God and welcome to the fold, brother. Bea and I were wondering how a born-again Christian was working in the lions' den."

"I signed the recording contract before I met the Lord."

He laughed at that, a joyous sound. "Have you ever heard of Chris Rodriguez?"

"I don't think so."

"He's been a guitarist with Michael W. Smith's band. He wasn't a Christian when he started playing with the group. Smith took him on because he was a great guitarist. But they got to talking on the road, he and the rest of the band. After one of their performances, when they were all back on the bus, he asked Jesus into his life."

Denny gave me an understanding smile and another pat on the back. "How about if you translated for one of your other band members. Would that be all right?"

"No problem. The sound engineer's Italian, too."

He thought it over. "That'll be okay for the ministers, the two of you with him doing all the talking. But for the interviews we'll need to use musicians."

Denny pulled out a leather-bound pocket calendar and leafed the pages. "We've got two possibilities. Albino's playing a couple of dates here in July, we could put you in as a guest attraction. He's also playing around Turin for about a week, starting the day after tomorrow. But I guess that's too soon to get everything together, right?"

I shrugged. "The band's on a break right now. I could see."

His eyes lit at the news. "We'll have to really move if it's gonna work. You'll need to meet with the ministers today, tomorrow at the latest. Think you can get your sound engineer down here that fast?"

Jake's reply was relayed to me by Mario, who arrived on the next morning's flight. "He said to tell them yes."

"That's it? Yes what?"

Mario shrugged, grinned. "Yes to whatever they want, I guess."

"But what about Como?" I had difficulty believing it was all that easy.

"Yes to that, too." Mario eyed me. "How you been holding out, Maestro?"

I ran a hand through my hair. "To tell the truth, I've been too busy to worry about it much."

Mario laughed at that. "Amazing how the Lord works these things out for us, isn't it? He makes our way straight, just like He promised."

Denny and Mario hit it off immediately, two technicians who easily lapsed into a language all their own. I left them at it, saying I was late for a date in the lions' den.

Ricki greeted me in the studio's front room. His normally friendly expression was drawn into somber lines. "Got some bad news for you, Maestro."

I knew it instantly. "Coppa's going with another guitarist."

Ricki didn't bother to deny it. "You know how important it is for us to feel like a family in here. Giorgio was really disturbed by your not wanting to join us except for the takes."

I searched within myself, was immensely glad to find that my strongest response was relief. "So he's dropping me right now? I don't have to play at all?"

Ricki misunderstood my question. "We don't want any trouble, you understand. We've already spoken to Antonio, told him we'd pay full rates."

"He must have been really excited over the news." I made a mental note to call him that night and apologize.

"Listen, Maestro, is everything all right?" His eyes showed concern. "You know, we all think a lot of you. If there's anything you need—"

All of a sudden the only thing I wanted was to be away. "Everything's fine, Ricki." I picked up my guitar, offered my hand. "Tell everybody I wish them luck, will you?"

A red-eyed and grumpy crew pulled into Turin the next morning following an all-night fourteen-hour drive. Mario and

I played the jolly hosts after the landlady took one look at Jake and fled to her room.

Once they were all in bed, Mario and I returned to ICM to meet the Italian musicians. Luca Genta played backup to Albino Montisci and was beginning to work on his own songs as well. Luca reminded me of paintings of Medieval martyrs. It was hard to imagine a more angelic face, a warmer voice.

Albino Montisci wore the mantle of his growing fame with humility. His face and eyes spoke of enduring difficult times, his voice of an understanding beyond worldly wisdom. He played for us cuts from his latest album, and from the first bars I knew that here was another person trained in classical music. His music was incredibly powerful. At times I had to grit my teeth to keep back the ache. To hear such adoration spoken in my mother tongue touched me very deeply.

> *Corro verso di te,*
> *Che m'importa del pensiero*
> *Della gente?*
> *Restino a guardare*
> *Mentre io corro da te*
> *Lascerō mille cose*
> *A Chiamarmi ivano!*[2]

> I shall flee towards you,
> What does it matter
> What other people think?
> Let them stand and witness
> While I flee towards you,
> A thousand different desires
> Shall cry out to me in vain!

Albino accepted our praise as though it were being given to the wrong man. He asked me about myself, and I confessed that I too had studied classical. He was clearly pleased, and asked if I would like to play on a couple of songs with him.

Mario laughed at that. When we turned to question him, he shook his head, said for us not to mind him, he was just marveling at the power of divine chance.

We let the others sleep as long as possible. Albino's group

---

[2]Albino Montisci, "Verso Di Te," from the album "Voci di Liberatā"; copyright © 1989 by Italian Christian Media SLR.

helped take our equipment over to the club and set up. It was a garish nightclub of immense proportions called Hiroshima-Mon Amour, and Denny warned us that many of the expected eight hundred people would not be Christians.

"A lot of the regulars come no matter what," he told us. "We've done this a couple of times before, and it goes over okay. Soon as some of the hard cases hear it's Christian they leave, but there are so many others waiting to get in that the place stays packed. The owners don't mind long as the music is quality."

"And the Word is spread where it might otherwise not be heard," Albino added.

"There should be groups from a dozen or so churches here tonight, and some of the gung-ho types will be trying to minister during the breaks. Last time we ended up having a dawn prayer session out in the parking lot after the place closed, brought nineteen people to the Lord."

Mario and I roused the band ninety minutes before the prayer session was to begin at one of the local churches. We had a great time force-feeding them coffee and rushing them through showers in the guesthouse's single bathroom.

Jake declined Mario's invitation to drive with an out-stretched palm. "Gonna have to study the lay of the land a little more before I drive around here again," he rumbled, and sleepily climbed into the passenger side. "Almost suffered a couple of major seizures just gettin' us into town."

Pipo was the only one who was cheerfully awake. "All I need is a little home-grown pasta and I'm ready to roll."

Amy looked at him askance, said, "Your stomach must be teflon-coated. How you can think of solid food right now is beyond me."

"Maybe the sister oughtta be thinkin' a little more 'bout what she's gonna be tellin' all those people waitin' to hear her speak," Jake said.

"The Lord's just gonna have to do this one on His own," Amy told her husband. "The better part of me is still back there in bed."

But by the time we made the introductions and completed the sound check and ate a quick bite at a local restaurant, smiles were back in place. We followed Denny's car to the church, a happy crew.

Il Centro Cristiano del Pieno Vangelo, the Full Gospel Christian Center, was one of Turin's larger evangelical churches. When it proved impossible to find affordable space above ground for their growing numbers, they purchased an old underground parking garage and converted it.

Amy was gracious in her greetings, and even while working through me as her translator her effect on the gathering was clear. Jake was content to stand in the background and accept awed glances in stone-faced silence. When the introductions were completed and we were all seated, one of the local ministers led us in prayer, then handed it over to Amy. She smiled at me; I nodded my readiness.

"I carried a lot of questions around with me before coming to the Lord," Amy said. "A lot of pain, too. But even when I wasn't hurting, I kept wondering about these things. I hated these questions, I really did. They disturbed me so *much*. I'd look around at all the other people I knew and they seemed so cool, so cynical. Did they ever have these doubts racking their brains? Probably not. I really admired them for this. They seemed so much more *comfortable* than I was."

She paused to brush a strand of hair from her forehead as I translated, then went on. "One of the big changes that has happened to me since becoming a Christian is how I really look at these questions of mine. Now they seem like lifelines to me. They were the only things that kept me halfheartedly searching for something more."

"Say it, sister," Jake murmured.

"A big question for me was, who am I? What purpose does life have? Am I just going to keep on as I am until I get old and sick and then just die? Why am I here?"

Amy opened her Bible, said, "I was wondering if somebody would please read for us Psalm eight, verse four right through to the end."

There was the sound of pages turning, then a soft-spoken voice read in Italian:

What is man that you are mindful of him,
The son of man that you care for him?
You made him a little lower than the heavenly beings
And crowned him with glory and honor.
You made him ruler over the works of your hands;

You put everything under his feet:
All flocks and herds,
And beasts of the field,
The birds of the air,
And the fish of the sea,
All that swim the paths of the seas.
O Lord, our Lord,
How majestic is your name in all the earth!"

"We wear His holy crown," Amy went on. "Genesis one, verse twenty-eight, says we were created in His own image. What does that say to you?"

"That we're important," a young man answered shyly, and I translated for Amy.

"We know who we are," Amy said, nodding to him. "I think even in my darkest moments I knew that there was something greater than myself that kept urging me to look in another direction. We know what we need, but the only real answer scares us to death. Why is that? Can someone tell us?"

Albino answered in halting English, "Because we want to be gods."

"We want to run our own lives," Amy agreed. "We want to run wild and free just like all our friends. We want to party. Like the song says, we just want to have fun. Why not? What is there that's stopping us?"

"His word," someone replied.

Amy nodded. "Can someone please tell us where?"

There was a scrambling through pages, then, "Romans twelve, verse two, says, 'Do not conform any longer to the pattern of this world, but be transformed by the renewing of your mind. Then you will be able to test and approve what God's will is—his good, pleasing and perfect will.' "

I finished translating back into English for the band, then waited while Amy swept the gathering with her deep gaze. Then she said quietly, "Let us bow our heads in prayer."

. . .

We played three more concerts over the next five days, all to capacity crowds. The outdoor concert at the Parco Rignon attracted almost two thousand people. Following that was the Teatro Massaua and then the Big Club. Many in the audience were not Christians; there was only scattered applause when Albino or Amy, with me translating, spoke of faith. But the distinctly faith-oriented lyrics of Albino's and Luca's songs did not seem to bother the crowds at all, and the music itself was greeted with tremendous applause. Clearly they were able to stomach the message so long as it was wrapped in a music with which they could identify.

The day before we were to begin our gig at the Como club we said goodbye to new friends and drove directly up to my cottage. It was much too small for all of us to stay there, but I wanted the band to share in the joy of my homecoming and to know that it was open to them all. The winding road that rose from Como and made its way along the steep-sided lake enchanted Amy with its breathtaking beauty. When we arrived at the cottage she did a skipping dance across the garden, stopped before the wall, looked out over the lake, and hugged herself.

She spun around, raced back to give Jake an excited embrace. "This is what I've been looking for all my life and didn't know it."

Jake turned an immobile face to search me out. From behind wrap-around shades he asked, "Think maybe you got room for a couple of guests?"

I could not help grinning. "Do I have any choice?"

Amy ran over, hugged me as well. "Can we pack this up and take it back with us?"

After making sure the others were comfortable in rooms at the town's only guesthouse, I took them all to a restaurant just over the Swiss border. Il Grotto Antico was a four-hundred-year-old water mill converted into a lantern-lit inn, and the trip took us along Lake Como, over some steep Alpine foothills, and down the length of the Lago di Lugano.

Amy banished Jake to the van's fold-down backseat. She craned and pointed out the window with childlike wonder. Snow-capped peaks reflected in crystal blue waters brought cries of delight. A tiny village's train station was rewarded with, "Look! An old-timey choo-choo. I love the ones with elbows!"

Throughout the meal we waited for news from Jake as we had waited every free moment since his return from Holland.

There was no reaction from the ebony giant, no sign at all that he was even aware of us. The only words he said came as we discussed a late-night drive around the Lake di Lugano to Campione. Better be getting on back, he advised. We've got a sound check and a full day of practice ahead of us. Looks were exchanged among us, but the hope was too great to allow for guessing.

I gave Amy and Jake my grandparents' bed and moved into the little alcove under the roof. Bringing this new faith to my hometown had troubled me; it was a public declaration to the people and the place that meant the most to me in all the world. Little whispers of doubt and indecision had returned whenever the thought arose. Yet as I lay in the darkness of my little room under the eaves and listened to Jake's rumbling gentleness and Amy's sparkling laughter, I knew I had done what was right. It was time to show my new colors.

Alessandro's greeting the next morning was subdued. He looked enormously weary as he shook hands and led us into the restaurant. He leaned against the reservations station while we inspected the two steel girders that stood like stone-colored masts against the sagging wall. Interlaced steel plates fixed by cables and iron stays held back the inward-pressing stonework. The contractors were right about one thing; with their coating of dusty gray paint, the new works would hardly be noticeable at night.

"Looks like one major headache over there." Jake's voice rumbled upward as he leaned back to eye the distant ceiling.

Alessandro turned to him, said in heavily accented English, "So you're the one who stole my Maestro."

"Not me, my man," Jake said, his gaze still on the ceiling of glass. "His Lord's just called him home."

We set up quickly, the work down to a smooth-running routine that required little discussion and less hesitation. By the time we were plugged in and tuned up, the room was filled with waiters and cleaners and *conoscenti* who had stopped by to wish Alessandro luck with his opening. The bearded bear walked over to the edge of the stage, asked Jake if we could play one song so everybody would then get back to work and his grand reopening wouldn't be put off until next month.

Jake looked around, got the nod from us. " 'Soldier Of Fortune,' " he murmured, naming a song by DeGarmo and Key.

"Say something, Amy," Mario called from his place at the back of the room.

Amy pulled the microphone from the stand. "Test, test. Unaccustomed as I am to speaking in public . . ."

Mario adjusted the levels, gave Jake the thumbs up. Jake nodded to Sameh, who clicked us into the song.

It was a solid rock of a number, one that allowed us to power full-on. The cynical expressions of the waiters dissolved into grins. The street-wise crowd at the back with Alessandro lowered their sunglasses, looked at each other, looked at us, moved forward.

When we finished the room echoed to cheers and excited voices. Even Alessandro sported a sad smile as he walked toward the stage. He spoke to me in halting English so we all could understand, "You think maybe you could tell me what I'm supposed to do after you leave?"

"Pray for guidance," Amy answered for us.

He looked her way, decided she was serious. "I don't think I remember how."

"That's why we're here," Amy said.

"You have an answer for everything?"

She smiled at that. "Just the things that matter."

We took a break halfway through the practice session. I joined the others in the kitchen for coffee. When I returned I found Jake and Alessandro leaning against the stage and talking in low tones. They were so engrossed in their conversation they did not see me. I waited beside the velvet drop that hid the kitchen entrances and watched them for quite a while before I realized they were talking about me.

"I've never seen anybody able to hold a crowd like him," Alessandro was saying.

"Gianni's got a talent you don't see so often," Jake agreed. "It's not just that he's a good guitarist. He's versatile, you know what I mean? Usually somebody talented like that, they get trapped in the groove that comes easy. Gianni's arrangements are like his playin'. I never know where his next song's gonna come from."

"It's more than talent," Alessandro replied. "There's a special power about Gianni when he's up there."

"The man's got appeal," Jake said. "When he plays, the audience follows him like their eyes 're trackin' a magnet. Amy's got it too. It's a light that shimmers around them when they're on stage. Talent like that, a performer's either got it or they don't. Most don't."

"I wish I knew who to replace him with," Alessandro said, picking at a blistered palm.

"Only advice I can give you is what Amy said earlier," Jake replied. "Every problem I've turned over to the Lord has been solved in His own special way. Then when the weight's off me I can see there was a reason for it, some lesson I needed to learn."

Alessandro looked over at the two new stone-colored girders, said, "I find that a little hard to believe."

"I hear what you're sayin', man," Jake said easily. "It's one of those things you can't understand 'til you see it from the inside."

As quietly as I could I turned and walked back into the kitchen. It gave me a warm feeling to see the power of faith move into this part of my world.

With Alessandro's agreement, I limited myself to one opening solo set, which I did on the Chet Atkins acoustic. As always, I entered the stage without introduction. The applause was loud, and throughout the room people called to me by name. I smiled and waved, surprised at the ease of it all. I was back where I had begun, playing before the same crowd I had fled from, and I had not given the first thought to the need for a smoke-filled barrier to protect me. I sat down on my backless stool, adjusted the guitar, smiled once more, and began.

I drifted easily from song to song, needing no conscious decisions to guide my flow. I did not pause until forty-five minutes later, when I placed the guitar back in its stand, waved to the shouts and whistles and applause, and walked from the stage.

It felt immensely pleasing and terrifically strange to return to my dressing room and find the group waiting there. I accepted their compliments and Amy's hug, allowed myself to be brought into the prayer circle, found myself marveling at how different it all felt. As usual Jake opened the prayer, and as it worked its way around the group I felt a growing desire to speak. My heart was stuttering when it came my turn, but I knew it was time for my voice to be heard as well.

"I thank you, Lord, for bringing me to this point," I said. Amy gave my hand a hard squeeze and held on tight. "I never thought I would feel sure enough of an invisible presence to speak out loud, but here I am. You exist, Father, and you have changed my whole world. There could be no greater witness to this than the fact that I am standing here, in this place, speaking to you in prayer. Thank you, Father, for reaching down and saving me."

A happy crew walked out on stage about an hour later. The room was packed to capacity. All the tables were moved aside, and people pressed up right against the stage. At Jake's suggestion Amy came out with us at the beginning of the set, since she and I were the only ones of the group that anyone in the crowd would recognize. We would start the second set with Hans's solo.

Our entrance was greeted with a tremendous noise. Amy was wearing a sequined blue gown, and as she raised her hand and waved to the crowd a myriad of sparkling diamonds winked across the back wall. Without preamble Jake nodded to Sameh, and we started in with a high-powered rendition of Mylon Lefevre and Broken Heart's "Give It Up." At the close we swung into the Imperials' "Promised Land" before the audience could react. Immediately we followed that with "Heaven" by Bebe and Cece Winans. When we finished the third song, the audience demanded to be heard.

Amy smiled through their noise, and when the crowd quieted she looked my way. I licked my lips, nodded. We knew it was a secular crowd we were facing here. We were going back to the way we had done it in the big Turin clubs. The verbal ministry would be short, sharp, decisive pauses after every second or third song. I would translate at the end of each sentence, speaking rapidly but clearly. Then we would swing into the next song before the crowd cooled.

"We are so very happy to be here, to be greeted by such a wonderful audience," Amy said, and waited for me to catch up. "We are called Natural Light, and I'd like to take this opportunity to thank Alessandro and our friend Giovanni here for making it possible for us to perform for you."

The spotlight swiveled and searched and found a beaming Alessandro waving from his place by the reservations desk. He had stationed himself there to greet everyone as they entered, then found himself unable to come forward because of the crush. The crowd gave him a loud ovation.

"You are looking at one happy man," Amy said, smiling at him. "May we join with all the others here in wishing you and your club many years of success."

When the spotlight and crowd had turned back to her, Amy went on. "There is a very fine band in the United States named First Call, and as they say in one of their songs, the reason we sing is to praise the One who gave us His Son, so that we might all know the freedom of eternal salvation."

The instant I completed my translation, Jake swept down his hand and we leapt into Kathy Troccoli's "Holy, Holy."[3] It was a good move. We were able to preach the Word to those who otherwise would run for cover by giving them no time whatsoever to react. Amy danced the length of the stage, singing with that heartfelt power that was all her own. Holy is the Lord, God Almighty, she sang, and I watched the audience slowly gather back from the shocked stillness where our words had pushed them. Holy is the Lord God Almighty, Amy sang, and I endured the stunned glances cast my way that even the spotlights could not erase.

I will sing a song of praise to you, oh Lord, my God and King, Amy sang, and Pipo pounded and danced and smiled as Hans and Karl swayed in step and belted out the accompanying overtones. You are the Prince of Peace, Amy sang, and I saw that while some in the crowd balked at the music's direction, most responded with smiles and hand-waving and swaying bodies. In your light I find a new joy dawning, she sang, and the band and the crowd moved to her song's magnetic quality.

To you, oh Lord, my God and King, I lift up my soul, we sang in unison, and I felt a thrill of *rightness* lift me beyond the club's earthly confines. This was my public declaration. This was my gift to those who needed what I had found. This was my service for the One who had seen fit to save me from myself.

. . .

Mornings and afternoons we used the empty club for practice. Occasionally Alessandro would be there with salesmen and trades-people, sometimes the cooks or waiters would come out front and smoke and smile and tap their feet and clap between songs. But mostly we were left alone. We began after breakfast and stopped when light streaming through the glass roof turned the courtyard into an oven. The massive air conditioners switched on automatically in the early afternoon, and by the time we returned from our siesta and stroll through the city, the place was once again comfortably cool. We stopped when the sky overhead became streaked with the burnished gold of another sunset, and joined the kitchen crew for dinner and conversation.

Jake pushed us all very hard. There was little free time and less relaxation. The tension and sense of unexplained urgency was with us always. We finished playing at one in the morning, arrived back in Torno about two, slept until ten, had breakfast together at the cottage, then drove back to the club. It was a grinding pace, but no one complained. No one even asked the reason for it, or questioned why we were concentrating so hard on our own music. Jake did not give us a reason, and we did not ask. There was something about his reserve, some intense quality to his drive for perfection, that gave us the patience to wait until he was ready to tell us whatever it was that wound him up so tight.

I wrote another song during that time, working through the quiet midday hours while the others slept. This time there was no ready acceptance of my work. Everything was questioned, pulled apart, adjusted, reworked. I stood in silent compliance, redoing parts as requested, too caught up in the pressing tension to argue. The result was good. Very good, in fact; focused and tight. The song was entitled "Light Me Up," and was a tune with simple lyrics inviting the Holy Spirit to come and transform the singer's life. The melody was saved from being straight disco-funk by fancy drum work and alternating percussion, and by a solo that matched my harsh rock-like guitar with Karl on alto sax. The result was both powerful and polished.

Late afternoon in the middle of the third week, we were finally satisfied with the song. All eyes turned toward Jake. There was no need to say it. It was time to hear what was pushing us so hard.

Jake took his time unstrapping his guitar. He wiped his face with the sweat-stained towel, draped it across his shoulders, motioned for us to gather at one of the stage-side tables.

A final sunbeam narrowed its way between two neighboring buildings to angle a pillar of fire through the glass roof and across the stone-faced courtyard. Pipo and Hans sat on the edge of the stage with their legs dangling down. The remainder of us pulled chairs up in a broad circle.

"Time for the next step," Jake began. He gave his face another swipe with the towel. "Got us a record company in Holland who wants to give us a chance."

"And a producer," Amy said, her eyes on Jake.

"Dude by the name of André Fredricks. Some of you may have heard of him."

"Sure," Mario said. "He mixes all the Gospel Holland television shows. Did Larry Norman's 'Live' album last year."

"Man is buildin' a strong name in the Christian music scene," Jake said.

"He's supposed to be the best in Europe," Mario agreed.

The room was so quiet I could hear a single car drum by on the cobblestones outside the club. High overhead a bird perched on the edge of the courtyard wall sang a plaintive note. Someone laughed inside the kitchen. The air conditioner breathed quietly in the distance.

"Best deal I could get," Jake said, talking to the linen covered table. "Company's called Spark Music, based in central Holland. Flattest place you've ever seen. Guy who runs it's called Gerrit Aan't Goor—hope I said that right."

"You're doing just fine, honey," Amy said, reaching for his hand. "Just fine."

"Yeah, well, he works with this lady called Leida Glass. Two real strong Christians, real committed to gospel music. Started out a few years back importing records for Word Music. Then they signed on some local acts. Recorded in local studios, used the same distribution network they set up for Word. Did pretty well. So now they want to try and work out a deal with Word. The idea is, see, they'll distribute us here in Europe, and get Word to handle us in the States."

Grins were popping out around the table. Jake's sweat-sheened seriousness held us back from shouting, jumping up, racing around the room. Pipo was content to grasp hold of the stage, lean back, and release a silent cry toward the distant ceiling.

"We've got us a special price from the studio in Dusseldorf where Mario, Pipo, and I work. Gonna go for a whole album, nine songs. Gotta push hard."

Jake raised his head and raked us with a warning glare. "Let's get two things straight right here, right now. We do *not* have time for mistakes."

"Or money," Amy added quietly.

"They're takin' a big chance on us. Biggest risk they've ever taken. You hear what I'm sayin'? We are their trial run. Even with the discount this is gonna strip the cupboard bare. Lotta hopes are ridin' on our bein' able to get it right the first time. Lotta dreams, lotta people's faith bein' put on the line."

Pipo started, "What if—"

"There can't be any what if's," Jake replied, his voice a rasp. "Nine songs, three days per song. Two days at the start for the guide tracks. Twelve days for mixing. Anybody who gets us off schedule ain't long for this earth."

He let the silence hold us until he was sure the importance was clear. I thought about having my songs put on display before all the world. I looked around the table, saw serious faces and inward-looking gazes. Jake's somber urgency had touched us all very deeply.

"There's one more thing," Jake said, drawing us back into the circle. "This album is gonna be an act of faith. Right from beginning to end. Egos and selfish desires are gonna be kept outside the studio. Prayer is the name of the game."

"And thanks," Amy murmured, her eyes on Jake.

"This is a miracle, and that's no lie. When all was lost and hope was gone, the Lord came through and turned the world to light. Remember that. This ain't something we've done for ourselves. This is a gift from on high. And we're gonna reflect that in our music and in our work."

Amy swiveled around in her seat and reached up for Pipo's hand. Silently we joined hands around the table and bowed our heads. We waited a moment, and it dawned on me that Jake was not going to speak.

In silence we prayed for that binding force, that cleansing power. Help me to set myself aside, I prayed, and felt the silence come alive. Help me to do your will with this gift. In Christ's holy name I pray.

.   .   .

Wednesday morning I excused myself from practice. Jake was not at all pleased with the news, and pressed hard. "We got exactly three more days here and fourteen in Dusseldorf before the hammer falls," he told me.

I refused to yield. "There's something I have to do."

Amy walked over, slid her arm around Jake, looked into my face, and said quietly, "It's important, isn't it, Gianni?"

I nodded. "Something I've been putting off for too long."

"Gianni's not the kind of man to do this unless it was really important, Jake."

The hardness left Jake's eyes. He told me, "Try to be back for the afternoon practice."

On a hill protruding from the heart of my little village rose the church of Torno. There were other chapels, other places of worship or prayer or gathering or gossip, but this was *the* church.

Twin staircases flowed down either side of an ancient balustrade like two graceful arms. Between them stood a supporting wall and a time-worn fountain that dated from the eleventh century. The town treated these stairs as their public domain. In the afternoons the ice-cream man set up his stall across the street, next to the tiny bar and dusty piazza where my grandfather used to sit with his cronies. In the summertime young people paraded majestically back and forth from the stairs to the ice cream seller and back again. The sweet sound of Italian spoken in the flush of youth was a continuous chorale until dusk. On weekends it lasted until midnight.

On Sundays to climb the stairs meant to run the gauntlet of the town's entire church-going population. Here new babies were presented, love publicly declared, scandals inflamed and settled, business transacted, life enhanced, feelings aroused. It was an enclave, this heart of the town, where life's theater was displayed for all to see.

The church's jumbled interior was the perfect child's fantasy. The marble floors and stone walls and high ceilings drew up all the coughs and sighs and droning voices and returned them in the endless echoes of one giant voice saying anything a child wished it to. Everywhere there were doors covered in red velvet, leading off to mystical places. The light was soft and still and cool, broken into a thousand shades by the stained-glass windows. The colors moved and floated with the clouds that drifted overhead. In alcoves stood statues that would come to life under a child's gaze and accompany him on adventures through the church's hidden ways.

When I was very young, my grandmother once told me that the church was where God lived. The church was dressed in such finery, she said, as a sign of respect to the Master of the house. In my wide-eyed wonder I imagined the bells to be the voice of God. And why not? They were certainly the loudest sound in the village, a melody that could be heard everywhere. They sang in a language that only the priests could understand, I decided. That was why priests stood in those fancy robes and talked to the people of the village. They were explaining what the bells had said that morning. They came out front to interpret, then went back into the hidden rooms to be with God in His home.

I sat in the church that Wednesday morning and remembered without pain. My Bible was open in my lap, and from time to time I would search out a passage, taking tiny tastes and savoring the simple joy of understanding.

For nine long years, Wednesday morning had been the only period in my drug-addled week when I had allowed myself to remember all that had come before. Here in the cool confines of this church, I had been able to bring out the sound of her voice and the touch of her hand and recall them without the pain that had left me sweaty and heartsore when dreams had invaded my lonely nights.

Now I sat in the same pew that had harbored my few moments of relative peace, and I felt closer to my grandmother than I had since her death. Not because of the place or because of the memories. Because of finally sharing her faith.

I walked from the church and stood on the broad terrace, looking down on the dusty central square, on the cafe with its rusty tables and feeble patrons, on the flock of motorcycles where the young people gathered to laugh and flirt, on the lake's deep blue that sparkled up between the houses, on the distant mountains. I took a deep breath and said a silent prayer. It was time to go.

A path of three hundred and fifty weathered stone steps led from the church up the steep hillside to the cemetery. I stopped halfway up to catch my breath, and turned to look out over the unfolding vista. Already I was above the village's highest point. The lake beckoned and shimmered, its surface ruffled into a million glinting mirrors by the breeze. The breeze tossed my hair with gentle fingers. I stood and inhaled the fragrance of mountain wildflowers and remembered the other times I had climbed these same stairs.

The first time had been for my grandfather's funeral, and I was saved from the blackness of his absence by my youth and by my grandmother's strength. For my grandmother's funeral there had been no one to turn to for help. Certainly not the fresh-faced priest sent to officiate over the final farewell of a woman he had never met. Certainly not my father, who had not come, not called, not tried to contact me during the dark days following her death as I had struggled with the German bureaucracy. On that day, I had climbed these stairs utterly alone. Not far above the point where I now stood, I had finally stopped and turned around, unable to continue.

I had been so afraid that day, afraid and alone. The void inside me had shrouded a terrifying pain. I had been too fearful of facing that pain to continue. I had stood there on the stair feeling nothing but the dread and the dark emptiness until the priest had returned down the stairs.

I remembered that day very clearly, the way his cassock had dragged on the ground, making the rustling sound of dried twigs in the wind, the way he had grasped the black-bound prayer book to his chest as though holding a shield between himself and me. I remembered the way he had looked at me with irritation and curiosity, as though I had sent him up the stairs on a fool's errand. But the priest had seen something in my eyes that had stilled the words before they were spoken. He had turned away from me with a slight shudder, and then hurried on down toward the village and life and friends and safety. I had remained standing frozen to the stair until darkness and exhaustion had finally driven me back to the empty cottage.

Now I stood and looked into the distance and felt the chains fall around my feet. I turned and continued up the stairs.

My grandfather's father and his father before him had been stonemasons. That was as far back as the family memory had gone, to my grandfather's father's father—three generations who had resided in the tiny village and scraped a living from the heart of the mountain.

As I pushed through the squeaky wrought-iron gate another image surfaced—that of a young child watching a very weary old man wash his hands at the kitchen's stone sink before seating himself for the evening meal. Why was my grandfather a stonemason, I had asked in my little piping voice. The smile that had creased the ancient features had taken the last vestige of strength the old man had possessed. When I was a child your age, he had replied, the greatest hope of an uneducated man was for a job. Any job. I did it because I could, he had said, but you must remember this, little Giovanezzo. It is not what a man does that is the measure of his worth. It is what he carries in his mind and heart. It is what he builds his life upon.

Little gravel paths wound among the graves. Most were family plots adorned with wide, highly polished tombstones. Upon the older markers were photographs printed upon metal, and then enameled onto the stone. I paused to look at the pictures of stern-faced people, all dressed in somber black. Most of the graves had summertime flowers planted around the marker. I strolled and enjoyed the peace and listened to the birds singing and wondered at the absence of fear and pain.

A familiar figure looked up from where he was raking a gravel path, and his rheumy eyes opened wide. He dropped his tool and came over as fast as his old bones would allow.

"Signor di Alta, buongiorno, buongiorno." He wiped a dirt-stained hand on filthy trousers and offered it to me.

I shook the weathered hand. Signor Bernasconi had been the warden of the cemetery since before my grandfather had passed on. He received a pittance from the church, and an occasional paltry sum from patrons who wished him to help care for the graves of relatives. He lived in a minuscule cottage that came with the job, two cramped rooms built into the corner of the cemetery wall. I asked Signor Bernasconi how he had been.

He waved the question aside with the stiff-armed gesture of an old man, as though it was silly to ask such a thing. "You'll be wanting to see your family's plot. I've kept it just as I promised, have no fear."

I realized he thought I was checking up on him. Until then, our contacts had been restricted to occasional meetings in the village cafe. Whenever I had seen him I had slipped fifty thousand lire, about thirty dollars, into his pocket—certainly more than he was receiving from anyone else in the village. He had never said anything about my never having visited the grave. The money had been taken with a simple nod and an assurance that the graves were all in good order.

I allowed him to grasp my sleeve and lead me toward the cemetery's lone tree. My great-grandfather had built the cemetery wall on the occasion of his own father's death—he had had no money to pay for plot or funeral, and the church had decided that a retaining wall was more than sufficient payment. The plot he had chosen was shaded by a tree that had grown massive and gnarled in the passing years, and was surrounded by the music of birds who nested in the crowded branches. I stood at the base of the plot and took time to assure Signor Bernasconi that all was fine and nicely done, marveling all the while at my heartfelt calm.

Once Signor Bernasconi had accepted my gift and shaken my hand again and left me alone, I turned and inspected the graves. The headstone was a light pearl-gray marble, fashioned by my grandfather's father for his wife's burial, large enough to include most of the family plot. At its center was a bas-relief of two angels kneeling and praying, with a name and date and picture of a stern-faced woman between them. The photograph of my great-grandmother was faded to smoky shadows, but the one to its right, that of my grandfather, was still very clear. I stood in front of my grandfather's grave and remembered the feel and the smell of him. I remembered the way he had explained faith to a hurting little boy, then turned and watched a leaf fall from the gently waving tree.

My grandmother was buried to the right of my grandfather, just as she would have wanted. I stood before her grave for a very long while, lost in memories and love, wishing there were some way to tell her of this healing.

Not until I turned away from the grave did it occur to me that perhaps she already knew.

CHAPTER
14

The two weeks between our return to Dusseldorf and our entry into the studio flew by. We had time to go through each song very carefully, studying our parts, making minor changes, becoming utterly comfortable with the music. Yet there was not enough time to lose the edge. The prospect of recording our music was with us always. We lived, ate, breathed, and spoke only of our songs. One moment, two endless weeks of grueling practice stretched out in front of us. The next, and it was time.

The van was very quiet when we pulled up in front of the studio. Jake cut the motor and leaned back. We sat and listened to the engine ping and waited for Pipo's car to appear with the rest of the band.

"I'm scared," Amy declared.

I nodded. It felt very different, going into the studio to make my own album, to put my own music down on tape.

"I'll tell you what you're gonna do," Jake said. His deep voice carried a soothing calm. "You're gonna walk through that door and show the world what the good Lord has given you."

"No chance," Amy said. "My heart's going to give up half-way across the street."

"Just go in there and sing as you always do," Jake said.

"This is your last and final warning," Amy replied. "You sure you want to lose me so soon?"

"Whole world's gonna hear the Holy Spirit at work," Jake said.

"One last gasp, clutch the old ticker, keel over, and that's all she wrote. Next thing you know I'll be tuning one of those little harps, trying to find a couple of angels who want to praise His name to a funky beat."

"Here they come," Jake said, and opened his door. "Ready?"

"You go ahead," Amy said. "I want to sit here and enjoy life a little while longer."

Mario pranced around and opened the van's sliding door. "Hans has never been in a full-blown studio before. I'm gonna give him a quick tour. You wanna come along?"

Pipo came around to Jake's door, grinning from ear to ear. He said to Amy, "All those years I thought ecstasy was something that'd have to wait until I saw St. Peter's face? Forget it. This is a major rush."

Amy groaned. "Can we have a little respect for the dying?"

"Lady's got a slight case of the nerves," Jake explained.

"Aw, hey, that right?" Pipo tried to make a serious face. "Don't worry, doll. They got machines in there to make a foghorn sound like major talent."

"This is your way of making me feel better?" Amy looked at Jake. "Do I have time to wring a conga player's neck?"

"Ain't worth the trouble," Jake said.

Mario led me and Hans across the street. There was a cloudless blue sky overhead and the air already tasted of coming heat. The trees lining the street spread their leafy canopies in utter stillness. It was all a gift, laid out especially for us this day. I would carry the memory of this moment with me for the rest of my life.

The building that housed the studio had a facade of heavy gray stone. Mario walked up to the glass-and-metal door and worked the buzzer. A large brass plaque announced that the first two floors were taken up by the studio—Stephan Kramer, proprietor.

The door buzzed. Mario pushed it open with a flourish and bowed low. "Welcome to dreamland."

He directed us into an enormous outer office where a girl with long hair and bluejeans punched at a computer console. The wall behind her desk was decorated by three framed gold records signed with illegible scrawls. The girl looked up, spotted Mario, yelled for Stephan in a bored voice, returned to her work.

A chubby man in his early thirties appeared at the door of an inner office. His eyes were squinted against the smoke rising from his cigarette. His close-cropped hair was already gray. Pale, puffy features spoke of late nights and little exercise.

He nodded at Mario, asked, "Where's Jake?"

"Outside. Amy's having a nervous breakdown."

"It happens," he said, hitched at his pants, and headed for the door.

"I wish I could find some way to reach that man's heart," Mario said quietly, watching Stephan stride from the room. He shrugged off the somber moment. "C'mon, guys, let me show you around."

Mario led us down a hall, stopped in the doorway of a glass-fronted room. He waved a hand at four massive tape machines. "Here you got your basic ATR's, audio tape recorders."

"Why are there four?" Hans asked, holding back as though afraid to enter the room. The machines rose up as high as my chest, decorated with gauges and flashing lights and crystal diode counters. The pair of larger machines ran two-inch tapes through a complex series of spindles that bounced softly as the tape started and stopped.

"The two big ones are Sony 48-track recorders, or multi-tracks, or MTR's, take your pick," Mario said to Hans. "You record your different instruments one by one on the MTR; then you play all the instruments back together and mix, getting the balance of sound just right. What you've got at the end is a stereo mix, which is what you hear on the record. The stereo mix is put on the master machine, those two smaller ones there. You gotta have two master machines to make safety copies."

I glanced at Hans's face, saw the nervous confusion, recalled how scared I had been the first time I worked in a studio. There were so many new impressions, so much strangeness to the scene. Most musicians felt a complete loss of control over their music when entering a studio for the first time. They felt overwhelmed by the massive banks of controls, the sterile isolation of the recording room, and the constant stream of commands coming from the producer. It brought out the worst in some, pushing them back to a level of immobile hostility. In others it brought out the best, spurring them to reach deeper than they ever had before, urging them to play to the utmost of their ability.

A good producer—and there were not many of them—used this alien setting to develop a sense of bonding with the musician. Time was of the essence in a studio; every extra moment spent building the sense of teamwork meant more money down the drain. A good producer became the interpreter; he or she took the dreams and unfinished songs and roughed-out ideas, worked them through this strange new world with its vast array of frightening equipment, and transformed the dreams into reality. The essential element here was trust. The musicians, many of whom had spent years playing together and yearning for the moment when they would cut their album, needed to trust the producer so completely that they would place the single most important element in their lives—their music—into this stranger's hands, and do so willingly. A good producer used the studio's strangeness to impress upon a new group how important this trust really was.

Mario opened a thick cloth-covered door, revealing a second door. Through it I could now hear a faintly thumping bass. He swung the lever and pushed, and we were awash in music.

Inside the second door was a small landing with three narrow steps leading down to the main floor. The walls were a beautiful pattern which alternated brick, rosewood paneling, and the same cloth baffling that covered the doors. The floor was carpeted except for a polished wood square where four chairs stood. The ceiling was high and set with recessed lighting.

At the room's center, spanning its entire width, was a massive control board. It was built like a fifteen-foot-long desk in the same rosewood paneling as the walls. It angled up from a line of levers interspersed with tiny square buttons to row upon row of multicolored knobs. Above them were gauges and madly dancing power-level indicators. The top of the desk was built as a level shelf, and supported two computer monitors frozen in graph-like displays. Spreading out on either side of the computer screens were three pairs of bookshelf speakers.

Two men were seated before the console, enclosed on three sides by their equipment. They listened, adjusted knobs and levers, listened again, talked with their hands. The man nearest me reached toward the MTR remote, the control for the tape machines in the other room. It was a lighted computer-type counter whose lowest numbers spun so fast I could not read them. He punched a button and the music stopped.

He looked at Mario, asked, "You guys ready to start?"

"Almost." He motioned at us, said, "Like you to meet two members of our band, Gianni and Hans. Guys, this is Jurgen, Stephan's number-one sound engineer. He's gonna help André mix our album."

Jurgen had a droopy Zappa mustache and weather-beaten features. Weary blue eyes crinkled with a hint of a smile. "Hope you won't give us as much trouble as this one did."

"Not a chance," Mario said, winking at me. "We've got a Power on our side."

"Right." The two engineers exchanged glances. Jurgen asked, "You mind if we go through this a couple more times?"

"Go ahead. I just want to show them around."

Jurgen nodded to his assistant, and the music poured out once again. He adjusted the master-volume lever, and the sound diminished to a level where Mario could make himself heard.

Mario pointed to the wide rosewood shelves that extended from the console like a pair of electronic arms. "These are known as your effects racks," Mario said. "Top machine is the small reverb unit, then a multi-effects unit, a chorus flanger, a digital delay processor, aural exciter, then the graphic and parametric equalizers. Against the back wall, the computer console there, that's the sequencer. We use an Atari here, with a Cuebase software system by Steinberg."

The outer door opened to admit a stranger. Jurgen nodded to him, reached to the MTR tape control, and shut off the music. In the silence Hans asked, "What do they all do?"

"Make you sound the best they can," Mario said. "Right, André?"

"Just your ordinary miracle machine," the new man agreed, and offered Mario his hand. "How is everybody?"

"Except for a slight case of nerves, we're raring to go." Mario turned to us, said, "Guys, this is André Fredricks. He's going to produce our album."

André had a strong face, handsome in a careless sort of way. His gray eyes appeared to look for reasons to smile. His voice was quiet, his manner very reserved. He shook our hands, studied us carefully. He carried himself with an air of utter professionalism.

"Hans hasn't had a chance to spend much time in a studio," Mario explained.

"None at all," Hans corrected.

"I was just showing him around."

André nodded and looked at me. "You've had some studio experience, is that right?"

"Never on Christian music, and never in Germany," I replied.

"Experience is experience," he said quietly. "Have you ever worked with any groups I might know?"

I named a couple of the better-known Italian groups with whom I had recorded. The light in his eyes focused in tighter.

"I have some of their albums," he said. "This is very good news."

Mario laid a proprietary hand on my shoulder. "The Maestro is one of the best guitarists I have ever heard."

"Is that what everyone calls you? Maestro?"

I felt my face grow red. "Mario labeled me with that when I was a kid. I've never been able to shake it."

"Wait 'til you hear him play," Mario said, moving my shoulder back and forth. "You'll see why."

"I look forward to it," André said in his quiet way, clearly holding back. "Well, perhaps I should go see if Jake is ready to start."

He gave the two sound engineers a friendly nod, turned and walked from the room. Mario said to us, "He's the best there is in Europe, Gianni. I'm really glad Jake got him to come down and work with us."

"He seems like a real professional," I agreed, very reassured by the man's attitude.

"Back to the tour." Mario pointed to a tangled web of wiring attached to the side of the console. "That's the patch bay. It connects the different outboard gear to input channels. You want to use the compressor on the guitar, which you've got coming in on tracks two and sixteen, right? So you connect the machine to those tracks only, then maybe the aural exciter to track twelve, multi-effects to four and eighteen, and so on."

I leaned over close to a very scared-looking Hans. "You

really don't need to worry about any of this. Relax and enjoy the show."

He scanned the room, taking nothing in. "I never thought it would be so confusing."

"It's not your job to know how all this stuff works," I assured him. "Just play the best you can, and leave the rest to the producer."

"These are the reference systems," Mario said, indicating the small speakers on the console. "When you think you've got the mix right, you play the song through these little speakers before doing the master tape. It gives you the chance to hear how it'll sound on somebody's home system."

He pointed to two giant speakers imbedded in the front wall, said, "Urei professional monitor system. Best in the world. Nineteen thousand dollars for the pair."

He grabbed Hans by the arm. "C'mon, guys, time to see where it's all gonna happen."

We passed behind the console and along the side wall to a second cloth-covered door. Mario pulled it open to reveal a short hallway and a second door. One wall of the hallway was set with a series of shelves, all filled with more blinking, flashing machines.

"Big Lexicon Reverb Units and Room Simulators," Mario explained. "Lexicons to a pro."

He pushed open the second door, stepped through and switched on the lights. "This is it, guys. The recording room. Also known as the sound room, session chamber or live room."

On the left as we entered were forty or fifty sets of headphones hung neatly on individual racks. Hans pointed and asked shyly, "What are these for?"

"You'll see," Mario said, and gave me his number-one grin. "What do you think, Maestro?"

"It's fine," I said, and it was. A real professional setup.

The room was large, perhaps twenty meters long and ten wide. There was the same brick, cloth and rosewood pattern to the walls, the same calm effect from recessed lighting. The floor was hardwood and brightly polished. Through a thick window set in the side wall I could see Jurgen and his assistant working at the mixing board. But when Mario closed the connecting door the room was so quiet I could hear the pounding of my heart.

The entire right wall was lined with microphones and

stands, along with a number of little circular screens with a very fine mesh. Hans asked Mario what they were.

"For the singers, you know, to protect the mikes. Some of those babies cost two thousand bucks a pop. You get somebody who sprays out his words, you let him do it on something that won't matter if it rusts."

Near the back of the room stood a series of mobile walls on big rubber rollers. Beyond them was a baby grand piano.

"Movable walls, for setting up chamber effects," Mario explained to Hans. "One side is mirrored, the other baffled. Gives us a chance to decide what kind of effect we want. Use them with drums, singers, pianos, hollow-body guitars, percussion, sometimes with horns."

The door to the control room opened, and Jake stepped inside. He gave the room a brief glance, said, "We're gonna use Stephan's room for a prayer time. You guys ready?"

André ruled the studio like a quiet tyrant. He never lifted his voice above a murmur, never showed ruffled feathers over the great mish-mash we made in setting up. He simply did not notice our mistakes or our nervousness. It helped us immensely. Tempers that might have become frayed gradually eased. Smiles began to reappear. The tension cooled, the excitement became a game.

Spacing in the live room was crucial; everybody needed to see everyone else and also be able to see the window to the control room. We were positioned in a wide semicircle with Sameh against the back wall, protected on both sides by the movable baffles. Amy stood in the center.

Microphones sprouted throughout the room like trees in a metal forest. Sameh's drums used eighteen, Pipo another eight. Amy had five taped together and slung from the same stand; André said he'd use the initial takes to see which one best suited her voice.

There were no amps. The guitars and keyboards and all the mikes were plugged into a squat box on the floor under the control-room window, covered with jack inputs like an enormous pincushion. Mario took over one plug at a time, calling out the input numbers to André, who noted them down on the long sheet laid across the mixing board.

When we finished with the setup, André came in. "We'll need a couple of hours to set the levels for drums and percussion mikes. Then we'll start on the repertoire you want to use on the album. You all need to become used to hearing your music through the headphones.

"The time some of you have had in the studio before doesn't matter so much here. It's always different when you're cutting your own album. You'll feel stiff and self-conscious at first. It's perfectly normal. We'll just keep at it until everybody feels comfortable."

From the tone of his voice, it sounded like a speech he had given a hundred times before. He went on. "We'll run through all the songs as often as possible today. The day after tomorrow we do it without horns, keyboard, guitar and vocals, taking down bass, and drums. You'll still be hearing the others, but they won't be playing anymore. I know this is standard practice for those with studio experience, but bear with me. I like to lay all these things out at the start. We have to get one microphone user at a time down on tape.

"Days three and four, then, are bass and drum tracks. We'll put in a few of the percussion tracks here as well. Day five we start with the other instruments on a song-by-song basis. Has the order of songs been arranged?"

"Mario's got the list," Jake said.

"Right. Guitar first, then keyboards, then horns, the remaining percussion, vocals, backup vocals, special effects. There is a good chance that we may be bringing you all back up again, and I want to mention that now. Song restructuring is often required once the studio work has begun. A lot of songs are just too long in their pre-recorded state. I'm hoping we can avoid a lot of that, since I understand both your songwriters have studio experience. But it can still happen, and if it does, we need to work through these changes as friends.

"I may need to suggest chord alterations if I find the song you've got is too close in sound to an existing melody. I may feel that a new bridge is required, or something else to jazz up the standard melody you've set out. Whatever it is, I need your honest input. But just as important, I need for you to feel as if I am doing this because I want your songs to be as successful as possible.

"Join me in the mixing room whenever you like. Tell me whatever is on your mind. I need your input. I want to hear how you feel each instrument is supposed to sound. Anything you think is important, I need to hear it. My job is to take these feelings and work them into a form that will be commercially successful."

André looked at Jake. "Anything else?"

"Time pressure," Jake said.

"They'll find that out soon enough," André said. "Questions?" No one said anything. "Okay, drums and percussion stay up, everybody else move downstairs. I'll let you know when we're ready to start with the whole band."

Downstairs meant out the side door of the live room, across the courtyard, through a door decorated with a sign saying "Ready Room" and a poster for the movie "Top Gun," and down a flight of stairs. The basement was enormous and contained a television-video corner, a floor-to-ceiling bookshelf full of films, a pool table, a kitchen, a practice room equipped with a portable mixing board and sequencer, and numerous comfortable sofas and chairs. It was carpeted, quiet, comfortable, and very calming.

Jake drew me into the little kitchen alcove, said, "Should have done this sooner, but with one thing and another I didn't pick them up 'til last night."

He drew out a sheaf of papers from his jacket, unfolded and flattened them on the counter. "You got two choices. You can take my word for it that this is a fair deal, or you can have a lawyer check it out. Either way's fine with me."

"What are they for?" They looked like my old studio contracts, with the dozen pages all containing places at the bottom for signatures and stamps.

"Song rights. Fifty-fifty split. I hold the right to give ten percent from each of us to the producer and another ten each to the band if we end up making a lot of changes here. License rights here for the album only. Everything else stays in our hands." Jake inspected me. "You understand what I'm saying?"

"I think so."

"Maybe it's better if you go see a lawyer, let him spell it out. Don't want anybody ever feelin' like I pulled a fast one."

I thought it over, held out my hand, and said, "You got a pen?"

Jake showed no emotion as he reached in his pocket again. "Gotta sign every page."

"I know." I completed the pages, folded them up and handed the packet back. "Thanks, Jake."

"I'll make copies for you and get the copyrights registered." He put the papers away. "Sure feels good doin' business with people who trust each other."

I nodded. "It sure does."

Two and a half hours later André called us all back upstairs and set us to work as a group. Our first couple of songs sounded absolutely miserable. We were so ragged I found myself wondering whether the whole idea wasn't some enormous mistake.

André wasn't the least bit put off. His calm, almost bored voice came over the headphones after the second song, "Don't fight it. Expect that for the first couple of hours you're going to sound like a cat who's been left out in the rain."

"Another hour of this and I'll be climbing the walls," Pipo said.

"I sounded better when I was three years old, singing in the bathtub," Amy agreed.

"Try to stop thinking," André said. "Strange as it may sound, it's the best thing you can do for your music. You're all busy trying to figure out how you need to sound on tape. It's too early for that. Just play the songs and concentrate on your feelings."

After ninety minutes of straight playing we took our first break. The mood was a little lighter as we trooped downstairs; we could all hear the sound coming together. The earphones felt less heavy and strange, and I was beginning to grow accustomed to hearing our music over them. Our music. Our album.

André joined us, leaned against the wall by the kitchen alcove, and waited for us to settle down with coffee and drinks. "Now comes the second step. You need to try to recapture the feeling you had the first time you played each song. That magic of discovery needs to come back into your music. The listener needs to feel as if he's there and taking part."

Hans wiped his face with a towel. "What happens after that?"

"The man makes you sound as good as you possibly can,"

Jake said, reaching for his own cloth.

André nodded, added in that calming voice, "If it goes right, you'll do the finest work you've ever done in here. We keep doing each track over and over until we're sure, all of us, that we've gotten the very best you have to give."

. . .

Eight very tired and sweaty bodies left the studio that night. Eleven hours in the studio, with a fifteen-minute break every hour and a half, had left us without a dozen words between us.

I barely had energy left to undress before sprawling into bed and conking out. I awoke several hours later, absolutely famished. Jake heard me rummaging in the kitchen and joined me, wearing his shirt, underwear, and one sock. Between us we demolished a bag of apples, half a kilo of cheese, and almost an entire loaf of bread. Then I went back to bed and slept until Amy waved a cup of coffee under my nose.

We were back in the studio by ten the next morning. It was rough going at first, with everyone stiff and grumpy and out of sorts. Soon enough, however, hearts started pumping faster, faces began to wear a sheen of sweat, the air started smelling of hard work, bodies started moving, and grins began to appear. The feeling was there. We had passed some invisible hump. No longer were we bored by playing the same song over and over. It wasn't just another exercise. This was the real thing. We were in the studio, making our first album.

André felt it, too. When we broke at midafternoon for sandwiches and coffee he told us it was time for phase three.

"All rules are hereby canceled," he said. "Nothing is taken for granted anymore. Start from the idea that nothing you've played has been exactly right. Question every note. Experiment."

It troubled us all at first. There was a return to the awkward fumbling of the day before. It distressed me to watch the others slip changes into the music. Yet slowly, slowly, we began to relax. The music was becoming tighter, and we could all hear it. All of us were stretching, searching, finding the path that suited us best. Hesitantly I began to respond, experimenting with plays that brought greater power to what they were doing.

By the following afternoon we had succeeded in playing

each of the songs another dozen times. There was a looseness in the room now, a sense of deep understanding. André clearly agreed. "Sameh, Jake, and Pipo are the only ones I'll need to see for the next two days. The rest of you can do whatever you like—stay and listen or go relax. Put your instruments up, come and go as you please. It would be nice, though, if everyone could plan to spend at least a couple of hours in the recording room with me. No special time, no order or anything. Just come in and let me hear what you think of the songs as we work on them. Think of it as a time of sowing seeds."

The rest of that afternoon I spent in bed. By early evening I was drawn back to the studio. I missed the atmosphere, the sense of being at the heart of something powerfully creative. I spent the next few hours watching Jake, Pipo, and Sameh alternate in the live room, sweating and pumping and working hard. I talked with the others as they came and went. André remained very quiet, preferring to watch and listen and let us discuss among ourselves. Yet his presence was felt by us all. It remained both a stimulus and a challenge. It called us to search deeper than ever before. It drew us out, stretched our musical talent in ways and directions never before considered.

I spent the next morning and early afternoon lazing about the apartment, dozing and leafing through magazines and playing brief runs on my guitar. When the phone rang about four-thirty I started guiltily, as though caught doing something improper.

It was Mario. "André's ready for you, Maestro."

"When?"

"Right now. We've got about three takes left before you're on. Grab your gear and come on down."

I was slightly breathless as I clambered from the taxi and pulled my guitar from the trunk. I walked through the empty outer office and tried to calm down. Even after all of the experience I had had in studios all over northern Italy, I was scared.

I pushed open the double doors and entered the control room. Jake sat in one of the chairs alongside the back wall. He was dripping sweat and drinking a Coke with shaky fingers. Sameh sat propped against the wall beside Jake, his head hanging down between his knees, a towel draped loosely across his shoulders. His shirt was plastered to his body.

I asked, "Where's Pipo?"

Mario sat with legs propped on one of the effects racks, chewing on a pen. He gave me a vague wave without looking up from the papers gathered in his lap, "Downstairs drowning in the shower."

The mixing board was covered with paper. André stood over a long sheet, making tiny notes in the graph-like blocks. "Which ones do I have down for guitar?"

Mario dropped his feet, leaned over another page on the console. "Five and eleven. You told me to ask about the voice gate."

"Later," André said, and looked at me. "I want you to hear something."

"Come sit down, Gianni," Jake said, and waved me to the seat beside him.

André hit the rewind button on the MTR remote. Mario grinned, leaned over and punched my shoulder. André hit the stop.

"Okay," André said, "we're going to start with 'Playing for Keeps.' This is take one from two days ago, your second day in the studio. Concentrate on just the bass, drums and percussion."

He pushed the play button. The music rushed out. It was very strange to hear my own music come pouring from those giant speakers, with André standing over the immense console, calmly sipping his coffee, occasionally adjusting a knob. So clinical, so professional. It was a totally different experience, hearing my own songs being played in the studio. Little ideas that came from my head and heart were being squeezed and fashioned and smoothed and polished and made ready to give to the world.

The music sounded good. The three of them played well. But there was an uncomfortable moment here, a missed beat there, a gap that should have been filled.

When it was over André hit fast forward, consulted another chart, hit the stop, said, "And this is the one we're going to use."

I was shocked out of my fear. The song was transformed. They played with uncanny precision, running along a path totally of their own making. Mario mouthed the words to Amy's voice and bounced in his chair. He turned and gave me a thumbs up. I agreed. The song was fantastic.

When the song was over Jake looked at Sameh. "Think it was worth it?"

Sameh raised his head, gave a tired smile. "No question."

André said to me, "This is what I want you to do."

I licked my lips, said, "I'll try."

"You ain't gonna just try," Jake said, rising to his feet. "You're gonna go in there and burn."

Mario grinned at me. "Blow me away, Maestro."

"Clear out for a while," André said to Jake and Sameh, and to me, "Go hook up, Gianni."

I played four solid hours without a pause. Over and over the same song, until I felt as though the notes had been pounded into my brain. Four hours of one song.

Something was not right. The guitar simply did not fit to the slow churning beat of the song. It clashed almost everywhere. I had tried everything but smashing my guitar against the wall, and still could not find the sound I felt we needed.

I refused the others' invitation to join them for a late dinner. I was not hungry. Instead I walked the streets, trying to clear my mind of the clutter of sounds. I stopped in a little corner shop that served coffee and grilled meats and had round chest-high tables where people could stand. I need your help, Father, I thought as I stood and looked around, listening to the prayer in my mind and feeling the distance between me and the others in the shop. I pray for all of my brothers and sisters here, I heard myself silently say. Look at the vague hopelessness in their eyes, Father. How can I help them when they don't want to hear? Is the music an answer? If not for them, for someone else? I felt myself both shielded from these people and joined to them by my prayers. A sense of calm grew around me as I stood there sipping at a drink I did not taste, eating food I did not want. Help me, Lord.

When I returned to the studio, I pulled out my Ibancz steel-string guitar and began playing runs. By the time the others arrived I knew what was needed. I had been wrong, using the Stratocaster. The sound was too dominating. I was going to play without a pick, strum with a fingernail grown long for classical guitar, and hold myself back as tightly as possible. André gave me a careful look when he saw what I had in mind, but did not say anything.

As soon as we started I knew I was finally on the right track. I began pulling out everything possible, stripping off every unnecessary note and putting nothing in its place. Most of the song became a series of gaps connected by little double-note slashes. The verses had simple trills at the end of each line, and the chords were nothing more than a quick-wristed flash of sound.

An hour and a half later I was almost satisfied. I leaned toward the voice mike and waited for André to signal that it was on. "I need to ask Jake something."

André nodded through the window, asked, "Is it about the solo?"

I nodded. "I have an idea," I said, and ustrapped my guitar.

I found him in front of the television. "I want to change the song and use the classical in the solo."

Jake thought it over, asked, "Mind if I listen in?"

Amy stood up. "Can I come too, Gianni?"

"I don't mind." Having two friends there would help a lot.

We worked at it over an hour. There were so many things to try, so many different ways I could play it. My moves became almost mechanical, as though only part of me was there.

At the end of a take André flicked on his mike and said, "It's almost one o'clock, Gianni. One more take and we'll call it a night."

I nodded dumbly and wiped my face. It was too much trouble to search for words.

"One more time," André repeated. "Push it hard as you can."

The control room's mike was attached to a metal arm coming from the center of the mixing console. Jake leaned forward, holding his face turned so he could speak into it and see me through the thick-paned window at the same time. "Everything you've got, Gianni," he said.

"Light up the room," Amy called from her place against the back wall.

There were two mikes for the acoustic guitar—one directly in front of the guitar's mouth, and another a meter away at my right. I adjusted my position so that I was centered in front of the mike, eased the headphones from where they were pressing painfully onto my ears.

"Let's hear your very best this time, Gianni," André said.

Play, Professor Schmitz had said. Don't think. Just play.

I leaned over my guitar, set my fingering, gave a sharp nod.

I knew immediately that I finally had it right. There was no question, no doubt, no worry about a wrong move somewhere. From the first moment, the guitar, the music and I were all one. I did not think about what to play. I did not think at all. The music chimed throughout me. I played what was. Each note went exactly into the place that was made for it.

When the song ended I kept my eyes closed, savoring the moment. I understood. The repetition and the exhaustion had been necessary to break down the barriers and tap that deepest well.

When I opened my eyes they were all watching me—André, Mario, Amy, Jake. I felt such a bonding with them. Such a powerful unity. We were all part of this, building something far beyond our puny human reach. There was a divine purpose here. I knew it more clearly in that moment than ever before. It all seemed so clear, so marvelously simple.

Amy said something; I saw her lips move, but the mike was still off. I tapped the headphones with my finger. Amy turned, said something to André, who jerked slightly as though coming awake. He punched a button and I heard the answering click.

Amy asked, "Can you hear me now, Gianni?"

"Yes."

"I'm really glad I was up here to see that."

"So am I." So close. The feeling just kept on building, the Holy Spirit so real that seeing it with my physical eyes could not have made it any clearer.

"I . . ." She hesitated, looked at Jake as though asking for him to say it for her. But Jake was still looking at me. Amy turned back. "Every time I hear this song, I'm going to remember this moment."

I nodded. There wasn't any need to say anything else. I understood.

"I'm not afraid anymore," she said. "You just showed me how it's got to go."

Jake turned to her, asked, "You mean it?"

She nodded, her eyes still on me. "I'm gonna knock 'em dead."

Jake looked at André. "Think maybe we could move up the

vocals, start 'em first thing tomorrow morning?"

André shrugged. "Why not? Guitar's sure as goodness done. You ready, Amy?"

"Yes." Her eyes never left my face. "Will you stay up here with me, Gianni?"

"Sure."

"Just to remind me, you know, what I'm supposed to do."

"I wouldn't miss it for the world," I told her.

. . .

Lead vocals for that one song took the better part of the next day. Keyboards, percussion, backup vocals, a chiming effect with the sequencer, and horns ran well into the evening. We followed Jake's lead and tried not to worry over how long it was all taking.

The next morning we gathered in the control room, jamming in behind the mixing board, and listened to the raw takes. The music had not been mixed, there was no clear balancing in the songs. But the power was there. The song had been transformed into something enormously better than what we had originally brought into the studio.

Without being asked, André played it through five times. I concentrated on each instrument in turn, and found transformations on every level. Jake had taken what before had been a simple bass run and changed it into a sharp one-tone punch in time to the bass drum. He stayed on the one note until the chord change, then moved to another deep note and continued striking the beat hard with his thumb. On the refrain he alternated the steady rhythm with a sharper, staccato beat. Bam, bam, pause, bam-ba-ba-ba-bam-ba-ba-ba-bam, still droning out the same deep note. I saw what he was after. It emphasized that key driving force, that steady beat marked by Sameh's bass drum. I had not noticed it when I was playing, but now I could see how the short punches were accented by my flicking guitar movements.

The sharp punching action was imitated by Hans and Karl on horns, by Lothar's racy little keyboard chords, and by Pipo. He had held back incredibly, playing the congas as an alternate beat only at the end of each verse, then slipped a whisper of the triangle in on another track.

And over it all were laid Amy's vocals. She was the swooping force that tied us all together. In direct contrast to our sharp punching sound, she soared. I looked around the room. Everyone was moving their hands, tapping fingers, nodding agreement. Such little things, minor changes when taken one at a time. Yet joined together they amplified the song's power tremendously.

André stopped the music, gave us a chance to chatter excitedly, then signaled for us to calm down. In his quiet voice he said, "This is what you need to be doing with all your songs. You see now how it should go, and what can happen. We need to start working for more speed now. Your fears and hesitations need to be left at the door. Try to come into the studio ready to reach deeper than you ever have before, right from the very beginning."

The words sobered us. The eight remaining songs stretched out before us like an impossible task.

"Sometimes you find a song that sounds okay live but just won't hold up when it's on tape. You can't become discouraged by this. Don't feel as if it has to be dropped. Try instead to find a way to rework it. Every time you hear it, ask yourself, 'How can I make this better?' "

André checked a number on the sheet in front of him. "I'm going to play all the remaining songs for you now. Once again, when a song is down on tape like this, you find sometimes that it is a little weak. Don't let it discourage you."

He made an adjustment to the master volume and went on. "You must listen with the attitude that it is basically a good song, but it doesn't have that special catchy something you need to make it commercially successful."

We avoided one another's eyes as the songs spun through. It was a good thing André had prepared us. After hearing the completed tracks of "Playing for Keeps," it was extremely disappointing to hear what we had down for the others. The bass, drums, and percussion sounded polished and tight as he was playing the tracks intended for the final cut. But the music hung upon them was sloppy. The cohesive force needed to make them sparkle was missing. And there was a sameness to some of the melodies that shamed me. Too many of them sounded cut from the same dough.

It was very quiet when the music stopped. The mood of exhilaration had vanished. André told us, "Once again, all of you need to put preconceived ideas aside. We don't have time for the breaking-down process again. We are a team, out to make the very best music we can. In order to do this in the time we have, we are going to have to work on absolute trust."

"And faith," Amy said quietly.

"Faith in the Lord, trust in each other," André agreed. "The two cannot be separated, especially not here. We are a family out to do His work, to spread His Word."

He nodded at Jake. "Now might be a good time for us all to join in prayer, don't you think?"

We did our R&B number next, a rock ballad called "Like a River." The going was as swift as it had been tough during the first song. I walked into the live room fairly certain of how it needed to be played. After an hour of takes André and Mario agreed that it was done. Lothar was upstairs for even a shorter period. When he came down, he looked confused. He struggled to find a way of explaining it, finally said, it was there waiting for me as soon as I walked in the door. By evening André was ready to start on the vocals.

Amy emerged four hours later pale from exhaustion, and announced she was going home for some serious vegetation. We spent an hour doing the backup vocals, ran through a couple of possible special effects, and closed up shop before midnight. The atmosphere had brightened immensely since that morning. It seemed possible that we might finish the album after all.

That night, tired as I was, I could not sleep. There was something nagging at the edges of my mind. Every time I began to drift off it would return, a whisper of something left undone.

I was heating water for tea when Jake came stumbling into the kitchen. "What's up, Gianni?"

"I didn't mean to disturb you."

He waved it aside. "You ain't the only one with music on his mind."

Now that he was there, I was glad to have someone to talk with. I told him of my nagging doubt and the frustration of not knowing what it was.

He listened to me in silence, stifled a yawn, and said, "Sounds to me like we need to take it to the Lord, Gianni."

I felt a vague sense of defeat as I lowered my head. I was tired, and the return to the studio was just a few hours away. It angered me that I couldn't work out what needed doing.

"Our dear Father in heaven," Jake began, setting a sleep-loosened hand on my shoulder. "It's really something to see you at work, helpin' us get our songs ready for release. We ask your help in makin' this the very best music we can, Lord, because we really want to do this for you. My brother Gianni is in need of rest, Father. He has to be back in the studio tomorrow, and he is tired. But there's something here that he feels needs seein' to, and he can't figure out what it is. We ask your help. Guide my brother to understand what it is you're callin' him to do."

His eyes still only half-open, he stood and yawned again. "Did He speak to you, Gianni?"

The clarity of what had been pestering me was so sharp that it shamed me. "Yes."

"Great." Jake shuffled back toward the bedroom, "Oughtta get yourself on to bed, my man. Gonna be a big day tomorrow."

The song for that day was "Powerline," a heavy rock-funk song with no holds barred. I played my tracks well, but with the detachment I had known in the Italian studios. It sounded polished, and the finished work was well done. But I needed to be elsewhere. As soon as I was through, I pulled Jake from what had become his regular station against the control room's back wall.

I led him into an empty corner of the front office. "I need to rework 'If Only You Could Know.' The song's just not right."

He seemed to have been waiting for me to say it. "Song lacks something, that's for sure. What you got in mind?"

"I don't know yet." The music was polished, all the lines fit well, but the song as a whole was weak. "The melody's okay. It just doesn't carry the power it should."

"I like that song a lot," Jake agreed. "Singin' it in four languages, man, it gives me shivers every time I hear it. But—"

"Something's missing," I finished. "I think it'd be better if I could go off by myself for a while. Maybe I'll head over to Mario's."

The ebony mask stayed in place. "You do what you need to do. We'll cover for you here."

"You think André could make me a cassette of the song?"

"No problem," Jake said, and patted me on the shoulder. "Been hopin' you'd want to do something with that song. Really feel like we're diggin' for gold here."

It was not until late afternoon that I realized what I was looking for. I felt a thrill run through me as I caught that first glimpse. All day I had been looking for a flaw in the song. That had been incorrect. The song was not flawed. It simply did not take advantage of the potential. It had a text in four languages, showing that the message of salvation applied to all people, of all the world. The music, however, was strictly western-style pop-rock.

When Amy had decided to sing it in the different languages, I had simply extended the same music I had fashioned for Jake's original English words, changing the tempo where necessary to fit the new words. That had been wrong.

If she was going to sing in different languages, there had to be some special twist to the music that *accented* the foreignness. I needed to alter the melody, transform it into something that would balance with the new verses, make them sparkle.

I had to take my excitement outside, walk off the edge. Something told me that the end result was going to be really special. When I left Mario's apartment and stepped out into the crisp air of early evening, I felt that I could not walk fast enough. I smiled at passers-by, wished there were some way I could share the joy of my discovery.

It came to me as I was walking across the park, the faintest hint of unheard sound that stopped me in my tracks. The inner voice sang its tuneless melody, drifting through the fullness of my heart with a crystal clarity. I held my breath and tried to still the pounding of my heart, afraid that the slightest motion would cause it to fade away. It was the first time I had heard that lilting music since before my grandmother died.

The melody in my mind and heart clarified, and I realized that I was hearing the finished piece. I stood in the cool night air, mesmerized by the sound of that song which I had thought was lost and gone forever. Faith healed the wound, sealed this cracked and broken vessel, and filled it with unending light; and now it gave form to the song of my heart. The gift of service and the gift of talent combined within me to create something drawn from a world far beyond my earthly senses.

I do not know how long I stood there. A long time. Long enough for my legs to grow so tired that I sat on the cold, wet ground. I did not need my guitar. I was not the least bit afraid of forgetting what I was hearing. Over and over the song played itself through, filling out and strengthening. The other instruments chimed in, clearly marked in my heart's passages. I knew *exactly* what was to be.

I took time to answer the gift with a prayer of thanks, then I stood up and ran.

I was out of the taxi before it stopped. I pushed the studio's buzzer, danced a frantic shuffle until the door sounded, raced up the stairs and through the front office and into the control room. Amy was in the recording chamber, resting between takes and listening to André through the headphones. Mario sat beside him and chewed on his mangled pen. Jake and Pipo were sitting against the back wall. The perfection of those four being there to share the moment made me laugh out loud.

To Jake I said, "I figured it out."

"Been prayin' you would," he said.

"Figured what?" Pipo asked.

"Can you get Amy out of there? This can't wait."

"Man looks a little fired up, don't he?" A hidden smile put a glint in Jake's eyes. "What you think, André? We got time to hear what he's got in mind?"

"Would somebody mind telling me what's going on?" Pipo asked.

"I need my acoustic guitar," I said to André. It was hard to slow down enough to put the thoughts into words. "And three mikes. The third out farther than the second, with a mirror wall behind it to bounce the sound. And a Lexicon hooked up to both the second and third, to bounce the sound even more."

André looked at me for a moment, then leaned toward the console mike and asked Amy, "Would you mind taking a little break?"

"Doesn't sound like I've got much of a choice, does it?" She smiled at me. "We've been praying for you, Gianni."

"Yeah, well, it worked."

"Look at that little two-step the man's doing," Pipo said. "What you on, Gianni?"

"He don't need drugs," Jake said, his voice like distant thunder in the small control room. "Too full of the Spirit to have room for anything else."

"I want to play two runs on the acoustic, both the backup and the lead parts," I said. "When we do concerts Lothar can play on the keyboards, but I want to put down both tracks with the hollow-body."

André asked, "You want to use the sampler for the rhythm sections?" That would be standard practice. A sampler took a bit of sound, then through computerized reproduction would make a loop so that the sound became continuous. This would be like a single run, or a drum sequence, played over and over and over, right through the song.

I shook my head. "I want to do the whole thing straight."

He looked at the wall clock. "You don't think it'd be better to start this tomorrow morning?"

"It won't take that long," I replied.

The five of them shared a glance, then broke out laughing. "It's okay, Maestro," Mario said, rising to his feet. "C'mon, let's get you strapped in before you explode."

As soon as the mikes were in place and the stool set up and the guitar tuned and the sound levels set, I told them, "This is the rhythm section. I'll need two more tracks for the lead."

"I understand," André said, the clipped words his only indication of being touched by the excitement. "What do you want to hear as you play?"

"Drums, percussion, bass, and Amy's voice." I did not even have to think about it.

They all stared at me. "That's it?"

"That's all I need."

He inspected me again, nodded, made his adjustments, said, "Say when."

I poised over the guitar, took a breath, told them, "Now."

The rhythm would be a straight rendition of a flamenco-style strumming, thumb and three fingers flying over the strings in a constant blur. The notes fell like raindrops, pouring from the guitar in a soft summer storm.

The bridge and solo were accented with sharp heel and fingertip explosions of sound, a half-breath of power before being cut off so cleanly that it left the listener wondering if it had ever been there at all. Then back to the soft rainfall of notes, falling all around the sweetness of Amy's voice.

We ran through it four times. As the last take ended, I did not look up. The music was back, singing in my mind and heart so clearly that I half expected the others to ask about it.

Instead Amy said, "He couldn't have practiced. His guitars have all been sitting there in the corner the entire afternoon."

"I doubt if there's a half beat of difference between any of them," André said to no one in particular.

"That was incredible, Maestro," Mario said quietly. "Really fantastic."

I nodded my thanks, said to André, "I'd like to run that through the sequencer."

He understood immediately. "And choose a sound from the synthesizer and match them up, right?"

"Something that would pull it into a strong electronic flow," I agreed. "Not distorted, though."

"Just enough of a change to make the listener unsure whether he was really hearing a guitar," André said, nodding at me through the window. "I understand, Maestro."

I waited until André had finished with his note-taking, then said, "I'm ready to give you the solo now."

There was no laughter, no words. I lowered my head to focus on the guitar and the music in my mind, but I could still feel their eyes.

I had to wait a moment while the tape was rewound, a level set for my solo tracks, then, "Ready when you are, Maestro."

I took a breath, flexed my fingers, and gave them a nod.

This time, each note was carefully measured. Much of my solo was played with two and three fingers plucked together, my left hand racing up and down the entire length of the guitar's neck. It was a delicate melody played in counterpoint to Amy's voice, its sparse notes and carefully accented timing a strong balance to the rainfall of the rhythm section.

I did not hesitate, or wonder, or even need to think. It was all laid out clearly in my mind and heart. All the years of practice, the study, the effort, were drawn together in the tight focus of this moment. And soon it was over. Too soon.

There was a long silence after the song ended. Finally Jake said, "I do believe we've got it."

"Maybe," André said. "I need to wait and hear it with the vocals redone."

"Don't need to hear another thing," Jake replied. "That's it. That's the one."

"Maestro," André said. "Could we please run through that one more time, just to make sure we've got it?"

"No problem," I replied.

"Got what?" Pipo asked.

"Our single," Amy said.

"What we got here is a major event," Jake said.

"I've got tingles up and down my spine," Amy agreed.

André turned his head toward me. "Do you have parts worked out for all the other instruments, Maestro?"

"Yes." Brief staccato runs for Karl on alto sax, more spaces than notes; a brief lilting melody for Hans on flute; a hint of wind-pipe overlay by the keyboards; it was all there.

"Including Amy?"

I looked at her through the glass, saw my reflection more clearly than their faces. The light in the control room was dimmed, and the window's triple panes both reflected and blurred my features. I wondered that the change within did not show. "If it's all right."

"If it is as beautiful as what I've just heard, I'm sure it will be fine, Gianni," she replied. "I won't sleep a wink tonight."

"Who said anything about sleeping?" André was busy with his papers and switches. "The fire's lit and the Spirit's among us. Why stop now?"

Amy laughed at that. "You mean an all-nighter? Like we were all back in school?"

"Absolutely," André replied, giving me the thumbs up to prepare for the second take. "Let's use the flame while it's burning strong. Hit it, Maestro."

CHAPTER

15

Two days after we had completed the studio work, while the others were still busy worrying over details with the record company and getting in the way as the cuts were mixed, I called my father. I had known I was going to do it since my return from the gravesite. He replied with a lengthy silence when I told him who it was. I asked politely if I might come by and see him the next day. When I hung up the phone, I found my hand was shaking and my muscles tensed from the effort.

That night I could not sleep. I knew what I had to do, but I did not see how it would be possible. I prayed about it with a sense of dread, knowing that I was called to do something for which I did not have the strength.

I got up, went to the bathroom, prowled the apartment. From my guitar case I pulled out the latest lyrics Jake had given me, entitled "A Cry in the Dark." He had passed them on just before we entered the studio, saying with a grim smile that there was no reason not to hope for another album after this one.

As with all good songs, the message was simple and direct— a man trapped in the ways of the world, asking if there wasn't something more to life. The refrain was a call from on high for the man to come to Jesus.

I wandered through the living room, headed for my place at the dining table, and paused in front of the bookshelves. There were a dozen or so large picture books of European cities, souvenirs of places where Jake and Amy had visited. I had seen Amy curl up in the corner with several of these books and spend hours lost in remembering and rediscovering.

I pulled out the one on Florence, the only book she had on an Italian city. I began leafing through it and came to the section on the Academia. I spent a long time staring at the picture of Michelangelo's David, turned the page, and went no farther.

On opposing pages were photographs of two other sculptures by Michelangelo, both entitled "The Prisoner." At first I thought they were unfinished and wondered idly why two uncompleted sculptures had been given so much coverage. Then my exhaustion began to fade.

The sculptures *were* finished. The two men, cramped into the agony of impossible positions, were imprisoned in the stone. Their muscles bunched and strained against the immovable force that held them fast. Their eyes were unseeing; all their attention, all their concentration, all their energy was focused on that which held them. Their *lives* remained unfinished, parched of power by their entrapment.

I scrambled for pen and paper, spread the lyrics out on the dining table, propped up the book in front of me so that every time I raised my eyes I could drink in the power of those creations.

Here were two men, isolated and blinded by their agony, just as I had been. They were trapped in stone so solid and overwhelming that both were held for eternity. Lost in their own separate worlds of pain. Struggling madly for release. Searching, fighting, straining to loosen the burden every way they could. I bent over my paper and began to write. That imprisonment was to be the basis for the melody.

I stopped and stared at the paper in front of me, struggling with the torrent of emotions that pressed for release. There was more than just the song demanding my attention. I fought to clear my mind, and continued structuring the song.

The bridge would be a trumpet shout calling to be heard. *Here is hope,* it would say. Here is joy for the asking. Turn to Christ and know freedom. You are trapped because you are looking in the wrong direction. *Turn around.*

I became caught up in the frenzy of creation, of release. A

need was building within me to show others what I had found, to reach back into the darkness and give others a hand, a light, a sign that they too could find freedom.

I knew why I was called to this song. I understood, but I pushed the thoughts as far away as I could until the work was completed. I knew if I stopped and recognized what was building in my heart and mind I would not return to the act of creating.

In the melody for the verses there was the slightest hint of conflict between the instruments, a tugging in different directions. Not enough to intrude, but to taunt with this inner struggle of blind desperation. Searching everywhere but the one place where an answer could be found.

The refrain was a single unified blast of sound. It was an acclaim of unrestrained power, a call that demanded to be heard. All chords were major, all voices were in harmony. Heed my call, it said. Here is a beacon to light your way.

I looked at the pictures once more. So different, those statues, and yet so alike—trapped in the same awful pattern of hopeless struggle, while the call to freedom yearned to be heard.

I stumbled to my bedroom, stripped off my clothes, lay down and pulled the covers up over my head. Now that the work was over, I allowed the realization that had accompanied the song to return.

My father was imprisoned in a stony coldness of his own making, yet I found it hardest to offer him what had been granted me. Why? I knew the answer, had known it from those first early days of faltering prayer. I could offer it to him only when I had forgiven him. And I could not forgive until I had left the pain behind.

If the desire to help was only extended to those who did not hurt me, then I was not living Christ's message. I did not need my Bible to find the words. They rang clear and true through the darkened silence of my room: Even the greatest of sinners loves those who love him.

Finally, finally I knew the solution to this impossible problem. The answer lay in surrender. It seemed so simple in that moment of utter fatigue, so clear now that I was not seeking to do the act myself. It was necessary for me to forgive my father, just as completely and utterly as the Lord forgave me. How was it possible? Only by allowing God to heal me of my pain. Only by offering up my doubts and struggles and memories and burdens, and asking Him to free me of what I could not carry on my own. Only by surrendering my will to Christ, by allowing myself to be an instrument of *His* will. I needed to show my father the same grace and salvation that had been shown to me. I did not have the power to light up his darkness, any more than I had been able to light up my own. But the Lord could. I lay in my bed, drained by the rush of creative effort, and understood what I was to do. I gave thanks for the beautiful simplicity of the answer until sleep crept up and claimed me.

The next day as I stood before the heavy entrance door to his apartment building, my hand clutched a crumpled piece of paper. On it I had written a Bible passage I had found that morning. It came from Mark, chapter eleven, verse twenty-five: "And when you stand praying, if you hold anything against anyone, forgive him, so that your Father in heaven may forgive you your sins."

I stopped with my hand outstretched toward the buzzer, prayed yet again for strength. I pressed the bell, waited for the release to sound, and entered the downstairs hall. Immediately I was struck by the smell of cleanser and dust and memories.

My heart was hammering and my breath rasping in my ears when I arrived at the landing and met Anna. She appeared unchanged. The same blond hair hung limply to either side of her face, the same silent irritation greeted my arrival.

I entered the living room and was shocked to stillness by the change in my father. His hair was almost entirely gray. I stood in the doorway and looked down on a dried and wrinkled shell of a man. He sat slumped against one end of the hard sofa and stared with red-rimmed eyes at the flickering television.

I walked to the television and switched it off. My father followed me with his eyes, but made no comment as I returned and sat down beside him.

"There are some burdens too heavy for us to carry alone," I said, and the power of that simple truth made me stop and swallow hard. "Recently I have thought a lot about those early years. I think I understand what drove you away from me. It was probably there for me to see all along, but I was too much lost in my own pain to understand. Or want to understand."

I stopped and waited, wondering if the man behind those dull, empty eyes even heard me.

He stirred in his seat and asked in a hoarse voice, "You are still a musician?"

I nodded. "We have finished work on our first album this week."

The sigh drained the support from his body, and his shoulders slumped still farther. He turned back to the blank television screen, watching as though it were still on.

I pressed forward, knowing it would never be easier than now, knowing it had to be said, forcing my voice to remain level, willing my body to cease its trembling. "I have found a source of strength and healing, and I want to share it with you. I have seen that by accepting Jesus Christ into my life I can be freed of the pain, and the blindness the pain caused."

His gaze did not turn from the television. Almost without moving his lips, he murmured, "Another musician."

"You blame yourself for my mother's death," I said, knowing it was true. "You've spent your life running away from it, and where has it gotten you? If I can find the strength to forgive you, couldn't you come to do the same for yourself?"

He did not look my way as he said, "It won't bring her back. Nothing will."

"It might bring you back, though," I replied.

My father looked at me in silence, his dark eyes revealing nothing. With the feeble motions of a man twice his age he rose to his feet and shuffled from the room. I waited, caught in the silence of a place void of life.

He was gone for a very long time. I heard muffled voices coming from their bedroom, and the thump of something heavy being dropped to the floor. I waited because there was nothing else to do.

When he returned he carried several sheets of yellowed paper in his hand. He sat down, gave me another long look, and handed the pages over without a word.

My hand was shaking slightly as I took them. I knew without knowing what they contained. I willed myself to maintain control, and began to read the unfamiliar script.

My Dear Caroline,

It was wonderful seeing you in New York last month and talking over old times. It's hard to believe that ten years have passed since we giggled together through Dr. Anderson's voice class. Your life and your work with the theater there sound terribly exciting to a little provincial girl like me.

Please excuse me for taking so long to reply to your wonderful invitation, but I wanted to wait until a performance took me away from home, so that I would have time to sit and write and think about these things in peace. I hear what you say about coming to New York, studying with the masters, working as an understudy, and being ready, always ready to make that big step.

I cannot tell you how it pulls at my heart to come and live there. And your offer is more than generous. It would be wonderful to raise Giovanni in an exciting, cosmopolitan environment. But it is something that I just cannot even consider.

My singing engagements are already taking me away from home four or five times a month, for two or three days at a time. My husband cannot or will not tolerate my absences. Every time I tell him about a new booking, every time I get ready to leave, every time I return, he is furious. Absolutely livid. You cannot imagine the rage.

No woman in Italy would think of pursuing her own career, he shouts at me. Let alone a career that takes her away from her husband and her child. He says that a lot. It means nothing to him when I say that this is America, I am American, and things are different here. He's never adjusted to life in America. He feels out of place and lonely here. My going away like this only makes it worse. I really think it's the biggest reason behind why he doesn't want me to go. And that's why he hates my music.

In America, my husband is a man without a country. I love him too much to be able to lie to myself about what my return home has cost him. You should see his face when he starts talking about Como—it is the face of another person. He lights up with that old soft smile, the one that I first fell in love with and see so seldom nowadays.

You would have to hear the things he says when he compares America and Italy to understand why a move

to another American city would simply be impossible for
him. The summers are so much nicer in Italy. The bread
tastes better in Italy. I haven't had any good sausage since
I left Italy. They call this wine? Look at these people fighting in the streets, there's just no sense of quality to these
people. The drugs these people take, they don't even care
about their own minds in this country. How could they
allow such brutality in a game like American football and
put it on television for all the children to see? Do they
have no shame in America? Look at these skirts, only a
putana would dress like this in Italy. These people have
no morals and no shame. If any daughter of mine acted
like this I would throw her out of my house.

I hear his voice like a chant in my mind even when
he is a thousand miles away. Every word is an accusation.
You did this to me. You. You and your selfish American
desires, your demand to put your own career ahead of our
life together as a couple. The worst things are the ones
that are never said, the yearning I see in his eyes before
I turn out the light at night, the ache in his soul to return
to Italy. I know these things, and I am afraid to speak of
them. What can I say? How can I make it better without
agreeing to return? How can I return and still have my
music?

I feel torn in two. I love my husband and my son. I
love my music. I would rather die than do any of them
harm, and yet as I live now I harm them all. My singing
suffers because I should be giving more time to it, not
less. I should have a place to work at home, practice five
hours a day, arrive at sessions and concerts and rehearsals relaxed and at peace. None of this happens now. I have
to sneak from the house and rush through my lessons and
exercises. I am the last to arrive for rehearsals and the
first to leave. Always whatever time I take is too much,
too much. Always I am away too much.

If he could only be honest with himself, he would recognize that he is just as lonely when I am there as when
I am gone. His fury is still there when I return, and it
forms a permanent barrier between us. He says he hates
my music, but I don't believe it. What he really hates is
my being away. He attacks my music because he sees it
as the cause. It has gotten so bad that lately he will not
even allow me to play a record or the radio in the house.
He can never let go of the anger over my leaving him. I
wish. . . .

I looked up from the pages and fastened my attention on the window, staring blankly until I realized that it had begun to rain. I stood on shaking legs and walked over, wanting a moment of solitude to gather myself. I stood in the corner of that silent room, listening to my tumbling thoughts and watching the rain streak the glass before my face.

Why had my mother left this letter unfinished? I ached for her, for the pain she conveyed in her words, and for the childhood years I had lived without a mother's touch. This letter spoke of a woman whom I barely knew. My mother had remained a gentle lullaby that I would strain and strain and barely hear in the darkness of my bedroom. For me her voice was a soft whisper that sometimes woke me from a deep sleep and then vanished into silence, her kiss a memory of butterfly wings drifting across my cheek, her arms an unanswered yearning. I stood and looked down at this letter from a woman I had never truly known, and missed her terribly.

She had wished, she had hoped for something and then decided to return home with this letter and see if she might speak to her husband. Yes. She returned home and she tried to talk with my father, but the talk turned to argument and the argument to fury. I stared out the rain-streaked window and remembered my parents fighting those nights after I had been put to bed. She fought with my father that night of her return. She fought and then she fled into the night, into the snowstorm. And she never came back.

The letter's last phrase echoed over and over again in my head. *He can never let go of the anger over my leaving.* What truth there was in those words, for then and for now. She left him for good, and his anger and his guilt and his pain destroyed him. It would be so easy for me to hate him. So very easy. The thought was like a taunt to my aching heart. I have every reason to hate him. My life has been warped by his burdens. His burdens, not mine. I have spent a lifetime carrying the memory of punishments he inflicted upon me for things which I never did.

Yet there was no anger, no need for hate. Even in the depth of my sadness I could marvel at this. It was the clearest possible way of being shown that I was not alone. Here was a gift from far beyond myself, something that I could never have realized on my own.

I turned back to my father, the words still chiming in my mind. *He can never let go of the anger over my leaving.*

"You never hated my music," I said, glad that there was still some strength to my voice. "You hate what makes you feel alone."

When he did not reply, I returned to my place on the couch. "That's why you fear my talent too, isn't it? The music would take me away too, leaving you alone. But you're already alone, aren't you? You've lost yourself in a labyrinth of old hate and pain, and there's no room in there for anyone alive, not even for yourself. So I was lost to you before I ever arrived in Dusseldorf. And your rejection of my own music was just something mechanical. Something you did because you had to, not because you felt anything for me."

I leaned forward in my seat, holding his gaze. "I forgive you," I said quietly. "I only wish there were some way I could show you that Christ could give you the strength to forgive yourself."

There was nothing else to be said. I sat and watched my father as his gaze scattered across the room, touching everywhere, seeing nothing. My pain was gone, and with it my need to hate him. I felt scrubbed utterly clean inside.

I looked at this bitterly sad man and realized that here was what forgiveness would always mean to me. I would look back to this moment when describing the freedom that true forgiveness could bring, and remember what it felt to lay my burdens aside.

Heavenly Father, I prayed to myself, my eyes still on my earthly father, I pray for this man who cannot pray for himself. Grant him your healing. Show him the way back home.

I sat and looked at him a moment longer, but no more words came. I rose to my feet, asked if I might come visit again and pay him my respects. My father did not answer, did not turn my way, did not even signal that he had heard me. I turned, left the room and the apartment and made my way down the stairs and out into the fresh summer rain.

I was free.

CHAPTER
16

Six weeks after the mixing was completed I had lunch with Fraulein Rohr and Herr Scherer. It was a happy-sad time, sharing all that had happened, smiling over the good memories, pausing for silences over what was no longer. We ate at a little Italian restaurant not far from the school. Herr Scherer spent much time reminiscing about the meal my grandmother had cooked for us.

Of the two, Herr Scherer had aged more. What before had been heavy and solid now sagged without support. His beard had only faint flecks of red among the gray, and much of his hair was gone. A deep weariness filled his eyes and touched me deeply, and it was at him that I looked when I spoke of my conversion.

Yet it was Fraulein Rohr who answered. "Your grandmother would be very proud of you, Gianni. Both for your music and for your faith."

She was a little wispier, her wayward hair slightly more clear in coloring, the wide blue eyes surrounded by a few new wrinkles. Yet it was hard to believe that ten years had passed since the last time I saw her.

"Do you remember when my grandmother invited you to Mass with her?" I asked.

She gave me her old gentle smile. "Do you know, I have often thought of that very thing. The way she spoke of faith made

God seem so real, so close I could almost touch Him."

"You can," I said. "Why don't you come with me one Sunday? Both of you. There are a lot of Germans in our congregation."

"I think I might like that," Fraulein Rohr replied softly. Herr Scherer fiddled with his coffee spoon and made no reply.

Fraulein Rohr went on. "Aren't you excited about your big concert? I don't think I'd sleep a wink. Imagine playing in front of five thousand people."

"We don't know how many will show up," I warned. "There is space for five thousand, that's all we've heard."

The album was to be launched in two days with a major concert sponsored by Gospel Holland, the Dutch Christian television network. Along with Spark Music, our record label, they were bringing together a number of local groups for a six-hour concert. The entire performance was to be video-taped, then edited down to a two-hour special program. It would be televised the following Saturday evening to a four-country audience estimated at five hundred thousand. We were promised a full forty minutes of air time if our performance met their expectations.

The concert was planned for Venlo, a city near the Dutch-German border, rather than at the normal television concert hall in Hilvershum, in an effort to attract as many of our German fans as possible. Earlier that same day we were to have one song filmed for a video at the local station. The video was intended to premiere on the prime-time Gospel Holland talk show. We were to be billed as a major new international talent, a discovery from Europe that would help spread the message worldwide. A lot of publicity had been generated by the idea of a gospel group made up of four different nationalities, all singing in English, making their debut album in a German studio with a Dutch producer and record label. We had spotted posters in several cities where we had played, and had many people come up to us at concerts to ask when the album was being released.

Jake had been pushing us very hard, both in preparation for the concert and for the television-studio taping. Spark Music had decided that "Love Enough To Share" would make a better single for the European market than "If Only They Could Know." We all disagreed with the choice, but took strength from

Jake's calm acceptance and said nothing. That was the song they were going to synch in the Venlo television studio.

Synchronization meant that our music was to be played off the album to ensure its quality, while we pretended to sing and play along. This was standard practice for music videos. Preparing for it had been boring, repetitive work made acceptable only because it was intended for television. Audiences in Holland, Germany, Belgium, and northern France all watched that program.

"The concert will be sold out," Fraulein Rohr said with absolute assurance. "And just imagine, on television as well. I can't thank you enough for the tickets."

I smiled at her and said to Herr Scherer, "It would be great if you could come, too. With your wife, of course."

He did not look at all comfortable. "I've never been very big on church music, Gianni, much as I would like to hear you play."

"I think you might be surprised," I told him. "This isn't exactly what you'd expect to hear in a church."

"Of course he'll come," Fraulein Rohr said. "If his wife and I have to tie him up and drag him, he'll be there."

He studied me with a hint of the old light back in his eyes. "Do you remember when I told you that you would need to get used to playing in public?"

I nodded. The memories were both fresh and freshly cleansed, the emotions no longer there to snag me. "My grandmother prayed me through that first concert in Fraulein Rohr's classroom. I don't think I could have made it without her prayers."

"You never told me that," Fraulein Rohr exclaimed.

Herr Scherer shook his head. "Religion pops up no matter what I say."

"It's the most important thing in my life," I said simply.

His gaze sharpened. "More than music?"

"I can't separate the two," I replied. "Not any more."

The television station complex was enormous, covering an entire city block of downtown Venlo. It was full of people rushing around with loud voices, all calling urgently for things that

I couldn't understand. We were hustled into a large chamber strung with more lights than I had ever seen before in my life. Three cameras were set on elevated cranes, positioned to the front and sides of the stage. It was as quiet and calm inside the studio as it was chaotic outside.

A man in beige gabardine pants and patterned silk shirt came over and shook hands with Jake. The rest of the band gathered round. Jake introduced him as Siebren Rijpma, the program producer and announcer for Gospel Holland. Jake had made it clear to us that Siebren's personal interest was exceptional, and we tried to show how grateful we were for the opportunity he provided. Siebren had kind eyes and an angular face. When he found a reason to smile, which was often, he glowed with a light that made all of us want to laugh with him.

We were joined by a gray-bearded balding man in his midfifties. He wore jeans and a T-shirt advertising an outdoor rock concert from twenty-five years ago. He stood and listened quietly as Siebren introduced him as the chief cameraman and began explaining how we would be positioned on stage.

The back doors slammed open. A young man in charcoal gray suit and tortoise-rimmed spectacles came hustling toward us, clipboard in hand. Ignoring the band completely, he started barking choppy little sentences in Dutch at Siebren and the cameraman. He read from his clipboard, pointed at various things around the room, ordered them around some more, glanced at his watch, barked again. Siebren and the cameraman both looked at him with the quiet astonishment they would have shown a monkey at the zoo. The young man glanced once more at his clipboard, nodded as though satisfied that nothing had been forgotten, turned and bounced away. As soon as the doors had closed behind him, Siebren started back exactly where he had left off. I decided that I was going to enjoy working with these two.

We were fortunate in being able to book the studio for two hours, Siebren said. It would give everyone time to relax and learn synching. We would not actually be recording sound, he explained. The song Spark Music had chosen as our single would be played through the speakers set up to either side of the stage, and we would play in synch to it. We were not to worry about the time, he stressed. It would be far better to run half an hour late, no matter what our gray-flannel friend just said, than rush and make a mess of our debut.

The idea was to give us a low-cost video that could be distributed for album promotion, Siebren told us. Jake nodded, said respectfully, "We covered all this yesterday."

The pair showed astonishment. "Covered what?"

"We've been playing that song and one other over our PA and practicing the synch along to it."

"For how long?"

"Absolutely the longest and most boring three days of my entire life," Pipo replied for us all.

"I listened to those songs all night in my sleep," Amy agreed.

"Worse than being in the studio during the final mix," Pipo said.

Siebren and the cameraman exchanged a glance, turned back to us. Siebren said, "You guys want a job?"

"Go teach the other bands how to come in prepared," the cameraman agreed. "Save us about a million hours."

"No thanks," Jake replied.

"Not on your life," Pipo agreed.

Siebren thought it over. "You have anything you'd like to do with the extra time?"

"Maybe we could do a second song," the cameraman offered. "Use it on the next show if the response is good for the first one."

A light powered from Jake's eyes, but he said nothing. Clearly this was what he had been hoping for.

"They ought to get a reward for coming in prepared," Siebren agreed. He asked Jake, "Did you have a second song in mind?"

Jake looked at me. "Tell them your idea."

I hesitated. It seemed silly now.

"Gianni had an idea for doing a second song," Amy told the pair. Then to me, "Go on, tell them."

I took a breath. "We have this sort of ballad, called 'If Only They Could Know.'"

"I know it," Siebren said. "I listened to a demo copy of your album last night."

"So did I," the cameraman said. "And I like your music, by the way."

"That song sent chills up my spine," Siebren agreed. "I really liked the way it went back and forth between the different languages. Really drove the point home."

The atmosphere loosened considerably. I went on, more easily now. Siebren listened to me in thoughtful silence. When I finished he looked at the cameraman.

"No problem from my end," the cameraman replied. "Maybe use a second camera with high-speed film for the band, do some off-color lighting." He nodded a decision. "Grainy film for the band, slow sweep from instrument to instrument, real precise lighting for the pair."

"Why don't you send someone to see if we can borrow a sound room for an hour?" Siebren suggested.

"We'll have to start fast on the lighting," the cameraman agreed, and left.

"There's a good chance we won't be able to get this done," Siebren warned us. "There won't be time or money to bring you back if something goes wrong. If you prefer, we can use the extra time for more takes here on the stage. That way we'll at least be sure of having one solid piece for the show. Or we could go ahead and try 'Love Enough to Share' here, then move into the sound room and use that as a back-drop for 'If Only They Could Know.' "

All eyes turned toward Jake. "The more I think about it, the more I like Gianni's idea."

"Me too," Siebren said, letting the smile show. "Did you bring the outfits?"

"In the van," Amy said.

"Like I said earlier, anytime you people want a job, you know where to come." He paused, asked us, "Do you think we could spare a moment for prayer?"

"Don't see how we could do without it," Jake said.

After the prayer, Siebren's manner became brisk and efficient. We were directed to the stage and placed far apart, each person restricted to a little box of space with heel and toe positions marked in chalk. We were shown which direction to face, where to hold our heads and instruments, how to avoid shadows through crouched body movements.

While Siebren walked Amy through her steps, the rest of us submitted to the discomfort of makeup and hair spray. A number of people moved around us, taking light readings, talking through headsets to people we could not see, adjusting the cymbals so they didn't catch the light, drawing lines for the men wearing cameras on their shoulders. One man with a shoulder unit came up so close I could see my reflection in the lens. When I started to back off he told me quietly to hold very still, then to turn my head, then to move as though swinging through a solo. As I did he curved around me, shooting my face from different angles. He moved back a step, focused on the guitar neck, told me to finger a run. I did. One of the men on the camera cranes swung over my way, coming down very close and shooting me from a higher angle. The first cameraman crouched down in front of me, swiveled the eyepiece up so he could balance the video-cam on the floor and shoot me from as low as possible. Their movements were carefully coordinated, and I realized some unseen individual was directing them through the headsets. The other band members watched gravely. None of us had ever been through anything like this.

Out of the corner of my eye I caught sight of Mario standing beside the stage. When the cameras were finished with me and pointed toward the next man, I unstrapped my guitar and went over.

"I can hardly believe this is happening," Mario said, drinking it all in with round eyes.

"You're telling that to me?"

"They said I could watch it from the control room. The producer's a great guy. He's doing the concert tonight, said I could handle the mixing board if I wanted. Seems that André Fredericks called and told him I would be the best man for the job."

I leaned over the edge of the stage. "Better grab hold. Your feet aren't even touching the ground."

He grinned. "Hey, Maestro, remember the first time you played for me?"

I didn't have to think. "You were standing with my grandmother in the doorway watching me practice."

"You weren't practicing. You were on your way to the moon."

I smiled in reply. Now that it was back, it was hard to remember how I survived those ten long years without hearing the inner song.

Mario noted the change in my expression, said, "This is no

day to get serious on me, Maestro."

"I was just thinking."

"I know you were. You want to think today, you think about how it feels to be saved."

I looked at him. "I never thanked you, did I?"

He did not need to ask what I was talking about. "Don't thank me, Maestro. Thank God."

"I do," I said. "Every day."

"Gianni," Amy called. I turned to see her shrug off a shapeless raincoat, revealing a shimmering white sequined dress. The move was greeted by whistles and applause from the light technicians and cameramen. Amy smiled, raised her hair up with both hands and swung around in a slow dance step.

Pipo grinned at Jake. "I thought the pros never noticed anything like that."

"Wrong network," the chief cameraman replied.

Siebren stepped lightly onto the stage. "Let's try to get some of that steam on tape, shall we?"

Mario grinned, gave me a double thumbs up, and raced for the back doors.

Siebren looked up to the glass control room set high in the back wall. He was not wearing a headset. He said in a loud voice, "Anybody up there awake?"

The orange ready-light above the smoked-glass panel blinked on and off a couple of times.

"Wonders will never cease," Siebren said loudly. "Think somebody might be able to find the CD? The right one?"

The orange light went into a paroxysm of blinking. The chief cameraman adjusted his headset. "Willy asks if you might want to take time for a little stroll outside."

Siebren grinned at the opaque glass. "I hear they're looking for somebody to cover the drought in Somalia."

"Willy says they're all ready to roll," the cameraman said.

"I thought they might be," Siebren said, and turned to us. "Since you've already practiced synching, perhaps we can do away with playing the song through a few times."

"Yes, please," Amy said.

"I'd get down on my knees, but there's not enough room back here," Pipo agreed.

"Why don't we go ahead and start then," Siebren suggested,

his voice nonchalant. "I'll just stay down here for the first filming to make sure everything runs according to plan."

An electric thrill ran through me as the cameramen moved
into position. I saw the others stand a little more erect, adjust
straps and instruments one last time, tense for the start.

"Everybody ready?" Siebren asked, and looked at each of us
in turn. "Fine. Watch the yellow light, please. It will blink four
times, then 'Love Enough To Share' will begin on the fifth blink.
Drums, conga, horns, singer, please feel free to make as much
noise as you like. That's the nice thing about not doing it live
on the show. Does anyone need a light to count time?"

"Not anymore," Pipo said.

Siebren looked back at the control room. "Four blinks, then
start, yes? Not fourteen."

The cameraman said, "Willy says okay."

"No, he didn't," said a voice from overhead.

The cameraman shrugged. "It's what he meant."

The ready-light blinked; one, two, three, four, and we began.

We had done the song countless times over the past three
days, hammering away in sheer boredom until all awkward-
ness over synching had disappeared. I blessed Jake's tireless
work today as I played with only part of my mind, the rest
occupied with Amy swaying and singing her heart out, Pipo
hammering and grinning, the three camera cranes swinging
and swooping, the man with the portable video-cam kneeling
at my feet and then rising to shove it in my face, Siebren standing at the stage's corner, pointing out things to the control
room, men scampering along fragile bridges overhead, lights
flashing and focusing and filling the stage with colors.

When the song ended Siebren stood in thought for a moment, turned to the control panel, and asked in a loud voice,
"How did it look?"

The cameraman closest to me said, "Willy can't decide who
looked better, the girl or the kid here."

"This I've got to see," Siebren said, jumping down lightly
from the stage. "Five minutes, everybody. Please don't leave the
stage."

The five became ten and the ten fifteen before Siebren's
voice crackled from the enclosed speakers, "All right, positions
everyone. We will do another couple of takes and perhaps

change a few things." He waited a moment for us to settle, then said, "On the fifth blink, as before."

We did three more takes, the cameras switching positions each time. The only moment of nerves for me came on the third take, when two of the cranes and one of the shoulder cameras were all pointed at me throughout most of the song. Then we did four more takes where they flooded the stage with smoke that glowed as the floor lights ran through complex patterns. Amy's steps raised multicolored swirls that swayed in time to her dance.

At the end of that take Siebren's voice came through the speakers once more. "Lady and gentlemen, your preparation has made our job infinitely easier. From all of us, thank you."

Pipo whooped and danced out from behind his congas, kicking streams of smoke up over his head. The rest of us stood and watched his war dance and grinned our enjoyment of having a big step behind us.

Siebren came through the back doors and walked to the edge of the stage. "The sound studio is ready. How many of you need to change clothes?"

"Just Gianni and Amy," Jake replied. "We thought the rest of us would stay casual."

Siebren thought it over. "And the two here are in frilly evening shirts and tuxedo trousers, is that right?"

"A matched pair," Jake agreed.

Siebren looked to where the chief cameraman stood beside me. "I like the contrast."

"Especially with the studio for background," the cameraman agreed. "Old wood and funky curtains. Maybe we could start and end with sweeps through the control room."

"Great idea," Siebren said, unleashing his grin. He turned back to us, said once more, "So long as you understand it might not be workable in the time we have."

"Might as well give it a shot," Jake said for us all.

"I agree. All right, those of you who do not have to change, perhaps you could give us a hand moving the equipment." He looked at me and Amy. "I would be most grateful if you two could please be quick."

"You heard the man," Jake said. "Get a move on."

Ten minutes later I was seated on a stool in the very center of the largest live room I had ever seen. It needed to be big. The place for Amy and me was surrounded by lights on tripods with little white umbrellas to soften the glare. It was hot. I felt little prickles of sweat breaking out as the makeup girl worked on my face. Just outside the lights, Amy stood patiently while one girl powdered her face and another braided silver threads into her hair. The chief cameraman was holding a light meter to my face while two men with shoulder-cams walked in and out of the light tripods getting their movements down and talking through their headsets.

The chief cameraman came up and took the acoustic guitar I was holding. As he carefully polished the face, Siebren appeared in the control room doorway and clapped his hands once. "Pay attention, please. I want you all to know that we have less than an hour to get this right. We have no monitors, so we won't have any idea how this is going to look until it's too late to change anything. We're going to do as many takes as time permits and hope for the best. If this does work, it will largely be because you came in prepared."

Siebren thought a moment, then asked the cameraman, "Did I forget anything?"

The cameraman shook his head. "You remind me of a man waiting for his first baby to be born."

Siebren gave the room one more glance. "That's it, then. Good luck, everyone."

The cameraman handed back my guitar. "Try not to touch the face. Fingerprints will show up strong under these lights. And don't swing it too much while we're filming. We've got to keep it at an angle where there's no glare."

Amy moved in between the lights, allowed herself to be positioned by the cameraman. He told us, "You two are going to have to be close enough for us to shoot both faces together." He turned me slightly. "Let's see if we can get the neck of your guitar and the finger action in there as well."

He turned to where one of the cameraman crouched and focused up on us, asked, "How does it look?"

"Dynamite."

"Try for a side shot," he said to one of the men hovering outside the circle of light. He turned back to me, said, "Gianni, that's your name, right? Yeah, well, don't you dare move. Don't even breathe more than you have to."

"All right."

To Amy he said, "Try to hold your swaying down to about this much." He held his two hands up a short distance apart. He looked at the cameraman who stood at my right shoulder, asked, "That about right?"

"Maybe a little more."

Siebren called from the control room, "No, let's keep it down to as little as possible. We can't redo a shot if she moves out of the frame."

The cameraman nodded, said to Amy, "We need to have you and Gianni in silhouette, with the kid's finger action kind of framing the bottom part of the picture."

Amy appeared surprisingly calm. "I understand."

The chief cameraman walked to the control-room door, picked up his video-cam, said to the cameraman beside Amy, "I'll take the single face shots, moving back and forth between the two. You stay put and concentrate on the side shot."

"Right."

Siebren said from the doorway, "You gentlemen have your positions marked? Fine. Cover as many angles as you can. All right, everybody set?" He turned to where Willy and Mario were seated behind the control-room console. "Watch my hand, everybody. Five, four, three, two, one, go!"

My initial case of nerves passed swiftly. With the hollow-body I could actually hear myself play, which had not been possible with the Stratocaster used on "Love Enough To Share." It was both easier and more fun to follow my part exactly. Amy stood beside and slightly behind me, her face pointed forward, her eyes half closed as she sang. The power of her voice sent chills up my spine.

We had time for nine takes before Siebren stopped us with, "You are to be congratulated, all of you. If this hasn't worked it will not be because of lack of effort. I think all of my crew will join me in saying what a pleasure it has been to work with professionals."

"Likewise," Jake called.

"Thanks a million," Pipo chorused.

"Before you break I would like to pan an entrance and an exit through the control room," Siebren said. "All cameras please leave the studio. Everyone else please hold as still as you can."

The chief cameraman walked slowly and steadily in and out of the live room, through the control room, back and forth several times. We held still and followed him with our eyes.

Siebren clapped the man on the shoulder, said to us, "We have less than ten minutes to break camp. If Natural Light would please help, they would earn our eternal gratitude."

.   .   .

The sound check for the concert was made much easier by having the same camera crew work with us as in the studio. It was a good thing, too. The auditorium was the largest hall that any of us had played in; the empty seats rose up in a seemingly endless wave. The promoters were expecting a sellout crowd. I looked out through the cavernous hall, tried to imagine the place full of people, could not.

We were scheduled to play two hour-long sets with an hour's break. In between our two sets one of Holland's gospel choirs would perform. We were not particularly excited about having our time on stage split in two, but the Gospel Holland people had pleaded long and hard with Jake. They wanted us to cushion the choir on either side, and show them on television singing to a full house. Jake told us afterward that he had not felt in much of a position to refuse them anything. We agreed, and said nothing more about it.

There were three men with shoulder-cams weaving their way among us, another positioned directly in front of the stage on a raised platform, and a final camera back on the distant balcony. Lighting and mixing boards were so far away that I could not make out Mario's face. It was a very big hall.

Amy came up to me after the sound check, asked if I wanted to sit in on the press conference.

"Not if I have to say anything."

"You really don't like being singled out, do you?"

"It's not that. Everything I've got to say I say in my music."

She looked at me, decided, "We all have our different gifts, Gianni. I still need you, though."

"Isn't Jake going to be there?"

"Of course he is. Times like these, I need both my men."

A bespectacled dark-haired young woman who looked enormously harried greeted us as we left the stage. Her name was Monika, she said, and she was working as press aide to Siebren, the show's producer.

"The last thing we expected was to have the secular press show an interest in what we were doing here," she told us. "But this concert has been sold out for several days. I guess they wanted to find out what's going on."

Amy took the news with no visible display of nervousness. "So what kind of questions should we expect?"

"Who knows?" She brushed her limp hair back. "The secular press in Holland is so far away from the religious press that it may as well be on Venus."

The pressroom was a large dining hall with one wall of glass overlooking a rock garden. Long tables, each set for twenty people, stretched out in orderly rows. The table closest to the entrance was filled with perhaps a dozen people. They fiddled with note pads and microphones and spoke quietly among themselves. Heads swiveled at our entrance, but there were no smiles, no expressions of friendliness.

Monika gave them a nervous grin. "I would like to introduce the leaders of Natural Light, Jake and Amy Templer. And this is their lead guitarist." She glanced at the paper in her hand, pronounced incorrectly, "Giovanni di Alta."

We went around and sat in the three open chairs directly opposite the center of their group. Tape players were switched on, microphones pushed in our direction.

The interviewer sat directly across from Amy, a tired-looking man in faddish clothes with ash-colored hair cut in a punk style. "Do you find a very great difference between a normal rock concert and one of your own?"

Amy laughed. "Which are you saying is normal?"

The interviewer seemed uncertain how to continue. "I mean, have you ever gone to rock concerts that weren't, like, Christian?"

Amy shared a smile with Jake before replying, "One or two."

"Well, did you notice any real difference?"

"They're two different worlds," Jake said.

"There is such tension and negative energy at secular rock concerts, such a potential for extremes," Amy said. "The violence you see sometimes is just an offshoot. Billy Joel did an interview not too long ago where he said that a successful concert was one where the first three rows of chairs were totally demolished. Look at Prince, or any number of heavy-metal bands. The definition of success for a secular rock group is that they work the crowd up to such a frenzy that they lose control."

Six arms stretched across the table, and two more reached in from either side. Their microphones pressed tightly around Amy's face like a battery of accusing metal fingers. It was not like approaching the microphone on stage. There was a cynicism here, a sense that they were hoping something would go wrong.

The microphones turned back toward their appointed spokesman. "So how would you describe your own music's direction?"

"With Christian rock there is a sense of being lifted upward," Amy replied. "The difference between gospel and secular rock music could not be greater. Look around you tonight and tell me what you find. Ask yourself if you have ever seen so many open-hearted smiles in a secular concert. Joy, peace and excitement all at the same time."

The microphones moved back for the question, "And what do you feel causes this difference?"

"The million dollar question," Jake said.

Amy reached out her hand to Jake. "May I have your Bible, please?"

She turned the pages, found the passage, and looked up. "This comes from the sixth chapter of Luke:

Each tree is recognized by its own fruit.
People do not pick figs from thornbushes,
or grapes from briars. The good man brings
good things out of the good stored up in
his heart. For out of the overflow of his
heart his mouth speaks.

She stared the interviewer directly in the eyes. "We give from what the Lord has given us. It is as simple as that. We celebrate because we are saved, and call for others to know the joy that we have found in Him."

We arrived backstage after dinner and went directly to our minuscule dressing room. We had not been there more than a few minutes when one of the roadies came in and asked for me. He passed me a slip of paper. I opened it, and felt the years fall away.

"Where is he?" I asked.

The roadie motioned with his bearded chin. "By the side entrance. Didn't want to come into the hall."

"What is it, Gianni?" Amy asked.

"I've got to go see someone," I said, and followed the roadie from the room.

He was waiting for me in the light of a slow-motion summer dusk. He stood as far from the laughing, jostling crowd as he could and still remain in view of the side doors. He wore exactly the same clothes I remembered—dark suit, over-starched white shirt, thin dark tie, glinting spectacles. I steeled myself and walked over.

"I heard from several of my students that you were back," Professor Schmitz told me. "I refused to believe you had stooped to this level until they brought me a poster of this concert."

I was too busy facing the flood of memories to reply. I waited for the chill of remembered pain to accompany them, was both surprised and reassured to find my calm untouched. It was the greatest possible gift I could have received at that moment, a gift so natural, so quiet, I could only appreciate its power by remembering how it once had been.

He misunderstood my silence. "You are right to be ashamed. To take a talent such as yours and apply it to the boorish repetition of modern music is worse than absurd. It is a crime."

His voice had the same flat deadness that I remembered, the eyes their same blank stare. Professor Schmitz paused to pick a cigarette from his inside pocket, light it, and drag deeply. His words poured out with the smoke.

"Where is the challenge with this trash, boy? How can a musician face himself in the mirror after prostituting his talent with such nonsense?"

I found my voice, immensely pleased to discover that it contained the same peace as my heart. "Do you recall a discussion when you told me about the masters being holy men? You said that they saw their work as an offering to God. Do you remember that?"

Professor Schmitz's eyes narrowed as he inspected my face. "Perhaps."

"This is the same," I replied. "At least it is for me."

The reply seemed to confuse him. "I heard of this, but I could not believe it."

"How often did they play their music?" I kept my gaze level with his. "How much did they have to rein in their talent in order to fit the gift to the recipient? It was not that the music was any worse or that the listener was less important because he or she had never learned to appreciate more complex forms of music. It was a new era, and it required a music which spoke to the people who were alive at that time. It is the same here today."

"This is worse than I thought," he muttered, dropping his half-finished cigarette to the ground and crushing it with his heel.

"That is what I am trying to do," I persisted, feeling more sure of this than anything in my entire life. "I am trying to fit an eternal message around a contemporary beat, a pattern that will touch the hearts of people alive today."

"There is no blindness worse than that caused by religion," he snapped.

"Perhaps you feel that way because of a lack of understanding through experience," I said, not needing to search for the reply. "Would you be willing to pray with me for guidance?"

"Don't be absurd," he replied. The fingers that searched out another cigarette trembled slightly.

"There is a place here for each of us," I told him. "A service that awaits everyone. All of our talents have been created for a divine purpose. You with your disciplined precision and me with my love of emotional flow. Having one gift does not make the others incorrect, and you were wrong to deny me the right to play creatively."

"I taught you as I was taught," he snapped. "As you needed to learn."

"In a way," I agreed, "you are right. I learned discipline from you, and only now do I understand how important that lesson is. Before I was too caught up in the pain you caused me by trying to separate my creativity from my need for discipline. Only in faith have I seen how each of these is crippled without the other."

"Faith." He spat out the word. "The greatest lie man has ever concocted. Another word for allowing emotions to wreak havoc, with no check whatsoever."

"Faith has given me the strength to admit to the value of your lessons in discipline," I countered. "And to thank you for them."

He looked at me a moment before replying. "My world was destroyed through emotions. Man has yet to progress to the point where he deserves this power of his feelings. He twists them and distorts them in an endless quest for personal gain. He destroys anything and everything in his path. Were it not for emotions, the world would know peace, for emotions fuel the evil hungers. I play without the distortion of this cancer. I refute it. I seek it not."

His voice had a droning timbre, a flatness mirrored in the cold depths behind his glasses. "Mankind must grow beyond the power of evil before he may earn the right of emotions."

I marveled at my calm. I was truly protected. Neither the memories nor the deadness in his voice could touch me anymore. I straightened, replied quietly, "I understand."

"You understand nothing."

"You faced your past alone, and you created a lie," I replied. "So did I. As long as we do it ourselves, we'll never understand, and never get it right."

I leaned up closer to him, said quietly, "You're wrong, Professor. Dead wrong. You're killing yourself, and one day you'll succeed. Is that what you want?"

He did not back off. "My most gifted student, the one who could truly have achieved world-class fame, and what is he doing? Playing cheap rock and roll with a bunch of religious fanatics. Have you not seen enough of what fanatics can do? You, who suffered through year after year of a place you despised? Can you not see that we still carry the burden of our past mistakes? Mistakes forced upon us by fanatics, who appealed to the fanatic in each of us? It is a danger, a disease, and you are the one who is dying."

"There is a way out of your hatred and your fear," I said. "I know it because I've seen it. But unless you are willing to let go of what you hate in yourself, and what you hate in others, you'll never be free. That's what has driven you all these years to kill the emotion in others."

"What on earth are you talking about?"

"Forgiveness."

That brought the anger out. "Had you known a tenth of what I have lived through, you would laugh at the word."

"Perhaps," I said. "It seemed impossible for me, too. But I've learned that if you allow Jesus Christ into your life, He is able to forgive for you."

"As a young child I watched a group of monks herded up and led away in the back of an army truck. They never returned. When I was eleven the war ended. Some time later I learned that the monks were all executed in Dachau. This is what your passion and your emotions offer you, boy. It is a sacrilege, do you hear me? It is a waste of a talent that comes to earth only once in a great while. You have a responsibility to this world and you have a responsibility to yourself to make the most of it."

"I am," I replied.

"By doing what—by playing this trash? By succumbing to the same fanatical disease that has plagued mankind since he first stood upright on two legs? Have you read no history? Has not every warring nation on earth appealed to their gods?"

"They have," I agreed. "And they hold their victories up to show the strength of the one they follow."

I raised an open hand in front of his face. "I hold out my joy to you, Herr Professor. I would give anything to be able to share this love and this eternal light with you."

I dropped my hand and stepped back. "Now, what do you have to share with me?"

.   .   .

The crowd greeted us with a roar that I felt in my chest. Jake walked to the front of the stage, his guitar slung upside-down behind his back, hanging from his left shoulder. He raised his fist and outstretched forefinger toward the ceiling; to my astonishment I saw hundreds of fists rise in reply. His own call was shouted back to us by a thousand voices.

"Praise the Lord!"

Amy walked up front and center, waved and smiled a hello. Jake gave us the nod, and we swung into "A Cry in the Dark."

The applause was loud and long when we finished. Amy called her thanks, waited for quiet.

"It is only when the Lord is in your life that those deepest of dreams come true," Amy told the crowd. "When the Spirit soars, when there is love enough to share."

Again Jake nodded to Sameh, who counted with his sticks and swung us into "Love Enough To Share." The cameraman nearest me dropped to his knees, swung up the eyepiece, focused in from below. I looked out at the mass of waving arms and could not help but smile.

The crowd swayed ever so slightly, many with eyes shut tight on a world that meant so little. The music spoke to something deep inside, communicating a joy that was far beyond anything here on earth.

Amy did not let up as the one song ended. There was no need to pause in the giving. We counted down and moved into the only song of that first set which was not an original of our own, Michael W. Smith's "All You're Missin' Is A Heartache."

Jake stepped back as the particle beam searched out my face. I watched the reflection from my guitar flicker out over the darkened hall. Sound began to fill the gallery as Mario lifted my power. A moment of building crescendo, and Sameh pounded out the beat. Jake swung down the neck, and on the lowest note the band struck the first chord. I played the discord, the endless desire for that which taunted us, the prince of this world. And Amy began to sing.

Many in the audience raised hands over their heads, many voices sang out the words. I ached for them, and for those who would not hear. True joy was not of this world. The answer was not in what we could see or taste or touch. We were taunted, my instrument cried. We were struck with the desire of falsehood. The temptations were all around us. We wanted to sin so badly. But we resisted. We tried. We were called by a higher voice.

And in the moments of peace, we saw why. All we were missing was the lie.

The response was fierce when we ended. Amy stood and allowed it to wash over her, waited until the crowd calmed down enough for her to speak.

"We are so very happy to have you all here with us tonight," Amy said, her voice still a bit husky from the effort she put into the last song. "So very happy."

She smiled to their applause, walked to where her Bible lay

open on the playback speaker, returned with it to the microphone. She held it up with both hands and said, "I'd like to introduce you to a friend of mine."

They laughed and clapped at that; she laughed with them. "Heaviest book in the world, so heavy a lot of people never find the strength to pick it up. It takes a strong heart, a lot of determination, and discipline. But those who read it know it's really a love letter."

There was a thunder of agreement. Amy raised the Book again. "A love letter written just for you, from the best friend a person could ever have. His name is Jesus Christ, and He's waiting to lead you home."

It was a beautiful experience, to stand and see the shining faces beyond the lights. They seemed so eager, those eyes watching us, so happy. I listened to Amy's words, watched the crowd in front of the stage grow, felt myself smiling a welcome.

"I look out today, see so many happy faces, and I praise God for this chance to share an evening with you. So many faces, so many different people. Where is everybody from? I know there are a lot of our brothers and sisters from Holland out there, and Germany, of course. Do we have other countries here?"

A voice from the front row called out, "Belgium!"

Another, "Basel, Switzerland!"

A shout from the back boomed, "Manchester rules!"

Amy laughed with the others. "Not here, mate." She waved to the applause, asked, "Who else?"

"Japan!"

"The kingdom of Texas!"

"Italia!"

A black man stood on his chair in the second row, smiled at us, shouted, "Lagos, Nigeria!"

"Welcome," she said, and smiled at his bow and wave. Then to the crowd, "Welcome, all of you. Five thousand people from all over the world, gathered here to party and praise God."

She searched for a passage, held it with her finger, and said to the crowd, "I read something earlier while I was waiting to come on tonight."

She waited for calm, and went on. "This comes from the seventh chapter of Revelation, verse nine: 'After this I looked and there before me was a great multitude that no one could count, from every nation, tribe, people and language, standing before the throne and in front of the Lord.' "

Amy closed the Book. "He's waiting to bring us home—all of us, no matter where we're from or what we're facing. He's there to help us through the hardest times, there to give us strength and light through our darkest hour."

.　　.　　.

We had time for a moment of calm, a joyful reflection over how well the set had gone, before Siebren appeared in the doorway of our dressing room.

"Willy's put together a little something I think you're going to enjoy," he said.

We hurried with him around the packed hall, down a connecting side passage, through the cable-strewn television monitor room, into a small back chamber. He stopped before a single monitor and video, waited until we had all jammed into the room.

"This is just a rough cut," he warned. "There's a lot left to do before it'll be ready for release. I just wanted you to have a chance to see what we've got to work with."

Amy drummed with her heels. "Put it on before I burst."

He smiled at her, switched on the set, pushed the Play button on the video, scrambled to one side so he could see both us and the screen.

Siebren had done us proud. The opening shot started from far back and swooped in fast and smooth as the beat caught hold. As the song continued to mount, the camera moved to each of us in turn. We watched Sameh trace a blur of racing sticks over four of his drums, then Pipo cocky and smiling and shuffling as his hands did a flurry on the congas, then Jake with muscles bulging as he thumped out the bass line.

"Is this for real?" Pipo clambered down on his knees and moved up closer. A chorus of shouts moved him back out of the way.

Amy sang her heart out. She smiled and beckoned and danced, the sheer joy of it all shining through. The picture cut to Lothar and focused on his hands, cut back to Amy, then over to Karl and Hans and the little two-step they had worked out for the show. At the end, Amy dropped her head so that her hair fell all around her face, and the camera swooped back out to that first far-distant shot.

The room erupted. I was so busy trying to shield myself from Mario and Pipo pounding my back that I only caught a glimpse of Jake standing to one side, somber and unmoved. Siebren waved us quiet, shouted us down, waited until the room had calmed, and pushed the Play button one more time.

The picture blurred, swirled, focused just as Karl, Lothar, Pipo and I began the opening bars to "If Only They Could Know." The picture passed through the studio's control room, sweeping by the massive control panel where Siebren and Willy and Mario wore headsets and adjusted knobs and consulted scattered sheets of paper. The camera moved steadily on through the door into the sound room, its grainy picture looking harsh and sweaty. There was a swift shadow-glance at Karl looking ready to blow his first run before the camera ducked under a forest of lights and suddenly switched to utter clarity and focus in on Amy's face just as she started to sing.

There was so much love, so much joy. Her eyes looked directly into the camera, the brilliant lighting accenting that beautiful mixture of café au lait skin, high cheekbones, slightly slanted dark eyes, and jet-black hair that spilled down over her shoulders.

Slowly, slowly the camera swiveled and opened, moving slightly over to one side, bringing into vision the guitar's tuning keys, then the guitar's neck and a hand doing a swift yet graceful dance over the frets, down farther and back a little more, and just as Amy hit the final notes of the first verse I came into view.

Immediately the camera shifted to a grainy slow-motion circle through the room, blurring and shifting to each musician in turn. Flashing faces came into clarity only when they approached the microphone to sing backup on the refrain. Then they moved back into half shadows as they played, as though they were only meant to be half seen.

The camera returned to Amy as she started the next verse, this one in Japanese, and the lighting on her face shifted slightly, just enough to darken the shadows of her cheekbones and throw her eyes into deeply slanted valleys. Her eyes gleamed from the screen, looking totally alien, enormously magnetic.

The bridge again, and the camera took in Sameh playing smooth brush strokes, Pipo doing a subtle swaying as he fingertapped the congas, Jake looking strong and huge and playing his bass with what looked like caresses.

The rough grainy film made the players seem only partially separated from the wall.

My solo was next, and the picture sharpened from grainy and ghostly to crystal clear and brilliant. I did the first run up the frets, and instead of following my hand, the camera backed off and blurred the run. It held a freeze-frame shot that showed a hundred hands and arms stretching the entire distance, covering all the neck at once. The first thunder-strum and the picture snapped back into focus, allowing a clear image of the next flurry of notes reaching up the neck, then again blurred as I moved back down, this time painting a multiple frame with my entire body, then again lashing into clarity as the solo ended with the three hard down strokes.

The third and fourth verses were devoted to switches back and forth between Amy and me, freezing and flowing the picture every time I did a rapid move. All the bridges and refrains had the grainy look of an ancient photograph as the screen panned the other players. Then back to a long shot of my six-bar run, ending with an angle over Amy's shoulder and down the guitar's neck and directly into my eyes. Close up on Amy, back underneath the lights, a swift smoldering glance at the others, then out the door and through the control room as the sound died away.

Jake was the only one who did not join the laughing, shouting clamor. He nodded to Siebren, who was too busy being smothered by the others to notice. He waited out in the hall for us to join him, then walked ahead and apart from us as we made a noisy procession back to our dressing room.

Once we were all back inside he closed the door, motioned for us all to take a seat, waited in dark-faced silence until we had calmed down.

"Spent a lotta time ridin' out the need to turn my ambitions over to the Creator," Jake said. "Tough lesson, one I don't aim on lettin' go of so soon. I was in there lookin' at that video, and it hit me hard that we might really be a success at this. I don't mean some local hero, either. I mean a *name*."

Clearly he was speaking what we had all sensed. It was one

thing to feel it and dance around it and be excited without really voicing the reason. It was another thing entirely to have the fact laid out cold.

"Gotta look deep here and now," Jake went on. "Gotta decide while there's still time. Who are we doin' this for? Are we gettin' excited over some little bits of film because it makes us look good, or because it gives the Father a clearer voice for somebody in need? Who are we shoutin' for? Us or Him?"

He reached in his back pocket, came out with his tattered Bible, started turning pages. "Something came to me while I was watchin' that second video and seein' the world open up in front of me. Yeah, here it is. First Timothy, chapter six, verses seventeen through nineteen." He paused and flashed a glance at us, then read:

> Command those who are rich in this present
> world not to be arrogant nor to put their
> hope in wealth, which is so uncertain, but
> to put their hope in God, who richly
> provides us with everything for our
> enjoyment. Command them to do good, to
> be rich in good deeds, and to be generous
> and willing to share. In this way they will
> lay up treasure for themselves as a firm
> foundation for the coming age, so that they
> may take hold of the life that is truly life.

I looked around the room, saw heads nodding in thoughtful agreement. Amy walked over toward Jake; he flinched as though expecting a blow. Instead she put her arm around his waist, held him close.

"Don't want to spoil anybody's good time," he murmured. "Just felt like it was something that needed sayin'."

"You know what you are?" she asked him softly. "You're our mirror."

"Just wanted to make sure we were bein' happy for the right reason," he said to the floor.

She hugged him tighter. "Where would we be without our Daddy Jake?"

A knock sounded at the door. Siebren stuck his head in and smiled. "Five minutes to showtime."

When the door closed again, Jake looked up. "Had something I was holdin' for later, but maybe I oughtta say it now. Talked to Youth With A Mission out of Amsterdam the other day. They're leadin' a music mission to Poland and Russia in two months. Wanted to know if we'd come along. Can't pay enough to cover our expenses, but it sounded like a pretty good deal. We'd be hittin' nine cities in Russia, Krakow and Warsaw in Poland, on the road four solid weeks. Lotta of risks involved. Pilfered equipment, problems with the authorities, bad food, gettin' harassed for preachin' the Word. The gospel ain't been freed up by Glasnost, least not yet, far as I can tell. Didn't feel like this was a decision I could make. Wanted to lay it on the table, ask everybody to take it to the Father in prayer."

I looked around the room, studied the faces, saw that the others had already made up their minds too. I wondered how it was possible for my heart to hold so much.

Jake stood, slipped from Amy's grasp, and headed for the door. He walked down the hall, a solitary figure ahead of us all. I hurried to catch up, fell in one pace behind him. The closer we came to the backstage doors, the louder the clamor became.

Siebren scrambled down the stairs; his face lit up in relief as he saw us. "I was just coming to get you. They're ready for you to go on."

Jake nodded and walked by him, wrapped in his isolation. I stayed as close to him as I could. We passed through the doors and past the clapping roadies and smiling cameramen and out onto the stage. The audience roared as the spotlight caught us. I watched Jake reach for his guitar, his gaze on the floor at his feet. My own fingers fumbled with my strap as I hastened to be ready. I slid the guitar up and over so that it hung down behind me, and as he started forward I fell into step beside him.

The spotlight caught the surprise as he looked down at me. I met his gaze, waited. Suddenly a grin spread over his hard-carved features, and a heavy hand landed on my back.

"Let's do it," he shouted.

"Ready when you are," I said, reaching up to grab his shoulder.

Together we walked forward and raised our free hands clenched in fists, forefingers outstretched toward the sky. With the audience roaring back at us, we called out the words:

"Praise the Lord!"

ACKNOWLEDGMENTS

My beloved wife, Izia, has given up her career as an international corporate lawyer to assist me with both the writing and our mission work. Besides her extremely valuable research and all of the commercial details she has freed me from, Izia has strived to create an island of calm in our home. She succors and supports me, granting me both the time and the energy with which to carry on this work. "But what we sought most of all from each other was the company of someone who believed this dream could become real."

It has been a continued blessing to have this opportunity to write about Contemporary Christian Music. During my own growth in faith, this music has been an instrument whereby the Holy Spirit has ministered to me and through me constantly. I would like to thank all the many artists whose work has remained such a tremendous source of joy and inspiration to me, and to so many others. Should they have the opportunity to read this book, I hope they will find similar joy and inspiration.

Research for each of my books has introduced me to a number of important contacts who have proven to be absolutely crucial. One of these for *The Maestro* was Chaz Corzine, manager to such artists as Michael W. Smith and First Call, and a partner in Blanton-Harrell, Inc. His willingness to assist me in the initial stages of my research was invaluable.

One of the real pleasures of writing is the opportunity to meet other brothers and sisters in the Lord, and to learn from their own walks in faith. Among the new friends I made while working on *The Maestro* are Marty and Vicky McCall, Bonnie and Dan Keen, and Paul and Marybeth Salveson. Marty, Bonnie and Marybeth make up First Call. Paul manages the First Call road work, and mixes for Margaret Becker when he has time. He is also a partner in one of Nashville's up-and-coming studios. Dan Keen is Manager of Writer Relations for a major song publishing company. Vicky McCall is an extremely talented artist. All of them are truly wonderful people, who shared their experiences and gave unstintingly of their time.

Zack Glickman, Russ Taff's manager, took time from what clearly was a typically frantic day to grant me a three-hour phone interview. His directives were extremely helpful in obtaining an overview of the Christian music industry.

The well-known Christian musician and songwriter, Bruce Carroll, is in truth a lay minister who sings his message with enormous power and talent. I learned a tremendous amount from him, both to apply in this book and to my life. It has been a real pleasure getting to know him.

The singer Jon Gibson was a great help, as was his associate Ramiz Yousef. The only problem I had with either was getting them to slow down enough to let me keep up. They juggle ideas and projects at dizzying speed. After trying to match Jon's pace for eleven hours, I collapsed from exhaustion. Anyhow, thanks a lot, guys. You are very special.

Larry Norman, one of the original artists of what is now called Contemporary Christian Music, let me tag along for a day of concerts and interviews, then gave up his only free morning before flying to Russia for a concert tour in order to talk about the roots of gospel rock. He was both a great source of information and a great personal inspiration.

As I mentioned in the book, Albino Montisci is an extremely talented Italian Christian artist, and a new-found friend. He gave generously of his time during a Holland tour, and hosted me in Turin when I went down to research that portion of the book. I highly recommend his music, which comes with an English translation of his powerful lyrics.

Domenico Manolio, Denny Hurst, and Beatrice Custer of the

Italian Christian Media Company deserve special thanks. When I wanted to see if I could develop Gianni's growth in faith during his return to Italy, they were there to assist me. They introduced me both to their work and to their affiliation with the growing network of evangelical churches in Italy.

Luca Genta, Marco Genta, and Emanuelle Saladino both tour with Albino and are recording artists in their own rights. I would like to offer a special note of thanks for the time and assistance which they gave me during my research.

Charlotte Hoglund is a rising star in the European Christian music circuit. I would like to thank her and her pianist, Robert Wirensj, for being so willing to help in developing a correct perspective on the European Christian music scene.

Stefan Ingman is both a friend and director of the Klangwerkstadt, which translates literally as "The Noise Factory." It is one of northern Germany's finest recording studios, and was used as the model for this book.

Sameh Mina and Martin Doepke are studio musicians with Germany's WDR 2 television station, as well as recording artists, and very close friends. They, along with Stefan Ingman, patiently put up with almost a year's worth of questions while I worked on this book.

Chaplain George Duncan and Chaplain Richard Hartwell, both ministering to the soldiers at Ramstein Air Base, were of great assistance in obtaining a solid understanding of a military chaplain's responsibilities.

As was described in the book, Gerrit Aan't Goor is Managing Director of both Spark Music and Crossbow Productions. He and his assistant, Leida Glass, went out of their way to assist me in making necessary contacts within the European Christian music industry. I can only hope that they will appreciate the book, and find that I have given a correct view of their work and their ministry.

Siebren Rijpma is the Executive Producer of a Dutch contemporary Christian music program called Gospel Holland. They have an estimated viewing audience of over half a million. Despite his extremely busy schedule, Siebren took time on a number of occasions to let me pester him with questions. I would like to compliment both him and his working crew—including the lighting and camera operators—for the wonderful sense of living faith with which they enter their work.

Bert Van Leeuwen was the announcer of the first Gospel Holland concert that I attended. He is a well-known television personality in Holland, and yet carries his faith with him in a clear effort to use his profession as a means of evangelism.

Evert ten Ham is both producer and announcer for several radio and television programs on Contemporary Christian Music in Europe. I would like to thank him and his wife Jolanda for giving me considerable assistance in structuring this book.

Eike Martens, Dave and Becky Durham, and Karen Lafferty are all members of Youth With A Mission's music outreach. Eike and Karen are based in Amsterdam, and Dave and Becky now work out of Lausanne, Switzerland. It was a great personal pleasure to have the chance to work with them. I would also like to commend both their work and the spirit with which they confront the needs of a world needing Christ.

Eddie Huff is both a Director of Youth With A Mission in Germany and one of Europe's finest Christian concert promoters. Eddie and his wife Vickie have become friends through the work on this book, and I remain very grateful for their kind assistance.

Tom and Ann Bourke work with the Navigators in Great Britain. Tom was willing to share with me a number of sensitive and personal experiences from his life prior to accepting Christ. This open-hearted honesty assisted greatly in drawing true-to-life characters, an essential component of an enjoyable novel.

Tom and Ann Perkins are also with the Navigators, ministering to men and women on several military bases around Kaiserslautern in Germany. Tom hosted me on a visit to the base, and allowed me to share in some wonderful times of Bible study and testimony with his family in Christ.

André Pouwer is in actuality one of Europe's premier producers of Christian music. He mixes both for television and records, and was kind enough to grant me time on several occasions. As with many of the other people with whom I worked on this book, I found our time together to be of great personal benefit, as well as of assistance in developing the authenticity of the story.

Reverend Bill DeLay and his wife Cathy are indeed the leaders of the International Baptist Church of Dusseldorf, which

Izia and I attend. I would like to thank them and the congregation for their support and Christian love. Many of the messages on salvation and prayer presented in this book are taken directly from Bill's sermons. I would like to also thank the Father for having led us to such a wonderful, Christ-filled spiritual home.

Reuben Blackwell, Vice President of the Raleigh Chamber of Commerce, is both a fine friend and a sensitive writer. Reuben has kindly assisted in the structuring of Jake's dialogue, in the hopes of making the man live in the minds and hearts of readers.

The village of Torno and the region of Lago di Como was introduced to me by Connie and Danilo Valente, two very dear friends who have opened their hearts and home to me for many years. I fell in love with this region fifteen years ago when they lived on the top floor of an ancient villa on the outskirts of Torno. I hope when they read this novel they will find that I have captured some of the flavor this region and its people possess.

My family has been of tremendous support during this long struggle. Despite the difficulty that some of them had in understanding why a successful businessman would give so much of himself year after year to what he felt was a call to serve through writing, they nonetheless continued their prayerful support and love. For this I am very, *very* grateful.

I would like to offer a special thanks to all of the family at Bethany House Publishers. They have gone out of their way to make Izia and me feel a part of their fellowship. We are truly blessed to have this chance to work with such a Spirit-filled publishing house. Special thanks must go to Carol Johnson, Editor in Chief, and Gary Johnson, Publisher, who have given freely of their most limited asset—time—and done so with the warmth and concern of true friends. Thanks also to Jeanne Mikkelson, Publicity Director, who works so hard to overcome the distance that separates us.

Reverend David Horner and Associate Pastor Mike Sparks of the Providence Baptist Church in Raleigh have been most helpful both with biblical guidance and encouragement. They are both firmly rooted in the Scriptures, and deeply love the Lord. Anyone who has questions related to his own spiritual growth (Paul McCommon, suggested as a spiritual counselor in the acknowledgment pages of *The Presence,* has recently accepted a position as missionary to Panama) should feel free to write them % Bethany House Publishers, 6820 Auto Club Road, Minneapolis, Minnesota 55438.